THE REDLINE HEIST

⊕ ⊕ ⊕

BAEN BOOKS
by MICHAEL MERSAULT

The Deep Man
The Silent Hand
The Presence Malign

The Redline Heist

THE REDLINE HEIST

* * *

Michael Mersault

THE REDLINE HEIST

A Baen Books Original

Baen Publishing Enterprises
P.O. Box 1403
Riverdale, NY 10471
www.baen.com

ISBN: 978-1-6680-7313-1

Cover art by Dave Seeley

First printing, February 2026

Distributed by Simon & Schuster
1230 Avenue of the Americas
New York, NY 10020

Library of Congress Control Number: 2025043280

Printed in the United States of America

10 9 8 7 6 5 4 3 2 1

For Timothy James
Perhaps every world I explore in writing now,
you and I discovered together years ago in settings constructed
of Lego blocks and other helpful mediums.
Hopefully these written accounts still evoke the glories of our
shared discoveries from so long ago.

CHAPTER 1

With all the skills she obtained in her infamous military career, Cherry Aisha could have found employment in any number of lucrative fields, even on such a backwater planet as Bethune, but instead she sprawled on a tall seat at the entrance to Manny's Playhouse, watching the eager reprobates stream by. She lacked the mass or height to be a truly ideal bouncer, who would primarily dissuade misbehaving party creatures by mere intimidation, but she supervised the string of bouncers beneath her to perfection, keeping the mayhem down to the optimal level Manny preferred . . . for gritty ambience or something. The crowd swirled by, spacers proudly sporting their distinctive orange vests, while frontier workers bore that over-spruced look, undermined by their sturdy attire, but city dwellers formed the majority of the mob, resplendent in their glow-rags and body paint.

Situated on the west side of Bethune's prime city, Torino, beneath the eastern fringe of the Gear, Manny's Playhouse didn't lack gritty ambience, and that grittiness provided unlikely qualities Cherry valued.

Manny's represented a job, a modest paycheck, and just enough challenge to keep Cherry's inner focus from intractably fixing upon the yawning abyss that had consumed nearly every other member of the Blue Light Brigade in the years following the war.

As her mind wandered around the brink of that same alluring abyss and its constant siren song, Cherry's gaze scanned over the marble-eyed patrons hurrying past her into the entrance, suddenly locking upon one man revealing the signs of intoxication . . . and more. Her augmented vision scan detected the telltale lump under the arm of that singular customer, and Cherry uncrossed her arms, motioning with two fingers. A pair of her massive underlings moved, snatching the long-haired merchant spacer out of line and giving him a gentle toss, sending him stumbling back into the flow of foot traffic moving along the thoroughfare where he fell. Cherry watched the operation dispassionately, her hired muscle stepping back to their posts, and she saw the long-haired spacer's thoughts drunkenly rattle through choices, his brow lowering as he suddenly settled upon the wrong option.

Without conscious consideration she exploded off her seat and crossed the distance in a burst of blinding speed, part of Cherry's mind dryly wondering why she even bothered. Her short knife was at the spacer's throat before his fumbling hand managed to draw the pistol from its concealed holster under his vest, but Cherry dimly realized that she felt no emotion, no fear, no excitement. She could nudge the razor edge of her blade through this man's pulsing artery, or she could spare his life . . . and neither option mattered in the slightest to her at that moment. Her growing zone of internal deadness now encompassed even this, it seemed.

The milling crowd parted around them, some looking on curiously, though Bethune remained a wild enough frontier planet that such scenes of modest violence weren't shocking.

"I'm sorry," Cherry said in a low, colorless tone as the man froze, her mouth near his ear. "You see, weapons aren't allowed in the establishment, old stick." Her knife just caressed the spacer's skin, blood seeping from the merest slice. "You hear me, love?"

The spacer's shaggy head nodded cautiously. "Y-yeah."

"Good," Cherry said, reaching her left hand around to eject the power cartridge from the half-drawn pistol. "I'll hold onto this, then. A little souvenir, like. Instead of your head, eh? You can even keep your adorable little weapon, see?"

Cherry straightened, her knife disappearing, and she slipped back to her perch beside the door, the confiscated power cartridge idly flipping in her hand. The shaggy spacer staggered up, pushing off through the crowd, but Cherry didn't look after his departure, already dismissing him from her thoughts. Instead, the abyss slowly filled her mind again, drawing, calling, waiting, as she went through the motions of a regular work night, acting like a regular person, wondering why even the modest approval of Manny should matter at all to her.

Originally, Cherry chose Bethune over other frontier worlds despite its burgeoning approach to urbane tameness because of its single claim to distinction within the Confederated Worlds. When scouts first mapped Bethune centuries earlier, they noted a number of unique terrain features including two tall hills shaped like nearly perfect pyramids, both situated a short distance from each other, a narrow valley between. Humanity being predictably drawn to interesting geometry, early colonists settled near the twin pyramids, attaching great significance to their appearance.

It was some years into Bethune's history before the superstitious fixation on the pyramids resulted in eccentric theorists mounting an expedition to tunnel through a hundred centuries of accumulated volcanic detritus and rock, seeking the mystical core of the pyramids and the deep meaning sure to be revealed. To the surprise of nearly every expert in human space, the lunatic theorists' tunnel blundered into an immense metal structure hidden within. The news exploded across human space, and speculation launched into the highest flights of fancy ever imagined.

It became quickly clear, Bethune's pyramids were of alien origin, possibly of ancient religious significance, and the nutters felt certain these pyramids must somehow be tied to the legendary pyramids of ancient Earth through strands of mystical consequence. Despite excited fervor from every university in human space and tremendous interest from the scientific and superstitious corners of the Confederated Worlds, it took decades to fully unearth even one of Bethune's pyramids . . . only to discover it wasn't really a pyramid at all.

While the exposed edifice possessed the appropriate number of sides to match human ideas of a pyramidal structure, the massive metal mechanism lay untouched by corrosion, the intricacies of its operation becoming clear, the implications unexpectedly alarming. The entirety of the unearthed alien artifact stood many times larger than the ancient earthly pyramids, but it was not a tomb or a temple. The first pyramid of Bethune was nothing more than the severed landing gear of some incredibly vast alien ship. Perhaps most troubling of all the facts emerging from the archaeological survey remained the fact that something had violently sheared these massive pyramid-shaped landing claws from whatever impossibly huge vessel once employed them. The only sensible answer suggested that they beheld the signs of some alien war from thousands of years in the past. The scale and power involved beggared human imagination, and perhaps this effect explained why widespread archaeology or salvage operations on Bethune never really took hold. Perhaps the mortal psyche recoiled from powers that so dwarfed and diminished every human effort in history.

Interest faded and the second pyramid had remained only half excavated now for more than a century, while the first pyramid became little more than an interesting appendage to Bethune's capital city of Torino, human structures now built in, under, and through the ancient landing claw... structures like Manny's Playhouse. The Gear served settlers of Bethune much like a boulder in the garden served so many squirming bugs.

Cherry Aisha viewed it in that light, the vile vermin squirming around her every night, her own existence representing just another particularly venomous bug among them all.

Cherry had thought that Bethune's tangible proof of an unimaginable alien conflict might provide relief from her own internal struggles. Seeing the solid, metallic evidence of a war that shrank all human strife to that of trivial scuffles by comparison, she thought, would help provide a healing perspective. Now, as she sat posted beside the entrance to Manny's Playhouse, glancing up at the smooth metallic ceiling high above her, the knowledge that she sheltered within a massive, ancient mechanism of war only solidified her feeling that *nothing* possessed any meaning. All human discord felt increasingly meaningless, her own trauma just as ridiculous as... as her life itself.

That line of reasoning did not provide any relief for Cherry, the abyss drawing nearer by the day, her excuses more transparent by the hour. She sat beside all the flooding human traffic who mindlessly chased their prurient appetites, and allowed the certainty to settle into her reinforced bones: Why shouldn't Bethune be her final destination... her *final* resting place?

These dark thoughts faded to the background as her autonomic scanning of the crowd locked upon a singular form. The man she beheld amidst the shuffling multitude possessed no individual quality that arrested attention, his clothing reflecting modest refinement, his demeanor elevated by expressive eyes and a smile that was both amused and mocking. But this man stood out to Cherry Aisha as if he were painted blue and wore a tail. Their eyes met through the intervening stir and Cherry saw his head nod slightly, that smile quirk. She knew what he saw, her straight black hair not that uncommon, nor her dark eyes and olive complexion. His look was one of recognition.

He plunged ahead through the crush, not moving toward the door to Manny's Playhouse, but steering straight for Cherry. She sat still, watching, the enticing void in her mind growing quieter as she studied the man.

One of her hulking subordinates stepped up to block the man's progress, but Cherry waved him back, and the stranger stepped near ... very near. Cherry's hands rested on her knees as she calmly regarded him, waiting.

He only delayed until they had a small bubble of privacy before speaking. "Might you be Lieutenant Aisha?" the man inquired, his voice confident, maybe overconfident, the smile quirking.

Cherry might have expected the stranger to say any number of things, but not this, unleashing flashes of sensation that roiled through her mind with that old, dead title. "Not anymore," she said, wondering how this man knew her true identity. No one on Bethune knew her true name ... except him, and knowing her name, he clearly took a risk, standing so near to her as he revealed her secret.

He regarded her for a moment, his expression holding a question, as if he detected the tumult within her. "I'm Warren Springer Stowe." He said the words like he expected her to recognize the name, but he only paused a moment before continuing. "Got somewhere to talk? I'd like to offer you a job."

He continued to smile down at Cherry as she steadily measured him. After a moment she said, "Who do you want me to kill?"

He held up his hands, the dismayed look on his face appearing genuine. "Whoa! No, no. Hah! Nothing like that." He laughed. "I'm all sunshine and bunnies, lady."

Cherry stared. She already had the job with Manny, and whatever this Stowe character wanted *had* to be dangerous, despite his words, or he wouldn't have sought her out. But ... curiosity, like a tender green shoot, seemed to emerge from the blackened soil of Cherry Aisha's heart. She turned her head, looking over at her oxlike underling.

"I will be away for a half hour or so, old fellow. Call me if there's any hullabaloo."

"Okay, boss," the muscle-head said.

Cherry looked up. "Well, Warren Springer Stowe, you've got thirty minutes to describe your sunshine and, er, bunnies to me, then. Shall we?"

"You peddle antiquities? Really?" Cherry Aisha said as she nibbled the kebab on her plate, her skepticism shining through. They sat in the darkened corner of restaurant a little farther down the Gear from Manny's, Cherry's back to the wall, Warren at her left hand. How Warren had unearthed her presence on Bethune remained a question that she allowed to rest.

Warren tilted his head and held up both hands like the arms of a balance scale. "In a manner of speaking, sure. Supply, demand, customers, vendors—business is business, mostly, right?"

Cherry chewed a morsel, steadily regarding him before saying, "I'm not, shall we say, well suited for dusting off old shit, ducky. What you want me for? Hmm?"

Warren rested his hands on the table, turning to watch a pair of party girls weaving through the dining establishment, their glowing skin-art flickering in the dim light, and Cherry scrutinized his profile. He wasn't quite her type, but he had a loose-limbed, easy quality that she grudgingly admired, and a pleasant smile. He drummed his fingers, focusing on Cherry again. "Sometimes I must, *shall we say*, obtain the antiquities I need from barbarians who don't properly value them. I think you might be perfect for helping me out on this one teensy little job."

"*Obtain?* You mean *steal*, don't you, love?" Cherry nodded now, understanding, wiping her greasy fingertips on a napkin. "I don't fancy a prison sentence, old fellow. The concrete décor, the limited menu, the closed spaces, the exclusively female company—not my cup of tea, see? Find someone else to steal your knickknacks, Mister Stowe."

Warren pursed his lips and produced a thin platinum card from his well-tailored jacket. "You know what this is?" He tilted it toward Cherry. "It is a million-guilder retainer card with Mundercast and

Mordaunt, good for any court in the Confederated Worlds. If we, um, bungle something, get our tails in a wringer, these guys will spring us out of lockup, *guaranteed* ... as long as we don't, uh, kill anybody." Warren smiled broadly.

Cherry stared at the platinum rectangle and its familiar icon. Mundercast and Mordaunt possessed a notable power that even someone like Cherry knew, their proficiency with the Law of the Confederated Worlds sufficient to tie regional courts in knots. Her eyes raised to stare at Warren. "A million-guilder retainer? What sort of bloody antiquities do you pinch then, mate? The crown bloody jewels?"

Warren chuckled, slipping the card back into his jacket and rubbing his hands together. "What do you know about the early expansion era from Earth? The, uh, Trillionaires?"

"Nothing. Are you going to give me a dreary old history lesson now? Can we skip ahead to the juicy bits, old fellow? I'm not a keen student."

"I'll be brief—"

"Praise be." Cherry sipped her drink, staring at Warren with a long-suffering expression.

Warren sighed patiently. "Okay, the *super*-brief version, then: The first supra-terrestrial industrialists were so rich that we can barely imagine it. There were only a few of them and they kept trying to outdo each other. Before long, some *old shit* from a particular era of Earth history became the real sign of wealth, and do you have any idea what it cost back then to get even a donut from the earth's surface up to their asteroid enclaves?"

"This is the super-brief version?" Cherry asked in a purr.

Warren waved a dismissing hand. "Anyway, these guys started buying up certain items and bringing them up ... especially certain ground vehicles from a very, um, special slice of Earth history."

Cherry perked up despite herself, puzzled. "Ground vehicles? Out to the Sol asteroid belt? Whatever for?"

"For prestige," Warren said. "Because they could, because only a handful of these antique vehicles existed on Earth, and these arseholes wanted to prove how cool they were by looting them from Earth and rocketing these heavy steel vehicles up into space. They ended up with entire museums of ground vehicles in the enclaves, one rich bastard trying to one-up another rich bastard . . . before the Super Cleanse, of course."

"Oh," Cherry said, her interest waning again. "I see. Useless old vehicles, sitting about in museums. Thrilling."

"That attitude right there"—Warren pointed his kebab at Cherry—"that's why I do what I do." Cherry stared at him with her eyebrows raised skeptically, and Warren shaped a rueful smile. "Well, I also do it because I love this old stuff . . . and I can make a lot of money from it."

Warren rifled in his nicely tailored jacket and brought out colorful images and words, evidently advertisements composed upon actual paper. "See these? These are the vehicles we're talking about. They just called them 'cars' back then." Cherry tilted her head to examine the two-dimensional pictures on the pages, seeing glossy ground vehicles crouched on black wheels, the passenger compartments enclosed within glass panels. "Practically handmade; internal combustion engines," he explained.

"*Internal combustion?* Is that the engine there?" Cherry asked, indicating the image of complicated mechanisms jammed under the bonnet. In her military career she had operated a vast swath of vehicles, so some professional interest flickered. "Must have had some slick logic controllers in there somewhere regulating all that mess, eh?"

"No. None."

"No logic controllers at all?" Cherry said, disbelievingly.

"Nope," Warren said. "These things are strictly mechanical, like riding a pair of scissors."

"Bloody death traps," Cherry said, sitting back, but she felt a gentle tug of attraction to the concept . . . riding about on a mechanical, exploding anachronism held a sudden appeal, freed from the digital babysitting that invaded nearly every aspect of modern human existence.

"Elegant, expensive deathtraps from an age we will never see again," Warren said. "They pieced these things together in ways we can barely understand now. You can still see the tool marks on some of the metal parts where some technician hand-fitted the parts so many centuries ago. It's just so great!"

A bygone age, nearly deleted, and these advertisements such alluring clues to the lives of their forebears; her gaze roved over the other adverts, seeing one advertising someone called *Mary Poppins*, evidently a pretty woman in absurd clothes with an umbrella in hand. Cherry eyed a number of words and numbers on the vehicle advert, tilting her head to read. "What does 1968 signify?"

"The year of manufacture, it seems."

She nodded, frowning as she continued to read. "And what's this 'HP' listed here?"

Warren looked at the listed specifications and leaned nearer, true enthusiasm lighting his eyes. "This is an ancient measurement that stands for *horse powers*."

"Horse powers?" she repeated, staring at him.

"Uh, yes. You know what horses are right? Yes? Well, the, uh, ancients admired the qualities of horses it seems. See...this description of a car called 'Mustang' there? A mustang is a sort of horse, and this sales babble goes on and on about the wild, untamed quality of the mustang and applies it to this particular vehicle. Observe this little horse icon on the car. See? The more power of horses a car has, the better. Neat, huh?"

Cherry finished her drink and shrugged. "I'll grant you there's a certain charm to animist superstition and all that. But what's the angle...what's *your* angle with all this?"

Warren popped the last morsel of kebab in his mouth and followed it with a sip from his glass. "In the centuries after the Super Cleanse when the Trillionaires were *absorbed*, their collections got scattered across a bunch of systems. The majority of these old things ended up in museums and other odd collections around the galaxy, where most of them are stuffed away in back rooms, utterly ignored."

"Aw, the poor things," Cherry said dryly. "And now you're here to save the sad little dears from obscurity, are you?

"Hah-hah." Warren smiled, his white teeth flashing in the dim light. "Yes, I suppose I am at that."

"Hmm, so charitable of you. And I daresay our modern Filthy Rich suddenly developed a taste for these things again?"

"Exactly. Exactly." Warren nodded, toying with his glass. "Our current wealthy bastards pay handsomely for an original car, and Bethune's got a couple very, very nice originals just gathering dust." He handed Cherry another picture of an ancient ground vehicle half covered by a rumpled cloth, literal dust sprinkled over it.

"This is on Bethune?" Cherry asked, surprised, trying to visualize where the image could possibly have been taken in Torino.

"Yep," Warren said. "The Pioneer Museum over on the north side of town."

"How very odd." Cherry contemplated the image for a moment before looking up. "I don't see how you could pinch such a monstrous huge knickknack, old fellow. Hardly fits in a pocket, does it?"

Warren smiled at her. "With a little help from the right person, we can get it out of the museum . . . and I can get it off the planet easy enough."

Cherry looked at the image of the target vehicle again for a moment. "You ever operate one of these *cars*, Warren Springer Stowe, or you just collect them, hmm?"

"Oh yes," he said. "I've probably driven more of these Old Earth cars than any person in the Confederated Worlds." Warren paused, his face illuminated by a sudden joy. "It's hard to describe the feeling, but . . . but there's really nothing quite like it."

Cherry Aisha looked up from the picture, intrigued by the genuine passion in Warren's voice. Passion, vitality. Life. How long since she had felt true delight about anything?

It was at that moment she realized that she was actually going to do this thing, without any solid idea of what the job really entailed or what it paid.

"Tell me your cunning plan, Mr. Stowe. I'm breathless with anticipation." Her tone could only be perceived as dismissive, but within her, the abyss lay quiescent for the first time in years, and it felt like a new spring season might be dawning for her at last.

CHAPTER 2

Warren Springer Stowe strolled along the narrow street with a spring in his step. Cherry Aisha seemed more calm and capable than he had even imagined, and far prettier than the old military picture he had seen. She resembled an image he had seen from Old Earth, a dark-eyed beauty with a funny red dot in the middle of her forehead. Cherry lacked the red dot, but she embodied the final piece of his scheme on Bethune, and with her on board, his plan was falling together, nearly ready to obtain this long-ignored treasure. He imagined that particular treasure waiting all these centuries . . . a 1968 Mustang left to rot like a piece of garbage. It was a crime against all that was good and right . . . and a hell of a lucrative opportunity.

So many automotive treasures lay forgotten just like this, due to that singular sociopolitical event in human history.

According to the history lessons, after the early expansion era from Earth, the great Techno-Socialist Republic coalesced, promising all the usual things, only at a greater scale, and success was *assured* through the use of the latest Artificial Intelligence technology. Unlike every other preceding utopia, the Techno-Socialists would employ an AI engine to adjudicate equity and guarantee fair outcomes for all. Like every other great socialist "republic," it inevitably expanded its control until any history that contrasted with the ideals of the new utopia became intolerable seeds of sedition. Unlike earlier utopias, the Techno-Socialists could engage in instantaneous deletion of information from virtually every data system joined to every network. The *Super Cleanse* purged images and information wholesale, destroying ten million times more data than all prior book-burning events in human history combined. In the wake of the Super Cleanse only scattered bits of imagery, data, and films survived. For future generations, this left only so many tantalizing clues of a beautiful, enigmatic era from humanity's past, and that era took on a legendary, fairy-tale status.

Warren Springer Stowe only represented one particularly passionate, educated fanatic in a galaxy-wide throng of devotees, but he liked to think his prized hoard of film snippets, images, and music comprised one of the most comprehensive collections around.

As he crossed the street, he looked at the flow of evening traffic milling around the vibrant nightlife of Torino, weaving through glimmering pedestrians on every side. One establishment had drawn his attention already, its antiquated ornamentation reminding Warren of some Old Earth pictures of a quaint desert city, with dark minarets and crenelated walls, while its name, Rick's Café, seemed detached from its décor in a puzzling manner. Although the image seemed a trifle confused, the operators of the bar clearly strove to evoke the feel of Old Earth, and Stowe couldn't resist a peek, despite the pressing business before him.

He pushed through faux wooden doors studded with stubby iron spikes and stepped within the dim interior. Rick's provided an old-fashioned bar running along almost the entire far wall, old-timey liquor bottles forming a mosaic behind, high ceilings rising above a spacious dining and drinking area. Equally old-fashioned tables and chairs dotted the tile floor, a white piano unattended against one pillar, a collection of live musicians performing a sultry song on antique-looking instruments. The whole aspect tickled a recollection in Warren's memory, feeling absurdly familiar from some fragment of Old Earth film, and he gazed about with satisfaction. This café could only be the loving creation of some other Old Earth fan, and he wondered what source material the proprietor used for his model. They clearly got their hands on some choice bit that had survived the Super Cleanse.

Even the tune moaning out from the band, low and moody, seemed to be lifted out of a fragment from Old Earth, its melody evoking yet another trace recollection in Warren's mind as the musicians appeared to actually play their anachronistic instruments. Warren only possessed a vague understanding of ancient musical implements, but he thought he identified a saxophone and a . . . clarinet among the ensemble, the musicians swaying as they performed.

Such attention to detail demanded a reward, in Warren's view, and he strolled to the bar, eyeing the chubby bartender with approval.

"What'll you have, sir?" the bartender asked, speaking with an unfamiliar accent, probably added for ambience.

"You have brandy?"

"Yes, sir. Brandy, or a delightful cognac."

Better and better.

"Cognac then, friend," Warren said, looking on appreciatively as the barkeep poured a generous portion from an actual bottle. Warren took the glass and turned to survey the varied clientele, wondering how many patrons understood even a fraction of the historical context they dined within.

The cognac rolled agreeably over Warren's tongue, the warmth flowing to his belly as his attention drifted to a severe-looking man and woman seated near the band, half-full glasses in their hands, their eyes fixed on Warren. A faint alarm rang in the back of Warren's mind, but his gaze moved on, noting the attractive woman in the band, her fingers flying over the silver keys of her . . . clarinet? Clarinet.

The severe man and woman still stared. Warren felt it, and he perceived their movement from the corner of his eye as they stood and approached, walking directly to him, halting a long step away.

"You are Warren Springer Stowe, aren't you?" the man asked.

Warren sipped from his glass, setting it down on the bar beside him before he looked at the man. "That's me," Warren said, glancing at his female counterpart. "And you two must be . . . what? A floor show?" Warren drew his small slender case from an inside jacket pocket, opening it to reveal his coveted supply of tobacco.

The man and woman shared a look. "I'm Bartson," the man said. "I'm the district attorney in this locale. This is Masters, my assistant."

"Oh, I see," Warren said, sprinkling tobacco on the small rectangle of paper and rolling it into a neat cigarette. "Bartson, Masters. Nice to meet you both."

Bartson's gaze drifted to the cigarette as Warren struck a small flame from his smoking case, puffing the cigarette to life. "That's not a class-one intoxicant, is it? They're not permitted on Bethune."

Warren inhaled and blew a cloud of smoke over Bartson and Masters. "Nope. Not even a class-two or -three intoxicant. It's called tobacco. It's an Old Earth thing. Only a mild little stimulant."

Warren struggled mightily to withhold a harsh cough. He had tracked down the seeds and grown his own tobacco after eagerly watching a number of surviving snippets of old film. The Old Earth people sure seemed to love tobacco, as far as he could tell, and he relished the whole process he saw in those old films, but the art and science was evidently lost. He figured either the seeds he bought were not the right species of tobacco plant, or his curing method remained flawed, because no matter how many times he tried smoking cigarettes, they tasted bad and made him feel lousy. They were great, however, for blowing clouds of smoke on people you didn't like. Maybe it would also make their clothes smell funny like it did Warren's.

Masters stifled a cough, waving away the smoke with a frown. "What are you doing on Bethune, Stowe?" Bartson asked, wrinkling his nose at the acrid tobacco smell.

Warren puffed the cigarette again and gestured broadly. "Rick's, man! This place is amazing." He laughed, exhaling another cloud of smoke. "And the Gear, of course. Alien tech. Very old. Very cool. And so alien, right?"

Bartson stared skeptically at Warren. "Right. We don't need any of your shady dealing here, Stowe."

"Shady dealing? *Shady dealing?* Really, District Attorney Bartson, you shouldn't buy all the mean-spirited rumors you hear. I'm a consultant and collector. Very respectable."

Masters had a sudden look of comprehension, whispering something to Bartson, who listened, his eyes widening. He focused on Warren with an accusing expression on his face. "You're here for Cathwaite's collection, aren't you?"

Never having heard of Cathwaite or any such collection, Warren said, "If I happen to look in on Cathwaite's collection, I can hardly be reproached, can I?"

Bartson's jaw tightened, his lips thinning. "If you in any way touch that collection, I will see you locked in a cell that will tickle that love of the medieval for which you are so famous."

Warren took another drag from his cigarette, again resisting the urge to cough, and smiled at Bartson. "No need for all this ruckus,

Bartson." He blew a smoke cloud over the two potentates. "You must not be aware, I am a licensed dealer and collector in every region of the Confederated Worlds, so relax."

Masters waved the smoke away, her eyes gleaming triumphantly. She opened her mouth to speak, but Bartson halted her with a sharp look, turning back to Warren. "You have been warned, Stowe. When you find yourself rotting in our delightful prison you will only have yourself to blame."

Warren wondered what Masters had been about to say, and he wished he knew.

"Prison? Not very hospitable soul, are you, Bartson? Show me where in Confederated law a citizen is forbidden from simply examining an ordinary collection, and I will happily spend all my time in Bethune right here in Rick's."

The two legal pukes turned on their heels, but not before Masters shot another enigmatic look toward Warren. There was a suggestion of triumph in that look, and Warren didn't like it. He watched them push through the outer doors of Rick's, and Warren extinguished his cigarette, rinsing the nasty taste away with a mouthful of cognac.

Bumping into the district attorney so close before a job didn't feel particularly good, but he was too close, with too much invested to pull the plug now. Besides, he was Warren Springer Stowe, and his level of genius could not be stopped by a couple small-minded bureaucrats.

CHAPTER 3

"Here's the south wall of the Pioneer Museum, see? Nice window and a little balcony there."

"I see it," Cherry said, looking at the pictures as they sat in Warren's hotel room in companionable darkness. "Even such a weary old pile as this will have sensors on that wall, and a detector for drones of any great size."

"I figured that," Warren said. "Otherwise I wouldn't need someone with your special skills."

"Show me the pictures from the inside."

Warren obediently brought up the selection of shots he'd obtained. Cherry scrolled through them, her professional eye sweeping each image, pausing on one shot of the museum's interior. "I see that one's an antique, but it isn't one of your *cars*, old fellow. What is it?"

Warren leaned to look, seeing the ancient two-wheeled vehicle in a dusty corner of the Pioneer Museum. "Oh yeah, that's a pretty special piece. It is a motorcycle. I've operated some Old Earth machines like this one, too. You've got to balance it yourself. No internal gyro or anything. They must have died in droves on those things back in the day, but it gives you a thrill you wouldn't believe . . . right until the moment you die."

Cherry liked the look of the vehicle, but she only nodded, continuing on, sifting the evidence of security systems within the Pioneer Museum. "I don't see how we're going to get this *car* of yours out of the museum, Mister Stowe."

"Through . . . here." He showed her a picture of the glass-encased front entrance. "I think I've got a way figured to clear this, but you get us in, and I can get us out, car and all. Trust me for that at least."

"I'm not a trusting soul, love," Cherry said. "But since your neck is on the line with me . . ." She turned her attention back to the images. "I don't suppose you have a shot of the roof, hmm?"

"Let's see . . . how about that?" He brought the image up and Cherry carefully studied each bit of it.

She nodded. "Okay. I will need to check a thing or two at the site, but this shouldn't be too difficult." She focused her gaze on Warren, measuring, and he grinned under the scrutiny. "You realize the local authorities may be watching you even now?"

Warren shrugged, laughing. "So they watch. These people have no imagination, no genius. And they've never tangled with someone like me before."

"Hmm, isn't that pretty much what everyone says just before everything goes wrong?"

"I'm not everyone," Warren said, winking at her. "You haven't had a chance to learn that about me yet, but you will."

"I suppose we will see about that," Cherry said dryly. "But speaking of learning about someone . . . how did you ever track me here, to Bethune?"

Warren leaned back smiling mysteriously at the abrupt change of subject. "I asked around."

Cherry didn't share his smile, thinking of who could be asked . . . who still lived. "*Asked around.* You are very brave, Stowe. What made you so sure I wouldn't value my privacy enough to keep your head as souvenir?"

"I don't buy all the horror and hype about the Blue Light Brigade . . . and I heard good things about you specifically."

"The *horror and hype*," Cherry repeated. She looked straight in Warren's eyes. "The worst things you heard were probably true and you took quite a risk." Warren just smiled. "And aside from my location, and my charming disposition, what did you hear?"

"Only that you were the best of the bunch from Blue Light."

Cherry snorted indelicately. "Whoever told you that was a fool or a liar." She thought back to all the candidates who had entered the induction to Blue Light, attempting to absorb the symbiote. There had been extreme athletes, elite warriors, and martial artists who had mostly failed to accept the symbiote, dying horribly as they failed. Those who had survived reflected no recognizable pattern. The ranks of the Blue Light Brigade eventually populated with a strangely diverse swath of human subjects, Cherry among them. Despite backgrounds that were often unimpressive, as hosts for the symbiote they became the most lethal fighting force in the galaxy, and among that force there had been shining stars, demigods. Cherry remembered their faces and names . . . and she remembered their fates, the most powerful among them yielding to the psychosis, the madness. "Perhaps I am the best of Blue Light still living," she said, her gaze focusing on Warren again. "But that isn't saying much. How many of us still live?"

"Not many," Warren said, standing up and fetching a flask. "Drink?"

Cherry looked from the flask to Warren's warm expression. "If you like, love. It's a waste, though. Alcohol has almost no effect on me anymore."

Warren shrugged, pouring a measure into a glass, handing it to her. He smiled a different sort of smile. "Care to spend the evening?" His eyebrows raised. "See just where this partnership can go?"

Cherry held his gaze as she sipped from the glass, feeling the liquor's heat on her tongue. She set the glass aside and smiled at Warren. "I must say, you are the first gentleman who has made such an offer knowing what I really am." She saw the flicker of dawning awareness in Warren's eyes. He clearly hadn't thought through the implications. "But I think not. Wise old souls have had a few things to say about mixing business with pleasure." The hint of relief in his eyes still hurt, after all this time.

He shrugged. "Ah well. Strictly business, then."

CHAPTER 4

The small probe did not display the proud emblem of the Maktoum Corporation, and neither did any of the hundred or so identical probes quietly sifting through the asteroids in Bethune's humble star system. Each of these probes bore dozens of optical eyes around their spherical skins, each eye tasked with tracking an asteroid until an interrogator pulse measured and sampled that individual asteroid. One by one, this particular probe identified and categorized floating chunks of rock, just like all the other Maktoum Corporation probes near Bethune.

Unlike all the others, this particular probe tracked and identified one very large, very unusual hunk of tumbling space debris, quickly picking out the key measurements, noting the odd discrepancies, and cataloging it with all the others. When the probe completed its task, it cogitated for a moment, sifting programmed instructions in the light of this new find. Unlike its sibling probes prospecting among the asteroids, this probe now disgorged its entire catalog of asteroid data in one long, coded burst, transmitting to a distant, waiting Maktoum survey vessel.

Shortly thereafter it received a special instruction signal, digested this for a moment, then actuated a self-destruct charge, detonating in a spectacular fashion, far from any prying eyes.

Only one of the three people crammed aboard the Maktoum survey vessel remained awake at the moment probe 61 sent its alert and accompanying trove of data.

Angel Rua had only worked for Maktoum Corporation for just over a year, but he knew his orders very well. Without pausing to awaken his fellow crew members, Angel double-checked the parameters and sent an alert upstream to the Maktoum outpost on Bethune. A moment later he sent the self-destruct code back to probe 61, just as his written orders required.

Angel could only guess what all the fuss could mean, and hoped he might eventually rise to a position within the company to be trusted with such strategic facts. For the foreseeable future Angel would remain cloistered in this miserable little survey vessel, hiding out from any observers, private or governmental, while the army of probes continued to survey, catalog, and upload their respective views of the asteroid field.

Out of all the asteroid belts in all the known star systems, why this clump near Bethune anyway? Though Angel had never set foot on Bethune proper, he knew it was a crusty frontier-type world, still mostly mining and agriculture, with little to recommend it aside from the peculiar alien Gear, for those who cared.

He sighed to himself as he glanced about the cramped confines enclosing him. Despite Bethune's supposed deficiencies, Angel fervently dreamed of a quick visit to the dirt ball. It would only a take a day or two, and he could walk around under an open sky, eat real food, maybe chat up a pretty girl . . . or chat up *anyone* aside from his two workmates.

But no . . . he knew their orders all too well. Hide out here on the fringe of the belt, upload the surveys, and when ordered, flip the switch on this whole star system, heading straight back to Earth over one hundred light-years distant. Angel knew he'd be lucky to emerge from this horrid little ship within three months, and not a single moment of excitement would likely break the boredom and monotony until then.

A moment later, the light began to flash on Angel's instrument panel as he received a coded message clearly responding to the data packet he had forwarded from probe 61.

When he opened the encrypted communiqué and saw the signature stamp from the Maktoum director of operations, Angel's mouth felt suddenly dry. One quick pass through the message made it clear that three months of boredom no longer stretched out before them, but Angel wasn't positive this sudden change represented an improvement.

Five minutes later, Angel roused his two sleeping associates with warranted gusto, extracting some choice language from both of them. "What? What the hell is so damned urgent, Rua?" McCardle demanded, sitting up in his bunk and fluttering his big, stupid hand at Angel.

"We've got orders," Angel said, enjoying the look dawning on McCardle's face. "We're moving out."

McCardle scrambled out of his blankets, a series of shocked expressions flashing across his face. "Back to Earth?"

"No," Angel said, gleeful to share the bad news. "We've been ordered to hunt down a rock."

Maktoum Corporation remained a family establishment although it had become one of the most influential and profitable commercial enterprises in history, with trillions in assets across dozens of planetary systems.

When managing director Sharif Maktoum suddenly appeared at the opulent Maktoum building in Bethune's capital, Torino, a flurry of activity flowed from the lobby entrance up to the fourteenth-floor management offices in a matter of moments. By the time Sharif strode into the conference room, all the section supervisors already stood at attention, Sharif's younger brother, Sami, at their head. The watchful expression in his eyes matched with a subdued look of exultancy that Sharif knew well and didn't trust. Sami felt he had achieved some notable victory, clearly.

Good, Sharif thought, it was about time Sami began to fill the shoes the prior generations of Maktoum luminaries had bequeathed to them both.

For the moment, Sharif ignored his brother, his gaze locking with each of the unit supervisors in turn. "Greetings to you all. I will not be on Bethune long, but I wished to let you all know that the next phase of operations here is of no little interest to everyone in our firm, even back on Earth."

Sharif thought he observed a number of relieved breaths among the assembly, and in the next instant he notched tensions back up. "While I am here, I am pleased to address any complaints or issues that may not have appeared in official communiqués. If any such issues exist, please speak up now."

Sharif knew that his own voice remained pitched comfortably low, his expression mild, but among the others he detected a faint undercurrent of... fear? From long experience Sharif merely stood quietly, allowing his senses to expand as the tension continued to increase. In a few moments it became increasingly obvious. All the supervisors except one wore wooden expressions, their eyes working hard to avoid looking in the same direction, while the final supervisor, a highly attractive female supervisor, wore a look that could only be called aloof. And Sami's smile had evolved into that mulish expression Sharif knew so well from their youth.

Ah, so this at least had not changed.

"Very well," Sharif said at last. "You may return to your duties." Sharif thought he heard an audible exhalation from the supervisors as they moved toward the door, Sami standing in place, his handsome features composed watchfully.

As the door closed behind the relieved flock, Sharif wondered, should he begin with *personal*, or *professional*? Personal... yes, personal.

Sharif drew a seat from the conference table, easing his lanky form into its yielding embrace, his gaze never leaving Sami's face. "Brother," Sharif began in his most gentle tone, "I do believe we both heard our father explain that one does not shit where one eats."

Sami's mulish lines appeared again, but that gleam of triumph still hovered about his eyes in a way that made Sharif uneasy. "Sharif, it's so good to see you also," Sami declared in a pointed tone, "and if your homily is meant to address my, um, romantic inclinations, I must say it explains that hangdog look your wife's always wearing." As Sharif opened his mouth to verbally eviscerate his younger brother, Sami held up a forestalling hand. "But none of that matters. Listen... I've got a plum in the bag, and this will make even you sit up and take notice."

Sharif schooled himself to patience. "If you refer to the imminent decision of the Bethune governing body, I've already—"

Sami swiped his hand sharply. "No, no. Not that. Your advisors have done their work well, and Bethune's falling into line, exactly as you planned, but I speak of something much... juicier."

Sharif's quick mind flitted through every ridiculous scheme Sami had authored in recent memory, realization suddenly dawning. "Not your ridiculous treasure hunting?"

Sami's triumphant expression returned in full force. "Not so ridiculous now, big brother." He jutted his head forward. "I've found it. Despite the piddling investment you allowed, *I have found it.*"

Sharif recalled the piddling investment constituted a few billion guilders that he never expected to see again. He also recalled a similar claim of victory on an entirely different sort of treasure hunt Sami had militated for a few years earlier, and Sharif couldn't resist the low-hanging fruit now.

"Perhaps you still remember an earlier *piddling investment*," Sharif said. "An army of forensic data specialists picking through the bones of pre-Cleanse data stores."

Sami flushed, recoiling. "I remember perfectly, but—"

"And you were so certain that if we could only locate these legendary fabrication files we would add a trillion guilders to our bottom line."

"I said that I remember!" Sami snapped.

Sharif went on as if he hadn't heard. "But it turns out that collectors will only pay vast prices for *original* Old Earth vehicles, not a new replication, no matter how exact to the original."

Sami moved, running his hands through his shining black coif, taking a distracted step away from Sharif. "I still think the book's not closed on that one. Those fabrication files will be worth a fortune eventually. When that market matures, they'll find out that Maktoum Corporation is the only enterprise in human space that can re-create genuine versions of those Old Earth vehicles."

Sharif sighed. "There is a chance—a microscopic chance—that these antique data files will be worth something eventually . . . even though there's no rational reason for anyone to operate such idiotic vehicles anymore, scarcely anywhere for someone to drive them if they wanted to, and their exploding fuel source is not likely to become commonly available even if they could." He stared at Sami until catching his gaze. "That microscopic chance is the only reason I haven't tried to offload the lot to some antiquities collector already."

Sami glowered at Sharif for a moment before saying, "Are you done now? Are you ready to be proven wrong . . . for once?"

Sharif couldn't resist a small smile. "By all means, brother. I yearn to be proven wrong."

Sami nodded. "You remember when I said that the real profit here on Bethune will go to whoever digs up some of the real alien tech?"

Sharif snorted. "Yes, Sami. But it's hardly a new idea. Every crank for the last century has claimed that the aliens who left the Gear lying about surely left something more valuable also lying about. And yet... the decades have passed without—"

"Until now," Sami interrupted. "Only it's not on the planet surface where everyone else was looking. I found it where the aliens would have to mine all the metals they needed for their enormous ships."

Sharif stared. "And what exactly have you found among the asteroids, Sami?"

"This." Sami unfolded a palm slate and handed it over to Sharif with a smirk.

As Sharif looked at the data and imagery scrolling across the slate, Sami went on, "You're looking at one of the biggest rocks in this system, and the Bethune system sports a lot of big rocks."

"Yes...I see," Sharif said. "And I see its mass is way off its mark."

Sami nodded. "More than seventy percent hollow. Which it would have to be if these aliens used it for a base."

Sharif handed the slate back to Sami. "A base? I think your enthusiasm is premature." He shook his head, smiling indulgently. "It is an interesting find, I grant you, brother, but it has probably just been carved out for minerals, with nothing more exciting to see than some ancient tool marks and—"

Sami thrust a finger out and waved it. "Uh-uh, brother. You're slipping. Look..." He handed the slate back. "Heat signatures, water vapor, and check out that isotope profile." Sami's expression took on its most triumphant gleam yet. "Somebody's generating power on this big rock, and we are about to figure out who..."

CHAPTER 5

It had only required about forty hours for the Maktoum survey vessel to close with their target, and all three crew members now stared at the huge rock illuminated on their scopes.

As ordered, they had matched velocity and bearing with the asteroid, then slowly circled its circumference, scanning with every instrument, and now they nervously prepared for the next step.

By now all three of them understood the only thing this asteroid could really be, all the indicators of ancient nonhuman construction sticking out like a variety of sore thumbs and other less complimentary swollen members, and this underscored the serious, historical nature of this next phase of their orders.

Of the survey ship's three-person crew, two were to don EVA gear, transit over to a feature that appeared to offer some sort of small entrance, and have their names forever immortalized. They would be the first human explorers to ever set foot in a functioning station of alien construction.

They even drew straws to see which of them would receive the honor of making history. Antoniy Keller lost the draw, selecting the long straw, leaving Angel Rua and Griff McCardle holding the short straws... and giving them their sudden chance at historical immortality.

Angel Rua would certainly have preferred to lose the draw and allow Keller to become famous instead. He didn't know all that much about Bethune, but everyone knew about the Gear, and the first question most people had when they heard about the unimaginably huge piece of alien vessel getting sliced off was: *Who the hell did the slicing?*

To Angel it seemed pretty likely that either side of that ancient conflict probably did a pretty good job of securing their facilities against interlopers and pests, even if the owners had been off on vacation for twenty thousand years or so, and he seriously considered resigning on the spot, refusing to go rather than face whatever unpleasant watchdogs they may have left waiting about.

It wasn't only the contract penalty he faced that drove Angel to the sticking point. As he stood in the survey ship's airlock listening to the air draining away, Griff McCardle poised woodenly beside him, Angel tried to calm his pounding heart with the image of his future stature within Maktoum Corporation. This action now would surely catapult him up through the ranks . . . if he survived.

On that cheerful note, the airlock's outer hatch began to cycle open, the immense mountain of rock appearing subjectively "beneath" them, its surface well lighted by Bethune's congenial sun.

Angel and Griff knew enough to approach the rock at a very cautious pace, vectoring toward the mostly smooth surface at a crawl until their boots touched down, seeming to accelerate rather sharply in the last instant. Angel almost keyed his radio to comment about the surprisingly firm gravitational pull when he remembered their agreement to maintain radio silence. Instead he followed Griff's cautious steps as he set off for their goal.

They had spotted the promising declivity during their external survey of the object, and their insertion point at the rock's pole offered them a simple route across a flat expanse to this shadowed notch. In just moments Angel saw Griff descending a modest slope, the rock seeming to bulge in beside them on the left and right.

In their flyby, the notch had not seemed so deep, but as they continued to follow the narrow course, the rock walls rose up high above them on each side. As Angel looked up to gauge their depth, he almost crashed into Griff, who had halted suddenly.

Peering past Griff's shoulder, Angel saw the clean rectangular depression in one rock wall and the shimmering metallic panel inset there, looking very much like a door.

They had hoped that advanced aliens from long ago still might employ something equivalent to hatches, airlocks, and the like, and they had brought the necessary tools to force entry into such a barrier. This proved unnecessary.

Even as Griff felt around the edges of the apparent hatch, they both staggered back as it eased open, a spray of thin vapor making it clear that it truly had been sealed a moment before. They shared a look, Angel seeing the pale, sweating face of McCardle through his faceplate before they both shuffled cautiously within and closed the hatch.

A greenish light flickered into life and they felt and heard the rush of atmosphere into the lock. Angel tilted his body back to look up. If the builders of this station scaled this door to their height in a manner similar to humans, then Angel guessed they must have stood over ten feet in height, which seemed rather small compared to the vast dimensions of the Gear on Bethune.

Angel silently wondered if the aliens who constructed this asteroid base might actually be those who blasted the Gear free from whatever ship it had been attached to. The difference seemed entirely academic to his fear-heightened mind.

His attention came back down as the inside hatch breathed open, revealing their first view of the station's inner workings.

An immense chamber expanded out before them, the smooth floor glowing with a soft aquamarine luminance. To the right they glimpsed smaller passages that opened onto this vast sweeping space, some angling downward, clearly ramps to lower levels, while to the left this huge chamber continued on to the indistinct distance.

As Angel moved to step from the airlock, Griff threw out a restraining arm, holding him back. Angel froze and Griff leaned forward with his multiscan, waving it over the glowing floor, testing for radioactivity. Griff turned his whole body to look at Angel, and Angel heard the crinkling sound of his EVA suit through the atmosphere surrounding them.

Only the soft scuffing of their steps and the sound of his own breathing came to Angel's ears as they approached the first of the smaller entrances, seeing a smooth ramp angling downward, the luminous glow continuing unchecked on the floor surface. With one shared look, they took the downward path, finding the passage nearly twenty feet in width, and perhaps a third smaller from floor to ceiling.

Angel slid a gloved hand along the arched wall, feeling its smoothness, though it seemed to have been bored through the asteroid's native stone, angling downward at about fifteen degrees on inclination.

Griff continually employed the multiscan as they descended, but Angel occupied himself only by counting their strides, reaching sixty-five paces when the sloped passage reached a broader tunnel, terminating as it leveled off.

Griff and Angel stood at the junction with this larger thoroughfare, alternately looking in each direction for some clue to guide their further exploration. At first Angel could not identify the slight pressure pushing him back, until he heard the whispering sound on his helmet.

"Wind?" he said, hearing his own voice loud inside the enclosing helmet.

Griff made a sound, staring to the left, and at first Angel couldn't understand what provoked Griff's attention. In the next moment Angel perceived the dark shape blocking a distant patch of the luminous floor, its blotting occlusion racing nearer. With a lurch Angel jerked Griff backward, managing two stumbling steps back into the sloped passage before the rushing force of wind roared about them. Angel looked up in time to see a large, box-like wheeled vehicle shoot past the opening, the roar of wind tugging them forward in its wake for a moment following its passage.

Angel staggered back to the junction, looking after the vehicle, seeing it disappear into the distance, and Griff appeared beside him, the multiscan in his hand.

When the dark shape finally faded from visibility Griff turned wide eyes toward Angel, his face contorted with some inexplicable shock. "What?" Angel said. "Just some automated system, right?"

"Not that!" Griff barked, his agitation clearly audible despite the muffling helmet between them. "Do you remember how long this asteroid is on its longest axis?"

"Uh, exactly how long?" Angel said, confused. "Not exactly . . . about—"

"Well, this passage"—Griff waved his arm—"is too damned long."

Angel looked down both arms of the immense tunnel before turning back to Griff. "Too long for what?"

"Look," Griff held the multiscan readout for Angel to see. "This should be the narrow axis, but just this bit we can see is almost as long as the entire rock is wide."

Angel heard the words and saw the numerals, but he didn't feel anything like Griff's evident agitation. "Some kind of mistake. That's all, Griff."

Griff shook his head and snatched the multiscan back even as they felt the telltale wind of another approaching vehicle, perhaps the same vehicle returning. "Come on," Griff snapped, leading the way back up the slope to their entrance point, but pausing to look back as the vehicle raced by again.

Angel hugged the right-hand wall as they ascended, freezing as a narrow entrance appeared beside him. "What the hell?" He turned to look at Griff, seeing an expression of Griff's face that multiplied his sense of unease. "This passage wasn't here on the way down, was it? We would have seen it." Griff shook his head, but Angel wasn't sure what that meant, turning his attention back to the small archway.

This perplexing new opening spanned only a little broader in width than Angel's outstretched arms, its floor glowing aquamarine like all the other spaces they had scanned so far, but he saw a faint ruby glimmer from the curving wall ahead, and that drew him forward.

"What's this?" Angel murmured, advancing a few steps to the curve until he could see the source of the light.

Angel only caught a brief glimpse of something like a large rippling carpet undulating upon the floor and wall before it twisted, a dozen glowing ruby eyes turning to transfix him. With a startled cry Angel fell back as the broad, flat shape flashed toward him, the impression of a beautiful, frightening symmetry etching Angel's vision before he utterly panicked. He turned blindly, losing all awareness until he felt himself suddenly seized and held.

"Damn it, Angel! What is it? What's wrong?" Griff's words finally penetrated and Angel realized only human hands gripped him.

"Didn't—didn't you see it?" Angel gasped, trying to see in all directions at once.

Griff looked past Angel into the narrower tunnel. "I saw the glow of some kind of red light, it got brighter and then you came crashing out... That's all I saw."

Angel didn't want to stand around discussing the experience, or go looking about for the apparition, so he urged a hasty return to the ship, hurrying back to the large central chamber as quickly as his legs and lungs allowed.

"You see?" Griff said at last, puffing along behind him as they approached the exit. "Look how far this chamber extends."

Angel glanced obediently at the yawning distance, but his focus remained on that waiting airlock. "I see, I guess," Angel said. "It's a long ways."

"It's too long; too far," Griff said, his tone strangely terse. "We've got to get to the ship and let them know."

Angel reached the airlock and held his breath in dread until it cycled, finally allowing them through. As the atmosphere dissipated from the lock, Angel touched his helmet to Griff's. "What does the . . . the size of the chambers matter compared to everything else that we saw anyway?"

The lock cycled open and they broke contact to negotiate the path back across the asteroid's surface where they found the survey ship still faithfully holding position. Angel didn't hear the answer to his question until they stood aboard, peeled out of their suits, and only then because it was the first thing Griff blurted out to the waiting Keller. "The damned thing is larger on the inside than it is on the outside!"

"What?" Keller asked blankly, his expression exactly matching how Angel felt.

"And something's alive in there too," Angel added, wondering why his contribution was deemed less important than some odd alien ideas of geometry.

CHAPTER 6

Compared to the high security structures Cherry had been *designed* to infiltrate, Torino's Pioneer Museum did not present any sort of challenge for her initial entry. Dragging Warren Springer Stowe along constituted a small hiccup in her usual methods, and the exfiltration demands for Warren's antique vehicle multiplied that hiccup into true heartburn, sticking with the gastronomical metaphor.

To his credit, Stowe seemed to bear the heavy, bulky backpack without strain, revealing a reasonable degree of physical conditioning under his polished, urbane exterior. Perhaps she wouldn't be forced to literally carry his weight, at least.

As Cherry stood silently waiting at the foot of the museum's darkened rear wall, Warren cleared his throat before speaking up. "So you're going to—"

"Be quiet," Cherry said, never turning from her fixed pose, staring upward. A moment later, she detected the flicker of movement at the crest of the high wall, her preprogrammed LTA drone dropping its small payload right on time while it stayed too high for the drone detectors.

With a flicker of intent, Cherry felt the symbiote shifting within her to compress and harden her fingertips even as she sprang upward, hearing Stowe's startled gasp behind her as her fingers and toes caught tiny imperfections in the stone high above Stowe's head. Two explosive leaps placed her at the rooftop where she found the security scanner muffled by the shroud her drone had dropped. Reaching carefully up within the shroud, she slipped the filter cap in place, knowing she only needed to fool the scanner for a few minutes. Only then did she spool the knotted line down for Stowe.

True to his assertion, he managed to clamber up the high wall with a minimum of grunting and gasping despite his encumbrance. This was good, because Cherry only allowed him a moment to catch his breath as she gathered up the knotted line and spoofed the sensors on the ventilation duct.

"In you go, Stowe," she commanded as she levered the grille open, waiting for him to crawl inside before carefully removing the shroud and filter from the security scanner. That would surely baffle the local constables, and the thought gave Cherry a fleeting pleasure... before the image of a survivor from the Blue Light Brigade reduced to such petty challenges stole that brief joy.

Cherry slipped into the duct and resealed the grille behind them before following Stowe's scuffling progress. "At the fork, bear right," Cherry murmured in a low voice.

"Right," Stowe replied, his voice muffled by the bulk of his body and pack filling the tight ducting.

He crawled along at a steady pace, passing several branching passages and two lighted vent grilles before Cherry called a halt. "Here," she said softly, "if you can turn around."

She double-checked the vent for any sensors before prying it loose, gripping it with one hand as she thrust her head and one shoulder through.

Right on target.

Beneath the vent a large, cluttered back room of the museum lay waiting in the half-light, and Cherry's augmented vision scanned every inch of it for any spectrum of active detection beams, seeing nothing of note. The museum staff clearly had not felt much concern over this storage room filled with oddities of a perceived low value, many shrouded under dusty slip covers. Their inattention to security, and their shameful valuation of Stowe's prized horse-car, should both receive some fresh institutional attention shortly, Cherry thought, grinning to herself.

She pulled back within the duct and rooted through her equipment, rigging a slender line through one magnetic piton. She leaned back out of the open grille to fix it in place until the green indicator illuminated. "Alright, Stowe," Cherry said, passing a loop of the line to him, "down you go, then."

Warren took the loop in hand and hesitantly scooted through the open grille, his heavy pack dragging along behind. Cherry gripped the tail of Warren's pack as he slipped out to swing on the thin line, easing the pack out to hang from Warren's quivering arm. Cherry spooled the line smoothly out, lowering Stowe quickly to the floor before his muscles gave out, following him down after dangling a moment to resecure the grille in place.

As soon as Cherry touched the floor she flipped the line sharply upward, disengaging the piton, causing it to drop like a stone into her waiting hand, while Warren looked on curiously. She turned to Warren as she spooled the line, saying, "Don't you have loads of arcane fiddling to do, Stowe?"

"Hmm? Oh, yes," Warren said with a sheepish tone, scrounging into his pack and drawing out several mysterious objects, one of which sloshed, clearly containing some quantity of fluid. Cherry didn't observe the remainder of his unpacking efforts, moving instead to check the two wide exit doors from the room, securing them against any surprise visitors with two precut lengths of steel cable. By the time she returned to Warren's side, he had his tools and equipment positioned about him, and he began removing the dusty cloth covering his prized antique vehicle.

He glanced over at Cherry. "I spoke to a retired tech who had the engine running on this thing a couple of years ago, so it shouldn't be too tough to get her operational now." Warren whipped the final breadth of cloth away to reveal this ancient prize as he finished talking, and Cherry eyed the vehicle critically in the low light. She found herself appreciating both its contours and that odd flavor of industrial simplicity it exuded, even as her innate sense of practicality scoffed.

Such an anachronism served no useful purpose in modern life, even if it didn't cost a zillion guilders to own it.

Warren opened the engine compartment and poked about, uttering satisfied sounds from time to time, and Cherry cast her eyes over the other oddities relegated to this realm of outer darkness, wondering what failed litmus test resulted in this shameful exile. An ancient leather jacket, framed under glass, rested to one side, a faded cartoon woman painted thereon, her large eyes and long eyelashes offering some strange allure. "Betty Boop," Cherry said quietly, reading the name beneath the image with a shrug. She stepped to a shrouded bulk squatting nearby and lifted the cloth to reveal the other sort of ancient vehicle, gleaming in black and chrome, though this one seemed unsteadily perched on only two wheels. *Motorcycle*, was what Warren had called the thing.

Cherry stood admiring the saddlelike arrangement for the motorcycle's operator when Warren spoke up.

"Like that?" he said, peering out at her from the Mustang's engine compartment, grinning. "Just an engine and a pair of wheels, with a tank full of explosive propellant right between your legs. Hah!"

Cherry tilted her head. "It's got a certain something. Really working for the whole horse thing, weren't they?" She leaned closer. "And who was this *Davidson* chap?"

Warren thrust his head back into the Mustang's engine compartment, his voice emerging from its bowels. "Uh, the fellow who made them, near as I can figure."

Cherry flipped a leg over the motorcycle's seat, sitting comfortably astride, her hands wrapping over the odd control grips. "And not a single gyro or logic controller?"

"Nope," Warren said, his head reemerging. "Not that I've ever seen."

She looked at the dusty, simplistic gauges between the handlebars, one of them revealing a series of graduated numbers that ascended to a zone marked in red. "What happens when your gauge reaches this red zone here, eh?"

Warren glanced up. "Oh that? That's the, uh, red line. When you redline it—push it too far, um, the thing can blow up."

Cherry shook her head. "Our honored forebears esteemed their lives even less than we do, it seems." She looked back at Stowe. "And you've operated some of the, um, motorcycles yourself?"

Stowe scratched his chin, leaving a grease mark. "A few of them, sure."

Cherry raised her eyebrows, considering him. "Mister Stowe, within your unimpressive exterior lurks a serious lack of self-preservation instinct."

"Hah!" Warren laughed, turning back to his tinkering, emerging from the engine compartment after a moment to heft a canister-like object from among his equipment. He moved to one of the strangely flattened wheels of the vehicle, seeming to freeze for a moment before reaching out to aggressively grasp the flattened portion. Stowe uttered a muffled oath.

"What is it?" Cherry asked, slipping from the motorcycle seat.

"Unbelievable!" Warren kicked the wheel. "These ignorant savages must have seen pictures of Old Earth cars sitting on flattened tires and thought that was their natural state." He kicked the wheel again. "You see this beauty? It's a solid composite, not an inflatable tire at all. I mean, collectors often use solids—but this set is actually *formed* with one flattened side; intentionally flawed. Tell me, who is that *stupid*?"

Cherry could see the dilemma immediately and began thinking through the implications as she said, "No one, I think. Anyone would know this thing needs to roll—even I can see that at a glance. So they must have proper wheels around here somewhere." Cherry moved to another cloth-shrouded form and peered under the cover.

Warren snapped his fingers. "Maybe you're right." He moved through the cluttered space, peeking under each cloth, behind every obstruction, but in mere minutes they realized the inescapable truth.

"So, what have you in the way of a backup plan, old stick?" Cherry inquired, staring fixedly at Warren's flushed face. "Because, as I see it, we've got about seventeen bloody minutes until we find ourselves in a little fix."

"Seventeen minutes?" Warren said, looking from the Mustang to his collection of tools and gadgetry. His gaze fell to the motorcycle where it squatted. "Can you—I suppose you can get yourself out of here okay alone?"

"Escape from the underpaid security yobs of a backwater museum?" Cherry inquired. "Though my heart fails at the thought, I think I can manage it somehow."

"Okay, okay," Warren said sheepishly, rubbing his chin as he thought. "I can scrape together a getaway myself. Sure I can. I got this. Chips are down, and Stowe springs into action!" He moved to his arcane equipment in a rush, dragging his pack up beside Mr. Davidson's motorcycle instead and pouring fluids in various portals about the steel-and-chrome anachronism.

After watching for a short time, Cherry pondered Warren's odds of successfully evading even the second-rate security he would face, feeling less certain by the moment.

Warren finished his tinkering and threw a leg over the motorcycle. "Umm..." He looked around the room. "If you could unsecure that door over there for me, that'd be great." Warren tugged his cap over his face until only his eyes were revealed. "Then it may be time for you scarper off. This thing's likely to be really loud, and we'll probably draw some attention when I fire it up."

Cherry loosed the securing cable from the door and cracked it open to survey the wide, shadowy corridor awaiting them. She turned back. "Your vehicle seats two, Stowe. I'll come along for a bit; see what I think of your silly antique thingummy in action."

"Are... are you sure about that?" Warren asked, moving the motorcycle awkwardly forward, pushing himself along with thrusts of his long legs.

"Indeed. If you cock it up too badly, I'll abandon ship and let you fend for yourself." Cherry couldn't see Warren's face, but the wrinkles appearing beside his eyes made it clear her words had provoked a smile.

"Alright," he said, placing one foot on a projecting peg-like member on the side of the machine. "Here goes." He threw his weight down on the peg, cranking it about, and Cherry waited for the advertised roar to bellow forth. Instead the motorcycle emitted a few paltry splutters and a trickle of gray smoke. Cherry folded her arms, leaning against the doorframe. "Umm..." Warren seemed to adjust a few controls before jamming the peg down again... and again... and again.

The process continued for some time and seemed more of an ancient exercise device rather than a means of transportation to Cherry. "Four minutes, Stowe," Cherry said, seeing the sweat dripping from around Warren's eyes, his chest heaving from exertion.

"Four?" he panted. "Okay. Almost got it." He spritzed some fluid into a metal orifice and gathered himself for another lunge.

At first Cherry thought this was yet another spluttering failure, then the sputters chained together, rising, coughing, turning slowly into a deafening roar. Sheathed in a cloud of smoke, Warren wheeled up to Cherry and she cast the doors wide. As Warren urged his metallic steed forward, she leaped lightly up behind him, tugging her own cap down over her face, peering from the eye slit.

Warren poured on the power with a jolt and Cherry seized the machine between her thighs, wrapping her arms around Warren's midsection as she heard and felt the bestial explosion of power.

Though objectively she realized their relative velocity could not compare to any number of vehicles she had operated, the impression of speed as they tore down the corridor, so low to the ground, the snarling exhaust echoing off the walls, made Cherry grin.

Despite the novel assault on her senses, Cherry's tactical mind remained fully engaged, tracking their route through the needlessly sprawling halls of the museum. Placing her mouth beside Warren's head, Cherry yelled, "Bear left... there!"

The ancient engine's roar subsided to a growl and Cherry felt Warren leaning the motorcycle far over as they rounded the corner, wondering how it maintained such stability without gyros.

As they came through the turn, Warren cranked on the accelerator again, the motorcycle straightening, and in the next instant Cherry caught a flash glimpse of a wide-eyed security guard as they roared past him. Cherry initiated a tactical timer at that moment, counting down the seconds until they would surely find themselves thronged by Torino's finest flatfoot ensemble.

Straight ahead Cherry saw the broad exit gleaming and she wondered just how well this two-wheeled contraption would handle the conditions they had planned for the Mustang's exit.

The transponder in Warren's pack linked with Cherry's pre-deployed system, and she saw the orange tracery of burning lines flash over the broad glazing of the exit a millisecond before it spiderwebbed, showering down like a waterfall of white crystals.

As they sped through the powdered crystal remains, Cherry felt the machine beneath her fishtail slightly, but Warren kept them upright. And they flew through the bare frame and out into the night air.

The sense of accomplishment died in a flash of bright light stabbing down from above. Cherry's augmented eyes looked through the blinding beam to see the only thing it could possibly be: a police Mako waiting up there to scoop them up. Inexplicably, impossibly, the police had anticipated their moves somehow.

Stowe and his assertions of genius...

Though Warren's vision could never resolve the sleek vehicle above through the glare, he clearly knew what they faced, whipping the motorcycle around the first corner and stoking even more speed out of the ancient engine, roaring down a narrow alley, the Mako's probing beam losing them for a few moments.

Warren yelled back over his shoulder, "I'll slow down so you can bail!"

Before Cherry could decline his kind offer, they saw the road ahead blocked even as the Mako swung in above them again, its light encircling them. An amplified voice declared something official sounding scarcely discernible over the motorcycle's roar, and Warren throttled back, sliding the two wheels to a halt just a stone's throw from a line of grim constables.

Warren reached over and killed the engine before dragging the hood from his head, tossing it aside. "Good evening, gents!" he called out, fishing in a pocket to withdraw his smoking case as a chorus of weapon-related clicks and buzzes rang out a warning.

"*Warren Springer Stowe*," an officious voice called. "*You are hereby arrested for burglary and theft.*"

Warren smiled, smoothly rolling one of his nasty little cigarettes, and said, "Burglary? Theft? My heavens, no! Just a little demonstration. Publicity stunt, that's all."

Cherry thought Warren was actually doing a fair job of calming the excitable hearts of these coppers, but when he struck a flame from his cigarette case, she discovered her mistake.

The universally eager trigger finger of the constabulary had been tempted too far. Before Warren could even touch his cigarette to the flame, two sap rounds struck him solidly in the gut, knocking him sideways, his limp body sliding to the ground.

Cherry struggled to keep the motorcycle from toppling over to crush Warren's slumped form, easing it down and moving to cautiously check Warren's pulse. As she felt the steady thump, she heard Warren groan, stirring to spit the crumpled cigarette from his lips.

Two figures stepped out from the perimeter light, their grating steps bringing Cherry's distracted gaze up. Cherry knew low-level bureaucrats when she saw them, and the man and woman staring triumphantly down fit the bill perfectly.

"Who are you, then?" the man asked.

Cherry slipped the hood from her head and shook her short hair out, latching onto the first ridiculous pseudonym that came to her mind, seeing those big, melting eyes from the old museum image. "I'm Betty Boop. And you are?"

"We're about to be your worst nightmare, Miss Boop," the woman said, smiling in a truly unpleasant manner, clearly even less aware of Old Earth pop characters than Cherry.

"Not so fast, Masters," Warren slowly growled out from his recumbent position. "My lawyers...gonna make mincemeat of you two."

Cherry really didn't appreciate the way the two stiffs began to smile then.

"Your lawyers, Stowe?" the man asked politely. "Do you mean the esteemed firm of Mordaunt and Mundercast? I believe they only practice within the *Confederated* Worlds, not independent systems like Bethune."

At Warren's gurgled sound of surprise, Masters smiled sweetly. "Oh yes, the official announcements will be everywhere tomorrow, but it's true: Bethune seceded from the Confederated Worlds. Your fancy law firm won't save you this time."

CHAPTER 7

They called this enticing new asteroid *Ajanib*, and Sharif immediately clapped a seal of high security over its existence.

"The timing, Sami," Sharif patiently explained. "Think how it would appear to certain paranoiacs among the Confederated Worlds' hierarchy... We encourage Bethune to part company with the Confederated Worlds at about the same moment we lay claim to some hunk of ancient alien tech right in the Bethune system."

Sami glowered at his older brother, entirely unwilling to be persuaded. Sami had no taste for hiding his light under a bushel, and now that he finally attained a galactic level of success, he naturally wanted to receive a galactic level of acclaim.

Sharif knew the expression on Sami's face all too well, sighing deeply. "Now don't get yourself in a state. Be reasonable and think about what I'm saying for just a few moments." Sami folded his arms, raising his eyebrows skeptically as Sharif pressed on. "How many politicians have you personally known, brother?"

Sami shrugged. "Many and many." Both brothers discovered early in life that no class of person was more eager to become their closest of friends—both being heirs to such an immense fortune—than politicians.

"Yes?" Sharif pressed on. "And think back across all those whom you have known... would you say any of them are likely to believe in an innocent coincidence where matters of power are concerned?" Sami's aloof expression faded somewhat, his eyes becoming thoughtful, remembering. "Or is every last one of them going to be dead certain that we have discovered the greatest secret in human history and we've orchestrated a treacherous method to keep it out of government hands?"

Sami frowned, leaning his head to one side. "We could easily explain that—"

"If they've already got an earful about your little discovery they won't believe anything we say," Sharif said, cutting Sami off. "This, brother, is the way wars stumble into existence."

Sami blew a breath through his teeth, but Sharif knew he had done his work. "So we will quietly find out what all Ajanib means for us, and after we've got that figured"—Sharif didn't say aloud the word they both held in mind, *exploited*—"we'll invite a cluster of top scientists from Earth or wherever to roam all over it, write their papers and such, while we go on about our business."

Sami could only reluctantly agree.

Unfortunately, they soon found that the exploitation phase that both brothers salivated over remained strangely unsatisfying.

The initial coterie of trusted company scientists slipped quietly out to Ajanib and conducted a hurried exploration and analysis, confirming the findings of the initial survey crew. Their reports, however, slowly drained Sami's overweening arrogance away. While the scientists discovered inexplicable *effects* within Ajanib, the scant technology and materials they uncovered represented only comparatively minor revelations for Maktoum Corporation's exploitation.

The scientific analysis infuriated Sami, even as it confirmed that the asteroid truly, bizarrely contained far greater internal volume than its external dimensions allowed. This effect seemed beyond their research, described as some "inexplicable superimposition of hyperbolic geometry" that had no discernible genesis to be reverse engineered. Sami's dreams of Maktoum cargo vessels containing ten times the internal volume suddenly dissolved.

The same dismal outcome unfolded with nearly all the odd technologies Ajanib seemed to promise. The base had operated autonomous mining or cargo transport vehicles through its hundreds of miles of passages, possibly for thousands and thousands of years, but they could locate no great computer brain controlling these vehicles. Artificial gravity, lighting, and atmospheric controls had clearly functioned for many centuries, but no fusion reactors seemed to be creating the necessary power.

Still, Sami stubbornly retained hope for months, expecting some great treasure vault of alien wonders to be discovered within the asteroid at any moment, and he had good reason for maintaining this lingering optimism. Their most gifted scientists seemed baffled by various aspects of Ajanib's wonders, particularly the strange hyperbolic geometrical effects found within, constantly describing the difficulty in retracing their steps to find certain chambers, or discovering new rooms where it seemed that they had previously searched.

When Sharif finally allowed Sami's "triumph" to be broadly revealed to the totality of human space, it had become more of a puzzling curiosity than a revolution in alien technology. In many ways it resembled the Gear on Bethune itself in this light, and the small trickle of scientists permitted to visit from Earth's universities only confirmed this.

Among the many burst bubbles, the report of an alien entity that Angel Rua encountered in the depths of Ajanib faded into the realm of myth, attributed to little more than heightened tensions and poor visibility through an unfamiliar helmet.

When Sami Maktoum finally made his way out to Ajanib himself, he could only bitterly grasp at a small thread of gratitude. Out of all the potential world-shaking discoveries in alien technology, Maktoum scientists had only isolated an amazing new lubricant that the automated mining car system employed, and this one humble product appeared likely to recoup the funds Sami had invested to find and secure the asteroid. As he walked from the large central section of Ajanib the surveyors had called the Plaza, this reflection didn't warm Sami's heart, and he still cherished a faint glimmering hope that Ajanib could become the astonishing success he had sought for many years.

When he strolled down a smooth ramp to one of the lower levels, a group of Maktoum scientists around him, Sami barely heard what they said to him, picturing his moment of glory when Sharif would finally be forced to admit that Sami's mercurial nature also contained its own fair share of family genius.

He popped out of his reverie for a moment to observe one of Ajanib's automated vehicles go roaring by them, seeing his frustrations embodied in its smooth gray chassis. How had these vehicles operated for thousands of years with simple automation alone? And why would such a technologically advanced race utilize wheeled vehicles at all? Just as Sami's mind pondered over the possibility of an alien's sentimental attachment to wheeled vehicles, the most brilliant idea of his whole life struck in a sudden thunderbolt of inspiration, almost blinding his natural vision as the ingenious images filled his mind, one after the other.

For once in his life, Sami saw the string of those earlier business failures in his life from a whole new perspective, each of them a necessary link in a chain that led to this fateful moment.

As he turned and looked at the miles of smooth tunnels, the galleries, the sheer enormity of it, Sami spoke out aloud, "It's perfect!"

The technicians and scientists around him didn't know what precisely seemed perfect to Sami, but they all felt naturally relieved... until they eventually saw Sami's plan take shape, their initial enthusiasm dying in one horrible unscientific instant of commercialism.

CHAPTER 8

Through the misadventures of his preceding years, Warren Springer Stowe had experienced only a few brief stints in jail, but those fleeting forays behind bars had given him a fair grip on the necessary skills. Those skills, combined with his lifelong fascination with peculiar people, served to secure his odd social position within Torino's rather barbaric lockup.

"Four queens, ace high," Warren said, spreading his cards across the crude metal table and smiling at his three poker victims.

Bailey muttered a vile curse and threw his cards down with a slap while the other two merely groaned, shaking their heads nearly in unison. "I'm done, man," one of them said. "You've cleaned me out."

"Ah, investing in your education never comes cheap," Warren offered as he policed up the cards, ignoring Bailey's seething presence entirely. "Just think how you'll be fleecing them when you get sent to labor camp."

The freshly shorn bleater perked up at the thought. "Hah! That's a good point."

Bailey still glowered savagely, but Warren only smiled as he arose from the hard stool. "Dear fellows, I have kept an important meeting waiting, so if you'll excuse me..." He pretended not to hear the grumbled aspersions, gathering his jail-scaled pathetic winnings and striding off to join a fresh-faced young man sitting on the nearby steps to the upper tier.

Warren extended his hand. "Guy, isn't it?"

The young man stood and took Warren's hand, fidgeting

47

uncomfortably in the red fabric that loosely resembled pants and shirt, the same horrid attire they all wore. "Yes, uh, Guy Betner, Mister Stowe."

Warren held up a hand. "No formality here, Guy. Call me Warren. That's formal enough compared to what Bailey was just calling me under his breath."

Guy looked past Warren at the still-fuming Bailey. "Man, I can't believe you aren't worried about him snapping on you."

Warren rubbed his chin, gazing across the dim and unimpressive space they called the "dayroom," missing the fiddly joys of his smoking case to occupy his hands. "This is your first time locked up, right?" Guy looked at Warren uncertainly but nodded. "Yeah, Guy? Well you'll find growling soreheads like Bailey in every jail and probably every prison too, to be sure." Warren smiled down at Guy. "You've just got to make it clear to all the Baileys of the world that there's easier meat to be had . . . and then you never, ever accept a threat."

Warren saw the skepticism on Guy's face, which normally wouldn't have mattered, but he needed Guy for a particular purpose, and soon. Guy moistened his lips before saying, "So you just have to be a bigger badass than everyone else then, right?" His tone hovered on the edge of disdain.

Warren chuckled, holding his arms out to his sides displaying his slender build. "Looking at my massive physique I'm sure it's easy to make that mistake, hah!" He winked at Guy. "But no, no, you don't understand what—"

At that moment a loud, unrefined voice interjected, "Stowe! I need those hots we was talkin' about, Stowe."

Warren turned to consider the unpleasant face of Calder, who shuffled nearer, fidgeting, shifting his weight from foot to foot. "Ah, Calder, friend, you see I'm in a meeting just now, so—"

"I need those hots *now*, Stowe, like we talked about," Calder growled again.

Warren smiled, feeling Guy's eyes on him. "When I'm done here, friend."

Calder knotted his fists and fidgeted even nearer, his face twitching. "*Now*, Stowe!"

Warren turned to Guy and said, "If you will excuse me just a moment, Guy, I will take care of Calder here." Guy nodded, his measuring expression seeming to transform into something closer to contempt, but Warren turned back to Calder as he rooted under his loose shirt with his left hand.

Warren's hand emerged, dropping two hot sticks on the orange-colored enamel floor. "There you are, Calder lad," he said, and then dropped a crude, jagged shank down beside the hot sticks with a metallic clank. "But pick it *all* up, you hear?"

Calder froze in his fidgeting as he spotted the makeshift weapon, his beady eyes flashing to find Warren's right hand tucked beneath the fringe of his shirt. "Pick them up, Calder . . . now," Warren said again, smiling.

Calder looked down at the hot sticks and the waiting shank, stepping back hesitantly. "I guess I can wait a little."

Warren stopped smiling. "You interrupted my meeting to get the damned things, so pick them up. Now."

Calder swallowed, fidgeting about for one tortured second before backing away, moving off across the dayroom, his shoulders slumped. Warren watched Calder's retreat a moment before stooping to scoop up the shank and hot sticks, tucking them away. He sighed. "Now, where were we, Guy?"

Guy's expression held no sign of contempt now. "You were saying you're not a badass . . ."

"Oh yes, precisely," Warren said with a wink, glancing across the dayroom. "Like dear Calder here, I didn't need to be more lethal, just very, very clear on my position."

Guy gnawed his lip, holding Warren's gaze. "And what if Calder called your bluff?"

Warren looked sharply at Guy, shaking his head. "It was no bluff. It's never a bluff." He looked to the far side of the dayroom and nodded his head toward the mountainous figure of Monk. "Monk tried me my second day here and found that I wasn't bluffing either."

Guy stared over at Monk for a disbelieving moment before looking back to Warren. "You *beat* Monk?"

"Beat him?" Warren laughed. "Lord no! As I understand it, he socked me up quite thoroughly. Fortunately, I slept through the worst bits of it, so I only had to contend with a few days of pissing blood, and of course this missing tooth." Warren opened his mouth and felt for his absent molar with a mournful frown. He closed his mouth and shrugged. "Anyway, getting thrashed by Monk doesn't prove I'm some kind of badass. It proves that I don't back down, and anyone wants to push me now knows they'll have to earn it the hard way, see?"

Guy nodded, his expression becoming thoughtful. "I guess I do." He looked down, deflated. "What a dirty, barbaric place we're stuck in now..."

Warren's smile grew. "You think so? I wonder if all this is what's always just beneath the surface every day, and society simply puts a fat layer of feel-good icing on the top so we can all pretend we're better than we really are."

At Guy's uneasy grimace, Warren chuckled. "Or maybe not. What do I really know? Not a philosopher, right?" He clapped Guy on the shoulder. "But I hear you served in the Scout services not so long ago, and that's what I'd like to learn about, if you're willing."

Guy looked up, surprise replacing the glum set to his lips. "Yeah, I was three years in the Frontier Scouts, and then decided Bethune was my kind of planet... What a damned mistake that was." Guy's face began to settle back into a morose cast.

"But tell me, Guy," Warren nudged, "don't you Scouts learn some rudimentary codes for, um... odd communication scenarios?"

Guy nodded. "We had to learn three or four ridiculous, antique codes, like, um, Skagway Semaphore, Cut-Key, and—"

"Yes, yes, yes," Warren interrupted, holding up a hand. "And can you still remember any of those, er, ridiculous codes?"

Guy shrugged. "My speed probably isn't that great, but I don't think I'll ever forget them, the way they drilled them into us." He seemed lost in the memory of it all for a moment, but slowly sharpened his focus back on Warren. "What would you want with antique codes anyway? No one really uses them, and the only people who know any of these are Scouts... and maybe a few odd military units."

Warren smiled, producing a piece of paper with lines of text scrawled upon its wrinkled surface. "This is a message I want you to encode in your various antique ciphers, Guy." He pointed at a crusty pipe that ran along one wall of the dayroom, disappearing through the dayroom partition. "See that pipe? I want you to tap out the encoded message on that."

Guy looked at the pipe, then at the scrap of paper, frowning. "I don't... You know that pipe doesn't go outside the building, right? It just goes through to the women's side of the jail."

Warren raised his eyebrows and looked at the pipe again. "Oh my goodness, really? Is that where it goes? Huh." He focused back on Guy. "Tap out my message on that pipe a few times for a couple of days, and I'll pay you, say, six hot sticks."

Guy didn't possess the gene for haggling evidently, and agreed instantly. "Deal. When do I begin?" He reached for the note, but Warren held it up, his smile fading.

"But, Guy, understand this: My business is mine alone. You understand me, my friend? Don't make my affairs the business of anyone else, right? I wouldn't like it,"

Guy's face settled into serious lines. "I understand, Mister Stowe."

CHAPTER 9

Cherry had never experienced an actual jail before, though she had been confined for months after the war, just like all the other survivors of the Blue Light Brigade. She immediately discovered that the two experiences held only a few similarities. Her military imprisonment constantly reflected the abject horror and loathing with which the Blue Light survivors were regarded by her so-called superiors in the military hierarchy.

Hail conquering heroes indeed, Cherry bitterly thought, remembering those darkest of days, shrugging at last. *We earned it . . . every bit of their fear.*

Now, imprisoned as an actual criminal miscreant, an enemy of law and order, Cherry found herself regarded more in the light of an evil child, denied most avenues for personal agency or volition, punitively restricted from common comforts and pleasures, but with obviously little real concern for any violent impulses Cherry might have. However, Bethune's authorities had no idea that they now entertained such a storied mistake of military hardware within their jail, and Cherry made certain of their ongoing ignorance.

She had arrived on Bethune without planetary officials ever being the wiser, utilizing the smuggler networks for all her travel, and when they processed her into Torino's jail, she had masked her fingerprints and retinal patterns. Her DNA profile remained a classified military secret back home, so the locals wouldn't find any satisfaction that way either. The fact that she remained adrift in the general female population of the jail meant that Warren Springer Stowe had kept his scream-hole shut about her actual identity, at least so far.

About fifty times every slow, boring day Cherry contemplated escaping, simply to get some edible food and a glimpse of the outdoors, but every time she managed to talk herself out of the impulse, only because escape would likely result in injuring or killing at least one or two Torino constables. Cherry silently wished that those military lab-coat stiffs back home could see how infinitely gentle she behaved when a couple of worthless specimens of humanity were all that stood between her and a decent meal.

If she examined her feelings candidly, though, Cherry could not argue that she waited with some degree of curiosity to see if Mr. Stowe would actually honor all his talk and legitimately utilize whatever influence he still possessed to free her. He certainly seemed to think Bethune's baffling secession from the Confederated Worlds would only prove a temporary setback. But as the weeks passed, Cherry began to wonder if Warren might be attempting to ditch her. She quietly vowed that if such a betrayal became clear it would become the most permanent mistake of Stowe's storied career.

Still . . . she had to acknowledge that the dark voice of the abyss that had once called so urgently now seemed strangely subdued despite the long, empty hours of incarceration. As the women in the dayroom began to screech about one of their frequent dramas, Cherry grimaced to herself. Maybe that dark internal call simply couldn't compete with the regular ruckus that now served as ambient noise in her confined little world.

Slipping off her hard, metal bunk, Cherry stepped through the open cell door into the dim and dingy common area they called a dayroom. Two women stood just outside their own cell doors, yelling and gesticulating in their tiresome fashion. "I told you I would kick your teeth in if you didn't quit that damned tapping!" the first woman shrilled.

"Are you completely out of your damned mind, Verna? I ain't tapping on shit. It's just them voices back in your head making you think everyone's trying to get you."

Verna, Cherry observed, was a sturdy red-faced specimen, shaped very much like a swollen thumb, and it seemed likely she was about to tackle her equally unattractive tormentor.

As Verna opened her mouth to begin another round of braying, the sound of metallic tapping began to ring out. "There it is!" Verna yelled. "You hear it, don't ya? Who's doing that?"

As several women began commenting on the tapping sound, Cherry lost interest and turned to return to her cell, but a sequence of taps rang out, and she turned sharply, listening.

A fellow prisoner slumped at a nearby table looked up at Cherry saying, "Whaddya think that—"

"Shut up," Cherry snapped, attuned to the sound ringing out from the pipe. As the woman sat mumbling quiet curses and threats, Cherry heard the coded message begin again, this time catching the whole thing.

Cherry strolled over to the exposed pipe, hardening a fingertip to a rigid point, and rapped out a short sequence of ringing notes.

Verna and several of the others looked suspiciously at Cherry, already prey to her earlier biting words, but she shrugged and trailed back to her cell, only allowing a small personal smile in the semiprivacy of its confines.

The coded message told her that for the moment Warren Springer Stowe ostensibly remained engaged in her well-being, and he evidently had hatched a plan.

Whether his plan worked or not, Cherry decided it was enough. She would let him live, regardless, just for the effort.

Now, how long must she wait for some change of scenery...?

CHAPTER 10

Maktoum Corporation had employed their full powers of *persuasion* to encourage Bethune's bid for independence from the Confederated Worlds, and now the Maktoum office on Bethune buzzed with activity, profiting from this fresh political reality.

Certain operations forbidden under Confederated Worlds law were launched, various revenue streams laundered, and assets of questionable provenance were dispatched to off-world buyers who streamed into Bethune on every inbound star liner.

This kept most of Sami's subordinates beyond busy, allowing him a free hand for hatching the most ambitious scheme of his life without tale bearers immediately grassing on him to Sharif. He wanted his vision for the mysterious asteroid base, Ajanib, fully operational (and hopefully profitable) before Sharif got wind of the unorthodox application that only he, Sami Maktoum, would ever have had the imagination and guts to attempt.

To accomplish this Sami had to bend a few rules—and not lie, precisely... merely suggest to various company department heads that Sharif had fully signed off on this new operation.

If Sami would have any chance of presenting his angry brother an inarguable business success, he would need to accomplish all this quickly, and that time pressure had the unintended consequence of driving Sami to heights of labor and productivity he had never known before. He remained in his office, or in meetings with suppliers, from early in the morning until late at night, striving to scrape all the necessary pieces together and have them operational in Ajanib at an unbelievable pace.

He sent materials and construction crews out to the asteroid to construct dozens of luxury suites, lounges, and galleries. He purchased a top-of-the-line universal fabrication system, and as it was being installed, he threaded a dangerous course through Maktoum Corporation departments to obtain the centerpiece of his whole new vision, the fruits of his earlier brainstorm: complete fabrication files from a certain era of Old Earth road vehicles. These ancient files he managed to secure despite a degree of skepticism from various Maktoum department supervisors that made Sami sweat, knowing Sharif would likely hear about it sooner rather than later. He felt sure that time ran down quickly, and Sami stepped up his frenetic efforts to an even higher pace. Success must arrive within months, not years.

On his checklist, Sami found himself in another tricky balancing act. He needed to begin client acquisition immediately, even though the operations on Ajanib stood far short of completion, and this presented an even greater conundrum. The client base Sami targeted populated the upper echelons of wealth and power—the very people Sharif might interact with on a social level.

If Sami advertised under the prestigious Maktoum brand, he would obtain an immediate badge of legitimacy...but also very possibly trigger an immediate visit from one outraged older brother.

After struggling mightily over the risks and benefits, Sami could only take the path of compounding risk. The Maktoum name adorning his enterprise was simply too valuable for an operation that *needed* top-tier clients in a hurry.

With the decision made, targeted advertising launched out to the ultra-wealthy of a dozen worlds and more, and Sami calculated market penetration, interstellar transit schedules, and construction progress advancing within the asteroid facility, Ajanib, timing everything down to the wire.

Almost immediately after initiating the advertising campaign, Sami discovered that he had nonetheless *mis*calculated, and for once in his life the mistake he made was in *undervaluing* the brilliance of his own creative vision.

Reservations poured in with shocking immediacy, some eager enthusiasts setting off for Bethune at once, and Sami faced a new terror, greater even than his fear of Sharif's wrath. Sami could not bear the thought of the embarrassment he would face as a mob of the wealthy elite arrived to experience the heady joys of Ajanib, only to find it an unfinished shell, in their jaundiced eyes nothing more than a sham. With this horror driving him, Sami made preparations to rocket out to Ajanib himself where he could drive laborers night and day, personally ensuring that the first paying clients to enter within the exotic confines of the alien asteroid would find exactly what they had been promised.

"I will be out at Ajanib for at least two weeks," Sami detailed to his assistant, Pushkin. "Forward all communication to my office there, but don't tell anyone that I'm off Bethune."

"Of course, sir," Pushkin said, his placid features composed, his hands clasped behind his back, effortlessly recalling every order Sami ever uttered without a reliance on notes.

Sami threw a few items from his desk into a satchel and paused to rub weary eyes. "Oh, yes . . . Pushkin, have we any experts available on antique Earth ground vehicles? I need one, fast."

Pushkin nodded as if this request was entirely reasonable. "I believe I mentioned the peculiar news that Warren Springer Stowe was arrested some weeks ago, and he's here in Torino, jailed awaiting a criminal trial."

"Stowe?" Sami repeated, remembering something about a stolen vehicle and some pathetic local museum. "I need someone who is *not* in jail," Sami said testily, "someone who's able to board a ship in . . . an hour and twenty minutes."

Pushkin pursed his lips, contemplating. "Hmm, there is a local collector—Cathwaite is his name, as I recall. Perhaps you could entice him somehow."

Being an heir to all the Maktoum charm and fortune, of *course* Sami could entice Cathwaite, especially since this Cathwaite embodied a burning addiction for anything related to Old Earth vehicles and culture. An hour and twenty-two minutes after his conversation with Pushkin, Sami and Cathwaite set off for the asteroid Ajanib.

"So you have really secured genuine fabrication files from the original manufacturers?" Peter Cathwaite asked for the fourth time, his bushy eyebrows lowered until they nearly touched the rim of the gleaming brandy snifter that he pressed to his lips.

"Yes," Sami patiently said, also for the fourth time, quietly pleased at Cathwaite's unconcealed awe. "Original, validated, direct from the top manufacturers of the era."

Cathwaite swirled the vintage brandy in his mouth, shaking his head as he swallowed. "God. How did that ever survive the Super Cleanse?"

Sami held up a palm. "We can only guess, but survive they did, and since most of the files represent vehicles from one, um, especially prized decade, our guess suggests a knowledgeable connoisseur stood behind the preservation."

Cathwaite perked up. "An especially prized decade? Which decade are we talking about here?"

Sami's own obsession with Old Earth vehicles—like most of his obsessions—had burned intensely but for a short duration, and now he couldn't readily recall all those countless details. Collectors only really valued ten decades or so of Earth history, back when most ground transport vehicles had been direct hydrocarbon burners, but which specific decades had become most prized again? Sami couldn't immediately remember, but he knew his fabrication files comprised the absolute cream of the crop. "Oh, you'll see soon enough, Cathwaite," he said, rather than reveal his shameful forgetfulness. He really needed about five hours of uninterrupted sleep, soon.

Sami managed to obtain that sleep and more before his ship reached Ajanib and he witnessed the most obvious first sign of his recent improvements. The utilitarian lock extension that they had originally added to the asteroid provided safe and functional docking for scientific vessels and supply ships, but Sami wanted his ultra-wealthy clientele embraced with suitable luxury from the moment they arrived, so an entirely separate docking arm now served as Sami and Cathwaite's introduction to the new face of Ajanib.

The ship's lock cycled to reveal a wide hallway laid out in teakwood with brass railings and accents; the *Nautical Look*, the architectural designer called it. Cathwaite nodded appreciatively. "Very nice, Sami, I must say."

Sami's on-site section supervisor, Belinda Athenos, greeted them alone, her posture rigid, but lines of fatigue combined with darkly circled eyes to present a picture of near-exhaustion. "Welcome to Ajanib, Director," Belinda said, bowing her head slightly. "We have two premier suites fully prepared, if you would like to—"

"In a moment, Athenos," Sami said, cutting her off. "We would like to go look over Build-Out first, if you could have someone take our things to our suites, please."

Sami prided himself on reading people at a glance, but the expression that flashed across the face of Belinda Athenos defied his interpretation, seeming a combination of exasperation and . . . fear?

"Yes, Director," is all she audibly replied, handing them each a small device. "Here are your inertial trackers. As you know, sir, the spatial geometry inside the station is . . . unique, and people get lost easily. With the inertial tracker you can always retrace your steps."

"Yes, yes," Sami said impatiently. "Now, if you can point me toward Build-Out, I will leave you to your duties."

Again an unreadable expression flickered across her face, but she bowed her head, meekly offering, "Continue to the mezzanine, straight ahead, then follow the ebony track. It will take you to Build-Out, and a few installation techs should be on hand if you have any questions there."

Before she finished speaking Sami was in motion, Cathwaite stepping up briskly at his side, Belinda Athenos left behind.

While the mezzanine space revealed the first glimpses of Ajanib's native materials to them, it also bore the refining marks of Sami's expensive renovations, a broad gleaming space with only the eyesore of stacked construction materials to detract.

Sami saw the path diverge ahead, with a sparkling white path leading leftward, a broad golden walkway continuing straight ahead, and a glass-like ebony track to the right. Following the right-hand path, they moved into a narrow corridor that continued about fifty paces to a luxurious control room equipped with a dozen semi-enclosed cubicles.

"Ah," Sami said, smiling. "Here we are." He only understood what he beheld because he had selected and purchased the equipment himself, but he had never actually utilized such a system himself.

Now, where were those techs she mentioned?

"So, how does it work, precisely?" Cathwaite asked, scratching his chin as he looked over one workstation.

Sami's verbal dexterity rarely failed him, and it threw him a lifeline now. "It's meant to be intuitive to use. So, you can be our first test, and we will both learn if it is as intuitive as advertised."

Cathwaite shrugged. "Okay, I'll give her a try. In the interest of science and all." He settled himself in the enveloping embrace of the waiting seat, and things immediately began to happen. A row of indicator lights illuminated, one after the other, even as a holographic display fizzed into life just before Cathwaite's bemused face. The dark wall facing the workstation glowed, Sami suddenly realizing that this "wall" was the view pane into the fabrication chamber itself that now stood under warm lights, waiting for its first creation.

Sami looked back down to see Cathwaite navigating through menus, murmuring as he did, "Incredible... simply incredible. Ford... hmmm... General Motors, Chevrolet..."

Sami heard the dimly remembered Old Earth brand names, wondering if Cathwaite's pronunciation was correct. If so, Sami had been mispronouncing "Chevrolet" for years.

"Can I...?" Cathwaite turned to regard Sami, his expression boyishly expectant. "Can I try constructing something?"

Sami had been assured all was in readiness. "Be my guest."

Cathwaite selected something called a 1968 Corvette Stingray, actuating it. Then Sami and Cathwaite watched as the universal fab-all came to life on the other side of the view pane, the lines of the vehicle coming together under glowing plasma injectors.

The moment of truth came quickly for Sami now. Would it all work as advertised?

CHAPTER 11

Sharif Maktoum prided himself on his ability to balance his professional duties with his role as a husband and father, attempting to emulate the lives of his own parents and grandparents before him in a longstanding family tradition. As a key part of this determination, Sharif worked from his Earth-based office as much as possible, attending every one of his wife's celebrated showings, where her paintings invariably drew critical and popular praise. He also made appearances at his daughter's polo matches and his son's triathlon events.

As his parents had demonstrated, these activities provided an almost mystical grounding effect that had kept generations of Maktoums productive and reasonably human despite the siren calls of immense wealth.

It was due to a heavy upcoming schedule of family activities that Sharif originally ignored the initial warning signs arising from Bethune.

First had been the call from Humphreys over in the Digital Properties department. "I just wanted to be sure I acted correctly, sir," Humphreys said in an apologetic tone. "Your brother indicated you had approved a substantial transfer, but I couldn't find a signature stamp from your office, so I—"

"Which property, Humphreys?" Sharif had interrupted with a sinking heart.

"Um, it's cataloged as Echo three four dash seven . . . a very large fabrication file series with—"

"Got it," Sharif interrupted again. "When did this transfer take place?"

"On the sixth, sir," Humphreys said. "A couple of weeks ago now, I guess."

Sharif had reassured Humphreys, ending the call, then decided that it was best to leave Sami to his devices for the moment, although he could only guess what harebrained scheme his brother pursued now. Sami undoubtedly believed he had found some amazing method to capitalize upon his earlier disastrous brainstorm, and Sharif would allow him a suitable quantity of metaphorical rope to eventually hang himself.

The second indicator of big ideas arising from the vicinity of Bethune hit Sharif's desk only a week later. A note from one of his most attentive bean counters flagged an unusually rapid increase in capital expenditures on the Ajanib project, detailing invoices from a troubling array of suppliers. The bizarre diversity of products and services puzzled Sharif as greatly as it irritated him, providing clues that seemed to run counter to each other. Was Sami establishing a top-shelf brothel on Ajanib, or some sort of high-tech prototyping facility? Whatever it was, Sharif knew he would need to address it personally.

With a long-suffering sigh, Sharif sent a message to his assistant, asking him to fit a trip to Bethune on the itinerary within the next eight weeks...but this rash of Sami-inspired revelations was not complete.

A week later, Sharif noticed an unusual degree of interest in his appearance at a prestigious gallery featuring some of his wife's latest work. She was the focal point of the evening, and yet several of the wealthy scions attending the event caught Sharif's eye with appreciative nods, smiles, and raised glasses, causing Sharif no small degree of puzzlement.

It was only as the evening wound down that he learned the unsettling truth when one of the Picot twins approached through the watchful screen of Sharif's security agents. "A master stroke, Sharif," Evelyn Picot said, smiling, "though a bit out of character for you, I must say." Sharif glimpsed the flashy animation rippling across Evelyn's palm slate, words scrolling over the image of antique Old Earth vehicles racing down the smooth, aquamarine tunnels of Ajanib.

Sharif didn't read every word of the high-end advertisement, but he saw the phrase "racing, high-stakes gambling, unregulated competition . . ." before the Maktoum logo, riding high, caught his attention.

Evelyn Picot stared at Sharif's face as the images sank in, saying, "You seem surprised, Sharif."

Sharif looked up to her face, his own expression as close to neutral as he could manage. "I *am* surprised. Sami is far ahead of schedule, it appears, and I didn't think the science teams had finished with Ajanib as yet."

Evelyn accepted this, shaking her head with a roguish gleam in her eye. "Another surprising benefit of this Bethune system's defection, ditching the Confederated Worlds, right?" she said. "A more adult tolerance for gambling and high-risk competition must be perfect for this sort of thing." She paused. "But those genuine copies of Old Earth vehicles . . . Where did you ever obtain certified fabrication files for antiques like that? Those must be worth a fortune."

Through a blank smile, Sharif said, "Sami certainly thinks they are worth more than I would have thought possible."

As soon as Sharif extricated himself from Evelyn Picot, he sent a terse message to his assistant instructing him to cancel anything that conflicted with a forthcoming trip. Sharif would be visiting Bethune as soon as he could feasibly get there. Until he faced Sami directly, alone, Sharif would not be pleasant company for anyone.

District Attorney Bartson strode into the holding cell that served as a meeting room, featuring a table bolted to the floor and chairs equally secured, where Warren Springer Stowe waited, seated on one hard chair, his arms crossed. Although the expression on Stowe's face seemed to retain a degree of the cockiness that irked Bartson to no end, the dehumanizing jail pajamas adorning Stowe's lanky body, and the rather pale, drawn cast to Stowe's features helped mitigate that feeling somewhat. Though Bartson would never willingly admit it to anyone, one key pleasure he found in an otherwise thankless job was the sensation he felt in moments such as this. For weeks Stowe had suffered under the deprivations common to "civilized" jails across human society, eating tasteless slop three meals per day, trying to sleep on a hard metal bunk, and all while clothed in a garment so obviously designed to humiliate. Bartson, however, breezed into these meetings, dressed immaculately, his hair finely coifed, the glow on his skin reflecting a recent luncheon at an outdoor corner café, frequently with a tall mug of dark roast steaming in his hand.

The contrast never failed to give Bartson a jolt of some lovely, primal energy, the delicious taste of true dominating power. When the subject of his domination was such an arrogant and wealthy prick like Warren Springer Stowe, it became nearly orgasmic.

Stowe sat silently observing Bartson as the folder in Bartson's hand was opened, spread flat on the table. "Well, Mister Stowe, since you refuse to obtain a licensed local attorney, it appears you will be representing yourself at trial." Warren said nothing, eyeing Bartson curiously, and Bartson smiled, going on. "In addition to the charges we previously mentioned, you will now also be charged with one assault."

Warrens brows lowered thoughtfully. "And whom have I supposedly assaulted, sport?"

Bartson sifted through his folder. "Hmm, his name is here somewhere. He was a guard at the museum, struck by flying glass. He's pretty badly injured, unable to work . . . I'd imagine he'll pursue personal damages too."

Warren smiled thinly. "It begins to become clear, I think. What sort of damages would you guess this nameless guard is seeking then, Bartson, old boy?"

Warren's knowing tone rankled Bartson, and he returned fire by taking a succulent gulp from his steaming mug and considering Warren with all the hauteur he could summon. "Unlike your endless escapades across the Confederated Worlds, here on Bethune no one is above the law, and now you will most certainly *pay*, Stowe."

Warren smiled more broadly. "I most certainly will *not*."

All of Bartson's warm satisfaction evaporated in an instant, thoroughly infuriated by Warren's stubborn hubris. "Then you will continue to enjoy jail life until your trial, where you will be found guilty. You do understand the severity of your crimes, don't you? When you are convicted you will spend at *least* eight years in our charming old-fashioned prison." Bartson took the opportunity for his own smile. "How's that for *paying*, Stowe?"

Warren shook his head. "You small-minded guys never really think about it all, do you? You can certainly make me *suffer*, that's true, but every day you will be spooning me your god-awful food, lodging me in your medieval prisons, watched over by shift after shift of guards for all these supposed years of my incarceration. *I* won't be paying anything; *your* citizens, *your* taxpayers will be paying."

Bartson snorted. "Public safety is in the interest of every law-abiding citizen, Stowe, and one of the few things taxpayers don't quibble about. Your sympathy for them is quite wasted."

Warren ran fingers through his hair, musing. "Oh, I don't know, Bartson. Someone might point out that prisons are great for employing minor bureaucrats . . . and also great for manufacturing lifetime law breakers. When a fellow thinks about it for a bit, there really is quite a lot to, um . . . quibble about."

Bartson felt his teeth grinding and forced himself to relax, taking a calming breath. "What are you trying to say, Stowe? You going to buy a marketing campaign decrying the evils of our criminal justice system? Even while you rot in a cell?"

Warren stared calmly into Bartson's eyes. "I just might."

Bartson stopped just short of slamming the table with his clenched fist, struggling for calm and measured words. They had seized every one of Warren's belongings they could find on Bethune without locating any substantial form of transferable wealth that could be used for leverage, but they knew he possessed a tidy personal fortune. "I think I mentioned our restitution-and-recompense system to you before. Spend your guilders on restitution and buy yourself a greatly abbreviated prison sentence. That will serve you far better than some pointless crusade."

Warren snorted. "Serve *you* far better, I hear."

Bartson felt a flush mount to his cheeks, and that angered him more than anything. He slapped his folder closed and stood. "I think this meeting is concluded. You and your accomplice . . . uh . . . Miss Boop, will be enjoying the pleasures of our jail for some time to come." He tapped the access plate and the outer door clanked open. He smiled with all the venom he could muster. "My case load is so heavy, I was forced to obtain waivers from the magistrate. You and your accomplice have your speedy trial rights suspended until further notice. Enjoy your time here."

Bartson turned on his heel, and if Warren offered a response it was lost in the cycling of the door. Masters stepped out from the observation room as Bartson stood fuming, her expression tentative. "That didn't go quite as we'd hoped," she offered.

"No," Bartson said. "Who the hell has a million-guilder retainer with a law firm, then won't spend a mere hundred thousand to get his ass out of a dungeon? And where the hell is he keeping his bankroll, anyway?"

Masters shook her head, mournfully considering. They both had mentally spent the fat bonus they would have received if Stowe only paid the restitution and recompense like any other sane wealthy person would.

Bartson and Masters walked silently down the echoing concrete hallway, attempting to figure some means of compelling Warren Springer Stowe to behave rationally. Bartson had all but promised his mistress that cozy little seaside cottage she longed for. Stowe's stubbornness, and Bartson's resulting pay cut, would not greatly impress a woman so universally admired, and Bartson would do nearly anything to retain her affections. Nearly anything . . .

CHAPTER 12

Sami Maktoum and Peter Cathwaite stood side by side as the final fabrication process finished and the conveyor deposited the gleaming golden vehicle before them. For Sami, the moment contained an odd tension that he could scarcely admit to himself. It was one thing to have a coterie of forensic data miners tell you that you possess original, certified fabrication files. It was quite another thing to invest billions of guilders (and likely incur the wrath of one's brother) on a gamble that had never been physically validated.

Now, with a sort of expert at his side, Sami waited nervously for Cathwaite's first comment, telling himself over and over that of course everything was perfect. The protracted silence as Cathwaite merely stared at the vehicle began to abrade Sami's reassurance but he bit his lip, refusing to display any uncertainty.

"Huh," Cathwaite uttered at last, causing Sami to interpret that sound into meaning . . . without success.

Cathwaite stepped up and gently touched the smooth surface of the vehicle's hood, turning sharply back to Sami. "When can we drive it?"

Sami throttled back his questions and forced a smile. "Drive it? I think we can try it now, Cathwaite. Just need to fill the, um, hydrocarbon reservoir here." Sami puzzled over the fuel-dispensing system for a moment before setting it in motion, a mechanical arm extending to the vehicle, its liquid payload jetting into the vehicle's internal tank.

When Sami looked back at Cathwaite it was to see him on his knees beside one of the rubbery black wheels. "Hmm, composite solids," Cathwaite murmured. "Not inflatable tires like the original vehicles."

"Yes," Sami said in a neutral tone, not sure what Cathwaite was indicating by this comment, whether a composite solid was good or bad.

"Aside from that," Cathwaite said, standing erect and smoothing a hand over the vehicle again, "seems exactly original. Like a time capsule." He opened the vehicle's door and slipped inside, placing two hands on the steering wheel. Sami fumbled with the unfamiliar door handle for a moment before climbing in, shutting the door behind him.

Cathwaite looked over the instruments and moved his feet about on the three odd-shaped pedals before reaching up to actuate the starting process. Sami had driven one ancient Earth vehicle in his younger years, and retained a clear recollection of a roaring engine noise as all those hydrocarbons exploded inside the clunky metal monstrosity. As Cathwaite triggered the ignition operation it seemed to utter a plaintive, repetitive straining sound that stopped abruptly as Cathwaite mumbled to himself. Sami looked over at Cathwaite with the beginnings of panic gnawing his guts, and Cathwaite actuated the starting sequence again, the straining sound rising two or three times before it coughed, roaring into life, the vehicle stirring and shifting beneath them as Cathwaite revved the engine.

Cathwaite grinned at Sami, moving the gear selection knob around with the accompaniment of some unpleasant grinding sounds, and eased the vehicle into motion . . . where it lurched sharply and fell silent. Sami looked at Cathwaite, who flushed, fumbling with the gear selector and the starter. "You have driven these things before, right?"

"Yes," Cathwaite said. "A couple of times, but never a Corvette . . . They're just too damned valuable to actually drive and . . . and honestly they're above my touch anyway."

Before Cathwaite could reinitiate the starter, a sharp rap on Sami's window caused him to jump. Belinda Athenos stood waiting, her pale and weary features wreathed in hydrocarbon smoke that swirled past her into the ventilation ducts. Sami fumbled with the door, shoving it open.

"What is it, Athenos?" he demanded, goaded into more than his usual easygoing air.

"Sorry to disturb, sir," she said, glancing uncertainly at Cathwaite before addressing Sami. "I just wished to caution you that you may want to restrict your vehicle testing to the oval track for now. We have experienced a few . . . issues down in the catacombs and the circuit."

Sami read her expression well enough to avoid probing the "issues" with Cathwaite listening. "Oh? Very well, Athenos. The oval track should suffice for the moment."

As Sami moved to close the vehicle door again, Belinda seemed to nerve herself to interpose a hand. "Director"—her eyes flicked to Cathwaite again—"if you could give me a moment of your time... soon, sir..."

"Yes, yes, Athenos," Sami said, maintaining his polite veneer with difficulty. "You will have your moment later. Thank you."

Sami slammed the door and Cathwaite triggered the engine into a fresh growl of explosive life. As the vehicle lurched forward, Sami saw Belinda's face swathed in smoke, her lip between her teeth, the expression in her eyes most unsettling. In the next instant Cathwaite managed to jerk and jolt the vehicle out through the access tunnel, operating the gear lever, accompanied by additional grinding sounds.

Three broad passages opened before them, each labeled with glowing holographic text. Cathwaite steered toward the leftmost route, driving through the glowing words OVAL TRACK, and immediately dropping down into the vast cavern.

"Oh ho!" Cathwaite chortled as he peered out at the broad expanse. "Beautiful!" The engine roared louder, the Corvette accelerating in a jerky fashion punctuated by gear-grinding lurches that made Sami's innards feel slightly uneasy. As they rounded the first gradual corner, the vehicle moving up the curved wall and still accelerating, Sami remembered the sensation that had so captured his emotions some years before.

Cathwaite poured the power on smoothly now and they seemed to blast into the long stretch of the oval, the aquamarine track flashing by close outside Sami's window, the engine's howl vibrating through his bones to the pit of his stomach. He almost yelled in delight, restraining himself with difficulty.

After flashing around the track a dozen times, Cathwaite slowed, the engine falling to a lower murmur, then applied the braking mechanism. Sami seemed to recall deceleration in his previous antique car experience had been devoid of any particular excitement, but either Cathwaite or this Corvette car handled deceleration in an entirely different fashion.

First, Sami felt himself slammed forward, nearly braining himself on the windshield, and when he overcame his initial shock he heard a protracted screeching sound, feeling the vehicle stirring strangely beneath him. To Sami's horror, the tail end of the Corvette seemed to break loose, coming around until the entire vehicle slid sideways down the track at a considerable velocity.

For a moment, Sami thought the Corvette would overturn, but instead it merely screeched to a halt, only tilting onto two wheels for a moment before thumping heavily back down.

Sami found that his hands clenched onto the seat like iron claws, and the inside of his cheek bled where he had unconsciously bitten it.

Sami slowly turned to look at Cathwaite, seeing the eccentric collector mopping sweat from his brow. "Need some practice with the brakes," Cathwaite said.

"Yes," Sami agreed. "Perhaps you can do some of that practicing after you drive me back to the Build-Out area."

Belinda Athenos contended with more than tight deadlines and challenging work conditions. "We've lost over twenty workers so far, sir," she explained, launching into a rather intense list of troubling issues besetting her.

Sami frowned. "What do you mean? They quit? Hire more."

"No, sir," she said, shaking her head. "They're gone, lost, and we've seen no sign of them."

"*Lost?*" Sami demanded, suddenly incensed. Despite the bizarre geometrical effects within Ajanib, it still only represented a limited bubble of livable space. "Find those slackers and fire them."

"We can't find them," Belinda said, and something about the haunted expression on her face chilled Sami's fire of indignation.

"Did you, um, inquire with the scientists?" The Maktoum Corporation science team still labored on—uselessly in Sami's opinion—and their living quarters and labs remained in a small utilitarian section of Ajanib segregated from his grand project.

It was Belinda's turn to frown. "The scientists resent our presence, sir. I can barely get a civil word out of them after they lectured me about all the history and science we are supposedly destroying every day."

Sami suddenly recalled a statement very much like that which had crossed his desk some weeks before, an angry science type blathering about "incalculable damage" and the like. In Sami's view the scientists had received their first shot at Ajanib and came up almost empty-handed. Now they wanted to squat on this valuable real estate and pretend that every little scrap of mineral was actually some huge scientific discovery.

"I see," Sami said, thinking. "I take it these disappearances occurred in the catacomb section, and thus your, um, earlier concern?"

"Yes, Director," Belinda said. "And now I can barely get workers to venture down at all, and a bunch are threatening to quit."

Sami waved a dismissive hand. "The scientists have been here for months and they're not losing anyone, so—"

Sami broke off as Belinda shook her head. "They've lost two people also."

"*What?* When?" Sami felt a sudden burning frustration. How had this happened without his knowledge?

"In the last twelve hours or so, as I understand it."

Sami took a deep breath, considering the situation, employing all the troubleshooting techniques an army of tutors had drilled into his head during his formative years, ticking through the probabilities one by one. "Were all the missing workers on foot when they disappeared?"

Belinda thought for a moment. "Yes, now that you mention it, they were."

Sami nodded to himself, murmuring, "No wounded, no bodies, no sign of a threat...?" He looked at Belinda. "It can only be some trick of the, the...whatever they call the alien geometric nonsense."

"But the inertial locator," Belinda said. "Everyone carries one, and you can always retrace your steps if you've got it with you."

Sami shook his head. "Only if the path you retrace hasn't moved since you walked on it, right?"

Belinda stared. "I don't know. Can that happen?"

"Who knows?" Sami said. "I'm guessing it's got to be something of that sort." He stood to his full height and flexed his fingers. "Now to get the workers back on track and feeling confident."

Belinda seemed to deflate. "With a pep talk, Director? I don't think it is going to help."

"I've got more in mind than just talk..."

CHAPTER 13

After his brief respite on the trip out to Ajanib, Sami began to feel the returning veil of fatigue clouding his thoughts as he applied himself to issue after issue threatening their fast-approaching deadline.

Beyond the dozens of construction and supervisory details, he faced this much greater threat confronting the entire project, sifting resources and hatching a plan as quickly as his desperate mind could juggle the numerous variables. Although he did not really need the scientists, nor particularly care about their goodwill, Sami decided to approach them first with his new safety plan.

Aside from their blanket protests against all his furious construction work within Ajanib, the meeting with the scientists proved far more fruitful than Sami had even hoped. They seemed surprised that a mere industrialist like Sami could formulate a plan that hadn't occurred to any of their lofty minds, and they seemed additionally gratified that he had cared enough to meet with them directly, even after months of his evident neglect. Of course he hadn't really cared about them at all, but a little goodwill from the eggheads might prove useful at some juncture.

The increasingly vital meeting with his skilled laborers faced Sami next, Belinda Athenos calling all the shifts together in the large space that served as the workers' dining hall.

Sami found the expressions aimed at him ranged from overtly hostile to the merely anxious, with most of the two-hundred-odd workers waiting with a sense of hopeful expectancy.

Good, not too far gone yet...

Sami began by praising the workers for the miracles they had already wrought within Ajanib in such a short period, his eyes roving over all the faces focused upon him, feeling the currents and energies confronting him. Rather than going straight to the besetting issue of the moment, Sami leaped into the business challenge the project faced, explaining the swiftly approaching deadline, when paying clients would begin arriving. "If this facility is not fully operational by then, I'm afraid all your miraculous work will be for nothing, and this project will be seen as the laughingstock of the galaxy."

A key element came to Sami's attention at that moment as a tall, angular man spoke out sharply, his expression something very like a sneer. "How can you talk about a timeline now, Director? We are losing people left and right, and you're focused on your damned construction schedule!"

Sami suppressed the smile that came to his lips, taking note of the angular man's face as he said, "That's right, I am. If we can't make the deadline, there's no point in any of this and we might as well shut down the whole project and send you all back to Bethune today." Sami let that sink in for a few moments, knowing these workers received a pay quadruple the going rates on Bethune. "I don't think any of us want that to happen, so I have created a plan to assure every worker's safety, and I've already proposed this plan to the science team, who have adopted the essential details, effective today, for their own people."

That made everyone sit up and take notice. The popular, fair-weather worship of scientists had its uses, a fact that Maktoum Corporation had exploited for generations. But Sami needed the voice of opposition to declare itself more directly before he cut them down and positioned himself as the magnanimous savior.

He thought through the perfectly fomenting words for a moment before speaking, striving for the perfect tone. "So, with all the new safety protocols in place we will immediately begin work, all three shifts in the catacombs and circuit areas, along with the work continuing on the mezzanine floor."

Sami had to resist his urge to smile as the tall, angular man sprang to his feet, just as Sami had hoped. "Oh, *we* will begin work immediately, will we?" the man yelled. "Easy for you to say, Director." He turned to glare at his fellow workers before turning back to Sami. "I'll set foot down in those damned catacombs when you prove to me it's safe, and not one second sooner."

Sami spread his hands, his face schooled to its most conciliatory expression. "Did I not just explain there is a new safety plan that the science team has already adopted?"

"You can talk about plans all you like, Director, but that's all it is: talk!"

Sami shook his head sadly. "Well I did intend to show you some of the hardware we will employ with the new plan, if you had given me a chance . . . But tell me now . . . how many of you here today share the views of this, um, strident fellow? Hmm?" Sami looked across the hesitant faces, seeing many share looks between each other. "Stand, please, if you agree with your comrade's position."

Six additional workers stood among the crowd, their expressions revealing various shades of rebellious indignation. *Excellent; even fewer than expected.*

"Ah, very well," Sami said. "You seven shall work only on the mezzanine level." He smiled at the remaining crowd. "The rest of you will now receive double your contract pay rate, and you will work wherever Supervisor Athenos assigns you . . . and I will personally join the workers assigned to the catacombs for the first shift."

Among the sudden murmur of voices he heard the chief agitator swearing angrily, his voice calling out above the babble, "I am a shift leader and you're paying plain laborers more than me, Director."

"Yes, I suppose I am," Sami said.

The tall man struck his fist on the table, his face suffused. "Well, we won't stand for it, you hear?"

Sami sighed heavily. "Yes, I daresay you won't." He looked directly into the angry eyes. "You are fired, Shift Leader. Clear your quarters and be on the next launch to Bethune."

The man spluttered and fumed, but Sami ignored him, addressing the greater audience, internally pleased with the perfectly planned outcome. He had found and lanced the infection before it got out of control. "This drone"—Sami reached behind him, lifting one of the camera drones he had specifically sourced for an entirely different purpose—"or one much like it will accompany every worker to the lower levels, and you will note how we have modified it here to spool a continuous line . . ."

With the work moving forward again, Sami still could not rest, first joining the laborers venturing down into the catacombs, as promised, then hurrying back to the utility lock for an important send-off.

As requested, Belinda Athenos awaited him, her expression no less pinched than it had been since Sami set foot within Ajanib, now with fresh worries to consumer her.

"Things are coming together nicely, Athenos," Sami said, rubbing his hands together. "You may relax a little now."

She shook her head. "We need at least forty more workers out here soon, Director, and—" She broke off as a nearby hatch cycled. Shift Leader Marsh entered, accompanied by two Asset Protection officers.

Marsh bore two large bags, which he dropped heavily as he drew up with Sami and Belinda. The passing hours had evidently stoked his sense of ill-usage into a white-hot core that shone forth from every rigid line of his person. "Well, *Director*," Marsh sneered, "you may think you've won, suckered your serfs into risking their lives to earn your family *another* trillion, but I'll have something to say about that!"

"Oh?" Sami said in a mild tone, smiling as the two officers tensed, clearly ready to tackle Marsh if his temper drove him to physical violence.

Marsh's pinched lips twitched into a tight smile. "Let's see how your precious deadline turns out when you can't hire a single worker from Bethune." Marsh stooped to lift his two bags, straightening to glare at Sami and Belinda. "As soon as I tell everyone what's *really* happening out here, no one will hire on, I guarantee you that!"

"But what of the nondisclosure clause in your employment contract?" Sami asked mildly, seemingly with bland curiosity.

"Sue me!" Marsh cast back over his shoulder as he stomped through the lock into the outbound launch.

Belinda turned her pale, fretful gaze onto Sami. "He's not wrong, Director. He can raise a big enough stink at about the same moment twenty Bethune families find out that they've lost contact with our twenty missing personnel." She shook her head. "The word will be out and we'll be lucky to hire a single worker before the deadline has come and gone."

Sami looked over at the docking port as they heard the launch detach, moving out from Ajanib on its way to Bethune, and he smiled, turning back to Belinda. "I don't think Marsh will be creating much of a scene until well after we have completed construction, Athenos. The man is a thief, and he will be arrested the moment he touches Bethune soil!"

CHAPTER 14

"Miss Boop, it is important you should know that Warren Springer Stowe blames you for the entire break-in and theft," Masters explained, her eyes tinged with pity, though her face held the firm cast of a civil servant pushed to unpleasant duty. "I'm sorry to say that with his accusation the court will most certainly find you entirely responsible for the crime . . . unless you can tell us otherwise."

"Oh dear," Cherry said, deadpan, sprawled on the cold metal chair in the interview room. "How monstrous."

"Yes," Masters continued, nodding slowly. "Warren Springer Stowe has made a habit of selling out his colleagues whenever things went wrong, so we *could* have reason to think *he* is actually the mastermind of this crime . . . despite his accusations toward you." Masters reached a sympathetic hand halfway across the table between them, and Cherry eyed the outstretched fingers for a moment before looking back up into Masters's eyes. "But," Masters continued, "if you refuse to tell us the truth, we can only go to trial with what we have . . . and what we have is just his accusation against you. He will get away with a slap on the wrist, while you are serving hard, lonely years in prison."

"Prison?" Cherry demanded, leaning forward, and Masters somberly nodded. "For a harmless joyride?"

The encouraging smile on Masters's face disappeared. "It was no harmless joyride, and we know it. We have the security footage from Stowe's hotel. You don't need a *planning session* for a joyride!"

Cherry blinked. "You have the security footage from Stowe's hotel *room*? Goodness. Planning session is what you call that now? How dreadfully unromantic, really."

Cherry felt gratified at the faint blush on Masters's cheeks. "Of course there's no security footage from *inside* the hotel room, Miss Boop." Masters looked away, chewing her lip for a moment before standing. "As soon as you're ready to tell your side of the story, let me know . . . but don't wait too long or Stowe will be long gone and leave you holding the bag."

Cherry nodded. "Betty Boop holding the bag. Sounds like the lyrics to a fetching new song, right?"

Masters scowled at Cherry and left without another word, and a few minutes later Cherry found herself escorted back to her jail pod, where the other listless drabs looked up from their card games with desultory interest.

Cherry ignored her pod-mates and strode over to the dusty pipe along the wall, her finger tapping out a quick rhythm. After a few moments a series of return taps rang out from the pipe and Cherry sauntered slowly to her waiting cell, her brow wrinkled in thought. So far Stowe had predicted every move Masters and Bartson had made, and Cherry had no reason to doubt Warren's honesty toward her . . . yet.

But her patience wore very, very thin, and her tolerance for betrayal remained scientifically undetectable.

Like many new arrivals to the jail pod, the lanky, angry newcomer paced about in a heated passion, loudly decrying the injustice he had received at the hands of the authorities. Warren did not doubt the fellow's general claims, simply because most of the jail's denizens received some measure of heavy-handed injustice, even if they were guilty of whatever infraction landed them behind bars. But the early, raw days of outrage from every new arrival became exceedingly tedious to witness, and unendurable if you accidentally became their confidant of the moment, so Warren avoided the fellow until he chanced to overhear a portion of the angular man's heated diatribe that fixed his attention like a bolt of lightning to a particularly attractive lightning rod.

"—This frame-up is straight from the Maktoums, you hear? They're out there making some kind of ridiculous racetrack for these antique vehicles and they're killing off innocent workers to do it!" Warren drifted nearer as the man continued. "It was them! The Maktoums! They hid things in my bags and claimed—"

"Antique vehicles, you say?" Warren interjected, taking an empty seat at the small metal table, displacing one of the newcomer's unwilling audience members.

The man stared suspiciously at Warren. "Who're you?"

"Me?" Warren smiled, folding his arms. "I'm Warren Springer Stowe."

The newbie squinted at Warren for a moment, his face clearing with a look of recollection. "I remember hearing about you a couple of months back. You're the one who robbed the Pioneer Museum."

Warren smirked. "Am I? And you're the one who robbed the Maktoums, right?"

"Oh," the man said, deflated. "I see what you mean." His gaze measured Warren's face skeptically and after a moment he offered, "I'm Josiah Marsh."

"Marsh? So, tell me all about it. Maybe I can help somehow."

It required only endurance on the part of Warren, listening to Marsh's labored recitation as it dwelled upon the Maktoums' coldhearted greed, the frightening mysteries of the Ajanib facility, and Marsh's own innocence of any crime whatsoever, little of which interested Warren in the slightest. But by patient questioning Warren eventually delved into the matters of real importance.

"My construction team—under my direct leadership—installed the fab system out there ourselves, got it working perfectly and under schedule," Marsh explained, his gaze growing distant as he undoubtedly remembered all his past efforts wasted on the vile Maktoums.

Before Marsh could begin a fresh condemnation of his oppressors, Warren pressed on: "But I imagine you never got a look at the fabrication files, since you were just installing the hardware, right?"

"What?" Marsh asked, returning to the present and drawing himself up. "No, no. Shorthanded as we were, we didn't have time for specialists, and I loaded the files up myself, checked every menu setting, and even ran off a couple small test pieces." His eyebrows lowered, clearly returning to the injustice of it all. "My team worked on almost every part of the mezzanine level, and we even began work in the catacombs when we started losing people...and then those Maktoums—"

"I'm sure you did," Warren interrupted, attempting to avoid another trip into the allegedly thankless treatment Marsh had received. "And in those menu settings there must have been dozens of option trees you had to verify on that fabrication interface too. That alone must have taken days for you to test."

"Uh..." Marsh refocused on Warren, the indignant light fading from his eyes. "Oh, there were, um, only five main sections, really. But I stumbled on a bunch of nested submenus in the interface that weren't anywhere on the schematic they provided for installation. Just luck I even found those."

Warren perked up, but restrained himself. "I'll bet they were surprised to hear that—hidden menus."

Marsh's brow wrinkled in recollection. "I don't think I got a chance to point it out to anyone." His forehead cleared as his lips took on a thin smile. "Hah! That's one thing at least that they didn't get out of me!"

"Very true, sport," Warren agreed. "But about these five sections in the fab system..."

The questions and answers went on until their dayroom period ended, providing Warren with a relatively firm grasp upon the Maktoums' Ajanib operation to contemplate as he reclined on the uncomfortable bunk in the confines of his cell.

Not for the first time, Warren felt an irresistible urgency to walk free from this jail, but now eagerness additionally driven by an opportunity he might never see again in his life. The Maktoums' intriguing new enterprise promised to create a venue perfectly matched to Warren's extremely exclusive skill set, and Warren saw precisely how they could financially profit from such an operation, but he saw even more clearly exactly what *they* had apparently overlooked. That knowledge comprised a value Warren could exploit...if only he stood free and clear of Bethune's lockup...somehow.

Warren's eyes suddenly flashed open and he sat up on the crinkling foam pad that served as a "mattress" on his steel jail bunk, the riskiest, most absurd plan rising within his mind. Point by point it illuminated in his thoughts, and he felt a growing certainty: If he was to have any chance at all to capitalize on the Maktoums' efforts, he must take the most awful chance of his life. And this meant first placing his fate in Cherry's hands . . . then counting upon a pair of separate long shots both coming together.

It would be all, or else it would be nothing but years of painful regret. But what other choice could he make? Besides, for Warren Springer Stowe, genius, success, and brilliance were the only outcomes possible!

As Cherry fetched the so-called breakfast tray with its glob of flavorless mush, she heard the rhythmic pinging begin, ringing out from the pipe along the wall. The guard and inmate trustee handing out the breakfast trays also looked curiously toward the sound, and Cherry frowned to herself. It seemed a foolish moment for Warren to attempt a message, and that meant it was all the more likely to be important.

As the beats continued to sing, Cherry decoded the message in her head, feeling a rare jolt of shock at what she heard.

Out of all the plans or schemes she had expected from Warren, this had never once crossed her mind, and her respect for him increased a notch.

The final words of the coded message had said *As soon as possible*, so Cherry did not waste even a moment, handing her tray to a grateful woman behind her in their shuffling line, and stepping up to the uniformed guard.

"Hey, I want to talk to Bartson or Masters . . . now," Cherry said. "I want to confess."

Those magic words had Cherry facing her targets in record time, their eager expressions poorly concealed. "Well, Miss Boop," Bartson said, "Stowe has already written a damning accusation against you, so whatever you might add now may not place you in the clear, but we are interested in hearing what you've got to say."

Cherry looked from Bartson to Masters, despising them for their seedy little prosecutorial games, and though Warren had not specifically suggested it, she thought a little pushback might just place her in the necessary bargaining position they required if Warren's plan was to work.

"Never mind, then," Cherry said, rising from her seat. "If you want to stick to your cheeky little lies, I've got nothing to say to you."

Both of them nearly leaped to their feet, sharing a quick look before Bartson said, "Now, now, Miss Boop. Don't be so hasty. We are willing to consider any information that you might—"

Cherry shook her head. "No *considering*, old stick. None of your game-playing either." She stared each of them in the eye. "I will give you Stowe; a full written confession with all the dirty little bits you're dying to hear. Understand?"

Bartson and Masters shared a frowning look, and Bartson said, "We hear you . . . and just what do you hope to get out of this?"

"I go free, mates. Time served."

Bartson shook his head. "Impossible."

Cherry crossed her arms. "Right. We're done talking, then."

Masters held up a hand, casting a cautioning glance to Bartson. "Miss Boop, what if you walked out of jail today on a deferred sentence? If your confession gives us what we need to make Stowe accountable for his crimes, then you continue to remain free on your own recognizance, but if your testimony is, um, lacking, you come right back."

Cherry made a show of weighing the options, but she already knew this move formed the best chance to achieve her objective. Besides, once she walked out of the jail, these yokels would only grab her again if she wanted to be grabbed.

She looked from Bartson to Masters as they seemed to hold their collective breath. "Give me that deal in writing with a magistrate's signature and we've got an accord," Cherry said, observing the eagerness evinced by these civil servants as they dispensed this vile dreck they cynically sold as justice to the masses.

Throwing Warren Springer Stowe to these petty wolves conjured uncomfortable feelings of betrayal in Cherry, but for now she could only look to the supposed goal, no matter how unrealistic it seemed. Stowe seemed unreasonably full of himself, but it was his own neck he placed on the block now.

CHAPTER 15

Cherry walked through the slight flow of pedestrian traffic in central Torino, well out from the Gear's shadow, feeling the cool breeze upon her skin, the sun's warmth radiating down at the perfect intensity, and she remembered the richness of these same sensations when she had eventually been freed after the war. Rather than drink it in, or go slake her various long-denied needs—like her need for a long soak in a tub—she attended to her goal; Stowe's goal.

The first leg in Stowe's plan required a connection to one of the superrich Maktoum heirs—Sami, by name—and the task of even reaching the actual eyes of a Maktoum heir represented a significant challenge in itself. Warren had extracted essential intelligence from Josiah Marsh, and this formed the key to any chance at navigating through the well-entrenched gatekeepers around Sami Maktoum. That intelligence Cherry intended to exploit now.

She avoided any tail that Masters and Bartson may have placed on her by the simple expedient of ducking into Torino's sole mercantile gem, the Merchant Expo, entering into an elevator alone, then immediately leaping up through the elevator's service hatch. Within the darkened shaft, Cherry calmly waited, riding the elevator upward, stepping lightly off upon a handy stanchion as the elevator continued on without her.

Moments later, she exited the Expo building from a loading dock and walked the short distance to the other edifice of Torino's modern pride: the Maktoum Building.

True to Marsh's description, a side entrance saw a steady flow of foot traffic admitting new hires on route to Ajanib or to diverse Maktoum labor projects around Bethune. Cherry joined in the flow, entering the Maktoum Building feeling reasonably invisible within the diverse admixture, moving through the doors as if she belonged.

Inside, the prospective workers dispersed, some standing in a line for what appeared to be an appointment secretary, others stepping into cubicles with interview screens. Cherry continued on until she strolled alone, ignoring the questioning looks aimed at her by the few perceptive office personnel until she reached the office she sought.

The vis-plate revealed the brief animation of a severe but smiling woman turning her head toward the viewer with a curt nod, the animation looping over and over while a name scrolled beneath: Supervisor Kashti Pura.

Cherry opened the door without hesitation and stepped in, closing the door lightly behind her. Kashti Pura looked up from her desk, the faint glimmer of her holographic output sparkling between them as she stared blankly at Cherry.

"I believe you are in the wrong office," Supervisor Pura said.

Cherry shook her head and slid into the chair opposite. "Negative, old girl. You hired my fiancé to work on some asteroid project, and now I've stopped getting his messages . . . So tell me, what's afoot, then?"

Pura grimaced, moving one hand, and Cherry wagged an upraised finger. "Uh-uh. If you call the security goons on me I will give that flock of new workers out there a bloody earful on my way out, see?" Cherry smiled as winningly as she knew how, "I swear I'll be as reasonable as soap. I just want you to tell me if poor old Cade is alive or dead."

Pura chewed her lip, considering. "Cade?"

Cherry nodded. "Cade. Cade Fettering. Master rigger."

Pura's hands raised slightly, her fingers flicking the sparkling air, and Cherry fixed her eyes on each movement, memorizing the strokes. The display glimmered, Pura's eyes scanning information only visible from her side of the desk. "Fettering . . ." she murmured. Something she saw made her eyes widen slightly and Cherry held her breath. This represented the make-or-break moment, where Marsh's inside information and Warren's calculations connected . . . and either succeeded or crashed disastrously.

Pura tapped her fingers on her desk, seeming to weigh uncomfortable options, choosing one at last. She stood from her ergonomic office chair as it whizzed about in the absence of her mass, and said, "Wait here just a moment, please."

Pura stepped out the office door, leaving it cracked open, and Cherry moved smoothly around the desk. She had been prepared to mimic Pura's security access code that she had memorized, but Pura hadn't even bothered to secure her workstation. That probably meant Cherry had even less time than she had hoped to achieve her goal.

Moving fast, Cherry accessed the intracompany messaging, and highlighted Sami Maktoum's icon. Her fingers flew, lacing the air, each stroke generating characters in a terse message that Warren had formulated back in jail, custom created to hook one Sami Maktoum.

Cherry sent the message and slipped back around the desk to resume her seat just seconds before Pura stepped back in, three burly security types in her wake. Cherry looked up at the four of them. "Called my bluff, did you?" she said, shaking her head. "Poor old Cade."

Pura stared down without sympathy. "You will accompany these gentlemen quietly to the exit, and we will then forget all this. Or . . . you can force them to seize you, whereupon you will be handed over to the constabulary and charged with a surprising number of crimes. Your choice."

"Does that mean Cade is dead?" Cherry said, unable to conjure any pretended emotions for her ersatz fiancé at the moment. The security thugs replied by stepping forward, and Cherry held up her hands. "Alright, boys. Relax. I'll come along quietly . . . beasts."

Once they had escorted her from the building and stood watching as she walked from the property, Cherry smiled to herself. She had succeeded as well as Warren could hope, and now a soapy tub and an excellent dinner beckoned to her.

For several days, everything seemed to go perfectly for Sami Maktoum. His safety plan had allowed work to resume in the catacombs, and neither labor crews nor the science team had suffered any fresh disappearances thus far, raising Sami's reputation among the diverse community inhabiting Ajanib. Additionally, word had come from Bethune that the hothead, Josiah Marsh, cooled his heels in jail while a new draft of workers signed on, ready to embark for Ajanib, untroubled by any tales of vanished workers.

They might just make the deadline before Sami's ultra-wealthy clients began to arrive, and Sami felt his immediate tensions subsiding, his natural exultancy beginning to resurge... only for a fresh disaster to strike.

Even as Sami had labored almost without respite, Cathwaite had kept himself thoroughly entertained, roaring around the oval track with ever-increasing skill and confidence, learning how to operate the antique Corvette better by the hour. But evidently Cathwaite's confidence eventually exceeded his skill.

Belinda Athenos messaged Sami, informing him that Cathwaite's Corvette lay in a smoldering heap, and the collector himself lay somewhere between life and death, ensconced in Ajanib's new medical clinic. When Sami heard the extent of Cathwaite's injuries—broken bones, punctured lungs, and a concussion—he could scarcely believe it. Did those Old Earth vehicles contain no safety systems at all? How could people have operated them so casually for centuries if the pernicious things were so damned deadly? Surely their earthly forebears could not have been as passively suicidal as all that.

In the next instant, all thought of ancient practices disappeared, submerged under a weight of dawning panic. If these *cars* were so horribly treacherous and deadly, his entire business premise might teeter on the brink of an unforeseen disaster, billions of guilders invested for nothing. The ultrarich hobbyists seemed to enjoy the sense of hair-raising risk associated with these Old Earth anachronisms, but he knew the demographic intimately well, and if just a few of them died in fiery wrecks within days of arriving here this enterprise would die right along with them.

Cathwaite's tenuous grip on life faded from the forefront of Sami's racing mind as he scrambled to form some solution to the dilemma. If Cathwaite could accidentally destroy himself on the comparatively safe oval track despite his familiarity with these old vehicles, Sami would need to somehow render the vehicles safer without neutering their daredevil appeal. Surely some sort of addition could be programmed into the fabrication system that could remain essentially invisible to the drivers... couldn't it? But how much additional time would that require? And what actual steps could be taken?

Therein lay the difficulty: Sami's only semi-expert on the old cars lay unresponsive, and no one else had sufficient familiarity to offer any insights beyond Sami's own poor knowledge. Could some modern safety device be capable of rescuing the entire Ajanib project? And could Sami discover it and include it within the tight time confines before him? He had no leeway, no time left to spare.

Another message arrived and Sami dreaded seeing its content, fearing it spelled out the final demise of Cathwaite. As he hesitantly accessed the message, Sami felt surprised to see it originated from Supervisor Kasthi Pura back in the Bethune office, and he wondered if she might unknowingly possess some sort of mystical precognition. Her opening line expressed some concerns about vehicle safety in the Ajanib project, and her final two sentences promised potential solutions to a problem Sami had only just discovered, mentioning that name again: *Warren Springer Stowe.*

Whatever the source of her insight, Supervisor Pura clearly embodied a greater asset within the company than Sami had realized, and he jotted her a quick reply, authorizing her to pursue the matter with Warren Springer Stowe and thanking her for the insightful observations.

With a solution evidently at hand, Sami checked the time and decided he could spare a moment to see Cathwaite in person. Perhaps the unlucky fellow might survive and spare Sami one more headache.

Supervisor Kashti Pura observed the message arrive from Sami Maktoum with a sinking heart. His demands generally translated into heartburn and longer hours for her, but this time she found his message to be utterly baffling.

Being thanked and applauded by either Maktoum brother formed a rare but delicious instant that often translated into fungible benefits, so Pura hoped she could somehow retain the credit he bestowed, even if at first glance it appeared Sami had mistaken her for someone else.

He referenced her recent message, and she knew she hadn't sent a message to Sami in many months, but just in the odd chance she had somehow *accidentally* authored some brilliant plan and subsequently forgotten its existence, she scanned through her sent messages...

The terse prescription lay there, Pura's own name and title in the signature line, and yet Kashti Pura knew she had never sent that message.

Ethics and integrity had formed a key foundation for all of Pura's career, and now she felt more conflicted than any time since her university days, facing a decision that should not have taken a moment to conclude. She could accept the accolades for an idea that she had never authored, or she could contact the director, explain that she had somehow allowed unauthorized access to her workstation, and admit that this plan he loved was actually created by some mysterious, unknown third party.

After a few tortured moments, Supervisor Pura wrote the message . . . thanking the director for his kind words and vowing to execute his exact orders immediately.

She would do her utter best to forget that the mysterious message was created by anything except her own hand.

Warren Springer Stowe received the order to meet Bartson and Masters, and marched through the sterile, echoing corridors to the meeting room. This time they did not make him wait.

They entered the small room wearing the smug expressions of two undertakers at the final meeting of a suicide cult.

"Bartson, Masters," Warren greeted in a neutral tone.

"Mister Stowe," Masters said, smiling. "Circumstances have evolved and we felt it only fair to give you an opportunity to tell your side of the story."

Warren shook his head, looking from Masters to Bartson and back. "I've already told you two, I have no story to tell."

"That's exactly what your associate, Miss Boop, *used to* say," Bartson replied with a smirk, and Warren stared in disbelief.

Masters expanded her smile. "Miss Boop wisely cooperated and gave us a full confession, detailing exactly how you masterminded the whole theft operation . . ."

"Sure she did," Warren snorted, rolling his eyes.

"Including these delicious little details," Masters continued, showing a scroll of images from the roof and vent of the Pioneer Museum. Masters glanced at Bartson before adding. "We were both suitably impressed that you scaled up the side of that wall. I didn't have you pegged as an acrobat."

Warren slumped back in his chair, the wind taken out of him. "You wore her down," he murmured. "Poor old Boop. You broke her."

"She merely saw reason," Bartson said. "But now you have a chance to share *your* truth."

"*My truth?*" Warren questioned in a skeptical tone. "Do you find that touchy-feely null-speak works with most people? Hardly seems likely."

Bartson merely smiled, holding all the cards. "Most people know when they are out of options; no chance at all." She shared a grin with Masters. "But pretty soon now you'll see there are only two options for you: You can get used to the idea of concrete décor for about the next decade, or you can buy a little mercy through restitution payments."

While Bartson held Warren's eye, smirking, Masters looked down at her palm slate, stiffening with a wordless noise. She lifted the slate, showing Bartson, and Warren suddenly gained the quiet satisfaction of seeing Bartson's jaw literally dropping, his face suffused. "This just can't be!"

"Problems there, kids?" Warren asked, hoping their agitation originated from the plan he had risked everything on. "Get some unwelcome tidings, perhaps?"

Bartson turned his furious gaze back on Warren. "You did this!" Bartson said through clenched teeth, and Warren felt certain Cherry must have succeeded in her mission, a warm feeling rising up from his belly. "But don't think you're going to get away with it, Stowe. One way or another, we're going to make you pay."

Despite the months in jail, the unkempt hair and jail garments, Warren's smile widened with pure delight.

CHAPTER 16

One of the quaint little assets megacorporations employed on many populated worlds outside Confederate space was that of indentured servitude. Depending upon the corporation and depending upon the laws of the hosting world, these servitude programs ranged from something slightly more severe than contracted apprenticeship, all the way to the next-worst thing to abject slavery.

With Maktoum Corporation on Bethune, their indenture agreement lay near the center of the severity continuum, and Warren Springer Stowe literally signed his life away with only a moment's hesitation. He hadn't known how Maktoum might secure his freedom, nor how they would hope to control and contain him, but an indenture was not what he had expected.

Still, with the indenture contract formalized, Warren found himself brusquely escorted from the jail, out of the Gear's great shadow, and loaded onto a Maktoum transport ship at the spaceport. Warren only had a few moments to appreciate the warmth of the sun and the feel of his own clothes before the accompanying constables roughly shoved him into the vessel jammed with artisans and laborers. After so many long weeks entombed in the Torino jail, his glimpse of clear skies and distant horizons seemed all too brief, ending as the hatches sealed him within the crowded ship, but a flash-glimpse among the passengers gave him a start of surprise.

Warren not only consoled himself with the awareness that he had achieved one near-miracle by pulling off this speedy coup, but also by the sight he caught of Cherry Aisha stoically ensconced among the mob of workers. For a moment, Warren wondered if Cherry had used her specialized skills to sneak aboard, or if she had simply signed on with Maktoum in some capacity. In either situation, he felt himself strangely relieved at her presence, wondering what impulse drove her to stick close instead of disappearing from sight and resuming her solitary freedom.

As the crowded vessel lifted from Bethune's surface, a less delightful idea dawned. Warren suddenly wondered if Cherry might have tagged along because she held some grudge against him. All he had done was botch their burglary and get her locked up in a medieval jail for many weeks where his promises of quick legal relief all failed... His keen memory immediately supplied historical images and facts from the Blue Light Brigade's final battle... also known as the *Slaughter of Panawaat*. He certainly hoped she cherished no grudge toward him.

The transit to Ajanib passed quickly enough, the Spartan conditions in the ship seeming rather luxurious compared to the tortures of jail, and Warren felt the gentle bump of their docking maneuver with increasing anticipation.

By this time, the few of his fellow passengers who had witnessed Warren's police escort had evidently shared the news, and as the column of workers moved to debark, Warren found he had become an item of universal curiosity. Some expressions seemed hostile or suspicious, but most seemed merely quizzical, and Warren found their regard amusing, smiling cheerfully at all of them, waiting to debark last.

Only when it seemed Warren remained the final passenger aboard did he realize he had never seen Cherry exit the Maktoum vessel. Evidently she played some puzzling game of her own, and she could clearly take care of herself.

When Warren trailed out through the utility lock, some steps behind the file of workers, he found a pair of Maktoum security types beside a worn-looking young woman who unmistakably awaited his appearance.

"Mister Stowe?" the woman said in a colorless voice. "I am Supervisor Belinda Athenos. You will accompany us to meet the director now, and your possessions will be delivered to your quarters."

I have possessions? Warren shrugged and followed along. "Alright then, Supervisor. I'm all yours."

He had little chance to appreciate the ancient peculiarities of Ajanib's interior configuration as he was hastily escorted from the utility lock, through unglamorous passages all illuminated by the subaqueous glow from Ajanib's native substrate, to a far more upscale section of the facility.

Clearly, recent construction had added dozens of suites, galleries, and lounges, all built from top-quality materials and assembled within existing chambers of the asteroid. Among them, one large mahogany door formed their destination, which Belinda Athenos opened and entered without ceremony, trailing Warren in behind her.

Warren noticed the security detail closing the door and remaining near outside before he turned his attention to Belinda Athenos and a gentleman he recognized but had never previously met: Sami Maktoum.

Sami remained seated behind a vast desk, his expression combining equal parts slyness, privilege, and petulance that seemed even more evident in person than it had appeared in various media appearances Warren had observed. Sami focused his keen brown eyes on Warren now. "Warren Springer Stowe," Sami greeted in a neutral tone. "We've heard so much about you." Sami indicated a seat on the opposite side of the broad desk without taking his focus off Warren.

Warren suddenly wished he had his smoking case handy, but he gave Sami his jauntiest smile and lowered his lanky body into the amazingly comfortable seat. "Have you now?" Warren said. "Most of it bad, presumably, and some of it probably true . . . which makes me wonder what prompted you to spring me from the dungeon and add my carcass to the Maktoum Corporation balance sheet."

Sami regarded Warren fixedly for a moment, his expression unamused. "Jails and prisons are such ridiculous anachronisms, Mister Stowe, don't you think?"

"Positively medieval," Warren agreed.

Sami's gaze roved over Warren's face before he said, "Yes, and highly wasteful, if you think about it for a moment." Sami smiled, his dark brown eyes beginning to gleam. "Someone breaks society's laws"—he gestured toward Warren with a negligent wave of his hand—"and this miscreant pays his *debt to society* by occupying an uncomfortable cell, guarded and managed by an army of people, all at public expense. In effect, the tax-paying citizens are fleeced *twice*."

Warren struck his own palm with a fist, sitting up. "You won't believe it, but I was saying pretty much the same thing to these two government stiffs not too long—"

"But," Sami interrupted, holding up a raised index finger, "these lawbreakers must go *somewhere* and do *something*, correct? And I think it is so much more intelligent and more humane for them to work where their abilities suit them, rather than, oh, just breaking rocks, digging ditches, and such demeaning things."

"You're going to make me all weepy," Warren said. "Quite the reformer, I see. Beautiful."

Sami regarded Warren, his lips thinning into a glare. "Of course, some lawbreakers just won't learn from anything but physical pain, Mister Stowe. We could always arrange some rocks for you to break until you can appreciate how fortunate you . . . might be."

Warren covered a yawn. "I don't think you've got the time for that, Sami—I can call you Sami, right?"

Sami ignored the question. "You read your indenture agreement, didn't you, Stowe?" he asked. "We have all the time in the world until you pay down your contract. We have your lifetime at least."

Warren shook his head, smiling. "I doubt it. I've only acquired a couple of skills worth anything much, and I'm guessing you've got a problem trying to get your fancy racetrack operational, or else you wouldn't be bringing me up here at all."

Sami's thick eyebrows lowered and he turned accusing eyes toward Belinda Athenos. "What did you tell him?"

"What did she tell me?" Warren interjected. "I just shuttled out here in a vessel packed with laborers. I kept my ears open." Warren hoped to keep Josiah Marsh's name out of the picture—not that he gave a cold damn about Marsh, but rather to keep Sami from guessing how much he really knew about Ajanib.

Sami turned back to Warren. "Don't bet too heavily on your value, Stowe. You're not the only expert available by a long shot."

"Hah," Warren said. "And yet here I am. What? Did you get someone killed in a crash or something?"

Sami's expression flickered through three quick changes, ending with a grimace. "No. He's not dead."

"Wait, wait, wait," Warren held up two hands, feigning a dawning awareness. "Tell me please . . . Some zero didn't smash a genuine antique Earth car to pieces, right?"

Sami shook his head, measuring Warren speculatively before speaking. "You could say it was *genuine* . . . but not *antique*."

Warren put on an air of bafflement. "That doesn't make any sense."

"Perhaps it is time I show you, Stowe," Sami said, rising from his seat, "and determine if you really have any value to our operation . . . or if I should find some rocks for you to break instead."

"This is the most advanced fabrication system money can buy," Sami explained to Warren as they walked through the gleaming selection kiosks. "And it is already loaded with certified fabrication files from the top golden-age vehicle manufacturers: Ford, Chrisler—"

"Chrysler, I believe," Warren provided.

Sami shrugged. "Chrysler, then; General Motors, Harley-Davidson, and Honda."

Warren turned to look questioningly at Sami. "Honda?"

"Did I not pronounce it correctly?" Sami said, impatience evident in his tone.

"Oh no, not at all. You pronounced it correctly. Go on, by all means, go on."

"Yes . . . well . . . with these files we can fabricate any vehicle our clientele might desire to drive, and give them a venue to test their racing skills against others"—Sami paused, his vision far away—"like a step back in time," he ended with a flourish.

Warren stared. "Very impressive," he said in a colorless voice. "No, really, it is. But racing?" He walked a half circle around the director, musing as Sami frowned, waiting. "Let me see if I understand what you have in mind.

"Your superrich patrons come to your odd little asteroid resort, download the Earth car of their fancy, and go roaring around a racetrack with a bunch of other nobs, using their dream car in a way they'd never dare with an actual antique. You charge a pretty penny for them to participate, maybe *sell* them their vehicle and garage it here for their ongoing use . . ." Warren mused for a moment, rubbing his chin. "Probably offer slick vanity vids of them daredeviling around for a nice upcharge . . . but that's still not enough coin-flow to finance this whole . . ." Warren looked up sharply at Sami. "Ah! Gambling, of course, and outside the Confederated Worlds too, so no limits, and the house gets a fat percentage."

Sami smiled modestly as he examined his well-manicured fingernails. "In a nutshell, and excluding a few other concessions we have planned, yes."

"But..." Warren smirked. "Turns out there's a rub, right? These Earth cars are so damned dangerous to drive fast, you're going to lose clients faster than you can replace them. Getting killed might give them a dose of cold feet, hmm?"

Sami's smiled appeared forced now, but he managed to say, "You apprehend the basic challenge, I believe."

Warren nodded, looking at the empty build-out kiosk close at hand. "I'll need to look into the fabrication file options first, but I think I can figure something to help all your pampered customers stay alive."

Sami couldn't hide the flush of obvious relief Warren's words brought him, but he covered it semi-skillfully, saying, "You may work off your indenture within this lifetime after all, Mister Stowe."

Warren chuckled. "Oh, I think I may do a bit better than all that, since you've entirely missed the biggest payoff this place can offer."

Sami's face lost its friendly expression, hardening. "Yes? Are you going to instruct *me* on the fine art of making money now, Stowe?"

Warren folded his arms. "Not for free, I'm not... but for a percentage, yes. I might."

CHAPTER 17

After her release from jail, and after accomplishing her final tasks for Warren, Cherry had soon decided that Bethune had lost its rustic charm as far as she was concerned. The idea of playing hide-and-seek with the local authorities held little appeal, and if someone became sufficiently interested in Cherry's peculiar lack of personal records, and asked questions in the correct quarters, her Blue Light identity *might* be uncovered.

The only nonclassified image of Cherry's face from Blue Light in circulation bore little resemblance to her civilian persona now, offering a distant profile shot of a soot-blackened shaved head amid the ruined city Blue Light had depopulated. But the existence of that image troubled Cherry. It tied her to her military career, and to the greatest war atrocity in recent decades.

Once she decided Bethune would no longer serve, Cherry had experienced a sensation she had not known in some time. Though it amounted to blatant self-deception, she labeled it "protecting her investment," since Stowe still owed her a pile of guilders after all, and she set about investigating Maktoum Corp's Ajanib operation. Just why had Master Rigger Cade disappeared, anyway? Why was Maktoum so twitchy about Ajanib, and why would they suddenly want someone with Warren Springer Stowe's rather specialized skill set out there? On these points, Warren's coded message in the jail had provided no clarity.

Over the course of one day, Cherry had uncovered enough intriguing bits to set her in motion. Inserting herself among the clutch of workers heading out to Ajanib held some challenges, but their haste and chaos formed a tableau in which her skills excelled. She managed to slip into the outgoing vessel, mixing with the diverse workers comfortably enough that her face became familiar to them, then upon arrival, ghosted out into Ajanib without detection. Even with her rarefied skills, she knew the pervading atmosphere of recklessness and alacrity was her greatest tool for success.

Once within Ajanib, her task became far simpler. Though she hadn't been able to follow Warren and his escorts, she set about exploring her new environment, locating the workers' quadrant by simply following the ones and twos who milled about the maze of aquamarine-lighted passages, trailing them back to the utilitarian complex of apartments, recreation sections, and a sizable dining hall.

Through her augmented senses, Cherry felt the oddness of Ajanib almost immediately, tilting her head from side to side and testing her footing cautiously. The gravity felt peculiar somehow, though neither noticeably lighter nor heavier than Bethune, and light and shadow both seemed slightly distorted to her vision as she made her way into the halls populated with workers.

Her nonchalance seemed to provide her key form of camouflage, shielding her from any untoward curiosity.

The only reason anyone eventually noticed Cherry originated from her lack of an inertial locator, one observant fellow glancing at her, then looking again. "Hey," he said, frowning, "where's your tracker?" He indicated the small box on his hip. Cherry looked down at her waistband as if she expected to see one sitting there. She shrugged.

"Lost it?" he said. "You're part of the new bunch, right?"

"That I am, mate," Cherry said.

"Well listen, this place is crazy. You keep your tracker on you all the time or you might find yourself lost forever on the way to dinner."

"Got it," Cherry said, turning to walk on, but her interlocutor wasn't finished.

"Get another tracker from supplies . . . right over there. Seriously." He pointed and Cherry gave him a jaunty thumbs-up, changing course.

Might as well grab one, for camouflage at least.

The supplies desk coughed up an inertial locator without a fuss and offered advice equally free. "If your first work assignment's in the catacombs," the small, officious fellow said, "stay close to your team, and be sure you've got a line running clear to the escort drone."

"Thanks, duck, I'll do that," Cherry said.

The supply fellow adjusted his shirt collar self-consciously, leaning closer to Cherry. "I'm Roland, by the way. I'd be happy to, uh, show you around."

Cherry winked at him. "I'll keep it in mind, if I come to need any showing about, Roland."

She waggled some fingers at him and strolled off as he called out in her wake, "But what's your name?"

Cherry called, "Mary Poppins," over her shoulder, pulling some half-remembered name she saw in Warren's ancient adverts as she moved on. She finished exploring the worker complex, settling herself briefly in a large cafeteria where a small clutch of Maktoum employees gathered, many of them familiar faces from the inbound transport. An unfamiliar woman held forth in a knowing voice that commanded attention: "—since all but one of the missing disappeared in the catacombs, that's where you got to be on your toes."

"They didn't say anything about this back on Bethune," one of the new hires grumbled. "They suckered us into signing on without saying a damned word about it!"

The experienced woman snorted. "So? Resign then, and head back to Bethune."

The grumbler sulked. "Give up my signing bonus and be on the hook for ship fare back? Right!" Other people Cherry recognized as new hires around him nodded, frowning.

"Listen to little old Gilda, then, and stow your grousing, okay?" the woman, evidently Gilda (though she was neither old nor especially little), said. "We haven't lost anyone since we started running escort drones and safety lines. So just do as you're told, and if you get assigned to the catacombs stay sharp, see?"

The conversation wandered into various mundane housekeeping matters that failed to excite Cherry's interest, so she set out to find a certain something that beckoned to either her sense of adventure, or that dark void of self-destruction.

A short walk revealed a series of expansive utility lifts that Maktoum Corp had clearly installed in recent days, a pool of small service vehicles charging nearby, arranged in neat rows, long racks of large drones lining one wall.

Though the lift didn't indicate any legend for catacombs on its control panel, Cherry naturally assumed one would place catacombs *downstairs*, sending the lift downward. When the doors opened she found her premonition fulfilled, a large glowing display revealed with a directional arrow and the word CATACOMBS set in place over a large, boxy, wheeled vehicle mounted like a trophy on an elevated stand.

Something about the vehicle arrested Cherry's attention and she stepped nearer, eyeing its odd dimensions as she realized it was larger than she had first thought, much taller than one of Stowe's beloved cars, and unlike any vehicle she had ever seen.

Her keen hearing detected the scuff of quiet steps and a faint whirring sound some seconds before a man and woman emerged from the broad entrance to the catacombs, a pair of high-end drones hovering attendance. They both carried instruments that seemed more appropriate for researchers than for construction workers, and at the sight of Cherry they both checked, eyeing her with obvious resentment.

Cherry looked about innocently. "Why the mean mugs then, hmm? What'd I do?"

At first they seemed bent on ignoring her, but the man stopped and turned his withering gaze on Cherry. "Do you see that, you philistine?" He indicated the boxy vehicle mounted before her.

"Easy now, mate," Cherry murmured. "Don't think I'm a filly-thing at all, and I'm sure as heck not blind. Couldn't miss this great lump here, now could I?"

"*Great lump?*" the man repeated in outraged accents as his companion rolled her eyes. "That 'great lump' is an example of the oldest wheeled vehicles humanity has ever seen, and *you people* have it mounted like some damned prize for your disgusting commercialism!"

Cherry pulled a face and looked back at the vehicle skeptically as the man stepped nearer, staring hard at Cherry. "Say," he demanded in an accusing voice, "what are you doing down here anyway? Looking to deface this historical treasure? Scratch your initials on an important alien artifact?"

Cherry looked back at him, shaking her head. "You got me all wrong, love. The *defacing* crew is on next shift. I'm on *desecration* duty, see? Found any religious icons for me to work over? No?" As the man tried to overcome a collision between outrage and surprise, Cherry went on: "Besides, looks like your historical treasure's made of the same fancy cheese the Gear's made out of on Bethune. Find it a challenge to do much defacing on it, I'd bet. Not going to carve many initials on it without a diamond awl or some such."

The two scientists stared at Cherry for a startled moment before the man said, "I'm Doctor Peter Maris, and this is my colleague, Doctor Tara Sang, but who the hell are you anyway?"

Cherry smiled. "No one special, duck. Just one of the new lot fresh out from Bethune, come to see these *terrifying* catacombs everyone's sniffling about."

Dr. Sang finally spoke, grousing. "*More* workers? Just what we need."

"Look now," Cherry said in a cheerful voice, "all that defacing and desecrating doesn't happen all on its own, you know. Takes willing hands, strong backs, see? And that's us."

Peter Maris eyed Cherry, his outrage fading as he measured her. "You don't seem like one of Maktoum's laborers to me."

Cherry crossed her arms. "I can't be the only stunning conversationalist of the bunch. Maybe you just never took the time to chat one of us up."

He shook his head. "It's nothing like that. Not a one of them would ever venture down here alone. No one would . . . except you."

Before Warren would explain his revolutionary concept to Sami, he needed to finish persuading the man that someone aside from a Maktoum might have a brilliant idea for Ajanib that he had somehow overlooked, and that took careful preparation. So, first Warren pushed Sami to finish explaining the technical bits of Ajanib's wares to him in greater detail, and Sami quickly warmed to the task, extolling the glory of his creation.

"As you have seen, we were able to repurpose existing tunnel networks and expand a few chambers within the asteroid, and even offer an oval track and a more complex circuit . . . but the catacombs always promised a . . . a richness of experience that made our offering beyond unique," Sami explained as they walked along, entering the opulent space labeled as the MEMBERS CLUB. Sami waved various holographic displays into life as they walked about the richly appointed chamber.

Warren took in the lush teak and brass furnishing, the old-fashioned bar and lounge seating, nodding with appreciation. "Exceptionally tasteful, I have to say, Sami. I'm impressed. Even got the old-timey glass bottles, like Rick's. Nice touch."

Sami frowned at the familiarity but went on, "As participants speed about through the miles of passages in the catacombs, spectators here can observe—and create wagers—on the activities unfolding below. Through drone cameras and some static camera positions, those relaxing here can take part in every drama advancing in the catacombs."

Warren felt his internal elation rising, but he worked to keep any sign of this from his face. Sami had created the ideal setup for the Big Plan Warren had dreamed up while languishing in Torino's terrible jail. The reality of Ajanib was nearly perfect, even more so than he had originally thought, and looking at the patchwork of scenes provided through various cameras situated within the catacombs, he gained a fresh insight, turning to consider Sami attentively. "I thought your so-called catacombs were just a king-sized racetrack, but I see I was mistaken."

Sami's forehead wrinkled and he glanced at the displays as if they might reveal something he hadn't noticed before. "Not a racetrack?" he said uncertainly.

"This is much better idea, a grander vision. I congratulate you and I must say I am impressed."

"Well...I am pleased to hear you say it," Sami said, nodding encouragement, his whole posture altered, his curiosity barely restrained as he waited to hear what insight Warren might offer. "Uh, what specifically would you say, uh, surprised you most about it?"

Warren nodded, walking from display to display, examining their respective views of the catacombs. "Yes indeed. Your target client isn't obsessively collecting every surviving film snippet from Old Earth *car races*," Warren said. "They're thrilled by the dramatized chase scenes from Old Earth entertainment shows, and those are the rare snippets every modern car fanatic collects. You see?"

Sami stared at Warren, clearly struggling to connect Warren's words to some accidental brilliance revealed within Ajanib's catacombs. "Well...yes," he agreed cautiously. "I suppose you're right...and..." Sami's voice trailed off expectantly.

Warren almost laughed out loud, but instead he stretched out his hands toward the displays and their various views of the empty passages below. "Here you have highways and alleys, on-ramps and junctions. Instead of a simple racetrack you have provided a venue to recreate every car chase scene ever displayed in Old Earth film dramas, and *our* clientele will gobble that up."

Sami's eyes glittered as he took this in, his gaze roving over the catacomb displays as if seeing them for the first time. "Yes," he said. "Yes, you are right, Stowe. Of course we are providing the fulfillment of fantasy, not a sterile practice of mere hand-and-eye coordination."

"That's the ticket, Sami. That's the winning ticket...or at least it would have been," Warren concluded, letting his hand drop as he shook his head, looking sidelong through his eyelashes at Sami. "If only..."

Sami chewed his lower lip for a moment, staring at Warren. "If only what, Stowe?"

Warren shrugged. "Never mind. I'm just indentured corporate property anyway. Don't you have some rocks around here that I'm supposed to be breaking?"

Despite Sami's tractability, Warren knew he was no abject fool. Now Sami could accept the bait and knowingly take the hook, or his pride could revolt at Warren's rather obvious manipulation and Warren could find himself breaking rocks for the next decade or more.

Sami continued to stare at Warren for a short time before turning to kill the numerous displays, one after the other, the Members Club suddenly dimming without their greenish glow. He turned back to Warren, the left side of his face shadowed, only his eye visibly gleaming. After a stretched moment of silence, Sami began speaking in a more constrained voice than Warren had yet heard: "It seems you like to take chances, Stowe. You like to gamble, and I know the heart of the gambler all too well." Sami sighed, looking down. "And now I propose to give you a gamble like you've never had before." Warren didn't say anything, waiting, and Sami finally added. "If Ajanib pays out, you'll be free...with a tidy sum. But if your contribution fails... we'll see just how long we can work an indentured servant until he dies." Sami turned away, casting over his shoulder, "Now that seems like an interesting proposition to me."

CHAPTER 18

Even with the agreement between Warren and Maktoum Corporation written up, executed, and witnessed, Warren didn't feel full of trust toward Sami, keeping a few cards in hand to play later if needed, but he knew he must start their working relationship off with absolute fireworks if he wanted to get Sami fully invested in *Warren's* vision.

"First," he explained, "I'll look into some safety upgrades on the fabrication side, so *our* clientele don't immediately incinerate themselves by accident."

Sami folded his arms across his chest, now exhibiting the first signs of buyer's remorse after Warren's initial effective sales pitch. "I don't seem to recall hearing you were an expert on fabrication systems, Stowe."

"Oh no, I most certainly am not." Warren grinned. "With all humility, Sami, I *am* the greatest living expert on Old Earth vehicles, and I think there are some settings in those old manufacturing files that someone like me might be able to tease out."

Sami huffed. "You had better be able to, Stowe, after all your talk. If we can't make these things safer—fast—all your other fancies are just so much high-flying nonsense!"

"A little faith, Sami," Warren said. "A little faith."

Sami's face revealed no hint of dawning faith. "And after you produce this miracle, then what?"

Warren examined his fingernails with a smile. "Have you ever heard of Roman gladiators, Sami?"

"Gladiators?" Sami repeated, tasting the word. "I seem to remember something about them. Did they race cars?"

"Mmm . . ." Warren scratched his head. "Sort of. They had little car-things dragged around by actual horses, I guess. But mostly they fought . . . these gladiator fellows, whacking away at each other with swords and such, while all the rich bastards—if you'll pardon the expression—watched and gambled, and so on."

Sami's eyes narrowed. "And what's that got to do with driving cars now?"

"The important question is, what's it got to do with making big piles of money, isn't it?"

Sami scowled. "Get to the point."

Warren stood smoothly up from his comfortable seat and began pacing about Sami's office as he explained: "Picture the scene . . . twenty, thirty, fifty cars in the catacombs going all out, every driver willing to risk *anything* to beat the others to the objective—"

"What drivers?" Sami interrupted, his scowl replaced by an emerging hint of interest. "What objective?"

Warren had a difficult time keeping the smile off his lips as he detected all the correct signs showing from Sami. "With so many cars in the biggest chase scene ever, the drivers sure as hell aren't going to be people who value their skin too highly—our gladiators, if you will." Warren paused in his pacing to wink at Sami before continuing. "And the objective? Think about it: Your gazillionaires have spent a stimulating morning puttering around the oval track, and now they're getting lunch at the Members Club."

Sami's eyes glittered as he stared at Warren's pacing. "Yes?"

"They're watching the displays as our gladiators hit the catacombs, one driving a Mustang, let's say, another in a Camaro, and so on, just like some Old Earth drama . . . But unlike the drama, there's no bank robber to chase, no convoy to despoil, no secret plans to transport. So our pet gazillionaire *creates* the objective—a privilege they might pay for, right?—and launches the gladiators off at top speed."

Sami nodded, his vision far away, entranced, seeing the scene unfold . . . and Warren wanted to kiss himself, but he kept the power flowing, his hands outstretched as he continued to weave the enchantment.

"Now the others in the Members Club see the gladiators zooming around, they see the objective, whatever it may be, and they have a pretty good idea which driver and car has the best shot at winning, so they prove their confidence by logging a big, fat bet on their chosen gladiator. Will ten thousand guilders be enough to convince their peers what a knowledgeable expert on Old Earth cars they are? A million guilders?"

All resistance, all reluctance had drained out of Sami, and his mind ran clearly though Warren's articulated vision, gathering power as it went. "Yes . . . yes," Sami murmured.

"And there would be more. So much more!" Warren continued, firmly in control. "A gambler in the Members Club may have selected a gladiator who doesn't manage to grab the objective, but perhaps they do reach the highest speed, or they wreck the most opposing gladiators, or cover the most ground, and these rack up their own points too, giving us all those delightful rankings and stats that everyone loves so much."

Sami's dazzled state hit some kind of internal snag, and Warren saw the Maktoum heir dragged back to reality. He squinted at Warren. "Where are we going to get even *twenty* drivers to serve as . . . um, these gladiators any time soon? I mean, think about it: You talk about *wrecking* opponents, but almost the only ones who know how to drive these things at all are people who *do* value their skins."

Warren stepped nearer, placing both hands flat on Sami's desk, holding Sami's stare with a confident smile. "That really would be a nasty fix, wouldn't it? Fortunately, Sami, you've got me in your corner."

"Oh?" Sami said, waiting.

"Sure." Warren straightened, rubbing his hands together. "We've got maybe three different pools of people to draw our potential gladiators from, and a new revenue stream on tap too." He held up one imperious index finger. "First, we've got a fair bunch of regular sods out among the worlds who drive cheap electric-car simulators who would gladly sign up to be a gladiator, and maybe even cough up some coin to purchase one of your new genuine copy-cars, especially if they had a chance to cash in big as a winning gladiator."

"But they—"

"Second," Warren continued, holding up two fingers as he talked over Sami, "I'll bet you could get a constant stream of poor indentured bastards who would sign up to be cannon fodder in exchange for release from their indenture agreement."

Sami slapped the desk. "But I'm telling you, they won't know how to drive the silly things! Where's the drama? Where's the big chase scene with drivers who can't even really drive?"

Warren laughed.

Sami scowled up at him. "I see nothing to laugh about."

"I'm telling you this all really would be quite the issue, quite the problem, quite the deal breaker . . . but Warren Springer Stowe is here, Sami, and I've probably taught more people to operate these old vehicles than anyone living. I'll have a class and get each new batch of gladiators literally up to speed. See?"

Sami took this in, turning his gaze inward to think a moment before nodding. "Okay, that might work."

"It'll work."

Sami turned back sharply, snapping his fingers. "But not in time, Stowe. I've got clients on the way, and we can't possibly recruit a bunch of suitable, er, gladiators, train them, and have them ready to compete before our first clients arrive. How many could we find on Bethune? One? Five?"

Warren just grinned, holding up three fingers. "That brings me to our third potential pool of gladiators that just happen to be in the neighborhood."

Sami shook his head, expressionless. "You can't mean . . ."

"You've got, what? Three hundred or so workers constructing all your fancy infrastructure here, right?"

"Give or take," Sami said, skeptically frowning. "But they'll never—"

"I'll bet we can get more than ten percent who'd be willing to try life as a gladiator in exchange for some more of these juicy Maktoum paychecks and a shot at the big prize."

"But their work is—"

"We'll hold tryouts during their rest period, and those with any potential will get an offer to drive. I could start training them right off, and by the time your clients arrive we should have some gladiators ready to roll."

Sami offered more objections, but Warren saw those as little more than grousing because someone without Maktoum blood saved his chestnuts.

Before Sami ever said it, Warren knew what the answer would be: "You can hold your, er, tryouts, Stowe, and see if there really are any among the workers who might serve. But first"—he thrust an index finger at Stowe—"you've got to fix these cars somehow so they don't kill everyone."

CHAPTER 19

"Important deeds are afoot, Miss Athenos," Warren declared, leaving Sami's offices with *his* grand plan fully embarked upon. Belinda Athenos awaited him, ordered by Sami to assist. "First...I need sandwiches and tea, stat!"

At Belinda's indignant stare, Warren added, "I presume you command some sort of minions for sandwich duties and whatnot, am I wrong? And, I need some time in Build-Out on the fabrication suite—all night if necessary."

Belinda uncoiled somewhat, nodding. "If you can find your way to Build-Out, I'll have someone deliver your food there."

"Excellent. English breakfast tea, if possible, and cream. The cream is essential."

"I'll tell them," Belinda said, her expression hardening again, undoubtedly unused to an indentured asset making any demands of her, an established, experienced supervisor of Maktoum Corp.

"My fate is in your hands, Miss Athenos."

Warren saluted her with an elaborate bow and set off for Build-Out, his mind sifting through the details he had extracted from that indignant shift leader, Josiah Marsh, back in Torino's jail. In the frantic push to complete construction on the fixtures and accommodations Sami had ordered, work crews labored in alternating twelve-hour shifts, the sound and sight of construction nearly ever-present, but here in the broad avenue to Build-Out, Warren seemed to inhabit a relative pocket of solitude and stillness...until he suddenly noticed someone walking quietly at his heels.

"D-damn!" Warren yelped with a spasm of nerves, before seeing the dark eyes and hair he recognized. "Cherry! You scared the hell out of me."

Cherry smiled. "Didn't soil yourself, did you, duck?"

Warren drew himself up. "Soil myse—? No!"

"Well, if you did, they've brought all your luggage the constables snabbled from your hotel room back in Torino. They've got it all stowed in a nice suite for you so you can get a change of knickers there if you want."

"I'm telling you, Cherry, I don't—wait . . . !" Warren brightened. "Do you happen to know if they brought my smoking case?"

Cherry gestured for Warren to continue walking and fell in beside him. "So they did, old fellow. You can go back to blowing your nasty stench clouds at will."

"Better and better," Warren said, rubbing his hands together as he turned to eye Cherry more carefully, realizing that she must not have harbored a grudge after all. "Didn't expect to see you tagging along this way, I must say, coming out here to Ajanib and all, but I'm glad you're here. Everything is coming together perfectly!"

"Oh?" Cherry said in speculative tone. "I got the idea you are now an indentured piece of Maktoum property, and likely to remain so for life. I believe that qualifies as transferring from frying pan to fire, or have I missed something, hmm?"

Warren swiped away a prospective life in servitude with a wave of his hand. "That? It is nothing. But I forgive your skepticism. You have had little chance to see my real brilliance at work."

They turned a broad corner, seeing the unoccupied fabrications suites ahead, each glowing with sparkling lights. "Mmm," Cherry said, "my months in lockup did rather dim your star, I daresay, and that after you somehow tipped off the coppers to begin with."

"Bah!" Warren snorted eloquently. "A provincial world and a change in government that caught everyone flat-footed. But now"—he smiled at Cherry and indicated the fabrication suite with a flourish—"I am in the one place in the galaxy where I absolutely *need* to be, so I can only guess that my subconscious is *even more* ingenious and prescient than my conscious mind ever suspected."

Cherry considered Warren for a moment as they strolled together into one of the semi-enclosed booths. "It's wonderful to behold, your self-confidence, Stowe. It's rather like some creature, whipped up by a mad scientist, unfazed as it's chased about by angry villagers."

Warren smiled warmly at her. "Why, thank you, Cherry. You begin to understand my greatness, it seems."

Cherry laughed. "And what is your greatness doing here tonight?"

Warren settled in, beginning to bring the fab system online, rows of lighted indicators illuminating as the holographic output sparkled to life. "I..." He bit his lip and punched up the main menu. "I am going to ferret out some safety features for the freshly manufactured antique vehicles, so any new drivers don't immediately kill themselves by accident."

"Oh?" Cherry mused, sitting on the arm of Warren's chair, observing his scrolling through the hundreds of arcane letter codes and options. "Is that so all your drivers can then head to these scary catacombs and get swallowed up by this dodgy alien rock?"

Warren didn't look up from his work. "Head to the catacombs, yes. Getting body snatched? I doubt it. No one's gone missing except when they're afoot down there. Ah!" He broke off, finding the nested menus just as Marsh had described.

Cherry leaned nearer to see a whole series of concealed option trees, turning to consider Warren's profile instead. "Have you even noticed the weird spatial dimensions here, Stowe?"

Warren bit his finger absently as he deciphered technical specifications. "Uh, weird spatial...? No, I can't say I have, but I have heard something about them."

"You mean you haven't noticed the way light doesn't seem to carry as far here?"

Warren looked up at her. "The light?" He thought back to the strange dimness visible in all the longer passages he had observed. "Yeah, now that you mention it, I guess I did see some of that."

"Well, before your grand plans get too daft, love, you may want to be sure your schemes even work here, right?"

Cherry looked up suddenly, her poise still relaxed. "Someone's coming, old fellow. I'd better scarper."

Warren stood and looked the direction Cherry indicated. "Probably my sandwiches and tea. Would you...?" He trailed off because Cherry was nowhere in sight, vanished in that alarming way she had.

With the delivery of sandwiches and tea, Warren went to work in earnest, sifting through options and forming certain of them into selectable packages that could be accessed in every fabrication booth within Build-Out, while leaving other options still hidden within the nested menus as a variety of concealed aces he may yet need to employ for his own betterment.

Then, on his own authority, Warren decided to structure a sample vehicle and set it to fabricate with the new test features. While he personally hungered to create one of his dream cars, like a 1969 Dodge Daytona, or a 1967 Boss Mustang, he chose an entirely different sort of car for this test bed. Thinking back through the dozens of antique vehicles he had driven through the years, one model stood out as the most forgiving car he ever operated, and it had offered delightfully numerous horse powers too.

He selected the 1969 Buick Gran Sport with the largest engine option and an automatic transmission. As a final touch, he made sure the non-original safety upgrade package he had just formulated was selected. Upon tapping the EXECUTE key, the view pane glowed to life, and Warren watched the particle injectors and fusion pulses begin to lay down gleaming trails of precise material, support members lifting or dropping to cradle frame, chassis, and engine of the vehicle as it rapidly came together.

Rather than sitting about waiting for the fabrication process to complete, Warren turned his impatient energy toward visiting his assigned quarters, going through the mostly unoccupied passages to the domicile wing where he found his rumpled luggage waiting as Cherry had said. As he unpacked, he found the cigarette case resting there, a simple note waiting within: *The goons in Bethune manhandled all your kit before I got it, duck. My own search was much gentler.* The note was signed *Betty Boop, aka Mary Poppins.*

Warren chuckled ruefully at the tangled chaos they had converted his belongings into as they had clearly sought some handle on his reputed bankroll. *Money-grubbing sods!*

He looked at the scratched and dented cigarette case in his hands, scarred from its drop to the ground on the night of his arrest, smiling before moving. With a series of deft touches, the concealed compartment opened from the side of the case to reveal his cache of data sticks and his preloaded Galactic Express card...and another small handwritten note:

What a darling little hidey-hole! Good to see that you are still in funds, since you still owe me loads. Boop/Poppins.

Irritation and amusement battled within Warren for a moment before the humor of the situation won out, provoking another laugh. Cherry was the most puzzling creature he had ever experienced, and he felt pleased she hadn't decided to saw his head from his shoulders. He extracted the slender jail shank he had managed to smuggle along, feeling a sense of satisfaction in the memento, even knowing that it would have provided no useful defense from his Blue Light partner. He set the shank aside and contemplated his new state.

As he selected a reasonably unwrinkled shirt and slacks from his disordered luggage, Warren cast an eye over his room and could only shake his head. Not only had his peculiar partner proven herself, she had helped him upgrade from a jail cell to a luxury suite. The fact that he was now allegedly the indentured property of the Maktoum Corporation made the joke all the better.

His laughter faded as Warren pondered the next steps necessary to keep Sami on track.

According to Torino time it was now well past midnight, and by morning Warren wanted all the pieces in place to keep Sami in awe of Warren's unlimited brilliance.

The Maktoum brothers might be trillionaires who rubbed shoulders with the galactic elite, but he felt sure they had never encountered a mind of Warren's immense caliber before.

This cheerful thought animated Warren as he rolled and lighted a cigarette, stepping out of his suite into a small crowd of startled workers hurrying by. Warren couldn't help roaring laughter, gusting smoke all over the workers, setting off to the Build-Out area and the new antique vehicle that should be nearing completion.

Sometimes being Warren Springer Stowe felt almost too good to be true.

CHAPTER 20

After his experience in the Corvette with Cathwaite, Sami felt more than a little reluctance in joining Warren for the test drive of Warren's proposed gladiator training car.

"C'mon, Sami," Warren said around the smoldering little roll between his lips. "You required safety features, and behold! This baby's loaded with them. Look! Safety harnesses, and this thing here's called a roll cage. And there's even more, including a couple of sneaky treats that you can't even see."

Belinda Athenos and a couple of workers stood nearby, forming their only spectators, and Sami refused to reveal any trepidation before his underlings.

"See, the doors even work still," Warren added, opening the driver's door of the large, heavy-looking Buick vehicle, and Sami couldn't begin to imagine why the doors *wouldn't* work on a vehicle that was literally hours old.

Sami matched Warren's movements to the best of his ability, slipping into the broad seat and fitting confusing buckles together, cinching them down tight. Warren looked over at Sami, the smoking stick jutting from his barred teeth. Sami pointed. "Aren't you, um... concerned about all the flammable, explosive hydrocarbons with that burning stick in your mouth?"

"The cigarette?" Warren asked, pulling it from his lips to eye its glowing tip. "Nah." The cigarette went back in his mouth, and he cranked the engine into roaring life, grinning maniacally.

Sami immediately observed the difference in experience between his ride with Cathwaite, and this launch, as Warren smoothly eased the growling power on, guiding the bulky car out to the oval track, leaving the observers up on the apron to watch.

Unlike the Corvette, Sami noticed this vehicle sported only two foot pedals, and Warren did not fumble about with the gear selector as they began to accelerate. The speed came on smoothly, Warren easily guiding the car around the track, the engine sound increasing gradually to a roar, then a howl. It all seemed too smooth, too easy.

Sami glanced at Warren, suddenly suspicious. "You didn't sneak logic controllers into this thing, did you?" he called over the bellowing engine noise.

Warren puffed out a cloud of acrid smoke. "Nope. All mechanical. Like I said, Sami, the perfect car for beginners to build some skill."

"Hmph," Sami said indistinctly over the noise, and Warren began to slow as they rounded their sixth lap, smoothly decelerating until the Buick's engine seemed to burble along in a manner that sounded almost civilized.

Warren brought them to a comfortable halt and looked over at Sami. "Ready to let me start training gladiators now, Sami?" he asked, jerking his head up toward the nearby apron where Belinda Athenos and a small gaggle of others looked on.

"Perhaps," Sami said, seeing Warren place both feet on the pedals, the car suddenly quivering as if ready to launch, the engine in a slowly rising growl.

"Hang on tight," Warren said, and the engine went from a growl to a roar in an instant, the car barely moving forward as the rear wheels screamed, white smoke pouring out around them.

Sami felt the car's tail end seeming to drift sideways an instant before Warren released the brake, launching them forward like some form of primitive rocket. Rather than continuing around the track, though, Warren spun the steering wheel, throwing the car into a screeching, smoking circle, terminating by modulating acceleration and straightening the wheel.

Just as Sami felt himself caught between excitement and fear the vehicle fell back into a quiet growl, Warren piloting them up the sloping wall of the oval track to the apron and all the waiting spectators.

"Well, Sami?" Warren asked, killing the engine, the sound of cooling metal audibly pinging as Belinda Athenos and the others stood back, staring with wide eyes, exhaust smoke drifting between them.

Sami unclenched his hands, looking from the astonished onlookers to Warren. He nodded, exhaling. "Okay. You may begin sifting workers for candidates." He frowned to himself. "I'll figure out the technicalities for employing your gladiators, then you'll have to get them ready for action—fast!"

Warren felt little surprise that so many of the laborers who had willingly taken mysterious high-paying work on the alien asteroid were sufficiently adventurous to try their hands at driving the antique Earth ground vehicles. He felt even less surprise that most of them seemed incapable of operating such a complex machine without the aid of the advanced logic units that had invisibly assisted them all of their lives. The subtle (or not so subtle) technological nannies interpreted human actions in nearly every mechanism modern humans employed, shielding human users from the harsh lessons earlier generations were forced to learn from unforgiving physical laws. Without this technological intermediary between the user and physics itself, most modern people seemed bent on self-destruction.

No matter how carefully Warren explained to a gladiator candidate, most still could not release their expectation that the controls on the Buick Gran Sport would interpret their intent, and it certainly *would not* obey an input that could actually harm them, right?

"Gently! Gently!" Warren yelled as the Buick slewed around, fishtailing from the abruptly spun steering wheel. For a moment, it seemed they might roll over down the track, the car sliding sideways at far too great a speed to predict.

The candidate, a genius named Roland, didn't seem to understand the risk. "Why isn't it going where I pointed the steering wheel?" he calmly asked as they screeched sideways down the track. "I don't want to go sideways; I want to go forward."

Warren held his reply until the Gran Sport slid to a lurching halt, jolting them both in their seats. He stared at Roland with the last shreds of his patience wearing thin. "You remember what I said about this thing using no logic elements, right?"

"Sure," Roland said, blinking calmly at Warren, his hands still gripping the steering wheel as instructed. "But I just turned this wheel where I wanted to go, like you said."

Warren took a slow, calming breath. "Okay, sport, just turn the wheel that way and push on the go-pedal a smidgen, and maybe we can discuss a few little items like, oh, inertia, momentum, and silly little things like that as we go..."

Most of the candidates weren't as difficult as Roland, and a few seemed almost miraculously suited to the primitive technology, including "little old Gilda," who drove the Gran Sport almost like she'd handled an antique car before.

"Nope," Gilda explained as she carefully piloted the Buick around the track, steadily chewing some gummy substance as she squinted out the window. "Never drove one of these before, but when I was a kid my pops had an old soil mover, and its logic systems got burned out before I was born. I cleared a lot of land back on Tyree with that crappy old beast before I got my first kiss. And that old thing felt a bit like driving this thing. Had to be real careful with it, 'specially side-hillin'."

Immediately after Warren conducted a mini-seminar explaining the concepts and controls to the whole group, he took each of the candidates out for test drives. While Gilda may have demonstrated significant immediate skill, many others were quick studies, comprehending the subtlety required after only a few minutes.

By the end of one long day he had sifted fifty-five candidates down to twenty-one solid options, and with those in his quiver, Warren went to Sami with the results. "Twenty-one students, Sami, and hopefully twenty-one gladiators by the time your fancy clientele arrives."

Sami's burning enthusiasm had already cooled somewhat, with a day of doubts gnawing his strained nerves, and Warren could immediately tell he would need to invest continual energy, stoking the furnace on this one if they were going to achieve the vision at all. Sami's trepidation could sink the whole thing through half measures.

"Twenty-one novices who might putter around the oval track with you right there to babysit them, you mean," Sami said, biting a fingernail as he scowled. "And they'll go from this pathetic display to speeding around the catacombs in just...days? I don't see it, Stowe. I don't see it at all."

Warren's grin remained. "We're a bit luckier than that. Almost all of the fifty-five hopefuls could *putter*, as you say. These final twenty-one show real aptitude." He produced his smoking case and began to roll a smoke as Sami grimaced, opening his mouth to speak as Warren continued. "If I get the right tools I'll have right around twenty gladiators ready to go, right on schedule."

Sami's irritated gaze moved from the cigarette forming in Warren's hands up to Warren's eyes, suddenly on guard. "Tools? What tools?"

"We're going to need cars right away if I'm going to train them in time, but of course we always knew that was part of the deal."

The mulish expression on Sami's face seemed to indicate he hadn't thought much about such an investment until this unwelcome moment. "You can conduct the training with just a few cars, Stowe."

"Twenty-one students; twenty-one vehicles, Sami, or we'll have your gladiators ready to go next year sometime."

Sami sat up suddenly, slapping his desk with one hand. "You demand a lot for an indentured asset, Stowe. It would be good for you to remember your place."

Warren chuckled. "Oh, I remember my place alright...*partner*." Sami flushed, and Warren went on. "And all my *demands*, as you call them, are building blocks for *our* success here. That is all."

Warren held a strong certainty that Sami's ongoing arguments stemmed less from the costly nature of the investment than they did from a need to curtail Warren's independence, or perhaps to remind Warren who held the reins.

"And I suppose you think you need to produce these, er, Gran Sport vehicles for every one of your trainees?" Sami said, glowering. "Do you have any idea how much material goes into such a large vehicle? Couldn't you use one of the smaller models?"

Warren shook his head. "Sami, wouldn't I just love to crank out a couple little Thunderbirds or maybe a Pontiac Ventura? Sure I would, but I'm telling you, all but one of these new builds must be Gran Sports, otherwise there's no way I can make our schedule."

The scowl didn't leave Sami's face as he drummed his fingers on the dark wood of his desk. "All but one? Why all but one?"

Warren shrugged, looking away. "One of the new trainees shows particular promise, and she will be well suited to a much, much smaller vehicle."

As Warren expected, Sami could only yield, though with poor grace, but Warren felt a sense of relief that Sami had pressed for no details on his one gifted trainee. Warren didn't want to attempt any explanations regarding Cherry, her status on Ajanib remaining a particular miracle, nor did he wish to explain why any student gladiator would ever want to try the catacombs on a motorcycle.

Any other student, or Warren himself, would likely face an inevitable and speedy death on a motorcycle, but Cherry evidently found some particular pleasure in her previous ill-fated ride on Harley-Davidson's machine, and she looked to improve on the experience, despite the risks.

Warren certainly could not tell her no.

CHAPTER 21

Through her habitual skulking, and shameless eavesdropping, Cherry discovered that the other Maktoum laborers suspected that she might be a management informant, planted to spy on them, which quickly began to work to her advantage. No one encountering her during her rambling ever questioned why she never seemed engaged in actual labor, and yet her continued presence excited no comment to their corporate superiors. She lodged in an apartment that had previously belonged to one of the workers gone missing in the catacombs, and she consumed her meals in the main cafeteria with the other crews.

For the moment, it served her well enough.

When she chose to join the other volunteers for test-driving the antique vehicle with Warren, she had a moment's concern that her identity might create a sudden interest from the head shed, but aside from a brief puzzled look from Belinda Athenos, it seemed the frenetic chaos of Ajanib still suited her needs delightfully.

The driving itself Cherry found less than thrilling after her original experience speeding around Torino astride the "borrowed" motorcycle. Even after Warren explained the full plan and the role of the so-called gladiators, Cherry remained unimpressed with the comparatively tame Buick.

"Get me a motorcycle, mate, and I'll try a hand at gladiating myself," Cherry said as she drove the roaring Buick around the oval track with reasonable proficiency.

"Gladiating on a motorcycle?" Warren said, taking his eyes from the track to stare at her profile. "That is far beyond sketchy, Cherry. You'll be killed for sure."

"Better and better," Cherry murmured just loud enough to hear over the engine and road noise. "You've sold me. Be a dear and make it happen, right?" That concluded the conversation and their initial test drive together.

Cherry kept the Build-Out section under casual surveillance throughout the evening, awaiting the inevitable outcome of Warren's meeting with Sami, and her vigil was rewarded before many hours had passed.

As Warren settled into a fab workstation, Cherry slipped quietly in beside him, observing his quiet work for a moment before saying, "So . . ." and watching Warren's startled jolt with a degree of amusement.

"Dammit, Cherry!" Warren yelped. "You're going to give me a heart attack one of these times. You should wear a damned bell or something . . ."

Cherry contemplated this for a moment. "A heart attack? Is this likely? I don't think I have ever shuffled someone off in that manner, so it would be an all-new experience, but on the other hand, I have developed an odd fondness for you."

Warren grumbled inarticulately and Cherry slid in closer, eyeing the displays. "Find me a motorcycle yet?"

Warren savagely cancelled open fields, opening new ones. "Might as well get it started on the fab," he groused. "It'll output faster than the cars anyway."

He sifted through a few menus and located a half dozen Harley-Davidson models and also a few vehicles labeled as Honda Fireblades.

"Fireblade? What's that?" Cherry asked, pleased by the name.

Warren stared at the scrolling data. "Hmm. I know what a Honda is—or was—but I've no clue what a Fireblade might be except it is some kind of motorcycle."

"Well, then, Stowe . . . let's learn together. I'll take it."

Warren shrugged, selecting the Fireblade model that featured the largest number beside the name, 954, which Cherry assumed surely equated to many powers of the horse.

The fab view pane glowed into life, and Cherry stepped from the console, moving nearer to the motorcycle quickly beginning to coalesce before her eyes. As components came together, Cherry shortly perceived that this Fireblade only resembled the museum Harley-

Davidson in the most general way. It featured two wheels and a low-slung saddle like the Harley-Davidson, and its reservoir of exploding hydrocarbons lay situated between one's thighs in the same suicidally daring fashion, but little else appeared similar to Harley-Davidson's machine.

By the time her Fireblade slid out of the finishing room, Cherry felt an almost erotic eagerness that seemed like a nearly forgotten remnant of her life before Blue Light, before the war.

Warren finished setting up the next vehicle fab before joining Cherry where she waited, comfortably straddling the new motorcycle. "I love it," she said, gripping the low-hung handle-grips as she looked at him. "Now show me how to operate this lovely thing."

At first Warren complained that she needed a helmet before he could begin to teach her the nuances of her new motorcycle. Cherry snorted derisively and badgered him into taking the plunge. Moments later, Cherry perched on the tiny uncomfortable seat behind Warren as he started the engine, its engine sound scarcely resembling the Harley-Davidson at all as it purred to life. Explaining each step, Warren put the motorcycle in gear and began tooling slowly about until she felt ready.

Finally she took the controls herself, even managing to keep from toppling over as she learned how to balance on two wheels without gyrostabilizers or any other modern technological aids. When she felt suitably prepared to try the oval track, Warren followed along in a freshly created Buick, and they slipped down to the track together.

Years earlier, when Cherry joined the military, one of her few natural qualities they had initially valued was a thing they had called *machine empathy*, and perhaps that quality functioned now as she learned to operate the Fireblade, slowly mastering the timing of the clutch and gear lever even as she began to push the speed higher and higher, the wind tearing at her, blurring her eyes even as the symbiote adapted her corneas to the assault.

Rounding the track, her body melded to the motorcycle gripped between her thighs, Cherry experimented with deeper and deeper lean angles as she cornered, noting the gyro-like powers of the spinning wheels as the tip of her knee grazed the aquamarine road surface for a moment mid-corner. Coming out of the corner, she rolled the throttle all the way back, hanging on tight as the Fireblade roared, launching into the straightaway. She jerked the clutch in, popped the gear lever, and rolled the throttle back on as she dumped the clutch, seeing the RPM gauge zip up to that magical red line. If her body wasn't locked so tightly onto the motorcycle, the sudden jolt of acceleration might have kicked her right out of the saddle, but instead the Fireblade's front tire rose up even as the motorcycle rocketed ahead, leaving Warren in the Buick behind.

As Cherry eased slightly off the throttle, her front tire touched down again, the handlebars giving one threatening shake before stabilizing, and she heard the roar of the Buick's engine drawing nearer as Warren strove to catch her.

Cherry glanced back over her shoulder and eased off the throttle to fall back beside Warren, looking over at him in his glass-and-steel cocoon as she hunkered low over the fuel tank behind the Fireblade's tiny windscreen. With a wind-tossed smile at Warren, Cherry actuated both brakes, hard, and the Fireblade decelerated with another startling suddenness that Cherry combated through the benefits of her highly classified military symbiote, the Fireblade beginning to fishtail beneath her until she eased off the brakes.

Ahead, Warren brought the Buick to a screeching halt... eventually, and Cherry geared down, coasting up beside him and halting with one foot on the ground. Warren stared at her and she saw her wild storm of wind-whipped hair for a moment in the window's reflection before he opened the door. "You're right," Cherry said. "I need a helmet."

Warren snorted, visibly incensed. "That's not all you need! You! You are lucky to be alive after all that. Maniac."

Cherry felt strangely pleased at Warren's emotion. It had been a long time since anyone who knew her true nature cared if she lived or died. "Am I?" Cherry mused. "I wonder... Anyway, Stowe, it's a bit harder than you might think to shuffle me off this mortal coil."

Warren glared at Cherry for a moment longer before looking away as he exhaled, running both hands through his hair. He turned back to her and shook his head. "You have got to be the fastest learner I've ever seen. Lunatic."

Cherry smiled. "A cheerful disregard for life and limb are my chief attributes, old fellow."

Warren pursed his lips, considering before replying, "That'll be important if you actually try to play gladiator on that thing. I shouldn't say it, but you're damned near skilled enough to try it even now, but my blood runs cold thinking of you fooling around in the catacombs between a bunch of jostling cars."

"Aw," Cherry said, still smiling. "Making me blush, Stowe. Such chivalry."

Warren's eyebrows lowered. "I'm serious. The rich sods spectating are going to love the smash-ups, trust me, and I've got these Buicks set up to give the drivers a good chance of surviving. There are no tricks on a motorcycle . . . One good crunch and you'll be cherry jam spread across the toast."

"*Cherry* jam. Nice, Stowe. Positively poetic. Such imagery."

Warren growled, putting a palm to his forehead and groaning. He spoke in a lower voice without looking up: "Do you know how shitty it is to give a damn about someone who's got a death wish?"

Cherry reached out to pat Warren's arm. "There, there, old stick. A death wish? Me? Nothing of the kind." As Cherry said the words she realized that for the moment at least she spoke the truth, the beckoning abyss now distant and quiet.

Warren looked up, measuring her with his eyes, and she smiled. "I really am more resilient than you think, Stowe. I'm like a cat."

Warren's mouth broke from its grim line into a rueful grin. "You've got nine lives?"

"Nine lives?" Cherry said. "Really? Poor, poor devils. No, I was going to say that I always land on my feet."

CHAPTER 22

By the time the first luxury yacht docked with Ajanib and disgorged its cargo of stupendously wealthy thrill seekers, Sami had led his people to work miracles within the asteroid facility. All the luxury features received their finishing touches, while the catacombs lay roughly ready for the gladiatorial contests to begin.

Although Warren Springer Stowe had delivered on his promise, providing twenty trained gladiators, Sami hadn't trusted his eggs to a single basket controlled by Stowe, hiring a few ringers from Bethune. These ringers possessed at least some skill with ancient vehicles, but more importantly to Sami's mind, they came with a rather mercenary, cutthroat pedigree that seemed like it would make Stowe's trainees look rather foolish. As much as Sami needed this operation to succeed, he felt an ever-increasing need to also wipe that smile off Stowe's face.

Having some professionals out-gladiate Stowe's pet gladiators seemed like a win all around, and Sami's five mercenaries already began to pay off as they flaunted Stowe's desires at every turn.

Sami had observed the initial meeting between Stowe and the "Bethune Five" with concealed glee as Warren offered to produce their vehicles in Build-Out, only to be shut down by their rugged leader, Hammerworth.

"We'll put together our own rides," Hammerworth said to Warren, sizing him up with clear disdain. "And they *won't* be any damned Gran Sports, that's a bet."

Sami withheld nothing from Hammerworth and his four comrades, and he felt validated in his selection as they managed to navigate the Build-Out system without assistance from Stowe or Sami, creating their five vehicles in short order. In response to Hammerworth's request, Sami ordered Stowe and his trainees off the oval track for the five new gladiators to polish their skills without interruption.

Instead of the pushback Sami expected, Stowe shrugged at the order. "They can use the track all they like. All our practice will be in the catacombs from now on anyway." But Stowe couldn't leave it at that. "Whichever of your hired soreheads survive the oval track can join us down there if they feel up to it."

Sami ground his teeth as he thought about Warren Springer Stowe the convict, the indentured asset speaking to a Maktoum heir the way he dared. Still...in Sami's calmer moments he could only acknowledge that Stowe had rescued the whole Ajanib project from several unexpected disasters, in addition to *transforming* the gladiator concept. Without Stowe's insights, Sami would also never have thought to use the fab system to create the maintenance tools and spare parts needed to tune and maintain these finicky old creations. Now they had a couple of fuel depots and maintenance stations in the actual catacombs so gladiators could affect quick pit stops without halting the all-important action.

Other little bits, like inter-vehicle communicators that could be monitored and broadcast within the Members Club, would *eventually* have occurred to Sami, but Warren's immediate grip on the dramatic power and his passionate depiction of it conveyed its own dynamic immediacy.

These contributions failed to improve Sami's perspective of Warren Springer Stowe, instead adding to the aggravation as Stowe's knowing smiles made it all too clear what he thought.

Still, as the first load of paying clients arrived, Sami turned all his considerable focus upon this critical culminating moment. If these initial customers experienced the unique combination of pleasures Sami intended, Ajanib would become the galaxy's most successful playground for the superrich. For this to occur, Warren Springer Stowe needed to fulfill every promise he ever made to Sami.

While more clients equaled more profits, Sami felt this first wave of only nineteen paying customers formed a perfect number to fine-tune the operation. There would be little pressure on the kitchens, servers, bartenders, and other workers who provided the human touch, and Sami could personally entertain and curate as needed with such a finite number, even as his own people got the operation up to speed.

Among these first nineteen Sami had only met York Rigby, the Gas Giant Consortium heir, before, and the other eighteen he knew only by reputation. Prabak Bhatt represented the wealthiest of the bunch, a multigenerational trillionaire and noted thrill seeker.

Savanah Westbrook's exploits in competitive water sports had become legendary a decade or more earlier, and she had evidently matured into new pursuits...such as racing antique ground vehicles. Sami appreciated her lithe athletic beauty, but something about her imperious expression kept him far from more carnal thoughts.

The presence of Klaus Benin among this initial flock of participants had surprised Sami somewhat. Klaus made his reputation first as a self-made business tycoon, and secondly as an inveterate playboy with *unique* tastes. He had been known to visit war zones on more than one planet, allegedly supplying weaponry to one side or the other in exchange for a little hands-on participation. The other members of the new clientele represented a fairly standard cross section of Sami's usual peer group, and he greeted them at the luxurious entry lounge with a troop of liveried porters at his left and right.

"Welcome to Ajanib, my friends," Sami intoned, spreading his hands with a graceful flourish as an underling provided inertial locators to each client. "If you will accompany me, the porters will care for all your belongings and see that they are delivered to your respective suites."

Only Savanah Westbrook found issue with this suggestion, retaining her two large bags and shooing away porters with a haughty flip of her hand. To Sami's eyes her attire appeared to be formed of glossy black leather that adhered to her body like a second skin, accentuating her height and contrasting with her severely trimmed white-blond hair, the overall impression of competent fitness heightened as she easily hefted her own luggage. As Sami turned to lead them from the lounge, he glanced back to see Klaus Benin at Savanah's side, the two seeming to engage in a rather intimate exchange.

Had they struck up a flirtation on the launch from Bethune? Or had they enjoyed a relationship at some prior time and place? Sami could only guess, but he saw it as a positive sign. He knew as well as any that romantic urges diminished one's reasoning powers, and at the present moment Sami's business stood ready to profit from any reckless indulgence.

"So this is what an old alien base looks like?" York Rigby asked, looking about at the aquamarine sections of the original asteroid surfaces as the group moved easily through the entrance area.

"Most of this section has been improved for human tastes, but those greenish glowing bits are all original . . . more than fifty thousand years old, they say."

"As old as all that?" York said politely, glancing about without much evident interest before focusing back on Sami. "And wasn't there supposed to be some odd spatial effect at work in here? I saw some mention of that somewhere or other."

Sami nodded, stifling his impatience. The old asteroid interested him far less than his new business venture. "You can see it even here if you know what to look for." They rounded the corner to see the mezzanine area revealed, Build-Out on the right, the entrance to lodging and dining on the left, Sami and York in the lead. "See, York, look at that light straight ahead at the end of the passage."

York squinted ahead as they strode along. "Oh, aye. Now isn't that an odd sight. Strange feeling to be sure, but must offer some interesting commercial applications."

It suddenly occurred to Sami that York's presence within Ajanib might be more in the role of a corporate spy rather than a pleasure-seeking industrialist heir. He glanced at York's impassive profile, hearing the other clients talking amongst themselves behind them, and could think of no reason to be anything less than honest. "We certainly hoped for some commercial use, but our scientists say it is a manufactured *effect*, not some functioning system that we can duplicate." They reached the grand entrance to the wing of luxury suites and Sami concluded with, "It does make for a delightful racetrack, though."

Sami paused, turning to address the others. "The concierge systems in your suites will supply all the necessary details you could desire, but there"—he gestured back toward the Build-Out section—"we provide a full catalog of the most desirable ancient model ground cars, complete with hundreds of original factory options that you can peruse any time you wish. But if you care to join me for a moment in the Members Club, I now invite you to lift a glass and obtain an excellent preview of all that Ajanib offers for your pleasure. If not, the inertial locator we provided you will show the path to your waiting suite."

Sami led the way and all nineteen followed him to the Members Club where, once again, Warren Springer Stowe's annoying fingerprints sullied an otherwise pleasurable moment for Sami. Nearly every one of the new clients seemed visibly impressed as they stared about the richly appointed chamber, the dynamic holo images at regular intervals around the periphery, attractive bartenders and servers needlessly polishing glasses or wiping immaculate tabletops.

On cue, the vehicles of Hammerworth's crew appeared on two holo images, their gleaming forms descending down the ramp from the broad apron onto the oval track, camera drones pacing them as they accelerated, five vehicles in a staggered line, the sound of their engines coming through the audio pickups.

"Two Barracudas, a Corvette, a Mustang, and . . . what's that first car?" York Rigby murmured as he stared at the unfolding scene, his detailed knowledge causing Sami to reassess his suspicion of corporate espionage.

"It's a Pontiac GTO, I believe," Klaus Benin provided, lifting a glass from a proffered tray, entirely ignoring the prettily smiling server as he coolly assessed the unfolding scene, while Savanah disdained the holographic displays entirely, her eyes on Klaus.

Sami moved to a broad table, waving a gleaming new display into life, textual information and numerical values scrolling. "Here you may assess the technical details on each of the gladiator's vehicles, including the factory options chosen at Build-Out. You can measure the odds of every contestant."

"*Gladiators?*" Prabak Bhatt inquired, sipping from his glass as he turned to Sami.

"Yes," Sami said, as most of the others divided their attention between the multiview images of the accelerating cars and his explanation. "These competitors risk death to engage in contests of driving prowess for our spectating pleasure. Gladiators."

Klaus Benin stared now. "I know something about those gladiators from antiquity, and they did more than just drive in circles."

Sami smiled, bowing slightly. "As the name implies, Mister Benin, the role of our gladiators involves much more than merely driving in circles also." He indicated other holo displays about the room. "If you glance at these displays feeding us views from Ajanib's vast catacombs, what do you see, hmm?" Sami looked at each of the nineteen wealthy clients in turn. "Do you not see the roads and highways of every Old Earth teledrama, the fragments of which we have all sampled?"

Sami saw puzzlement in some faces while others nodded appreciatively, and he continued, "Instead of a staged teledrama, our gladiators will follow the objectives created in this room, racing and battling against each other to meet whatever goal *we* in this room appoint for them."

"Battling?" Klaus Benin asked with an arched eyebrow.

"*Battling*," Sami repeated. "With the powerful incentives offered to victorious drivers, there will be unfettered competition; there *will* be casualties."

"Indeed, Sami, is that what we are seeing here?" Prabak Bhatt blandly inquired, staring at the holo display as a muted cacophony of voices arose from the inter-vehicle communicators.

Sami first felt a surge of temper at the sound of the drivers' voices, having strictly informed Hammerworth and Stowe he wanted no audible distractions during his first presentation, then he saw two of the vehicles clashing as they sped around the oval track, sparks flying. Sami heard a woman's voice crackling over the communicator, engine noise almost drowning her urgent cries.

"Damn it, Catbox! What's wrong with you? You're going to—"

"Stay off my line, Cleo," an imperturbable man's voice purred as the last two cars came speeding into a corner, the green Mustang nudging into the rear quarter of the black Barracuda.

The Barracuda's tail end swung slowly out of line, smoke rising up from the rear tires, the Mustang sweeping past a moment before the Barracuda flipped, rolling as sparks flew along with shattered pieces of body metal. The woman's voice arose in an inarticulate cry of pain and broke off as the inverted vehicle tumbled again, slewing chunks of smoking metal in every direction.

"Ten thousand says she's dead," Savanah Westbrook said in a dispassionate voice.

More from hopefulness than any other motivation, Sami said, "Ten thousand says she lives." And around him the others joined in on one side of the bet or the other.

Before the question could be answered by a safety crew running down to the wreckage, York Rigby stepped close beside Sami, his eyes on Klaus Benin, who stared at the carnage with an odd smile.

"Well, Sami, seems you've got all the ingredients for a delightfully ugly little drama here. Should make for a fabulous time, I'd say." York looked from Benin's disturbing grin to where he gazed hungrily at the holo image of a vehicle now engulfed in flame. "But I do wonder, where will it end, hmm?"

CHAPTER 23

True to Warren's prediction, one of Hammerworth's drivers got smashed on the oval track, though she survived with only minor injuries, but he derived very limited satisfaction from his prophetic accuracy. His next task as a grand director of this unfolding live drama seemed difficult enough without Hammerworth's crew clawing at each other and everyone around them, and their evident willingness to casually destroy anyone—even their own comrades—made the stakes all too clear.

The first event for the gladiators stood only hours away, their shrinking respite created as Sami's clients availed themselves of Build-Out: selecting, constructing, and driving their own authentic reproductions. For the moment, Warren expended very little attention on the paying customers after establishing the oval-track procedure necessary to keep them from accidentally (or intentionally) killing one another. His focus lay on the upcoming production and upon his personal students in the art of antique vehicle operations. None of them, save Cherry, possessed anywhere near the skill level he wanted to see before they faced the chaos and direct violence that seemed increasingly likely to beset them. But now the moment approached and Warren threw himself into preparatory steps.

With all the gladiators, except Hammerworth's crew, gathered around him, Warren went over a digitized model of the catacombs that, while not exact, presented a rough layout of the appointed battleground. "Cast your eyes and see where I've positioned each vehicle on the model here, okay, children?" Warren began. "There's a reason for choosing these starting routes, and you can see how I've got you dispersed."

Dennison, one of Warren's freshly minted gladiators, raised a finger as he frowned down at the model. "But where're Hammerworth's creeps going to be?"

"Wherever it enters their little pea brains to be, Dennison," Warren said. "But they've barely seen the catacombs, so they're not likely to reveal any sudden genius this way."

Dennison's face continued to wear a hesitant, concerned expression that Warren saw reflected from more than a few around the circle. "Listen up, all of you." Warren took a step back and raised his arms dramatically. "I have seen you all drive...and I've seen Hammerworth's lot drive, and most of them aren't any better than you are behind the wheel, so don't let all their tough-guy theatrics get into your head."

"They're a lot meaner than we are, though," Gilda said, chewing away on whatever it was she always munched on, her arms crossed. "That seems sure enough."

Warren saw Cherry idling out of the fringe of the group, her dark eyes looking from face to face in a measuring way, and he turned back to Gilda with a smile. "Meaner than some of you, maybe." The gladiators seemed to suddenly assess each other, looking for unexpected signs of meanness among their number as Warren went on. "That bunch are all operating straight power vehicles, all of them with three pedals, and only one or two of them really know how to properly operate the gears."

"We will be happy to mock them for their lack of skill...if we manage to survive, Stowe," Bandar, another aspiring gladiator, said in a snide tone.

Warren shook his head. "You don't get it. With those particular cars and their skills—or lack thereof—they'll be at a disadvantage at any section of the catacombs with tight corners and sharp speed variations, see? So find some tight spots, like here and here"—Warren stepped up to the model, pointing out a few of the sections constructed to resemble narrow city streets, with dead ends and ninety-degree turns—"and if you stay on the go pedal the way I taught you, those twits will be fiddling around with their gears while you're long gone."

All the gladiators except Cherry took this in, gazing down at the model in concentrated silence. Gilda broke the reverie, pursing her lips, that chewy gob in her cheek as she looked up at Warren. "What'll we do if they catch us on those straightaways or those big sweepers?"

Warren scratched his head and shrugged one shoulder. "Well, you sure won't outrun them, so you'll have a choice: try to block them or get out of the way and let them pass you."

"And hope they're not feeling too nasty as they pass you, right?" Gilda concluded.

"Something like that," Warren admitted. "But keep in mind, you don't make this kind of coin for nothing."

"That's true enough," Gilda said, smacking on her chewy mass again, "but I'd kinda like to make it for more than the last day of my life, right?"

With time ticking quickly down, Warren sought out Hammerworth and his people for the final briefing before the big launch, finding them together in an uneasy group. Warren saw they had made use of the fab program he had unearthed, all of them wearing the snug-fitting bodysuits, cradling helmets in their arms, just like his own gladiators.

It seemed immediately clear that Warren had stepped into the midst of some slow-boiling dispute among the five Bethune toughs, and for a moment he was ignored or unobserved, free to witness the cheerful camaraderie of their group in full force.

"Hammer, you going to let that flaming prick act like that?" Cleo asked in an outraged tone, her seriousness heightened by the bandage at the corner of one eye and a rather singed look to her blondish hair.

Hammerworth frowned at her beneath his heavy brows, and the one they called Catbox snorted, interjecting, "People are going to tell me how to act now, Cleo? Where's that in my contract?"

"Don't push it, Catbox," Hammerworth growled, turning his blocky visage to transfix the slender, loose-limbed Catbox where he sprawled at ease, his back against one wall.

"Or else what, Hammer?" Catbox yawned. "Going to put that ape-like strength of yours to some barbaric use? And me, the best driver you've got, getting all busted up? Doesn't seem likely."

Hammerworth took one quick step, his powerful hand snatching hold of Catbox's forearm, bearing down as he stared down at his victim. "I don't have to smash you, boy, and you'll still wish you were dead." Warren thought he heard the bones in Catbox's arm grating as

Hammerworth squeezed more and more tightly, Catbox going pale, his fixed grin trembling.

"I—I think you've made your point, Hammer," Catbox gasped out, and Hammerworth released him, stepping back as Catbox slumped, gripping his forearm.

The other two silent members of Hammerworth's crew looked up from the power struggle, Kira spotting Warren in the doorway. "Look, Hells, we've got company, of a sort," he said, nodding toward Warren as the other four all turned their focus on this new intruder.

"What do you want?" Hammerworth said, ignoring Catbox as he focused his brutish gaze upon Warren.

"It's getting close to the big moment," Warren said as he leaned against the doorframe, folding his arms. "Need to go over a few things."

Hammerworth strode nearer until well within arm's reach, and Warren didn't move a muscle, pleased to note that even leaning he still stood taller than the stocky beast. "Save the sermons for your little pets, Stowe. We know what we're doing without any nonsense from you."

Warren smiled. "Do you really? It is so tempting. You have no idea how tempting." Warren's smile became a smirk. "When the objective is selected up in the Members Club, and the scenario gets called, I'd honestly enjoy watching you five wandering aimlessly about the catacombs while my 'pets' scoop up the win."

Hammerworth's brows lowered while Cleo spoke up from her seat. "We'd better hear what he's got to say, Hammer."

Without turning, Hammerworth said, "Be quiet, Cleo," then pressed closer to Warren. "What's the trick, Stowe?"

Warren shook his head. "Instructions, Sport. Guidance. You may have noticed such things, say, on shampoo or the like, right? Apply, wash, rinse, and so on?"

"You are not as funny as you think you are," Hammerworth said. "Say something useful, or get out."

"Something useful..." Warren mused. "Okay, you'll hear the scenario called over the communicator line along with the location of the starting objective, right?"

"We know all that," Catbox said, still holding his bruised forearm.

"Of course," Warren said. "And since you all have the catacomb locations *completely* committed to memory, you'll be able to find your way directly to the objective, hmm?"

Warren let them chew on that image for a moment, noting the glances shot amongst Hammerworth's four teammates behind their leader's back. Hells spoke for the first time now: "So your little pets have everything memorized, then? Hardly. You've got a guidance system for them, right?"

Warren unfolded his arms, looking past Hammerworth and pointing at Hells. "A guidance system . . . of sorts, but for *every* driver who pays attention. Now listen: When they call the objective, one of your camera drones will position well out in front of you and lead you to it. If you're going exactly the wrong direction it'll show you a red illuminator until you get turned around. Got it?"

Hammerworth stared at Warren, measuring him with pure suspicion. "And why do you suddenly give a damn about us?"

Warren laughed. "Oh to be sure, I don't care about you at all. I just need this first scenario to go smoothly . . . and our clients won't find it thrilling if you five wander blindly around the catacombs. They've got to see some action."

Catbox smirked as he cradled his arm. "Do you think they'll find some thrills seeing a bunch of Buicks getting smashed to pieces?" he asked, his eyes glittering as he stared at Warren. "Because I'll tell you straight, I'm betting that burning wreckage'll make them feel all tingly."

Hells barked laughter and Hammerworth merely nodded as Warren turned, throwing over his shoulder, "So far the only burning wreckage they've seen is a Barracuda, and they liked it enough for a repeat. Good luck."

Warren went directly to the discreet chamber he had requisitioned near the Members Club to use as a sort of command center, and after assuring that his gladiators were fueled up and ready to enter the catacombs he settled into his next task.

He had gotten the room outfitted with monitors tied into fixed camera emplacements in the catacombs as well as the feed from camera drones. Unbeknownst to Sami, he had also rigged unmonitored direct communication to his gladiators . . . just in case. In this first and most vital presentation, Warren stood ready to conduct every step of the drama to the best of his abilities, but in addition he also monitored the betting action within the Members Club.

He would carefully play to the audience and produce the success he had sold to Sami. Warren's own freedom—his life—depended upon it.

He watched Sami enter the Members Club followed by a stream of his clients who had spent the earlier part of their day constructing and driving the vehicles of their choice with varying degrees of skill, and now their heightened tastes required fresh stimulation.

Warren checked the monitors, seeing the gladiator vehicles entering the catacombs, his own protégés first, each of them heading toward their assigned cruising ground, each Gran Sport bearing its unit number just like an Old Earth racer . . . or like a billiard ball about to get whacked. Before he checked on Hammerworth's crew, Warren spotted the small shape of Cherry's Fireblade accelerating away from the load-in zone, her body melded into the Honda like one continuous piece.

Hammerworth's crew entered the catacombs, but unlike the others, these five vehicles did not speed off to cruising zones, instead holding their positions at the junction of the three major arterials, waiting.

"Wouldn't know thrilling drama if it bit them on the face," Warren muttered to himself as he checked his view of the Members Club.

Sami had three of his clients at the three input tables, each positioned at the cardinal points of the club's perimeter, their cocktails in hand, the light glowing up from the tables into their respective faces. Warren knew what those three gamblers would be seeing because he had laid out the system himself.

Each was presented with unique options that they could select from. One saw a list of Victory Conditions, another a list of Team Scale options, and the third a list of Target Options. Their three respective choices would create the scenario and launch the gladiators into action.

Warren saw the Victory Conditions selection illuminate: ESCAPE TO THE BORDER. Then he saw Team Scale selected, and his heart sank: ONE AGAINST ALL. Statistically speaking, one of his protégés was about to be sorely tested.

The final choice pinged home: FIXED TARGET.

Those three selections joined together to create the scenario: BANK ROBBERY. Now whichever gladiator reached the location deemed "the bank," the position marked by a hovering drone, would receive the target bonus . . . even as they became the true target themselves, running for their life toward the demarcation line indicating "the border," where they would then be both victorious and safe.

Warren activated the communicator and spoke, addressing all twenty-six gladiators. "Alright, sports racers, it's a Bank Robbery; the bank is at the Y-junction in alpha sector. Good luck!" Out of the corner of his eye on one display Warren saw Hammerworth's drivers launch, their tires smoking as they headed out.

Warren opened his smoking case, withdrew a small data node from the hidden compartment, and linked it to his workstation. He found the old sound file he had obtained years earlier and linked it into the audio line. The ancient music from a long-forgotten band began to blare out an appropriate song, some kind of guitar driving a grainy jam, a vocalist from antiquity describing a fellow going the distance while also going for speed, and Warren watched as twenty-six ancient vehicles did just that. They went for speed.

CHAPTER 24

Bandar felt his hands sweating on the steering wheel of the Buick as he gripped it exactly as Warren Springer Stowe had instructed. His right foot pressed the speed pedal just the right amount, holding the low-growling vehicle to 50 on the analog gauge, the wide aquamarine-glowing arterial walls blurring by on either side, only an occasional turnoff visible to Bandar's eyes as it flashed past.

In the next moment, he heard the distinctive gong as the very first objective was called, and Stowe's voice came across the communicator only seconds later, explaining the scenario and location. After another moment, a catchy unfamiliar song began rocking out over the audio line, but Bandar had no attention to spare it.

Bandar saw one of the pacing camera drones pull ahead, and he didn't need the red illuminator to know he was heading directly away from the designated *Bank* location. He remembered passing the Y-junction only minutes earlier and he felt a mingled sense of fear and expectancy that he should chance to be the nearest gladiator, even as his right foot moved to the braking pedal, mashing it aggressively down until he came to a screeching halt. The arterial's width allowed him to slowly turn around in one slow sweep that Bandar thought would have made Stowe a little proud.

He pressed the speed pedal again, his excitement driving him to jam it to the floor, the tires screeching as the engine bellowed, blasting him back down the passage. The gauge on the dash showed 50, 60 . . . 90, and ahead Bandar spotted the illuminating glow of his objective, a drone holding position high up, its projector creating a shimmering golden wall of light. Bandar flashed through the glowing curtain, hearing another gong through the communicator as the song broke off and Stowe's voice came across in a very serious sounding tone: "Calling all cars, calling all cars. Bank robbery in progress, suspect heading from alpha sector, outbound for the border."

Bandar knew he had just become the *bank robber* in this scenario, all the other gladiators suddenly conscripted pursuers. While Bandar already secured a sizable bonus just by being the first to reach the objective, and each second he remained "free" added incrementally more to his account, the lion's share of the winnings remained to the final victor—either to Bandar if he reached the "border" marker, or to some other driver who "apprehended" him by closing within a stone's throw for a few critical seconds before Bandar managed to evade.

Despite his sudden flood of adrenaline, Bandar's thoughts crystallized on the image of his many pursuers racing from every direction to intercept him. This fat arterial formed the most obvious path for his flight, and surely it also served as the most likely route for his eager pursuers.

He remembered a series of branching thoroughfares to the right and left coming up, with more than one side path winding around to rejoin the arterial farther along, and in an impulse decision, he jammed on the braking pedal. The Buick squealed and fishtailed beneath him as it decelerated, but Bandar saw this intended turnoff flash by on the right before he could even try to make the corner.

The Buick lurched to a halt and Bandar fumbled with the shifter, moving it into reverse rather than going through a cumbersome turnaround. He just managed to weave around backward to the junction and slam the shifter back into drive when he spotted twin headlights closing fast. "Aw! Damn, damn, damn!"

He wrestled the steering wheel and stabbed his foot on the go pedal too aggressively, the Buick crow-hopping, the tail end slewing around to clip the passage wall before Bandar got it under control. Looking up at that ridiculous rectangle of mirror, he glimpsed the flash of lights pass by behind him, too slowly, but he rounded the curve before he could confirm the pursuit.

This smaller road offered a few tight curves and a couple of turnoffs, so Bandar couldn't push the Buick to its top speeds without a high probability of wrecking, yet he felt like the wolves nibbled at his heels, even though no chase vehicles were in sight.

A few moments later, a bright light flashed from that little rectangle of rear-facing mirror and Bandar saw the twin beams of a pursuit vehicle rounding the curve some distance behind. The camera drones orbiting his pursuer flickered as they swept through the headlights' reach, but Bandar couldn't make out any details of the vehicle itself. He hoped it was another Buick Gran Sport back there. His fellow gladiators would not hesitate to tag him out and claim the bonus, but Bandar felt sure that none of *them* would seek to physically harm him.

He felt no such assurance when it came to Hammerworth and his crew, and those lights behind could be anyone . . . drawing nearer.

Bandar gripped the steering wheel more tightly and pressed the pedal harder, hearing the engine's tone rising even as the number on the gauge spun higher and higher. Sweat ran down Bandar's sides as he whipped around a tight curve, his vehicle skittering, forcing him to ease off the speed slightly and wrestle the wheel back into stability.

Ahead he saw a junction he remembered from one of their training drives, a passage branching off to the left at a shallow angle. A sudden tone jarred him at the same moment, a pursuer closing within tagging range, those headlights abruptly close behind.

Bandar slammed on the braking pedal to make for the branching passage but felt a hard smack from behind that nearly spun his Buick into the sloping wall of the passage. He just managed to hold the fishtailing vehicle straight enough to steer onto the new passage, and the tag tone choked off as he broke away from his pursuer, catching a glimpse of orange sparks showering from the crumpled front end of a Buick Gran Sport.

For the moment, Bandar ran clear.

Within the Members Club, Sami saw the clear signs of appreciation by his clients as the three selectors chose the Bank Robbery scenario, and Stowe's grim announcements came over the audio line. Their initial excitement seemed to taper as the seconds passed with only disparate views of various gladiator vehicles speeding individually through the catacombs, the camera drones finally highlighting Bandar's Buick as the "Bank Robber" of the scenario. But a sudden bet placed by York Rigby generated a new source of stimulation: Would the bank robber actually make his getaway? Or would he be tagged out by his numerous pursuers? York bet a mere ten thousand guilders that Bandar could escape to the "border" waypoint, and the odds against Bandar made for a high-risk, high-reward calculation.

Then Bandar missed his initial turn from the arterial, the camera drones showing his clumsy backtracking to the turnoff.

"He drives about like you do, Prabak," Savanah said as she sipped a golden cocktail, staring unblinking at the holographic images.

Prabak only smiled at Savanah's jab, but for an instant Sami saw the flash of anger behind Prabak's dark eyes before he turned back to the display.

A murmur of voices drew Sami's gaze back up, seeing the view from another vehicle as it rapidly closed with bank-robber Bandar. "Who is that in pursuit?" Sami asked, stepping nearer to squint at the identifier.

"Says it is unit seventeen: Dennison," Klaus Benin murmured from Sami's side, his tone seemingly bemused.

Sami had hoped one of his handpicked Bethune toughs would be the scenario victor, not only to give Stowe a dose of much-needed humility, but also to provide a suitably thrilling conclusion to the event. He needed this conglomeration of connoisseurs to end the day eager for more, even if that meant losing a gladiator in a particularly brutal fashion. But so far Hammerworth's drivers hadn't found their way to the action, their unfamiliarity with the catacombs leaving them disadvantaged.

Looking from Bandar's camera view to Dennison's, it became quickly clear who possessed the greater driving skill, Dennison's smoother handling quickly closing the distance.

The gamblers stopped talking amongst themselves now as they watched between multiple holographic images, seeing Dennison's car growing closer and closer, Bandar's red taillights seeming to jig about unsteadily as he strove to get away.

A shrilling tone came over the audio line and Stowe's voice announced, "There's the proximity tone—four seconds to apprehension of the bank robber by unit seventeen."

Sami saw the flash of red lights as Bandar abruptly braked, and from multiple camera drones it was clear Dennison's attempt to evade came too late.

Around Sami, a few gamblers chortled as Dennison's vehicle

rammed Bandar, bits of body metal launching outward as a cloud of white vapor puffed up. Unit 17 spun around twice, lurching to a halt, while Bandar's wounded Gran Sport screeched about before sliding into a branching road to the left.

Stowe's voice rang out over the audio line: "Calling all cars, unit seventeen is out of commission and the bank robber is still running."

Sami's heart warmed as bets began to flow steadily now, each of them logging on the wager board, more than a million guilders currently wagered.

He only cast one glance at the single remaining view of Dennison's smashed Buick as the action moved on, seeing a tongue of yellow flame licking out from the shattered vehicle's hood.

Bandar felt the Buick's wounds as he drove, an odd vibration coming through his steering wheel and a disjointed feel as he rounded each curve, but he kept the speed up as high as he dared. If he could just rejoin an arterial he could probably sprint the final distance and cash in on that fat bonus.

His thoughts flitted back to the close escape he had just managed, trying to recall who drove car 17 ... Dennison, he thought.

Hope he's okay ...

A pair of headlights sweeping in from an elevated junction to the right pushed every thought of Dennison's fate from Bandar's mind, his pulse jumping like the tachometer on his dash as he gauged the speed of this new threat, his foot pressing down hard.

In his rapid assessment it seemed the chase car—another Gran Sport ... a bright red one, number 3—would merge with his path somewhat behind him, so if he could just keep ahead of tagging range, he might still make it to the border waypoint ... and to that big payoff. To have any chance at all he would need to push his wounded vehicle as fast as he could dare to drive.

The two routes came together, the red Gran Sport merging well behind Bandar, just as he had hoped, but as they roared through the large open area back into a tighter passage, Bandar felt the shimmy in his vehicle increasing. Looking up at the mirror, the twin headlights of the chase vehicle resembled a horizontal blur of white, the mirror shaking hard as Bandar accelerated. Only a minute or so more would get him to the arterial, but those lights behind grew nearer, the echoing roar of that engine sounding louder each second.

Looking from the road ahead to the quivering mirror and back, Bandar fought to keep the drifting vehicle centered up even as he saw the branching appear ahead, the sweeping entrances to the arterial opening to the left and right. Bandar steered right, barely keeping the weaving vehicle on track for the curve, snatching a quick glance at the pursuit vehicle getting nearer and nearer.

They shot out of the entrance onto the broad arterial, the open space giving Bandar the confidence to floor the pedal again, even though the shimmy began to grow so harsh his teeth rattled.

From out of nowhere a single bright headlight stabbed out for an instant behind him, then flashed past Bandar in a blur, an engine screaming like a turbine as it rocketed ahead, the tag tone blaring at the same moment.

Bandar managed a second's awareness that it was . . . what's-her-face, *Poppins*, on that crazy motorcycle thing as she held position to one side ahead of him, still getting the tag tone. That flash of awareness disappeared as he decelerated sharply to break off the tag tone, even as Stowe's voice announced something over the audio line that Bandar couldn't bother to comprehend.

The steering wheel rattled and jerked in Bandar's hands, the vehicle around him whipsawing back and forth before breaking loose to spin around even as the tunnel walls blurred on either side. For a moment, time slowed and he saw the red Gran Sport bearing down on him, now nose to nose, its tires smoking as it braked and fishtailed, sliding along beside him as he continued backward down the arterial. The red car's driver managed to twitch the steering wheel, drifting to a halt right beside him, the tag tone suddenly audible to the quivering, sweating Bandar.

"Bank robber apprehended, unit three!" Stowe's voice called out.

Bandar tried to moisten his dry mouth as he tugged his helmet free, looking over at the Gran Sport sitting just a short distance away, camera drones slowly orbiting them both.

Gilda smiled at Bandar, her jaws champing away as she raised her hand, one thumb extended upward.

Dennison saw his fat financial bonus disappear right along with Bandar's surviving taillight, his own number 17 Gran Sport thoroughly wrecked, but at least Stowe's assurances about the safety upgrades held true. Aside from a sore neck, Dennison couldn't detect any immediate sign of injury as he tugged his helmet free, but a strong smell of smoke stoked a rising sense of panic in the pit of his stomach.

He struggled out of the restraint harness as the smell increased and a visible glow of yellow flame leaped up from the Buick's shattered hood. The sloshing tank full of explosive hydrocarbon fuel situated somewhere beneath him suddenly possessed Dennison's mind with great urgency. They had told all the drivers to stay in their vehicle if they wrecked, and simply await the aid vehicle, but Dennison didn't fancy sitting atop a fiery explosion.

In a frantic surge he kicked the crumpled door open and staggered out onto the road surface, backing away from the smoldering wreck past a dead camera drone, evidently shattered by flying wreckage. One drone still orbited the wreck, and Dennison remained too focused on a potential explosion to wonder where the other two drones might have gone.

Exactly how explosive was this old fuel anyway?

Dennison backed all the way to one sloping aquamarine wall of the passage, staring at the burning Gran Sport before he noticed the glowing ruby luminance to his left. When he turned to look at last, tearing his eyes away from the leaping flames, he made only one startled sound before it was upon him.

CHAPTER 25

Sharif Maktoum swept into the Maktoum office building in central Torino with only the minimum retinue in his wake. This trip to Bethune had taken far longer than it should have, with what seemed more delays and transport issues than he had experienced in the prior decade combined, and his simmering temper nearly boiled over when he discovered Sami's absence.

"How long has he been working from Ajanib?" Sharif demanded of Supervisor Kashti Pura, his jaw clenching in suppressed anger. How could Sami spend even a *week* away from Torino at this juncture when all their plans could finally be executed? Bethune's independence from the Confederated Worlds might be a very short-lived phenomenon, and Maktoum Corporation had invested heavily in aiding their secession. They must recoup that investment without delay.

Supervisor Pura bit her lip, hesitating before saying, "Would you like me to confirm the date he departed, Director?"

Despite the veil of anger, Sharif knew he had placed Pura in the untenable position between the two brothers, asking her to inform on Sami. He bit back his initial impulse. "No, that will not be necessary. Thank you, Supervisor. I will go discuss it with Sami directly." He forced a smile past his wrath. "Do you happen to know when I can get a transport out to the asteroid?"

Supervisor Pura seemed to breathe more easily as she said, "The regular transport transits to Ajanib tomorrow, Director, or I can look into some other vessel that—"

"The *regular* transport?" Sharif said in a gently inquiring tone.

"Yes, Director. It brings supplies and workers out to Ajanib. Tomorrow there will also be a few clients aboard."

"Clients?" Sharif said in a sharp-edged voice, then seeing Pura's expression added, "Never mind. I'll take the transport and see for myself."

"Very well, Director," Pura said in evident relief.

"But, Pura," Sharif said, staring directly into her eyes, "I would prefer to surprise Sami, if possible."

Supervisor Pura nodded somberly. "Yes, Director," she said, and Sharif felt reasonably certain that this degree of loyalty she would surrender to him, at least.

All the gladiators except Hammerworth's bunch watched the camera drone footage over and over together, seeing the distant smoke-screened figure of Dennison backing away from the burning car, turning to look at something out of sight beyond the frame, his body visibly jolting just as the camera drone's orbit swept the view past Dennison.

"Where the hell did he go?" Muller demanded once again, voicing the unanswerable question that they had all posed. "The aid vehicle arrived at the wreck seven minutes later, right? Where could he have disappeared to in a little more than five minutes?" Other voices rose up among the gladiators but Sami's voice cut them all off, a hint of impatience leaking through his attempt at control.

"We all know the safety protocol in the catacombs, and anyone who ignores the protocol takes a big chance."

"Hmm," Gilda mused, her arms crossed. "Seems sorta hard to follow the protocol when that means roasting your ass in a burning car."

Sami had bigger issues to contend with, but he knew that any chance of building on the first scenario's success meant retaining his team of gladiators and getting them back in the catacombs soon. The need to placate these underlings grated on Sami's nerves but he worked hard to maintain his smooth delivery. "I believe I mentioned we will include a flame-retardant canister with every vehicle now, so every driver can follow the protocol and stay safe."

There were more under-voice grumblings but Sami swept on. "I must attend to our clients, but I want to say that I think this first scenario proceeded very well, despite Dennison's unfortunate disappearance, and I am sure you would all like a shot at a financial windfall such as, er, Gilda and Bandar have already received."

Leave them counting the money they haven't got yet . . .

The gladiators began to cross-talk on the happier topic of financial bonuses to come as Sami exited the chamber and made his way to the oval track where many of his wealthy clients tried to replicate some of the better moves they had witnessed during the first gladiator scenario. A pair of badly crumpled client vehicles to one side bore witness to the learning curve and to the effectiveness of Stowe's safety upgrades. No clients had suffered any injury so far and Sami felt his confidence surging as everything began to fall together.

Belinda Athenos moved from a cluster of spectating clients who stood about the apron, clearly feeling very twentieth century in their old-fashioned driving suits, cradling helmets in their arms. "Director, we are expecting the regular transport within an hour, four new clients joining us."

Sami nodded, glancing up as a client's vehicle roared by on the oval track below them. "Very well, Athenos. I will be in the Members Club overseeing a new scenario and you may encourage our new guests to join us directly if they wish. You may explain to them that a live driving competition is in progress."

Belinda Athenos dipped her head. "Very well, sir."

A moment later, the final two cars rounded the track, their engines winding down as they pulled off, coming up to the apron where the first, a Corvette Stingray, lurched to an unsteady halt, and then a Shelby Mustang GT350 followed suit, jerking and sputtering until it fell silent. In the momentary silence Sami announced, "If you wish to get cleaned up and join me in the Members Club, a fresh scenario will be ready to initiate in forty-five minutes or so."

"Excellent, Sami," Prabak Bhatt declared. He had been the only gambler who had bet on Gilda to win the prior scenario, and after wrecking his own car on the oval track, it seemed betting suited his skills more surely than driving. "It is a giddy anticipation to see how this next scenario reveals its surprises."

Savanah and Klaus Benin made no comment, walking toward the suites, so close together that their bodies nearly touched. Sami's gaze followed them for a moment, and though he reminded himself that romance was good for business, he couldn't help feeling a sense of aggravation, watching them. How could such a self-possessed beauty, like Savanah, be enamored with such a dodgy screwball like Benin? And *enamored* seemed an apt word for what Sami observed. The animal energy rippled between them like electricity.

His focus turned back to the business at hand. He needed to see Warren Springer Stowe and assure that all was in readiness for the fast-approaching scenario.

The three clients chosen at random as selectors took their seats and each made their choice on their respective menus, the scenario logging and beginning a moment later. The scenario gong rang out and Stowe's voice came over the audio line, "All units form a convoy and complete one full circuit of the catacomb perimeter. Scenario is ... *Spy Versus Spy*. Three target locations in succession, each location providing the *Secret Plans* of the objective. Three chances to obtain an objective. First objective will appear when the perimeter circuit is complete."

When Sami first heard Stowe describe the Spy Versus Spy scenario he could readily connect it to Old Earth entertainment film fragments he had seen, but he had doubted how effectively such a scenario would resonate with viewing clients in the Members Club. Those doubts redoubled now as every display within the club merely revealed gladiator vehicles streaming into the perimeter route, slowly forming a long chain of speeding vehicles, twenty-five units long, offering no immediate conflict, no drama, no tension. Sami felt a chill sweat break out as a protracted moment of near silence filled the Members Club, a few of the gamblers turning away from the holo displays to converse with their tablemates.

Then all twenty-five vehicles began to accelerate, plus that odd motorcycle thing at the tail of the chain, as they rounded a bend, passing close to a static camera position, the roar of twenty-five engines drawing nearer, and twenty-five gleaming ancient vehicles whipping past the camera like projectiles from an automatic weapon. York Rigby made an appreciative sound and Sami looked over to see him staring at the display, nodding slowly. "Now that is quite the sight," he said, several gamblers around him agreeing.

Sami couldn't understand the sudden appeal, but evidently the simple view of these antiques speeding en masse in such a way tickled the particular fancy of the true enthusiast.

The gong sounded again and Stowe's voice pronounced, "Secret Plans deposited, Charlie sector, the corner of First and Green."

On the holo display it was like the explosive break in a game of billiards, vehicles steering for turnoffs, others continuing to accelerate on the perimeter, while others jammed on the brakes, sliding to a screeching halt.

"Oh ho!" York chortled as two gladiator vehicles tangled, both of them spinning out of control on the perimeter as that motorcycle dodged through their steaming wreckage.

"That lovely black GTO—unit twenty-six—he is on the scent, it seems," Prabak Bhatt declared, placing a fat bet on Hammerworth himself. Other gamblers began posting bets and Sami's internal relief surged, seeing the wager board filling up with delightfully large figures.

A stir at the entrance to the Members Club signaled the arrival of Belinda Athenos and Sami focused his smile toward her, looking for the new clients in her wake. First he noticed the strange, rigid cast to her expression a moment before his brother's figure came into view, Sharif's fulminating gaze transfixing Sami where he stood.

The moment of reckoning had arrived, just as Sami had known it would in his innermost heart, but far sooner than he had hoped, and all the dodgy actions he had taken to create this masterpiece now rushed back into his recollection. The sudden tumult of cheers and shouting around him only managed to pierce through Sami's frozen intellect when Sharif's eyes looked up into the Members Club, his expression perplexed.

Sami glanced back at the holographic displays, seeing two gladiator vehicles freshly wrecked and a green Mustang in the process of ramming another Gran Sport into a spinning crash, as the clients cheered and placed more bets. When Sami turned back to Sharif, the look of rage on his brother's face had softened, a measuring, calculating look in his eyes.

Some of the gamblers caught sight of Sharif now, calling out greetings, and Sami saw him plaster on his most urbane expression, nodding or waving to various acquaintances as he approached Sami. Before Sharif could say anything, Stowe's voice came over the audio channel: "Unit twenty-six has captured the Secret Plans from the first objective. New objective is in place: Secret Plans deposited at the roundabout, alpha sector." The wager board chimed, showing settled bets, won and lost, and the gamblers began placing new bets while that green Mustang—Catbox, that was the lunatic's name—wrecked yet another Gran Sport. The clientele went wild, many of them placing side bets on Catbox as he seemed to focus solely on eliminating competing gladiators.

Klaus Benin turned from the action and stepped over to the Brothers Maktoum, with Savanah Westbrook trailing along beside him, her glass in hand. "Sami, Sharif," Klaus greeted, sipping from his own glass. "It seems you really have created something promising here." While Sami ground his teeth at Benin's stinting praise, he welcomed even the presence of such a twit as Klaus because it momentarily kept Sharif's unpleasant talons off of *him*.

Sharif filled in for Sami's frozen silence. "Thank you, Klaus. It really is amazing what one can accomplish when one gives no thought to the expense or any low thoughts about earning a profit." Sharif didn't look toward Sami as he spoke but each word lodged like well-aimed arrows in Sami's affronted ego.

Klaus smirked, sharing a look with Savanah, who rolled her eyes, before he said, "No need to pretend modesty with me, Sharif. Once you fine-tune your offering here, this promises to be the entertainment powerhouse of the known worlds."

Sami felt his loathing of Klaus suddenly dissipate, looking to see how Sharif took this estimation to heart. "Fine-tuning," Sharif repeated, either as a statement or a question, his expression entirely neutral.

An avid gleam suddenly illuminated Benin's face. "Yes, fine-tuning. I mean, these bumper cars are plenty of fun, but if you really want to bring the thrills you should give these gladiators teeth and claws—period-correct teeth and claws." He produced a data stick between two fingers, holding it up. "You've got that platinum-grade fabrication system constructing the cars, and I'll bet the anti-weapons protocols aren't installed out here away from Confederated World busybodies... And I've got the fabrication files for some antique armament that would make this whole operation go next level."

Sharif looked from Benin's face to the data stick and back. "Interesting. We will have to discuss this more, soon." Klaus bowed his head in a short jerk and turned back to the voluble gamblers all glued to the unfolding drama nearing its conclusion.

Sharif directed his focus back on Sami now, his expression unreadable. "You have been very busy, brother," he said.

Sami hated the shrinking sensation he felt under Sharif's pointed focus, and responded with less smooth deliberation than he had visualized when he had imagined this eventuality. "That's right. I've been busy. And I've created something no one else could have—not even you."

Sharif revealed a hint of cynical amusement as he said, "Yes, only you could have invested billions to convert a priceless alien artifact into an amusement attraction, right?"

Anger flared, fueling Sami's retort. "You heard Benin: this is bigger than some amusement ride." A roar of cheers and shouts brought Sami's eyes around as he said, "And look at the wager board; there's—" He broke off, shocked at how the amount had multiplied in just a few minutes of heavy betting activity. "There's fifty million guilders wagered with just this small handful of clients in one night."

Sharif's eyebrows raised as he focused on the wager board, the numbers continuing to shift as the scenario drew to an end and Stowe's voice called out the third and final objective fulfilled. The panoply of holographic displays flashed with speeding vehicles, and the gamblers turned their attention to each other, some toasting successes or losses, others moving their hand through the air, simulating the movements of cars.

Warren Springer Stowe emerged from his little control center and Sharif locked his gaze upon the lanky enthusiast, seeming to sift his memory for a half-remembered recollection. Warren jerked a thumb at the wager board and winked at Sami.

"That's Warren Springer Stowe, isn't it? What in Sheol is he doing here?" Sharif demanded.

Sami swallowed, finally saying, "He's an, uh, indentured company asset, Sharif." He worked his mouth for a moment before adding, "And a . . . a minority partner of mine in this operation . . ."

CHAPTER 26

Cherry leaned against a wall in the back of the room, watching and listening to the gladiators—minus three who weren't present due to injuries sustained in the scenario, compliments of Catbox—as they replayed and decried the dirty tactics Hammerworth's crew employed in the action.

"They hunted us down, smashing anyone who had a chance at an objective, clearing the way for Hammerworth to clean up," one of the more timid gladiators moaned.

"They didn't smash everyone," Gilda retorted in a dry voice, though her own red Gran Sport was also one of Catbox's victims. "Muller got through to an objective and cashed in."

Cherry felt a degree of personal satisfaction over Muller's victory. She had played a close daredevil game with one of Hammerworth's drivers—Cleo in her Barracuda—and allowed Muller to slip through to the waiting objective unscathed. But he had been the only exception.

Twelve Gran Sports had been taken out by Hammerworth's crew, with only one of his drivers, Hells in his Corvette, wrecked doing it. Of course the green Mustang Catbox drove barely survived the scenario, so battered and mangled that he needed an entirely new vehicle from Build-Out.

"Where the hell is Sami, or Warren, anyway?" Bandar asked in an indignant voice. "They should be here explaining—"

"I'm here," Warren declared as he strolled into the room holding a pair of tiny model cars in his hands. "Now everyone can untwist their knickers and take a breath."

161

"Warren and his itty-bitty cars are going to untwist my knickers, everybody," Gilda declared, arching an eyebrow. "Right out in front of everyone? Never knew you were such a naughty exhibitionist, hon."

A few of the gladiators chuckled at Gilda's wit, but most remained far too tense to smile. Warren winked at Gilda before holding up the two small cars. "Very pretty, Gilda, and not that far off the mark, really. I'm about to teach you all how to give the, um, *business* to any car that rubs up against you; how to give it, and keep them from giving it to you."

Warren raised the cars with a flourish. "Observe. I call this the *Stowe Maneuver* . . ."

Cherry smiled to herself and slipped away to check on other parties who might be tempted to untoward hijinks while Warren and the gladiators all remained out of the way.

Before long, she figured Ajanib would surely be equipped with more elaborate security systems and protocols, but for the moment Sami depended upon a dozen or so company security officers and the most basic area surveillance cameras. This allowed Cherry almost unfettered freedom to indulge her unending curiosity.

She slipped unseen into Hammerworth's section of rooms at the far end of the worker area, discovering the five toughs engaged in their usual disordered attempts at planning, snarling at each other while Catbox tossed jibes at his mates whenever it appeared order might be restored. After listening for a time, Cherry moved on.

She wanted to discover the whereabouts of Sami and his newly arrived brother, but she detected no voices issuing from Sami's office or suite, and as she wove her way through the luxury wings she heard an intriguing, intermittent noise ahead, notching up her augmented hearing as she approached the door of a prime suite. Only a moment of listening brought her the conjoined voices of Klaus Benin and Savanah Westbrook, clearly at the pinnacle of a highly personal shared effort. Cherry smirked to herself as the summit was obviously attained, the appropriate calls to deity observed, and the aftermath of deep breathing and murmured accolades uttered.

Cherry was about to continue in her perambulations when she heard a communication chime softly ring out within the postcoital suite, so she waited to glean some idea of what caller might be reaching out to those two entangled power elites.

Klaus took the call, the caller's voice barely audible even with Cherry's preternatural hearing. "Sami," Klaus said, his voice scarcely sounding winded. "What can I do for you?" Cherry strained to hear Sami's words, only detecting the bare edges of vowels and consonants. "Hmm, yes," Klaus replied after listening. "Say, thirty minutes in your office, then. Very well."

The connection ended and Cherry listened hard, waiting. Savanah's sultry voice broke the silence. "Well?"

"The Maktoum brothers want to hear more," Klaus replied with satisfaction. "It seems I have set the hook after all. Things should become much more interesting now."

Cherry found that Ajanib's peculiar geometry worked to her benefit, shadows rising where they shouldn't be and light sources seeming to glow feebly beyond a stone's throw. These effects enabled her to easily observe Klaus Benin's arrival at Sami's office, and before the door fully closed she had crossed the spanning distance, her aural sensitivity ramped all the way up.

The thick office door presented no difficulty to Cherry and she quickly identified the voices of Sami, Klaus, and Sharif as they conversed. Though they clearly referenced visual images that she could not see, she pieced together the outline of their intentions and the planned time frame of their execution without much difficulty.

Cherry's emotions fluctuated only slightly, although these three men coolly formed a plan that would begin costing lives almost immediately. Her greater response arose from the clear exclusion of Stowe from their planning and the sense of stealthy betrayal their actions exuded, driving her desire to find Stowe and reveal these impending changes about to alter everything. Only her discipline kept her locked on the present mission, hoping to tap that precious moment when Klaus departed and the two brothers would surely open their minds to each other.

That moment eventually arose, after what seemed a needless sifting of unessential details, Klaus finally taking his leave.

Cherry awaited Benin's departure from her concealed place immersed in the shadows, and continued to impatiently wait until he walked out of sight before loping silently back to the door.

The conversation between Sami and Sharif was well advanced by this time, and Cherry scowled to herself, wondering what juicy morsels she may have missed, but the key payoff to her efforts arrived in the next instant.

". . . Stowe is too much of a purist," Sami said in a contrary tone. "He is not going to like anything about this."

Cherry heard a long-suffering sigh, surely from Sharif. "The opinion of an indentured asset should not factor into any decision we make, Sami, and I find your dependen—"

"He is a contractual *partner* in this offering, Sharif," Sami interrupted. "I told you that."

Cherry heard the nervous rustling of movement, picturing Sami fidgeting under his brother's basilisk gaze, before Sharif finally replied, "How you ever agreed to such a partnership beggars the imagination."

"Right," Sami snapped. "I'm sure if *you* had put this place together within such a demanding deadline, *you* could have found a better expert even more quickly than I did!"

Sharif chuckled softly. "Sami, Sami, Sami . . . I give you full credit for pulling innumerable rabbits from countless hats here, but if I had been the one assembling this place, I wouldn't have raced at such a rate because I wouldn't have been operating with such a shameful disregard for every company policy, trying to outrun the day of reckoning."

"Easy for you to say," Sami retorted. "You don't have an older brother questioning and sifting every project you undertake."

"That is true," Sharif said in a mild tone. "I had Mother or Father sifting every project I touched for the first few years, and believe me, I am a soft touch by comparison."

Sami fell silent, perhaps acknowledging the verity of Sharif's words. "Well, whatever the differences between us, I do have a binding contract with Stowe, and he has lived up to the letter of it, so we're stuck with him."

Sharif cleared his throat. "Contract or no contract, he can be sidelined, one way or another."

"And then find us another expert . . . where? And how long would that take, assuming anyone really could replace Stowe?"

A silence stretched and Cherry tried to visualize the invisible, unspoken dynamics on the opposite side of the intervening door. Sharif spoke at last. "Really, Sami, how much more can Stowe really contribute? By now he's surely given up most of the value he ever possessed."

"Do you think so?" Sami fired back. "And if the addition of Benin's toys causes some issue in the cars, are *you* going to figure it out? Or are you going to bring in an expert from Earth who takes a month or more to get here and costs us as much as Stowe when it's all said and done?"

"What kind of function issues could there be? Klaus seems very confident."

"Who knows?" Sami replied in an exasperated voice. "Do you know how finicky these machines are? And even if that goes smoothly, what about everything else Stowe handles?"

Sharif uttered another audible sigh. "Like what?"

"He trains and organizes the gladiators, he teases out safety upgrades, and you heard how he runs the scenarios."

"It doesn't take an expert to run the scenarios, surely, and hasn't he milked all the safety upgrades he could by now?"

"So you propose to hire two or three experts to replace Stowe. Is that what you're saying? Because it sounds like a much cleaner idea to just keep him doing what he's doing." Sami paused. "Is this some personal grudge, Sharif? Or what?"

Sharif sighed again. "Sami, do you not see how *unseemly* it is to be dictated to by an indentured asset?"

"I *made* him an asset, so I could get him out here when I needed him."

"Yes, perhaps, but you made him from the raw material of a criminal, and that's no better."

Sami huffed. "I still say you have no better option than Stowe. We just deal with his pushback as well as we can, maybe offer him a quicker path out of his indenture, and—"

Sharif interrupted with a sudden laugh. "Oh, no, no, Sami. A much better idea occurs to me." Sharif seemed to gather his thoughts as Sami silently waited until he began again.

"You know how to get Stowe to do exactly what we want with no effective means to push back?" The question was clearly rhetorical and Sharif went on. "We use the power of his servitude and place him in a position where his life is directly tied to the success or failure of the enterprise."

"I already have," Sami said dismissively. "It's in our contract. If the operation becomes profitable he can work off his indenture and score a nice percentage of—"

"Not that way," Sharif said. "I mean we put him right into the thick of it as a gladiator himself. We'll form official teams and he'll train the gladiators of his own team as a way to preserve his life, especially because the other team will be composed of ringers, pros, cutthroats."

"But, Sharif, if we make the changes Klaus is offering us," Sami said in a reluctant tone, "it may be a *slaughter* down in the catacombs."

Cherry could almost hear Sharif shrug. "If he's as good as he claims, he'll manage. If not . . . we're minus one pain in the neck."

CHAPTER 27

"What do you mean, it's time to get out?" Warren said, smiling as he fully focused on Cherry at last.

"Now listen close, Stowe, you ass," Cherry admonished. "I'm telling you that Klaus Benin bloke is providing some Old Earth weaponry, do you hear me? They're arming the gladiators . . . and the Maktoums are going to toss you into the middle of it."

Warren listened to her explanation, musing thoughtfully before saying, "Very interesting. What sort of Old Earth weapons are we talking here?"

"Does it really matter? Lethal ones. Benin's got genuine fabrication files for some old projectile weapons, and I heard enough to know Sharif hopes some of these projectiles get introduced to your vitals as uncomfortably as possible."

Warren didn't seem to grant Cherry's warning the attention she felt it deserved, instead looking off into the invisible distance, a bemused smile cracking his lips. "Weapons to mount in the cars themselves, I presume?" he said at last.

Cherry stared indignantly at Warren. "Have you ever actually seen people who've been shot to bits before? Loads of them have the most surprised look on their faces."

Warren turned his attention on Cherry, his eyes uncomfortably searching her face. "I understand," he said.

"I don't think you really do, old fellow," she said in a lower tone.

Warren continued to smile at her. "Are these weapons to be mounted?"

Cherry sighed. "It sounded that way, how they were talking about the effects on the cars and such."

"Hmm," Warren murmured, rubbing his chin as he looked away, suddenly smiling. "Sometimes my brilliance is almost scary, you know?"

Cherry shook her head, eyes rolling ceiling-ward. "Thicker than a whale sandwich!"

Sami expected rebellion, indignation, even threats once Warren learned of the planned changes besetting him, but Sami never imagined the cheerful enthusiasm Warren actually displayed.

"Mounting Old Earth projectile weapons, Sami?" he repeated upon listening to Sami's explanation. "What a splendid idea! Why didn't you tell me such a feature was available? The clients will love it!"

Sharif watched the interaction between Sami and Warren, and Sami glanced back uncertainly to gain some glimmer of his brother's thoughts before answering. "Well, er, yes, of course we think clients will love it, but we've only just become aware of these genuine fabrication files."

Warren nodded, looking away from Sami into Build-Out, where Klaus Benin worked away in one of the kiosks. "How are we mounting these weapons in the cars anyway?"

Sami cleared his throat. "We were just working on that, and thought you might like to give your input . . . um . . . seeing how you will be taking part in the next scenario, er . . . as a g-gladiator."

Warren looked back at Sami with a deep frown and Sami readied his arsenal of arguments. He had already experienced Stowe's moral force and strength of personality, and Sami did not want to look like a weak fool, especially in front of Sharif.

"How will the gamblers feel about that, Sami? Won't that create a conflict of interest, one of the *partners* also playing gladiator?"

Of all the objections Sami had visualized, the issue of ethical gambling constraints had never occurred to him, and for a moment he found himself without a ready answer. Sharif stepped smoothly into the breach.

"With full disclosure to the clients, we don't expect any issue that would counterbalance the benefits someone of your renown would bring to the scenario, Stowe."

"Well, perfect!" Stowe declared with evident satisfaction. "I'll finally be doing what I do best, and still improving this product at the same time. Best of both worlds." Stowe rubbed his hands together. "So what are we waiting for? Have we got some armed vehicles ready to test yet?"

"Umm, perhaps you can assist Klaus there," Sami suggested, still waiting for Warren's core of rebellious self-determination to reveal itself.

"Right," Warren said, and strode off to Klaus Benin's side.

Sami watched Warren for a moment before looking at Sharif. "He's not what I expected after your description," Sharif said.

Sami turned to study Warren where he hobnobbed with Benin. "That's not what I expected either. Not even a little."

Klaus Benin displayed obvious frustration as he labored on the fabrication kiosk system, and his discomfiture made Warren feel happy all over. "Get it all sorted out there, sport?" Warren asked in a cheery voice as he produced his smoking case and began rolling a cigarette.

Warren thought he heard Benin's teeth grinding before he leveled a cold glare at Warren. "Not quite. And you may refer to me as '*Mister Benin*,' Stowe."

Warren finished creating his cigarette and struck a light from his smoking case before he answered. "Oh? No formality is necessary between us, Klaus, friend. You need not refer to me as *Lord Stowe*, for instance, although I do rightfully hold that title." He puffed the cigarette into life. "A gift from her majesty, Queen Portia of that delightfully backward world, Elsinore. Lovely, excitable woman."

Klaus glared poisonously between Warren and the smoldering cigarette between Warren's fingers, but Warren looked beyond him at the fabrication display, reading aloud, "Browning thirty-caliber, Browning fifty-caliber, Lewis thirty-caliber, Thompson forty-five-caliber...hmm, antique weaponry systems, right?"

"Obviously," Klaus said in a scornful tone.

"Right...and if the weights listed are accurate, some of these weapons are pretty massive. Where're you planning to mount them on the cars?"

Klaus took a deep, calming breath and coughed as he inhaled Warren's secondhand smoke, angrily flapping the smoke away from his face. "That is what I've been working on—until you interrupted me."

Warren leaned nearer, the tendril of smoke curling up from his cigarette to invade Benin's nostril. "Looks like you haven't made much progress here, tiger," Warren offered as Klaus lurched back, coughing again, rising to his feet. Warren ignored him, saying, "Probably need to bring up a car fabrication menu first, like the Buick Gran Sport here . . ." Warren took over the controls as Klaus glowered, standing a few strides back out of cigarette range. "See, old boy, this Browning fifty-caliber is just too big to easily squeeze into—"

"How about the thirty-caliber?" Klaus interrupted, edging farther back and waving away the pernicious smoke.

"The thirty-caliber?" Warren said as he manipulated the controls. "We could probably mount two of them, one on either side of the—"

"Fine," Klaus interrupted again. "Do it. But make sure there's still room for the ammunition. See those boxes? One of those boxes must mount beside each Browning."

"Right, got it," Warren said. "And then we go over here, select some fixtures, adjust some geometry like so, and—"

"Yes, yes," Klaus said, drifting farther back out of Warren's growing cloud of tobacco smoke. "Put that together and we'll test it out. Do you understand, Stowe?"

Warren glanced sidelong over his shoulder, smiling to himself as he exploited his private access, Klaus having lost interest in the tedious and unusually smoky process.

"Oh, I understand alright, sport," Stowe said, making selections that suited his own desires, most certainly not all that Klaus Benin had in mind.

They conducted the first test within the confines of the oval track, only six people present. Aside from Sami and Sharif, Klaus Benin and Hammerworth stood on the edge of the apron, while Warren and his "assistant" Cherry occupied the armed Gran Sport that rolled down onto the track and centered up. A pair of large drones swept down the track ahead, a broad target dangling down between them, coming to a halt about two hundred paces ahead.

Warren looked up to Sami and received the nod. "Okay," he said to Cherry, "Benin showed me how to arm these Brownings. You just reach in there and grab that handle on the side that—"

"I know how to operate old projectile weapons," Cherry said, reaching deep under the dashboard to charge each of the Browning Model 1919 .30-caliber machine guns, the heavy metallic clangs announcing their readiness. "Okay," Cherry said, looking steadily at Warren. "You'll probably find this a trifle loud, old stick."

Warren nodded and reached to the grip-handle affixed to the Gran Sport's shift lever. He squeezed the handle and for a moment thought he had fabricated something incorrectly as the deafening explosion of fire buffeted his ears, the Gran Sport quivering as dual streams of glowing, arcing projectiles swept out from beneath the hood. One of the streams lanced through the distant target, the other string of glowing projectiles narrowly missing, passing by one edge. Warren released the handle, the firing ceasing immediately.

Warren grinned at Cherry. "Thought I blew something up for a second." He grimaced and shook his head. "My ears are ringing now."

"Yes. Loud." Cherry pointed downrange. "The left-hand gun needs to be adjusted inboard a trifle, duck."

Warren stuck a finger in his ear and wiggled it about. "Yeah, saw that. There's a little traverse adjustment beneath the gun. Give it a couple of clicks maybe." Warren looked up at the spectators and saw Sami gesture for him to advance.

"Ready?" Warren asked, giving Sami the thumbs-up with a jaunty smile.

Cherry finished her adjustments. "Ready, mate."

Warren threw the Gran Sport into gear and gave the small audience a flourish, white-smoking the tires as they launched. The drones began to advance at the same time, accelerating to stay out ahead of them as they rounded the corner and came around to the second straightaway.

As soon as they accelerated out of the corner, Warren lined up on the drone-supported target, knowing Sami and the other spectators would have a good view from up on the apron. He gripped the trigger handle and squeezed, ready for the thunder of fire now.

The guns roared, both streams striking the target at first, until the drones jigged to one side. Warren fired small bursts as he steered back and forth, trying to keep the dodging target lined up, dimly noticing they swept past the spectators as they blazed away.

One moment Warren saw the twin lines of flashing projectiles crossing through the target, the guns roaring, smoke issuing from beneath the hood with each burst, then they fell silent. Warren squeezed the trigger handle in vain and Cherry spoke up over the engine noise and the ringing in his ears. "Out of ammunition."

Warren laughed and brought the Gran Sport back around to the apron, steering up to the waiting spectators and drawing to a halt. Before Warren opened his door, Cherry eyed the small assembly, jerking her head toward them.

Warren looked, seeing Benin conversing with Sami and Sharif, a smug expression on his face, but Hammerworth's face wore an avid, hungry look he had seen a time or two in jail that he did not like.

"That one's trouble," Cherry said quietly. "I'll need to do something about him eventually, likely . . . him and that lunatic, Catbox."

Warren smiled through the window at Hammerworth, answering Cherry without turning. "You may be correct. I've made a little treat for you, if that eventuality should ever roll around."

Cherry turned to stare at Warren's profile, but before she could inquire more closely, he threw his door open and greeted the observers. "Sami, Sharif, was it as spectacular up here as it was down in it? Hmm? I mean, *wow!*"

Despite Warren's assurances, nearly half the original gladiators vowed to quit immediately upon hearing of the new weapon additions.

"I'm not a warrior," Bandar declared, tossing his helmet on the table in the midst of his peers. "I'm barely a driver, and I'm not letting these psychopaths get their jollies shooting me full of extra holes!"

"Bandar, friend," Warren said, sprawled loose-limbed in his seat, smiling, "I'm no warrior either, and I've no interest in getting my innards ventilated, but as you see . . . I'm driving."

Bandar frowned, glancing around all the hesitant faces surrounding them before addressing Warren. "You are an expert driver, Stowe . . . and you are . . . you are indentured. The rest of us are neither, and those are two big differences between us and you."

Warren's smile widened. "Don't sell yourself short, Bandar lad. You drive better every day. But as to this other matter . . . do you imagine I would swallow a violent death simply because I'm an indentured asset? Not likely! Got loads of living to do still."

"Whether we want it or not," Gilda interjected, "Hammerworth's pack of thugs'll get a vote on it. Maybe you can ignore bullets, Stowe, but them bullets might just not ignore you."

Warren sat up straight and pulled a small object from the inner pocket of his jacket. "I forgive your doubts, all of you," he graciously began, "because we've not worked together long enough for you to comprehend the depths of my cunning. But you will learn." He held up the object in his hand, revealing to all a tiny model driver's seat from a Gran Sport.

"An itty-bitty seat to go right along with your tiny toy cars, right?" Gilda said.

Warren dropped the model seat on the table where it clanked heavily. "That's a scale model of the drivers' seats I placed in each of your cars when the fabricator laid in these fancy new projectile weapons. A nifty armor matrix composite that *will* ignore bullets, Gilda." Warren scanned across all the expectant faces. "Hammerworth's toughs may shoot your vehicle full of holes, but we can sit there safe enough."

Bandar shook his head, staring at the tiny metal seat. "Maybe . . . as long as they don't hit us from the sides."

Warren shrugged. "I think I've mentioned before that one doesn't earn this kind of coin for petting bunny rabbits. It's a dangerous job, but if you do your part you should be able to keep your flickering candle of life alight."

Gilda reached down and lifted the small model, examining it critically. "I suppose you put those tricky little armor-seats in Hammerworth's cars too, right?"

Warren rubbed his chin, musing thoughtfully. "I knew I forgot something!"

CHAPTER 28

The service elevators brought the gladiators' Gran Sports down to the catacomb level, two at a time, where they assembled in one long row, Warren supervising a small crew loading the ammunition boxes into each car.

"Lock those down alongside the weapons, and feed the belts in," Warren said at the first vehicle. "Be sure to double-check them all before we roll." The crew mumbled their agreement, and Warren left them to it.

He strolled down the line of waiting vehicles, his helmet swinging in his left hand until he reached the final car: his own 1969 Dodge Daytona with its distinctive tail fin. Cherry sat astride her Fireblade right beside the Dodge, one foot on the ground, her helmet resting atop the fuel tank.

"Well, Cherry?" Warren said in a low voice, leaning against the Daytona.

She jerked her chin down beside her left leg where a metal bracket protruded. "I see you made a small modification to my Fireblade here. But I don't really see the point of it."

Warren shot her a jaunty grin and turned to open the trunk of his vehicle. "You know it's the easiest thing to program this fabrication system to build whatever I need and, say, simply construct it in the trunk of a vehicle." He reached in and pulled out a blocky, stubby weapon. "Happy Christmas, Cherry! I know, in your heart of hearts, you've always wanted an antique boom stick, and this here is a Thompson forty-five-caliber submachine gun."

"Stowe? A gift?" Cherry said in a neutral tone, eyeing the weapon. "You know the way to a woman's heart, clearly."

"It's really heavy, I'm afraid," Warren said, passing it delicately over, and Cherry took it lightly in hand, hefting it as if it weighed nothing.

"Ah, I see," she said. "It fits into these brackets here, out of the way until I need it." She clicked it into place and practiced freeing the weapon a couple of times. "Very nice."

"Didn't want you to feel left out," Warren said. "And for your stocking . . . A toy." He handed her one of the tiny cars he had created, then passed over a bundle of loaded magazines and pointed at the weapon where it rested. "It operates by—"

"I'm familiar with antique open-bolt projectile weapons, old fellow," Cherry interrupted, setting the toy car in her lap and popping the loaded magazine free with a negligent twist, eyeing the stubby cartridges revealed. "Phosphorus tipped?"

Warren shrugged. "In the fabrication system it calls them *tracer rounds*, and they are the only available ammunition option for any of the guns. Uh, Klaus said in the old days they made these tracers because it hurts more to get shot by them."

Cherry snorted, replacing the magazine and clicking the Thompson back into its brackets. "Most sociopaths aren't such bloody idiots." She slipped her helmet on as the engines began cranking up along the line of waiting gladiators. "Where is Hammerworth's crew entering from, anyway?"

Warren opened the door of his brand-new Dodge Daytona. "They didn't tell me anything, but it can only be the ramp down from the circuit track."

Cherry pressed the ignition button, her Fireblade thrumming to life. She turned to stare at Warren. "Stowe," she called out as Warren slid into his seat. He looked over expectantly at her. "Don't forget to arm your guns. You might just need them."

Warren laughed and leaned under the dash to arm both of the Browning .30-caliber machine guns before closing his door and strapping in. He patted the pockets of his jumpsuit, feeling his smoking case and the slender shape of the jail shank, a good-luck charm he retained with some sentimental favor. He took a deep breath and let it out, ready.

The camera drones lifted off from their rows of charging racks at that moment, the small swarm weaving over and around each car, occasionally dodging around a drone from another nearby car as they danced.

Warren shifted into first gear and eased the clutch, taking a slow lead into the mouth of the catacombs, a glance in his mirror showing the line of glossy Gran Sports filing in behind him. Bandar had eventually chosen greed over self-preservation, and only three gladiators ended up finding the lethal additions too frightening to face, choosing to resign as gladiators.

For just a moment Warren felt a cold thread of doubt slip through his vitals, and he hoped he wasn't now leading a flock of innocents to the slaughter. Another second or two spent enumerating all the reassurances he had given his protégé gladiators brought his natural confidence back on track, and he began to accelerate, shifting into second gear, then third, the Daytona surging ahead.

The start tone rang out over the communication system and an unfamiliar voice announced, "Scenario is Gangland Turf War." Warren frowned, listening, suddenly suspicious. As the announcer called out the unit numbers across the line, his suspicions were confirmed. The two gangs were divided between Hammerworth's five and Warren's seventeen. Sami was not using the selection system at all, clearly, opting to dictate the scenario, and Warren silently wondered how many of his gladiator crew would also realize the significance.

The next thought occurring to Warren concerned exactly how Sami might have structured the scenario so the gambling clients up the Members Club would see any degree of fairness in a five-versus-seventeen contest.

The only reasonable answer punched Warren in the stomach: ambush.

Sami would even the odds by allowing Hammerworth's people in early to get set. What else could it be?

As Warren's thoughts raced, picturing exactly where Hammerworth would try to catch them, Cherry's Fireblade suddenly launched forward, her engine screaming as she took off like a shot.

In Cherry's tactical mind, the perfidy of the Maktoums stood out immediately, and she felt suddenly certain the scenario had been carefully structured to eliminate the problem of Warren Springer Stowe in one simple step: partner removal via quasi-legal murder.

Milliseconds after hearing the scenario announcement, Cherry's entire aspect changed, from sporting participation to a military-style operation. It seemed crystal clear that she simply had five targets to neutralize before they might eliminate Stowe. Straightforward enough.

With the decision made, she dropped a gear on the Fireblade, hunkered low as she punched the throttle and dumped the clutch, rocketing forward, quickly doubling the speed of the other gladiators, her camera drones suddenly struggling to catch up. She went up through the gears and kept the throttle pinned wide open down the arterial straightaway, seeing the first gradual curve coming up fast, the lights of the other gladiator vehicles invisibly distant behind her. She barely eased the throttle at all, leaning the bike far over on its fat, grippy tires as she raced into the sweeper, allowing her line to drift up the smooth banked outer wall.

Just as she returned to full throttle, the curve easing around to the next straightaway, a car sitting dark and still along the inner wall appeared. Two streams of tracer-tipped projectiles spat out, striking low beneath her as Cherry's path clung to the outer wall. In a flash Cherry flew past, and she tried the communicator line, "One enemy gang vehicle sitting in ambush, left side at the first arterial curve."

For a moment she thought about going back to eliminate the ambusher, but a quick calculation kept her pressing forward. If she could simply find all five, their ability to ambush Stowe and the others disappeared, and then she could disable whichever she might.

Her first hint of another ambusher arrived at a fast-approaching intersection on the arterial, where a glimpse of a camera drone tipped her off. Moving too fast to stop, Cherry tucked down tight and kept the throttle pegged, flashing past the intersection before the two ambushers could react, their belated fire streaming more than a car-length behind her. "Two more ambushers, left side at the central intersection," she called over the communicator, then in the next moment, "Correction, one ambusher at the intersection—one outbound on the arterial."

Cherry saw the lights sweep around far behind her as one foe tried pursuit. She well knew that nothing on wheels could catch her on the Fireblade as long as she had fuel to run, but running away didn't suit her plans at all, and she had to assume Hammerworth's sods communicated also, likely attempting to box her in.

Only one turnoff joined the arterial before she reached the perimeter, and that junction approached fast. She made the split-second decision and seized both brakes, bringing the Fireblade to the brink of washing out as she bled speed hard and fast, glancing in her shuddering mirror to gauge the distance to her pursuing enemy. Plenty of range still.

The corner came up fast on her left and she released the brakes, throwing the bike hard over, her knee grazing the road surface as she whipped around. She straightened out of the corner and hit the throttle again, coming to a gentle curve before the chase cleared the arterial behind her, her orbiting drones finally racing back into place above her.

She entered a zone of simulated city streets, a grid of intersecting roads adjoining small open spaces like compact parking lots. Two quick turns put Cherry in position, her left hand reaching to free the Thompson, supporting it across her right wrist as she throttled down, coasting for just a moment.

The pursuit car roared around the slow curve, its tires screeching as it accelerated out to a clear lane for Cherry's shot. Cherry saw the driver's helmet twist sharply toward her just as she squeezed the Thompson's trigger, holding it down, .45-caliber tracers visibly walking down the side of the car, the Thompson thumping against her shoulder as it fired.

The car lurched and spun, striking one wall in a shower of orange sparks, rebounding to pile into another wall. Cherry reluctantly left the smoldering wreck without assuring that the driver had permanently retired, unwilling to act on her lethal training as a clutch of camera drones captured every vicious moment for the spectators. She clipped the Thompson back into its brackets and continued on. "One enemy gang vehicle out of commission," she called over the communicator, accelerating away.

Hammerworth's people might be moving to intercept her, Cherry figured, and if they had attempted to box her in they should be encroaching from one of the secondary avenues any moment...

She throttled back, downshifting to first gear, and slipped into a narrow lane, killing the Fireblade's engine and lights as she coasted to the corner of a simulated building front. She barely came to a halt when the white beams of headlights overlay the aquamarine glow before her, the deep growl of a powerful engine resounding through the narrow lanes. She readied her Thompson, stabilizing the bike beneath her with both feet on the ground, the gun firmly shouldered. She leaned forward, barely projecting her eye and the weapon muzzle around the corner.

If it hadn't been for a bloody camera drone circling out before her, the target of her surprise would have received a hail of bad news without a moment's warning. Instead the car, a black Barracuda, slewed in an instant, its twin .30-caliber machine guns spewing fire, two streams of tracers sweeping toward Cherry as she fired a sustained burst across the car's windshield, the glass shattering in a crystal shower.

The Barracuda ceased firing, its tires screeching as it slid straight into a simulated building with a heavy crash. Cherry refit the Thompson into place, started the Fireblade's engine and set off, announcing over the communicator, "Second gang vehicle out of commission."

She glanced at the smoking Barracuda as she accelerated past, but saw no sign of movement except for the waiting camera drones. Where could the remaining members of Hammerworth's crew be patrolling now?

The communicator crackled into life within Cherry's helmet, the roaring sound of an engine accompanying a desperate call. "Help! Got one on me!" It sounded like Bandar, and Cherry heard the *crack-ping* of projectile impacts punctuating his words. "Inbound . . . just past—" Bandar's words broke off with a cry and the channel fell silent.

Within the Members Club, Sami and Sharif observed the wagers doubling, quadrupling as the gamblers succumbed to the brutal drama unfolding below. Sharif wore that satisfied mien that Sami did not entirely like, and Klaus Benin kept preening every time some particularly flashy display of his antique weaponry excited the spectators.

And then there was this unexpected development as one of the amateur gladiators—that Poppins woman and her motorcycle—began defying the betting odds, all in such a startling, violent fashion.

Klaus Benin turned from watching the camera drone feed as Poppins riddled one car, sending it crashing into a wall, and strolled to Sami's side. The odd flush on his face and gleam in his eyes made Sami uneasy as Benin leaned in close. "Sami, where did you find this Poppins character? You really must introduce me."

"Perhaps, perhaps," Sami said, fighting the urge to step away, even as he wondered where they *had* found Poppins. "Mustn't distract her, and of course we wouldn't want any interaction between . . . er . . . gladiators and guests that, um, others might find objectionable."

Klaus eyed Sami with that haughty expression Sami hated. "I think I might satisfy any objections."

Savanah looked back from a lull in the action and moved through the other clients to join Klaus. "What are you plotting now?" she said, looking between Klaus and Sami as she sipped from her glass.

Klaus held Sami's eye as he replied, "Just wondering if Sami might have seeded the ranks with ringers."

A cheer erupted and they all looked up at the displays in time to see Poppins sending another car spinning out of control, a stubby weapon held one-handed as she raced along on the glossy red-and-black motorcycle.

"A ringer?" Sami repeated, staring up at the holographic imagery. "No ringers, Klaus, but she is most certainly becoming . . . interesting. Very interesting."

CHAPTER 29

"Gangland Scenario complete," the announcer declared over the communication channel as Warren led three of "his" gladiators through some of the tighter lanes of the catacombs, hunting for the final two members of their rival *gang*. "Return to start locations."

Warren reluctantly downshifted his new Daytona and glanced back at the three Gran Sports close in his wake, nodding to them as he angled for the approaching junction. He had wanted to catch Hammerworth or Catbox and handle them roughly himself, but it appeared they evaded his wrath . . . for the moment.

On the return trip, Warren spotted Bandar's Gran Sport smoldering on the side of the arterial, its rear quarters riddled with dozens of jagged bullet holes, and a bit farther along two more Gran Sports in similar condition. None of the wrecks showed any active camera drones, nor any sign of the drivers, and Warren maintained every confidence they had all survived their misadventures with intact skins.

Just before they reached the junction to their start zone, a black Mustang joined the ranks of the defunct, but unlike the derelict Gran Sports, it bore only one tight cluster of bullet holes through the driver-side windshield, the remainder of the vehicle seemingly unharmed.

Warren perceived Cherry's handiwork at a glance, Hammerworth's driver, Hells, nowhere to be seen around his Mustang.

Minutes later, Warren shifted down to first gear as they swept out of the catacombs into the broad assembly area, joining the other surviving Gran Sports already waiting there. Warren steered carefully into the next open spot, coming to a smooth halt at the end of the row,

183

his wingmates wrangling their way into position after much backing and forthing.

Warren noticed that only after all the cars were in position and the engines off did the arming crew come out with their cart, a pair of Maktoum security stiffs with them. It seemed he detected literal gunshyness at work, and he wondered if they had somehow overlooked Cherry's armament despite her obvious displays over the last hour or so.

As he formed this thought, Cherry's Fireblade came whipping into the assembly area, Cherry leaning the bike far over for a smooth, sharp turn into the narrow slot between Warren's Daytona and the next Gran Sport. Warren glanced at the crew to see them eyeing Cherry, but absent the caution he had expected to see.

One of them approached Cherry diffidently. "Miss Poppins, where is the firearm you had?" Only then did Warren notice that the retention clips on Cherry's Fireblade no longer held that antique Thompson gun.

Cherry removed her helmet and looked down at the empty spot on her bike with evident surprise. "Oh my," she said. "Must have dropped it in the catacombs somewhere in all the excitement."

The Maktoum flunky worked his jaw for a bit, but what could anyone say that would make the Thompson reappear? By the time the fellow retreated, Warren found Cherry to be the focus of all the assembled gladiators. For a moment Cherry surveyed them all as they stared at her, her expression neutral, then Gilda spoke up for all of them. "You sure did it, didn't you?" she said, her helmet in one hand, her other at her hip. "Put three—three!—of Hammerworth's pukes in their place!" The amateur gladiators around Gilda broke into hoots and cheers, and Warren felt genuine surprise at Cherry's self-conscious flush. It was the only time he had witnessed her discomfited by anything at all. Who would guess that a little jovial recognition would embody her hidden vulnerability?

"How'd you manage it?" Gilda asked, the others around her adding their own encouraging sounds.

Cherry shrugged, blowing the hair from her brow. "Luck, I guess," she said, and Warren quietly wondered how many dead eyes stared back at her from her memories of the Blue Light days. Three Bethune soreheads could not measure greatly as opponents in her experience.

Cherry found a more pleasing topic to pursue. "Bandar? Did he get the permanent retirement too?"

Gilda snorted. "A permanent stain in his shorts, maybe. He isn't bad hurt, but his armored seat got the full treatment. Whole lotta new ventilation in his ride, made him twitchy. Shaking like a jelly still, I'd bet."

"And Hammerworth's lot?" Cherry asked in a casual tone. "They survive?"

Mueller stepped up to the periphery of the gladiators. "I just heard: Cleo and Kira got picked up okay." He hesitated. "But . . . Hells goes back to Bethune in a bag."

Among the gathering both murmurs of satisfaction and some gasps of dismay arose, but Warren studied Cherry's expression for any sign of emotion, seeing nothing, neither sorrow nor pleasure.

Gilda spoke up. "Hells did his damnedest to kill Bandar and the others, so you won't see me shed a tear for his cold carcass." She shrugged. "But we'd better get abovestairs before dinner gets cold. Think we got some coin coming to a few of us too!"

Warren joined the other gladiators, for the first time a participant in the post-scenario scoring session gathered in their ready room. He glanced at Cherry idling against one wall near the service lifts, her arms crossed over her helmet, before scanning across the excited clutch of adventurers. There had never been so many electrifying extremes in a scenario to discuss before, and they waited for the wall display to populate with totals that might fill their respective bank accounts.

The display illuminated, first ticking through each driver's mileage totals: the more ground covered during the scenario, the more one earned, though petty sums compared to the big wins. Next it scrolled through highest average speeds, with the name MARY POPPINS at the top ranking as usual.

When the display populated with the listed victors, the small crowd's volume of cross talk rose an order of magnitude, and Warren would not have noticed the arrival of the newcomers if he had not observed Cherry's eyes dart and narrow. Warren turned to see Sami, Sharif, Belinda, and a couple of the Maktoum security stiffs standing just within the door from the Members Club. They all seemed to pointedly fix on Cherry for a moment before looking away, and Cherry caught Warren's eye with an inscrutable message across the crowded room.

Sami waved everyone down to a hush as he began speaking. "There you see the bonus levels from the Gangland scenario with some remarkable efforts . . . and sacrifices." He paused. "Of course the late Hells racked up a truly impressive total before he was, um, retired, and his winnings will go to his estate." Sami glanced at Belinda Athenos and cleared his throat. "As has so often been the case in these scenarios, Miss Poppins has risen to the top in a truly impressive fashion, but her immense winnings have created a, er, small problem."

Warren suddenly realized where this headed and he looked over at Cherry, seeing a thin, unfamiliar smile on her lips.

"Supervisor Athenos has attempted to credit Miss Poppins's accounts on several occasions and finally received notice from our office in Torino . . ." Sami turned to Belinda with a smile, holding out his hand. "Supervisor Athenos?"

"Yes, Director," Belinda said in a self-conscious tone. "The Torino office confirmed: there is no Mary Poppins on payroll, nor any Mary Poppins on the transport manifests for Ajanib . . . ever."

Warren felt his stomach clench, his mind racing for a quick solution to this problem that he should have foreseen. Cherry's next-level skullduggery likely could not have included tweaking Maktoum Corp's internal employment systems, and Warren should have inquired on that front, but it was too late now.

Sami stared across the room at Cherry as all the gladiators turned confused gazes from Sami to Cherry. "So, Miss Poppins, who exactly are you, and where did you come from?"

Before anyone could speak up one way or another, Cherry's hand dipped more fluidly than human physiology seemed to allow, rising and snapping taut, a flashing blade blurring across the room to strike Warren, sinking deep, even as the crowd of gladiators uttered a cacophony of confused cries.

As Warren toppled, he saw Cherry dart through the door to the service lifts, the security goons shoving their way through the startled crowd after her, and it suddenly seemed good for Warren to take a little rest . . . just a little rest.

Sami looked across his desk into Sharif's placid eyes, grating his teeth together in impotent anger. "It comes from all your sneaking about and rushing your work, brother," Sharif lectured. "To overlook the most basic security measures is really quite remarkable for someone trained as we were."

Sami had already enumerated all the reasons so many elements of the Ajanib operation remained unfinished, and rather than applaud the superhuman efforts he had exerted, the amazing results he achieved, Sharif could only point out the few small flaws that remained. "Yes, yes, yes," Sami said, roughly straightening the cuffs of his shirt. "That's all very nice, but it doesn't amount to much. So that savage little female slipped away into the catacombs. What of it?"

"On her little two-wheeled car," Sharif added.

"Well, yes, her motorcycle," Sami admitted, shrugging.

Sharif stared at his younger brother. "How long until she expends the fuel in that machine?"

Sami felt the heat rising to his face. "Um, tech—technically she may not expend it at all."

Sharif's lips compressed into a line. "Explain this to me, if you please."

Only Sharif could have this effect on Sami, making him feel an incompetent child. "There are two . . . uh . . . fuel depots within the, um, catacombs . . . so participants can refuel during lengthy scenarios if needed."

"*Unsecured* depots?"

Sharif's tone almost caused Sami's temper to explode, but he reined it in with Olympian effort. "Now why would I need them secured in a section of Ajanib where no one except gladiators willingly goes?" Sami demanded. "Because of the hordes of tourists? The many burglars prowling about?" Sharif's unperturbed expression of amusement only fueled Sami's ire as he went on. "Really, of all that I created here in such a short period, locking up the fuel that only gladiators and clients desire, within this asteroid where we control all access—"

"Not *all* access," Sharif interrupted.

"Whatever," Sami said. "But it doesn't matter if she *can* get fuel forever. She can't have much to eat down there, and she can't go speeding about forever." Sami folded his arms and gave his brother his most knowing look. "You've heard something about it: People who hold still in the catacombs tend to disappear . . . forever."

Sharif frowned. "I don't want her to disappear. I want to know who she is, why she's on Ajanib, and why she tried to kill Stowe."

CHAPTER 30

"What happened?" Warren mumbled as his eyes blearily opened.

An unfamiliar woman looked down at him with a professionally disinterested expression. "What happened? A few things." She jabbed Warren with something painful and he managed to keep his vocalization to a mere grunt. The woman seemed satisfied with her action, murmuring, "Mmm, first a nasty little blade got stuck into you . . . right here."

"Ow!" Warren, unable to restrain himself as she prodded him.

"Then you fainted."

"*Fainted?*" Warren said, outraged at the very idea.

"Then we patched you up," she concluded. "Which wasn't too bad. The blade penetrated deep, but didn't do much damage there, surprisingly. Missed the important bits of your shoulder and missed your collarbone too, which might have been better, honestly."

All this talk of Warren's lacerated anatomy made him feel a little queasy and he grasped for less visceral information. "And the, um, Poppins woman?"

The medico shrugged. "Still on the run in the catacombs, I guess."

Warren breathed a silent sight of relief. "Oh well. When will I be up and going again?"

The woman thought for a moment. "Honestly you could probably go now, but if you faint again, then the director—"

"*Faint?* I don't faint." Warren scowled up at her. "I surely passed out from blood loss."

She shook her head. "Wasn't that much blood loss at first."

"Then traumatic shock," Warren supplied.

"Hmm, yes. 'Fainting' is what you call that."

Warren heard a soft chuckle from nearby and looked over to see an unfamiliar fellow sitting on the edge of a medical bed, smiling at him. "Trust me, Mister Stowe," the fellow said, "that's not the worst shock to your ego Rose is likely to inflict."

"Uh," Warren said. "Are we acquainted?"

The man tilted his head with a rueful smile. "I'm familiar with you, alright. Have been for years. But there's no reason you should know a small-time Bethune collector like me."

Warren's thoughts cleared, awareness dawning even as he fended off another probing medical touch from Rose. "*Cathwaite*," he said. "You've got to be Cathwaite."

The rueful smile turned to an expression of pure chagrin. "Oh no! The only reason you could know my name is from my shameful, amateurish crash here."

"Not at all," Warren assured. "I first heard of you as a collector, truly."

"I'll leave you two to entertain each other," Rose said, sauntering off, humming to herself.

Cathwaite turned his gaze from Rose's retreating figure back to Warren. "What a reputation! I'll forever be known as the small-time collector who wrecked the first Corvette he ever drove." He hesitated and Warren let him speak. "It's this: pride. The only reason I've been fighting off Sami's attempts to ship me back to Bethune: pride." He shrugged. "I figure if I can only stay here long enough maybe I'll have some chance to redeem my reputation."

Warren's thoughts began to percolate more lucidly now and he saw numerous little connections branching out like chain lightning. "You and Sami must be good friends, then?"

"Hah," Cathwaite snorted. "I'd never met the Maktoums until Sami enlisted me to come out here." His frown deepened. "And now I fear I'm a bit of an embarrassment to him. He keeps me sequestered here, out of sight."

Warren struggled to sit up, discovering new nerve endings as he moved to a more vertical position, a plan taking shape. "Oh, fiddle!" Warren said. "You can do anything you want, if you think about it. Sami owes you." Cathwaite looked up, hope battling disbelief across his face. "Really, man," Warren assured. "If you hadn't demonstrated just how truly dangerous these antiques are, his clients would be dropping like flies instead of dropping millions on all of Sami's expensive treats."

Cathwaite's expression became illuminated with hope. "Did Sami actually say that?"

"Well, no," Warren admitted. "But Sami doesn't have much room in his heart for admiring anyone but himself. He can barely admit *I* did anything for this operation, and I damned near created it."

"Hmm," Cathwaite said indistinctly, looking down, silent for a moment before looking back up at Warren, his brow wrinkled. "Um, weren't you in jail not so long ago? I remember a bit of stir about you and some museum vehicle back in Torino."

Warren laughed and then grimaced in pain. "Indeed I was, and now—you won't believe this—I am an indentured asset of the Maktoum Corporation."

Cathwaite stared. "I hope you are kidding."

Warren shook his head. "Serious as an Extinction Level Event, brother."

"But that's . . . Damn, man." Cathwaite looked away, seemingly stricken speechless.

"It may not be as bad as all that," Warren said, waving away a potential lifetime of servitude with a swipe of his hand and an accompanying grimace of pain, clutching tenderly at his bandaged chest. "It's given me the perfect chance to structure everything here the way I wanted and still participate in the actual competitions. I have a very good shot at buying my way out of this . . . if the Maktoums don't decide to bump me off first."

Cathwaite's mouth worked into a hesitant smile, as if he thought Warren joked, then at Warren's serious expression his own mouth settled into a grim line. "You wouldn't think they'd actually try to kill you, do you? Is that what you believe happened today?"

"I think they might, *actually*," Warren said, deciding to add a little confusion into the mix just in case Cathwaite blabbed to the Maktoums, "and today *could* have been their work, though they acted all surprised about it."

Cathwaite shook his head. "I really hope you're wrong, for more reasons than one." He suddenly blushed, looking self-conscious. "That sounded callous. I'm sorry. It's just . . . just that Ajanib is like the fulfillment of a dream I've had since I was a kid, and I'd hate to see this place fail almost ... almost as much as I'd hate to see the Maktoums kill a man I've admired for many years."

Warren worked mightily to suppress the triumphant smile that threatened to emerge. All the pieces came together now, almost as if his subconscious cunning had engineered this unlikely moment.

"Cathwaite, brother, I'm touched," Warren said. "What a kind sentiment, and I feel exactly the same as you about Ajanib." He painfully scooted himself to the edge of his cot, closer to Cathwaite. "That's why I've been helping the Maktoums in every possible manner despite their dickish ways, and that brings me to an important question for you ..." Cathwaite appeared frozen with anticipation, seeming to sense the vitality of the moment. "If I can get you back in Sami's good graces, are you healthy enough to dive back into all the debauchery and merrymaking of Ajanib?"

"Into the debau—Uh, yes. I guess ... I guess I am."

"Excellent!" Warren said. "You'll have to keep a secret or two, and together we can make this place succeed, with or without the Maktoums."

When Sami ventured into the clinic on another of his irregular visits, Cathwaite sat up, fully dressed, waiting for him. Sami glanced over at the blanket-shrouded form of Warren Springer Stowe and Cathwaite shook his head. "He's out cold. Rose must have given him something and he hasn't opened his eyes since they brought him in a few hours ago." The collector sighed. "Which is terrible. I'd hoped to have someone to chat with finally."

Sami shrugged. "Rose reported that he'll be up in no time, so soon enough ..."

"By the time he's up and about I'll be gone," Cathwaite said.

Sami's eyebrows lifted. "Ready to return to Bethune now? The transport won't be leaving until—"

"No," Cathwaite said, cutting him off. "Not to Bethune. That won't work."

A deep line formed between Sami's eyebrows. "What do you mean exactly, Cathwaite?"

"Back in Torino everyone knows I came out to Ajanib, and there's going to be a lot of talk when I show up after so much time all busted up and limping this way."

"Okay ..." Sami said, waiting, staring fixedly.

"And I've already been out here so long I'm going to need a better excuse than that I've been driving around in circles all this time." Cathwaite went on, gathering his courage, trying to remember exactly what Stowe had said without glancing at Stowe's recumbent figure. "Your . . . your operation here means a lot to me, Sami. I want nothing more than to see it . . . um, flourish, and participating—now—with your clientele gives *us* the best chance for that." As Cathwaite observed Sami's expression hardening he rushed on, trying to maintain the low, calm tone Stowe had advised. "Your clients don't know how I got my limp, and we won't tell them, and after spending some time throwing money around here while I heal, I get the perfect excuse for my long absence from Torino."

Cathwaite tried to maintain Sami's intent gaze without looking away, just barely managing it until Sami finally blinked. "It seems you've been thinking, Cathwaite."

Cathwaite heaved a quiet sigh of relief.

"But," Sami went on, shaking his head as Cathwaite held his breath, "the offerings of Ajanib come at a pretty steep cost, I'm afraid. Not free, even for someone like you who provided a useful service for us."

"Oh yes?" Cathwaite said, breathing again, on solid ground. "Well, obviously I'm no trillionaire, Sami, but wouldn't my paltry five million keep up appearances for a couple of weeks at least, even while it's providing a pretty alibi to protect this whole operation?"

The expression on Sami's face made it clear he hadn't expected Cathwaite to possess pockets anywhere as deep as five-million worth . . . and if Stowe hadn't supplied him with an astonishing bank roll of his own wealth (as a Maktoum indenture?) indeed Cathwaite's pockets would have been far thinner.

It seemed to Cathwaite that Sami waffled for the sake of appearances at this point, finally saying, "Five million should be enough to make a showing. But be careful in your bets or you'll lose it all. And sitting around the Members Club with nothing to play most certainly will not work."

Cathwaite nodded, keeping the triumph off his face to the best of his ability. "I understand."

Though Cathwaite had Warren to thank for this windfall opportunity, he limped out of the medical ward behind Sami without a backward look at Warren's silent, attentive shape . . . just as they had discussed.

CHAPTER 31

"Are you sufficiently recovered?" Sharif Maktoum blandly inquired as Sami sat silently beside him, both of them seeming to critically measure Warren with their matching sets of dark eyes.

"Can't keep me down. I'm like a tiger." Warren raised both hands to simulate tiger claws and winced, relaxing his left arm. "Just a tweence sore still."

The brothers seemed disinterested in his tiger qualities or in his lingering degree of pain, Sharif still transfixing him with the eye of an inquisitor. "Tell me, Stowe," Sharif asked in a low voice, "why did the Poppins woman attack you?"

Warren stopped smiling and turned the pointed gaze back on them. "You tell me. The others say she came in on the transport with me, lived and worked with your people, and when you two come into the room and say the word, she spears me like a cocktail snack . . . and I hear you still haven't caught her. Seems kind of fishy to me."

Sami flushed and shifted uncomfortably, but Sharif sat calmly observing Warren's face until he ceased speaking before he offered, "Several people say that you two seemed, mmm, quite friendly, chatting and so on."

Warren solemnly raised his right hand. "Guilty as charged, and if you ask around you'll find that I'm *quite friendly, chatting and so on* with beautiful exotic women all over the Confederated Worlds. I've got priors." Warren put his right hand in his pocket. "And again I ask you two, with all her chances to cut my throat, why'd she wait until you came in and said her name, hmm? Very suspicious, especially when someone might feel like eliminating a partner that they might mistakenly believe has already served his purpose."

Sami chuckled nervously, shifting under Warren's accusing glare, saying, "Nonsense, Stowe! Of course we wouldn't—"

Sharif cut him off, never taking his eyes off Warren. "If she worked for us, and we had wanted you dead, it seems she had ample opportunity in the catacombs, but"—Sharif's lips formed a hint of a smile—"this is all pointless speculation. She never worked for us, and now she has evidently vanished into those catacombs without a trace."

"Oh?" Warren said, raising his eyebrows. "Then we'll likely never see the murderous tart ever again, disappeared like all the others."

"That's what *I* said," Sami offered, looking between Warren and Sharif.

"Perhaps," Sharif said. "In any case, Stowe, are you well enough to drive? Another scenario is planned for today, and we don't wish to let our clients down."

"Absolutely," Warren vowed. "Never better."

"Excellent. You have two hours for any preparation you might wish to make."

"Two hours it is," Warren said, drawing out his smoking case and beginning to roll a cigarette as both brothers stared at his graceful motions with unappreciative frowns. "But you know," Warren went on, "this Poppins woman seemed to hold more of a grudge against Hammerworth's bunch than she held against me. Did you ever think of that?" He put the flame to his finished smoke, and just as the brothers both opened their mouths to protest, Warren marched out, throwing a mocking laugh over his shoulder.

Cherry carefully steered her Fireblade through the tight side passages of the catacombs that would never accommodate a car, going down curving ramps, or weaving through concealed halls that bisected most of the arterials.

The scant camera coverage rarely had a chance to spot her, but at times she applied a heavier degree of energy to remain unseen. Reaching a well-trafficked roadway, Cherry stopped the Fireblade short and dismounted, snatching up her antique Thompson gun. Leaning out, she spotted a fixed camera module sixty full paces down the roadway, lifted the Thompson to her shoulder, and fired a single shot. The camera module exploded as a .45-caliber tracer slug slammed through its delicate componentry.

She fit the Thompson back in its brackets and threw a leg over her Fireblade, launching out onto the broad road. She was forced to stop once more and sneak up to destroy another camera, but after just a few minutes of cautious travel she reached one of the catacomb fuel depots unobserved by any snooping cameras. Not only would it supply fuel for her motorcycle, but a source of fresh water and toiletry facilities that Warren had insisted upon providing for the drivers.

After dealing with her immediate needs, Cherry found the tiny model car Warren had given her, placing it atop the fuel dispenser. With that single sign of her presence in sight, Cherry slipped her helmet into place, started the Fireblade's engine, and sped back down the roadway. Unless the Maktoums were more upset about her disappearance than she suspected, another scenario should be kicking off soon, and she wanted to be ready and in position before the catacombs became too busy.

When it did begin, Cherry, her Fireblade, and her Thompson would be poised for action.

Three more of Warren's gladiators quit after the prior deadly scenario, but surprisingly Bandar wasn't one of the quitters, taking his place in yet another freshly fabbed Gran Sport, and overseeing the arming of his twin Browning 1919 .30-caliber machine guns.

Warren watched Bandar and the others grimly preparing while he eyed and armed his own guns, surreptitiously checking to be sure the small package under his seat was well secured before shutting his door and firing up the Daytona's powerful engine. Smoking case and lucky shank rested in jumpsuit pockets, everything in place for the big event.

A moment later, all down the line engines roared to life, spewing gray exhaust, and Warren waited until the camera drones lifted off before he slipped the shifter into first gear, leading the way out into the catacombs.

The music system he had discovered within the fabrication menu trees definitely hadn't been period correct, but Warren had added it as a whim and now he linked a memory stick, starting one of his most cherished ancient tunes. As they began accelerating into the catacombs, the engine throbbing powerfully through his frame, some long-forgotten musical act called "The Cars" of all things began singing "Let the good times roll," and Warren grinned despite all the deadly questions he accelerated directly toward.

Was he correct in his thinking and Cherry's attack had been a way to distance herself from him in the eyes of the Maktoums? Was she wrong in thinking the Maktoums had been plotting his death all along? And how would Hammerworth deal with the loss of Hells at Cherry's hands? By exacting his terrible vengeance on Warren's gladiators?

Perhaps the foremost questions on Warren's mind surrounded Cherry's actual survival in the catacombs, and it suddenly surprised Warren to realize that her survival or loss held no direct cost for him, and yet it concerned him the most. Could she, with her Blue Light heritage, survive whatever odd phenomenon consumed every other solitary trespasser in the catacombs?

The scenario gong rang over the audio channel and Warren quieted his antiquated music to listen for the scenario specifics. The cultured voice of his replacement began speaking: "Attention gladiators, scenario is... *Odd Versus Even*. All units have sixty seconds to scatter before scoring begins."

"Damn it," Warren muttered to himself. It seemed another scenario unlikely to have been selected organically, and likely to result in a great deal of mayhem, but at least Sharif and Sami had not yet imported more cutthroats. He bit his lip, remembering that Sami had finally opted to sample live audio feeds from the drivers during the scenario to add greater drama for spectating clients... just as Warren had pushed from the beginning. Now anything Warren transmitted to the other gladiators, or possibly even said to himself, might well play for the entire Members Club crowd. While this feature provided a key element of Warren's current plans, he needed to limit his words to the bare essentials... for now.

Rather than scoot off the arterial and lose himself in a maze of smaller passages as most of the other cars behind him seemed to be choosing, Warren just accelerated straight ahead, counting upon the Daytona's speed to keep him out of any great danger for the moment.

The start tone rang out again, marking the official start of hostilities. Now even-numbered units and odd numbers would clash, each opponent vehicle disabled providing a rich bonus to the victorious driver. Catbox would likely score big in this scenario, doing what he enjoyed most, and driving an odd-numbered car made him a legitimate target for Warren.

A moment's contemplation brought Catbox's likely hunting ground to mind, recalling his prior tastes quite clearly. Most of his victories lay on the main route through the Town section, or directly off that main route.

Warren made a snap decision, downshifting, hugging the right side of the arterial as he stomped the brake pedal, whipping the wheel just far enough as he gunned the throttle, sliding into a sharp corner with a boatload of retained speed, his camera drones overshooting the corner and sweeping back after him.

He floored the throttle, shifting up at the precise moment of optimal acceleration, his eyes searching the passage ahead for any sign of headlights, ambushers. Hammerworth and his remaining drivers would no longer fear Cherry's wrath, but had their prior losses taught them caution?

The narrow lanes of the simulated town approached, and Warren resisted the urge to slow the Daytona, keeping the throttle floored, the engine roaring full-throated as he swept through a dozen bisecting intersections in a series of lightning flashes. He glimpsed the green Mustang to the right, stationary, dark and waiting, and only Warren's speed saved him, the tracers from the twin .30-caliber machine guns in Catbox's car slashing just behind him.

"Sweet mother of pearl!" Warren yelled, seeing the Mustang's lights appear behind him, launching into the chase. He smiled, downshifting and stomping the brake as he slid into a sharp turn. Everything felt just perfect.

Cathwaite had entered the Members Club not only feeling awkward due to his limp, but also out of his element among the wealthiest of luminaries from the Confederated Worlds. While he possessed a fair degree of wealth by Bethune standards, and the addition of Stowe's shocking largesse doubled his gambling bankroll, he knew that he was an infant among sophisticates, and this crowd instinctively detected this too, Sami utterly ignoring him.

As Cathwaite self-consciously took a seat and accepted a cocktail, those clients stirring around the Members Club eyed him with the thinnest veil of urbanity, and this strange weight of moral force began to wear away at Cathwaite until he nearly abandoned it all, fleeing back to his new suite. Just as he nervously clapped his crystal tumbler down on the glossy tabletop, lurching to his feet, the holographic displays around him all flowed into life. The clients all across the lush chamber turned, ignoring Cathwaite, and he looked up to see a dozen views of the catacombs, gleaming cars speeding through the aquamarine passages, camera drones pacing every vehicle.

A polished voice rang out, describing the scenario, but Cathwaite barely heard, caught up in the imagery he had dreamed of since childhood, engines roaring as the string of cars whipped past a fixed camera position. Another call came across the audio channel, and the gladiator vehicles scattered through the catacombs, and Cathwaite saw the distinct shape of only one 1969 Dodge Daytona, marking its progress.

Wagers began to flow immediately, and Cathwaite acted as Warren had instructed him, placing a ten-thousand-guilder bet on Hammerworth, a low-risk, low-reward gambit. By the time Cathwaite placed the bet, over a million guilders showed on the wager board, dwarfing his modest investment in seconds.

Now terse commands and warnings crackled through the audio channel, each overlaid by the distinctive howl of antique high-displacement engines. Pairs or trios of allied drivers sped through the twisting passages, each mile covered stacking up more guilders into their respective accounts even as they hunted their opposing numbers for the big bonuses.

"*Bandar, stay to the left! To the left! That corner's coming up fast,*" one tough-sounding woman called through the communicator.

"*I see it, Gilda,*" a male voice replied.

Around Cathwaite more and more bets were placed, the wager board populating steadily as gamblers avidly watched the displays and listened to the cacophony of calls coming through the audio channel. A chorus of cheers and hoots drew Cathwaite's attention to a pair of displays where he witnessed the anachronistic firepower of Klaus Benin's toys at work for the first time.

Camera drones on the eleven-car scanned back in its wake as it desperately sped down a broad corridor. A pursuing Corvette far behind fired its twin weapons, flame blossoming from the two hood apertures, staggered streams of glowing projectiles bracketing the eleven-car. The Corvette visibly closed the distance, firing again, both spurts of projectiles chewing into Gran Sport number eleven, sending it sliding into a sidewall in a shower of sparks.

Cathwaite swallowed as the cheers resounded about him, tearing his eyes away to seek out Warren's Daytona among the displays. He looked up just in time to see the green Mustang's ambush position, the burst of deadly fire narrowly missing Stowe.

"That Catbox fellow is going to rack up another kill," one gambler called out. "Fifty thousand on Catbox to take out that Daytona."

More gamblers focused on the drama, prior scenarios demonstrating that Catbox always provided quality violence. Cathwaite felt his mouth go dry; clearly Warren had misjudged his plan, and now was about to become another victim of this Catbox lunatic.

"*Sweet mother of pearl!*" Warren's voice yelled out over the audio channel, and Cathwaite could scarcely believe what he heard: the prearranged signal. How could Warren think such a thing even as he faced destruction?

Cathwaite opened his dry mouth and placed the bet, obedient to his instructions. "I'll bet . . . I'll bet the Daytona takes Catbox . . ." Several clients turned to smirk at Cathwaite, or stare in surprise that only multiplied as he concluded by following Warren's directions to the letter, "One million guilders on the Daytona."

Sami's brows lowered as he turned to stare at Cathwaite. "I-I always loved those Daytonas," Cathwaite choked out under the pressure of their stares. "And isn't that Warren Springer Stowe driving?"

One of the gamblers he recognized as York Rigby seemed to nod thoughtfully before turning back to observe the clash between Catbox and Stowe, while others snorted and muttered comments about tyros and amateurs that made Cathwaite blush. He could barely watch as the twin view of the clash began to unfold, the green Mustang accelerating hard, seeming to overhaul the Daytona quite readily, flying around a sharp curve, not far behind Stowe, almost ready to line up a shot.

Cathwaite shifted his attention to Warren's camera drone feed just in time to see an astonishing maneuver. The Daytona jigged, its tires smoking as its back end broke loose, sweeping around even as the car slid at high speed down the road, its twin weapon-muzzles coming about, angling...nearer, nearer...

As the green Mustang slid around the corner, two scorching strings of bullets swept across its engine compartment and windshield, blowing chunks of metal visibly into the air as the windshield shattered. The Mustang jerked and spun, heavily impacting one wall, and the Daytona stopped firing, lurching to a halt, smoke swirling up from the fire-blackened gunports.

"Very nice wager," York Rigby said, suddenly standing at Cathwaite's elbow. "What was that? Seven-to-one odds?"

Cathwaite gulped, feeling all eyes seemingly pinned upon him. "I-I am not really sure."

"Eight-to-one," another voice announced in an amused tone, and Cathwaite observed the speaker to be a cold, imperious-looking fellow, a tall athletic woman at his side.

"Eight-to-one?" York Rigby said. "And didn't you bet on Catbox, Klaus?"

This Klaus fellow took a drink from his glass, smiling a thin, thin smile at York. "Yes, I bet on Catbox. Who would have thought Stowe would still be such a factor, eh? I certainly did not, but luck...she is a fickle lady. Whom will she bless tomorrow? Eh?"

CHAPTER 32

As the green Mustang slammed to a disastrous halt, Warren didn't wait around, gunning the Daytona's engine and speeding away. Across the communicator channel he heard the calls and cries of conflict still ringing out, but only two of Hammerworth's crew remained driving odd-numbered cars, and it sounded like Gilda and Bandar were in the process of neutralizing Cleo at that very moment.

"*I'm on her! I'm on her!*" Bandar crowed, the roar of his machine guns coming across in bursts.

"*Missed, Bandar!*" Gilda's voice answered. "*She's going right, and…*" Gilda's guns hammered. "*Ha-ha!*" she laughed.

"*Got her, Gilda!*" Bandar cheered.

Warren nodded to himself. Now Kira alone drove an even-numbered car from Hammerworth's group, so only Hammerworth himself remained a valid target, but where would he hunt? And would Kira try for a solo mission of slaughter among the amateur gladiators?

As Warren contemplated his best chance for finding Hammerworth, he came through the City Street section, rounding a tight curve, his headlights sweeping across one of the two fuel depots emplaced within the catacombs. In that flash of lights Warren glimpsed a small red gleam that did not initially register, but a moment later he mashed the brakes, spinning the Daytona in a flash of throttle, his tires screaming.

He rolled back to the fuel depot and killed the Daytona's engine. The accompanying camera drones whirred around the depot in a slow orbit as he opened the Daytona's bonnet, the hot engine clicking and pinging as it shed heat, the barrels of the two Browning .30-caliber machine guns equally heated.

From the cover of the extended bonnet Warren peered over, confirming the presence of the palm-sized red car he had gifted: Cherry.

Warren tinkered with imaginary issues for a moment before closing the bonnet and walking back to the driver-side door, timing the drone orbits closely. As the space in the camera coverage arrived, he grabbed the small bundle from beneath his seat, slipping it beneath the Daytona's undercarriage.

For the time, it was all he could do for her.

In another moment, Warren gunned the big engine and roared back out, hunting that lumpy prick, Hammerworth.

Six Gran Sports had roared by Cherry's concealed position at various times since the scenario began and Cherry continued waiting and watching, seeking the perfect opportunity for her test as she sat comfortably astride the Fireblade. She had dealt with the static camera earlier, and now she faced only camera drones that likely focused on their target vehicles more than anything... if only the correct chance would arrive.

Cherry's augmented hearing detected the powerful engine, clearly *not* the distinctive sound of a Gran Sport, and a moment later a red Barracuda sped into sight, the odd geometric effects of Ajanib bringing the vehicle rather suddenly into the clear.

Kira.

Cherry raised the Thompson gun to her shoulder, aiming carefully... squeezing the trigger, the muzzle angled high. The gun thumped her shoulder as it spat a dozen heavy glowing slugs out, several striking the Barracuda's lead camera drone, dropping it like a stone... right through Kira's windshield.

As Kira's Barracuda jerked suddenly to one side, sliding, Cherry engaged the other drones, dropping them one by one in showers of sparks, ending their transmissions in a flash.

Cherry lowered the muzzle, dumping the rest of the Thompson's magazine through the Barracuda's grill and bonnet as it continued to swerve back and forth, until crashing at last. Changing magazines and clipping the Thompson into place, Cherry started her Fireblade and coasted out to the smoking wreck. She stopped and lifted the Thompson one-handed.

"Get out, Kira," Cherry said, her weapon rock steady, pointing through the shattered windshield at Kira's helmet-shrouded melon.

"Don't shoot, Poppins!" Kira said, his voice evincing all the terror Cherry knew so well from the bad old days. That was fine.

"Get out of the car, Kira," Cherry repeated. "And quit playing games with the communicator. I'm guessing it won't work since I shot a bunch of these lovely bullets right through your car's battery a bit ago. No power, old fellow. And that means no sneaky message about me."

Kira clambered out, nervously eyeing Cherry as he pulled his helmet free.

"Start walking," Cherry ordered, gesturing with her weapon, and Kira stared fearfully at her, slowly backing away. "Walk!" Cherry snapped, and Kira turned, casting glances over his shoulder as he trudged down the arterial.

He walked about fifty paces before clearly spotting one of the near-invisible side passages, leaping suddenly through the gap. Cherry waited a few moments before starting her Fireblade and idling slowly toward the tight opening, seeing a flash of ruby luminance even as she heard Kira cry out. In the five seconds it took for Cherry to turn her Fireblade through the gap, any sign of Kira had vanished.

Cherry bit her lip, her augmented vision scanning over the featureless passage, seeking clarity, listening, even scenting the air. After a silent moment, she muttered, "Very interesting indeed."

Within the Members Club, Cathwaite scarcely enjoyed the currents of grudging approval more than he had the earlier disdain aimed at him from his fellow gamblers. The dark-eyed, congenial fellow, Prabak Bhatt, had lost heavy on Catbox, but he did not seem to begrudge Cathwaite his simultaneous win, later winning back his coin betting on Gilda.

Cathwaite's only other bet, on Hammerworth, had netted a small pot of winnings as the team leader riddled a pair of Gran Sports at low odds before the scenario came to an end.

As the other clients swirled together in a convivial ménage, clearly discussing the scenario or their individual wins and losses on the wager board, Cathwaite looked on, feeling intensely uncomfortable.

The sensation of discomfort notched up as that same tall, athletic blonde sauntered to an empty seat at Cathwaite's table, seating herself as she blandly surveyed him over the salted rim of her golden snifter. "Who *are* you?" she asked. "Friend of Sami's?"

Cathwaite suddenly found his own glass and took a nervous swallow before saying, "Not really. I have a little collection on Bethune and Sami asked me"—he noticed Sami hovering nearby at that moment, clearly listening to every word though he looked away—"to come sample the delights, and here I am. Cathwaite's the name."

"Cathwaite?" Her eyes flicked over him, then fixed on his face. "I'm Savanah." She sipped her drink without looking away from him. "Collection, you say?"

Cathwaite shifted, suddenly finding the plush seat strangely uncomfortable. "Well, yes . . . very humble, modest—"

"Oh? How modest?" Savanah inquired under her eyelashes. "Fieros? Ford Escorts?"

Cathwaite shrugged dismissively, silently wishing he had a Fiero or an Escort. "Not even—not even as exclusive as that . . . I've got a couple of Hyundais and a . . . a Yugo."

Savanah stared at him. Cathwaite began to speak, nervously coughing. "Ahem, been trying to sell my little collection and upgrade, you see."

"I'd imagine so," Savanah said dryly.

York Rigby's voice intruded, "A few more lucky nights like tonight and you'll have guilders to spare for your new collection." Cathwaite looked up, startled to find York close beside him.

Savanah snorted. "Or lose it all on such a stupid risk. Betting on a Daytona of all things!"

Before Cathwaite could formulate a response York spoke again: "A Daytona *and* Warren Springer Stowe."

"Stowe?" Savanah said with a curl of her lip. "So he's a collector. A collector is one thing; this game is something else entirely."

Cathwaite looked from Savanah to York, seeing York smile. "Perhaps. Seems Stowe did quite well here."

Savanah tilted her glass, draining it in a single gulp, and looked about the room until she spotted Klaus Benin, standing from her seat to her full height. She looked down on York and Cathwaite. "Perhaps we can make a little side bet. How many more lucky nights will Stowe see, hmm, Rigby?" She strode away on those words.

York said nothing for a moment as he and Cathwaite watched Savanah's sinuous figure cross the room. He turned to Cathwaite with a knowing gleam in his eye. "Seems she offered that bet like a woman who's got a tidy grip on inside knowledge. Makes a curious gent wonder what Warren Springer Stowe will face next..."

CHAPTER 33

During the scenario scoring that followed, Warren learned that one of his gladiators had died in the scenario, ambushed by Kira, who had subsequently vanished, his vehicle and camera drones shot full of holes, but Catbox had survived his own wreck. None of the assembled gladiators mourned Kira's likely demise, but Sami seemed troubled by the man's mysterious fate, and Warren couldn't help himself, pouring on the coals. "Like I said, Sami, that Poppins creature has it out for Hammerworth and his brutes, and I'll bet she diced Kira into bite-sized portions and is dining on his sour carcass right now. And serves him right, shooting the soup out of Jonas like that!"

Aside from losing one of his own drivers, Warren felt every reason for cheer. He had bested Catbox in a straight contest, and his own driver bonus amounted to a pretty penny . . . though not nearly so much as Cathwaite had surely netted betting in the Members Club.

Sami seemed far less cheerful. "If she really was responsible for, er, taking Kira out, it is completely unacceptable. She is not a part of this operation anymore, and an unsanctioned wild card could overset our whole credibility with the betting clients."

Warren laughed, fishing about in his driver's jumpsuit for his smoking case. "You've got to be kidding, Sami. I'd bet anything the clients will *love* a wild card, as long as it brings along a spicy breath of carnage with it."

Sami's eyes snapped angrily. "Speaking of carnage, Stowe, our new drivers will be here on the next transport. Did I forget to mention them?"

Warren built a cigarette and shook his head. "I don't seem to recall you saying anything about new drivers, but feels like it might be a good idea since Hammerworth's running shy a couple of people already." Warren's words didn't stoke the angry response he had expected.

"I'm very glad you are so pleased, Stowe," Sami said with an expression of muted glee. "You can come along and greet the new arrivals in a couple of hours, and see how much you'll like them."

Warren struck a light to his cigarette, puffing it into life and blowing an incidental cloud of smoke into Sami's face. "Alright, I will."

Sami fled, coughing.

Doctors Peter Maris and Tara Sang shuffled carefully along together, each individually tethered to their own escort drone, both bearing a load of instruments slung over their respective shoulders. They gingerly maneuvered around scattered wreckage left behind by the aid vehicles, muttering unusually sophisticated curses at each piece of irreverent evidence they beheld.

"Barbarians! Ignorant damned savages! I wish they'd all go to blazes!" Peter Maris snarled.

Tara Sang nodded, shoving a scorched piece of jagged metal aside. "I heard one of them did just that earlier. *Snatched*, they say, I guess, or something of that nature."

Peter snorted. "I wish they were *snatched*. Nothing of the kind, of course. Must be some intermittent feature of the geometric—" He broke off, looking up, staring. "It's you," he said.

Tara Sang looked at Peter, then followed his gaze to see that slender, dark-haired woman astride her glossy vehicle, both ensconced within a barely visible side passage. She calmly observed them as she spooned what appeared to be peaches from a container, her expression passively watchful. "You're down here alone?" Tara said to her. "And no tether drone." Tara could not conceal the shock in her voice.

"Right-o on both counts, love," Cherry said.

"But why?" Peter asked, staring as she slurped the last of her snack, dabbing her mouth with a sleeve.

"I take it you don't chat up Sami and Sharif that often, then?"

Peter made a sound. "What's the point? Neither of them give a damn about our job."

Cherry shrugged, smiling slightly. "Oh, if you did speak with them, you might know I quit the desecration gig to become one of the—what did you say? Barbarians? Or was it filly-things? Either way, I'm racing about down in these catacombs now, entertaining the rich sods abovestairs and earning more coin than ever."

Tara shook her head, frowning. "But we understand there's no sporting scenario until tomorrow at the earliest."

Cherry swept a hand across the narrow panorama. "Little extracurricular scouting for tomorrow. That's all. Can't be caught napping. Er, I know you'll not grass on me to Sami."

Tara and Peter shared a look. "Oh? Sami would not approve of your, um, scouting?"

"Lord no," Cherry said. "We former desecrators are supposed to be cannon fodder for his team of bullies. Fortunes won and lost on the betting tables, right?"

"But how will you ever get back to your quarters? You can't possibly sneak your way back onto the utility lifts," Tara said. "They're *suddenly* following security protocols on those for some reason."

Cherry shook her head with a sigh. "I admit it—it's had me in a quandary. Just eating a snack here, wondering how I can get back to my room without Sami raking me over."

Peter glanced at Tara before clearing his throat and offering, "There is another way . . . if you can leave your vehicle down here, and you don't mind a little climbing."

"Climbing?" Cherry said looking up with a smile. "I positively *love* climbing."

The transport arrived with eight new drivers, but even more importantly, it carried a dozen wealthy clients with a combined trillion guilders in disposable wealth.

The success of the last two scenarios had stopped Sharif's snide comments, Sami now eagerly anticipating feeding his brother crow by the forkful, these additional clients forming the next link in Sami's chain of success. He handled them with every bit of the assured charisma he possessed, and only as Belinda Athenos took over did Sami notice Warren Springer Stowe leaning against a nearby wall, his arms folded across his chest, that annoying, knowing grin on his face.

"So," Warren said, "where are these fire-breathing drivers you brought on, hmm, Sami?"

Sami controlled his irritation with effort. "Klaus met them aboard the launch and he should be bringing them out any moment—ah! There we are."

Klaus Benin accompanied six men and two women, all evidently formed from a similar mold, from a common source. Where Hammerworth and his rough crew bore the look of tough, eccentric individualists, these new drivers barely seemed like individuals at all, their personalities ostensibly subsumed by an overserious team identity.

"Sami Maktoum," Klaus greeted grandiloquently, "allow me to introduce, uh . . ." He seemed to hesitate, glancing sidelong at Warren, "*Mister* Strayer and *Miss* Vogl." Sami noticed Benin's odd emphasis, suddenly realizing that he avoided mention of military rank, just as he had insisted that Stowe not be informed of the new drivers' planet of origin. "These two *manage* the team," Klaus concluded.

"Pleased to have you with us," Sami said, then indicated Stowe with the inclination of his head. "And you may have heard of Warren Springer Stowe."

"We've heard of him," Miss Vogl said, her eyes barely glancing, her voice touched by hints of a harsh accent.

"You're a *driving* team?" Warren said, not hiding his skepticism.

"That's right," Klaus interjected before Vogl or Strayer could speak.

Warren grinned. "So they'll assemble their own cars in Build-Out?"

"I think we have that handled, Stowe," Klaus said, turning as if to depart.

"Let me guess," Warren said. "All Camaros and Corvettes for this *driving* team, right?"

The eight new *drivers* shared surprised looks at Warren's comment, but Benin's face reddened angrily, and Sami felt lost in the unspoken undercurrents. *What did Corvettes and Camaros matter?*

Klaus Benin seemed momentarily bereft of speech, opening his mouth as Warren's hands busily constructed one of his vile cigarettes, but Warren spoke first. "Bought their skills on the ASFACC simulator, did you?" No one said anything, Klaus merely staring, and Warren stuck his cigarette in the corner of his mouth and looked sidelong at Sami, smirking. "You see, the ASFACC simulator system only offers Corvettes and Camaros. Hell of a lot easier than digging up a real car . . . and fuel . . . and someplace to drive"—he touched flame to his cigarette and squinted at the eight silent drivers—"on whichever interesting planet you're from."

Vogl and Strayer looked merely bemused by Warren's words, seemingly more fascinated by his smoldering cigarette than anything he was saying, but Klaus Benin's pallid face radiated anger. "Just worry about your own drivers, Stowe. You'll need all the luck you can get." Klaus directed his eight disciples toward the exit, and Sami found himself momentarily alone with Warren, stepping back from the cloud of acrid smoke issuing from his cigarette.

"Making friends wherever you go, Stowe?"

Warren laughed. "If Klaus—or you—wanted to be friendly you wouldn't have imported this lot of throat-cutters. They weren't hired for their good looks and charming manners, that's for sure."

"As you know, Stowe, skilled, willing drivers are hard to come by on short notice," Sami said in his most reasonable tone. "And without drivers to clash, we have dissatisfied clients. And dissatisfied clients means you get to be an indentured asset until you're eighty years old or so, right?"

Warren flicked his cigarette on the ground and mashed it out with his toe. "Eighty years old, Sami?" He exhaled smoke through his nostrils in a manner Sami found rather unsettling, staring straight into his partner's eyes. "I don't think there's any thought in your mind about me living even one more year. Or is it only Sharif and Klaus plotting my demise, while faithful, loyal Sami remains on Team Stowe?"

Sami chuckled nervously. "Stowe? Stowe! What an absurd thing to say! I've continually told Sharif what a useful asset—I mean *contributor* you've been."

"Hah!" Warren replied, seeming to change subjects abruptly in the next moment. "So how many days will your new drivers need on the oval track before they enter their first scenario?"

Sami blinked. "Days? Klaus assures me they will be *participating* in tomorrow's scenarios."

Warren's eyebrows raised. "Oh really? What remarkable faith you—or Klaus—place in their driving abilities."

"Klaus assures me that—" Sami began, only to be cut off by Warren.

"And Klaus is such an expert on driving, isn't he?"

Sami felt his face grow hot. "No, he isn't, as you well know. But why should you care? It's all the better for you and your gladiators if this bunch can't drive, isn't it?"

Warren stared at Sami with the most severe expression Sami had ever seen on his generally affable face. "No, it's not. The clients are here to see thrilling adventures in driving, not a bunch of unskilled tyros trying to compensate for their lack of driving skill with an excess of crude violence." Warren turned his back on Sami, throwing one last line over his shoulder: "You really shouldn't let a psycho nutter like Benin make business decisions for you, Sami. Can't end well."

As Warren strode along the corridors to his suite, he tried to imagine what this Vogl and Strayer would attempt in the catacombs, since he knew the limitations of the ASFACC simulation system all too well. They sure as hell wouldn't be outdriving anyone, and if they got too rambunctious they'd be lucky to keep their cars in one piece, even without opponents shooting at them.

Still ... all eight of them possessed that look ... soldiers or mercenaries or something of that nature. What would they do?

"You're thinking so hard I can smell it," a voice proclaimed from practically right beside Warren, causing him to jump with a startled, non-flattering exclamation.

"Erg! Damn it!" Warren gulped, stopping in his tracks. "Cherry? How did you—?"

"With difficulty, Stowe, with difficulty." She pointed at his chest. "Sorry about the knife, duck, but I thought it might throw a bit of dust in their eyes."

Warren touched the bandaged wound. "*Sorry about ... ?*" he murmured. "What are friends for, after all, Cherry? A little knife wound among chums, just warms the heart right up." He broke off. "What are you doing up here? *How* are you up here?"

"Got your care package down below, love, but ... I fancied better food and a cozier place to sleep. The science blokes were kind enough to show me a clever back door up from the catacombs."

"So by now Sami and Sharif will know what you're up to," Warren said, thinking fast.

Cherry shrugged. "Doubt it. The eggheads aren't on terms with Sami at the moment. Didn't seem to know anything about the *Mary Poppins Rampage*, even."

"Hmm," Warren said in simple eloquence, thinking of rampages past and present. "Did you, um, happen to delete Kira, by the way?"

"Not really. Just set him afoot."

Warren considered Cherry's enigmatic smile a moment before asking, "Then where is he?"

"Wherever people go when they get body-snatched."

Warren stared at her, looking for any sign of a joke, not seeing it. "R-really?"

Cherry nodded. "I didn't precisely see what snatched him, but something did. It hasn't tried for me . . . yet."

"Not the tricky alien geometry at work like we thought, then?"

"Nope. Thinking it may be an actual tricky alien . . . in the flesh."

CHAPTER 34

Cherry slipped back into the dim utilitarian research section early, retracing her steps back toward the catacombs only to find Peter Maris waiting. He seemed half awake, sprawled on a chair overlooking the chute leading below, perking up with a jolt as Cherry stepped near.

He stared at her. "Poppins," he said after a quiet moment, his voice scratchy with fatigue. "I wondered if you'd return . . . or if you'd stay up here sticking knives in people."

Cherry contemplated the scientist for a moment before saying, "Asked around, did you? And yet you didn't set the dogs on me. Why not?"

"You don't strike me as any sort of crazed maniac."

Cherry nodded, crossing one arm across her chest and resting her chin in her palm. "Ah, the hubris of the overeducated. I see."

Peter sat up sharply. "You're no cold-blooded killer, Poppins, and I can see that."

Cherry laughed. "Oh really, Doctor? But I *am*." She unfolded her arms and stepped near as Peter tensed in his seat, moving past him to the chute. "I'm just *very* selective these days." She reached back to gently pat his rigid shoulder and then lowered herself into the green-glowing crevice.

The climb didn't present any difficulty for Cherry, even with a small pack of supplies slung over her shoulder, and she quickly clambered down to the catacomb level. After Kira's mysterious snatching, she maintained a defensive poise, ready to strike hard and fast at the first appearance of a threat, but the silent caverns greeted her without any hint of an alien presence, and she found the Fireblade stashed just as she had left it. She pulled the Thompson from its secure brackets and checked the magazine before throwing her leg over the saddle and starting the engine.

Warren had described the new drivers imported by Klaus Benin, and Cherry felt less cheerful about this addition than Warren seemed to be. The Blue Light Brigade was not the only supersecret elite fighting unit created by one warlike world or another, and these eight newcomers sounded like they could be some such creatures. If Warren spoke true and these people could not readily compete as drivers, what other path to victory could they possibly seek?

Cherry's own actions in that prior scenario seemed like a model of behavior that Klaus Benin might choose to emulate with his stone-eyed crew, and as Cherry piloted her Fireblade through Ajanib's deserted catacombs she recognized the irony. She likely must now seek to combat a merciless style of ambush that she had accidentally inspired.

Hopefully Stowe discovered some hint of their intentions by sifting through the fabrication files before the scenario began. They only possessed a few hours until the truth would be made manifest.

Warren had his hands full from the time he awakened, preparing for yet another victory despite what must be impending dirty tricks on the part of Klaus Benin and his lackeys.

Fortunately, Cathwaite recalled his instructions, making a practice of visiting Build-Out, ostensibly shopping about through the fabrication offerings or observing the new builds of other clients. It served as no great difficulty to depart from a fabrication kiosk just as Cathwaite arrived, the collector's instructions passed invisibly along, but Warren's demanding tasks began long before this handoff occurred.

Sifting through the fabrication log, Warren discovered the vehicles Benin must have created for his new hitters, but the numbers didn't add up. Two 1968 Camaros and two 1969 Corvettes matched Warren's expectations perfectly, but two 1968 El Caminos also appeared in that same sequence of builds along with a selection of Benin's nasty antique projectile weapons. Where were the final two vehicles that they surely built for his new gladiators? And why El Caminos, since they didn't appear on any of the simulation systems he had ever heard of?

The final fabrication items listed in the log history seemed be some kind of tall mounting gimbals that Warren could not identify, but at least Cherry's premonition had proven wrong.

She had expected Klaus to arm his minions with the shoulder-fired Thompsons, or maybe the larger Lewis guns, much as she had employed her Thompson to such great effect, mimicking her own ambush techniques. While the choice of El Caminos remained a puzzle, and providing vehicles for only six of his new drivers made no sense, Warren saw nothing in the fabrication to alarm him.

His duties continued, briefing his own gladiators and getting everyone energized for the biggest event Ajanib had hosted so far.

Cathwaite read Stowe's detailed instructions and committed them to memory. So far the man had proven nearly infallible, his advice and actions making them both considerably wealthier, and Cathwaite would continue to follow his orders to the best of his abilities.

It seemed that the new crowd of ultrarich clients only made Cathwaite's task easier, providing a dozen fresh personalities where he now embodied a known quantity, if a rather boring one by the standards of these elites. At the very least, more clients increased Cathwaite's sense of anonymity, dialing his nervousness back a full notch.

This enabled Cathwaite to observe the new clients constructing and testing their new vehicles, thoroughly enjoying the sight of a 1965 Chevelle, a 1960 Thunderbird, and multiple versions and years of Corvettes and Mustangs as they each rolled out of Build-Out. He derived further pleasure observing that many of the new arrivals handled a stick shift and three pedals even *less* expertly than he had, one of them even managing to wreck his brand-new Mustang within just a few laps on the oval track.

Fortunately, no serious injuries were incurred and the clients naturally migrated to the Members Club for the impending scenario. Those who had just arrived could not begin to comprehend the spectacle about to engulf them, and the more experienced gamblers sipped their drinks and nibbled appetizers with barely suppressed anticipation.

Sami had dropped hints of an all-new spectacle to be revealed, and Klaus Benin rather ostentatiously declared he would abstain from wagers in this impending scenario since he had become so intimately involved in the composition of this new offering. All this made Cathwaite increasingly anxious as he contemplated Warren's instructions. He was about to risk a shocking stack of guilders on a scenario that sounded more and more like something Warren could not possibly have foreseen.

Cathwaite's thoughts tumbled together as the holographic displays around the room swirled into life, one after the other, the clients hushing to a murmur of low voices as the scenes began to lock onto the gleaming vehicles of Ajanib's gladiators.

Sounds also increased, the roar of a dozen powerful combustion engines increasing in volume by the second, filling the Members Club with its thrilling cacophony. Voices crackled over the audio channel, the backdrop of engine noise bringing the gamblers right into the drivers' seats as the two teams of gladiators advanced, accelerating.

Cathwaite heard Stowe's voice call out, *"Don't lag! Bring your speed up and... ready!"*

The scenario tone rang out, the announcer declaring, "Scenario is *Center Flag*. Secure the flag and advance it to the opposing border... beginning now!"

Cathwaite bit his lip and placed two wagers, expending four million guilders on pure faith, even as he tried not to think how long it had taken to earn a million guilders from his modest enterprise back on Bethune.

How can Warren Springer Stowe be so certain?

In the very next instant, Cathwaite saw the source of Klaus Benin's smugness and desperately wished he could cancel the bets he had just placed. There could be no way Warren had anticipated this. It would be a slaughter.

Warren figured the scenario would be something aggressive, without subtlety, and Center Flag certainly qualified. The first gladiator to reach the flag position would become the *flag holder*, and receive a tidy bonus, their task being to survive intact as they ran the gauntlet through the area held by the opposing team and deliver the flag to the far border. Doing so provided a heroic cash bonus, but seemed nearly suicidal to achieve, with any enemy gladiator successfully intercepting the flag holder suddenly becoming the new flag holder themselves.

As the announcer called out the flag position, Warren thought quickly through possible strategies, wishing Cherry still numbered among his official gladiators. She could have reached the flag long before any opposing gladiators made it, then merely run with the flag while her teammates cleared a path to the border. Now, just about the best Warren could hope would be to reach the flag almost simultaneously with his opponents, and this time it wouldn't merely be Catbox and Hammerworth, but Vogl and Strayer's team of unknowns too.

With the flag start position on the north arterial, it made for a head-to-head game of chicken that Hammerworth wouldn't savor, Warren felt, so he made a snap decision. "Bandar, you and your wing go straight for the flag. I'll take my wing through the south access and try to flank them, while Gilda's group takes the secondary to the east."

"*Got it,*" Bandar affirmed over the communicator, his voice sounding cheerful enough. Either he hadn't realized the potential storm he faced or the idea of that initial flag bonus elevated his courage to new heights.

Warren slowed enough that his two wing partners could stay with him into the turnoff, then he pushed the pedal hard, running up through the gears as he flew down the access route paralleling the arterial, his two comrades falling farther and farther behind as Warren's Daytona outpaced them.

He preferred to discover whatever awaited them well ahead of his underlings, both for his own room to maneuver, and to give them a chance to survive any nasty surprise.

Within Warren's mental clock it seemed sufficient time had elapsed for Bandar to have reached the flag, while Warren saw the wide-open space approaching that marked the turn back onto the arterial, or the Y-junction with Main Street.

The objective tone chimed across the audio channel and the announcer called, "*Flag taken by car eleven.*"

Another second elapsed and Bandar called out, "*I've got it! I've got it, and no sight of—No!*"

The rapid chatter of bullets ripping through metal came clearly over the audio line, Bandar's transmission cutting abruptly off.

Warren bit his lip as he approached the turnoff, punching his brakes and sliding the fishtailing Daytona around the curve at high speed just when he spotted a single vehicle, stationary at the verge of the Y-junction. He only had a moment to recognize the El Camino where it sat broadside to him almost straight ahead before he realized one of Vogl's boys crouched in the bed of the vehicle, a swivel-mounted machine gun pointed right at him.

The machine gun spewed fire, the stream of tracer bullets slamming into Warren's Daytona like a dozen sledgehammers.

CHAPTER 35

Cathwaite looked in horror between multiple holographic displays, seeing what he thought to be two El Caminos, one posted on the arterial north of the initial flag position, the other waiting at the Y-junction. Both seemed to feature some kind of swivel-mounted weapon in their shallow beds, a gunner crouched in position on each.

The El Camino on the arterial opened fire first, the thread of arcing tracer rounds lancing into the number eleven Gran Sport before sweeping across the other two Buicks in Bandar's formation. Glass shattered, sparks flew, steam and smoke belched out from perforated engine compartments.

Around Cathwaite exultant cheers and delighted hoots finally pierced his sense of shock just a moment before he saw the one and only Dodge Daytona speeding straight toward the other El Camino. He could say and do nothing as that wand of destruction erupted from the machine gun's muzzle, dozens of projectiles plowing into the Daytona that seemed to blindly accelerate straight to its doom.

As hammering rounds visibly ripped the life from Warren's car, it seemed to twitch to one side, the vehicle spinning around on smoking tires, now sliding rear-first toward the El Camino. Tracer rounds shredded the Daytona's rear quarters, stitching across metal and glass, bullets punching straight through to explode out the shattered front windshield. But nothing could stop the momentum, Warren's car careening backward, straight into the El Camino with a percussive crunch.

Cathwaite knew there could be no way Warren had survived the

223

hail of fire that punched through his car, but at least he received the dim satisfaction of seeing the El Camino's gunner flung high through the air, landing face-first on the unforgiving road surface.

After a still moment, orbiting camera drones revealed a struggling figure emerge from the smoke-filled Daytona, a fire-retardant canister in hand. Stowe somehow, miraculously survived, now limping about the wreckage, spraying streams of expanding foam into the nascent tongues of flame.

Shouts around the Members Club dragged Cathwaite's attention up to another holographic tableau in time to see the first El Camino, now the flag holder, potting another pair of Gran Sports before they could draw close enough to try shots from their own fixed machine guns. The arterial lay nearly clogged with smoldering wrecks, the El Camino gunner poised to deal out more destruction, surely until their teammates cleared an easy path to run the flag across the southern boundary.

As Cathwaite watched, one camera drone feed flashed red and went dark as it orbited the El Camino, then another. A third camera drone flashed but maintained a flickering, distorted signal, plummeting down, the last picture it transmitted revealing the El Camino gunner's startled face in shocking close-up just before it also went dark.

"What the hell is happening?" Klaus Benin demanded.

"It appears, dear Klaus," York Rigby drawled, "that someone has dropped a heavy camera drone on your pet killer's face. The biter has been bitten, as they say."

Savanah Westbrook put her hand on Benin's shoulder but he shook it off, his face pale in the flickering illumination from a dozen holographic images. "I know who has done this thing," snarled through clenched teeth. "It's got to be that Mary Poppins."

Hunched low over the Fireblade's fuel tank, weaving through the trackless maze of smaller passages, Cherry found herself actually angry for the first time in . . . a long, long while. Since Panawaat she had rarely allowed herself the luxury of anger, but when she spotted the swivel-mounted gun on an El Camino, it brought her back to the war for a palpable instant. Everything that came before this had amounted to dangerous games, mostly bent on disabling vehicles. This new innovation had been authored to *kill*, and Cherry knew Klaus Benin's sociopathic fingerprints were all over it.

Sami evidently hadn't thought to get the gladiator communication system reconfigured and Cherry still freely monitored the scenario chatter as she slipped about the catacombs, earlier hearing Warren's near brush with permanent retirement. She hadn't been able to intervene then, so she turned her ire upon the undamaged El Camino instead. It had taken only three shots, and three camera drones, before she managed to drop one on the gunner, firing her Thompson from one of the many small side passages. Now the communicator chatter told her that Warren's remaining gladiators were battling against the opposing team on a more even basis, even recapturing the flag from the gunner-less El Camino.

Cherry's winding route brought her to a crossing point of the north arterial and she only paused for a moment to check for cameras and traffic before gunning the Fireblade across the broad roadway.

Her unerring sense of direction brought her slowly to the Y-junction in time to see the aid vehicle scraping one deceased gunner off the ground before the heavier recovery vehicle scooped the bullet-shredded Daytona up for recycling. Warren appeared nowhere in sight, probably already bundled into an aid vehicle, and Cherry saw nothing more for her to accomplish in the catacombs, at least for the moment.

The immediate question now became unavoidable: If Cherry risked returning through the science quarter above, would Peter Maris manifest a tardy attack of conscience in the form of an official Maktoum welcoming committee?

As Cherry whipped her Fireblade through the route to this potential meeting, she internally shrugged. The security stiffs were unlikely to bring enough game to bear, at least initially, so she could simply retreat back to the catacombs and try her luck at getting body-snatched as she napped, as uncomfortable as that sounded. Adding to her calculus, Cherry felt a growing desire to visit Klaus Benin personally and test his thirst for violence in a more intimate, energetic fashion. She didn't visualize Benin surviving the test.

Stowing her motorcycle and Thompson gun in the same handy alcove, Cherry began to ascend the narrow chute up to the science quarter and whatever might await her there, listening between handholds for any indication of what vigilant lurkers might loiter above.

When Cherry emerged to find the seated figure of Dr. Peter Maris alone, she paused to eye him for a measuring instant before hopping up the rest of the way. "Shouldn't you be reducing pi, or whatever it is you science blokes do all day?"

Peter frowned, staring at Cherry before looking away. "I've only been here a short time. I . . . I thought you might return when the excitement in the catacombs died down."

"Good guess, old stick," Cherry said, dusting the knees of her racing jumpsuit before straightening. "Dying for a shower and a drink."

Peter fixed his gaze on Cherry, unsmiling, his jaw uncharacteristically clenched. "I can't allow that, Poppins."

Cherry put a finger to her chin and considered Peter. "Now, Doc, seems we already covered what a desperate, dangerous character I am. Wouldn't want to come between me and some flower-scented bubble bath, love. Not advisable."

Peter's rigid look did not relent. "You can bathe and dine and rest here . . . in the science quarter," he proclaimed in an unyielding voice. "But I won't allow you through to the Ajanib resort area to risk the lives of those people."

"*Bathe and rest in the science quarter*," Cherry repeated, raising her eyebrows. "By that you mean *your* quarters, don't you?"

Peter shifted uneasily, his face suddenly losing its righteous bearing. "Well, yes, of course, but I—"

"My, my, Doc," Cherry chided, "such drama over a little flirtation. Should've just asked me out. Got a soft spot for eggheads, I do."

"Poppins," Peter began in a somewhat choked voice, "I would take no such advan—"

"Tell you what, Doctor Maris," Cherry said, striding up close enough to touch Peter without effort, "I'll give you a rain check on the date, but I'll also give you the solemn vow of a proud Poppins: I'll not harm a soul while I'm taking care of a few little items up here. How about that?"

Peter shook his head, seeming entirely off any solid foundation he once possessed. "Poppins, I can't allow—"

"That's a dear," Cherry said, reaching out to lightly pat Peter's cheek. "Such a vow's quite a sacrifice for me, old fellow. You've no idea." She leaned back, smiling at his confused expression. "There's a bloke out there who could really be improved by losing nine pounds of ugly off his shoulders. But...a vow is a vow." She walked past a stunned Dr. Maris to the exit door, pausing to wag an index finger. "And we Poppinses always honor a promise."

"No, Cherry," Warren declared, "you really *can't* do any of those disturbing things to Klaus Benin just now. It would ruin everything."

Warren wore a patchwork of bandages and sported a few small blisters on one cheek as he stretched out on his luxurious bed, attired in loose slacks and a shirt unbuttoned from neck to waist.

"Look in the mirror, mate," Cherry retorted. "Klaus is already ruining everything—particularly you. And how many died down there today?"

Warren turned his gaze downward, fiddling with one of the bandages for a moment before replying. "Five died. Three of them were my people; then the two gunners. And four more of mine are in the clinic for their wounds."

"See?" Cherry said. "Don't play at war with this nutter sod. Don't act the foot soldier for his little slaughter. I'll just go win the war proper tonight by offing the bloody enemy general. Much better all the way round, Stowe."

"No!" Warren said in a firm voice. "Listen to me, Cherry." He held out a hand, lowering his voice. "Listen to me. Klaus Benin's worth around fifty billion guilders, and if he violently dies, even in this new independent system Bethune supposedly is, you are never leaving Ajanib alive, no matter how many tricks you have up your sleeves. You understand?"

Cherry stared expressionlessly at Warren before finally saying, "And then they will connect the dots to Betty Boop, and from Boop... to you, Stowe."

"That too," Warren admitted. "I'd be going to prison—probably for life—and you would be dead. Neither eventuality sounds very pleasant."

Warren said nothing more for several seconds, but broke the stretching silence with, "I've got a plan to stop him, and not only stop him but break him financially. You've just got to let me do this *my* way."

"Oh yes, Stowe," Cherry said dryly, waving her finger at all the torn flesh on his body. "Your way is working splendidly! I can tell because of all the blood. You never seem to understand, duck, it's not supposed to be *your* blood."

Warren smiled. "Cherry, when will you come to understand my great genius, hmm?"

Cherry snorted. "Perhaps when you stop getting arrested, shot, burned, or sold into slavery."

"Bah! Mere trifles for one of great vision," Warren said, staring up into some invisible image before his eyes. "Such great vision," he repeated, then frowned, looked back at Cherry. "Only tell me one thing, Cherry: Can you move a few weighty parcels down into the catacombs for me through your little lurk portal? Hmm? Tonight? It would be oh so helpful!"

CHAPTER 36

With Sharif's full support now, Ajanib saw an incoming transport or yacht nearly every day, new clients arriving, sometimes with a new gladiator candidate or two in company from Klaus Benin's private reservoir.

During the early hours of an Ajanib day Build-Out hummed with activity, clients creating their dream cars, one after another, taking their new creations to the oval track, putting them through their paces. With so many clients constructing their second or third vehicle, along with new clients building their first, the activity only paused during a few select hours of each Ajanib day, but Sami and Sharif largely left this process to underlings now.

"You must admit Klaus Benin's *production* was quite remarkable," Sharif said as the two brothers oversaw the swirl of vehicles roaring about the oval track below them.

Sami kept his focus fixed on the growling cars sweeping by below, frowning. "Remarkably brutal," he said, remembering the ghoulish expression on Benin's face as machine-gun bullets mercilessly ripped through cars and drivers alike. "Ajanib is meant to be about the adventure of the chase—driving! speed!—not just slaughter."

"Squeamish, Sami?" Sharif said, smiling. "I would think two hundred and fifty million guilders in an hour's wagers would settle your stomach nicely. Benin's toys created a frenzy of betting."

Sami tried to isolate his own internal sense of disquiet beyond a mere personal distaste for Klaus Benin, wondering how much of his emotional impressions had been influenced by the visions and passion of Warren Springer Stowe. "It is like pushing some filthy street drug, brother," Sami said at last. "Benin's slaughter is the hot-sell thrill of the moment, but we're forced to either keep multiplying the bloodshed, scenario after scenario, or lose the interest of our clients. We have ruined them, and we're only selling bloodlust now."

Sharif's smile broadened as he considered Sami, the noisy backdrop of roaring engines rising and falling around them. "Very eloquent, but I never thought to see the day you would be the voice of caution or moderation. It really is quite the moment, brother. We should mark the occasion."

"We *are* marking the occasion," Sami said, turning his troubled eyes on Sharif. "We celebrate with another slaughter . . . if any of Stowe's gladiators are fools enough to still participate."

Sharif contemplated Sami for a moment before shaking his head. "Shortly Stowe and his capricious gladiators will be superfluous, I believe."

Sami's brows lowered. "Now what have you done, Sharif?"

"I have secured the perfect source for gladiators who will not be nearly so choosy, and a near endless supply of them too."

"This sounds like another of Benin's innovations," Sami said, his lips twisting as he stared at Sharif.

"Partly," Sharif admitted, "but really *you* were the key inspiration."

Sami couldn't hide his skepticism. "Me? I was the inspiration?"

Sharif nodded slowly. "Convicts, Sami. You began shopping for talent among the miscreants, and I merely continued this shining tradition." Sharif turned his gaze on a particularly loud Pontiac GTO roaring by below. "A bureaucrat is coming out from Bethune to handle the fine details, but he's bringing our first load of new convicts—I mean, *gladiators*—with him."

Sami stared in shocked amazement. "That is insane, Sharif. Do you hear me? Who's going to teach these people to drive? And how long will *that* take?"

Sharif shrugged. "Benin's cutthroats already proved that you don't have to be any great driver to be a gladiator. So I supplied a simulator system for the Bethune's prison complex, they run hopeful candidates through it, and the best of the bunch are Ajanib-bound in a flash."

"To get butchered by Klaus Benin's mercenaries," Sami said in a flat tone.

Sharif placed a hand on Sami's shoulder. "We are providing more benefit to humanity than you seem to acknowledge, brother. Haven't you railed against the foolish wastefulness of punitive imprisonment? Here we put the incarcerated to exciting tasks and a remarkable way to earn their freedom, while trimming off the deadwood of society."

Sami shook his head, feeling strangely sickened by such a callous exploitation of desperate hopes.

"And you may not know it," Sharif went on, "but an equally troubling issue surrounds all these elite, engineered warriors who are left in dribs and drabs, jobless when wars end. What's to be done with them? So many of them create mayhem when left adrift, like those Para-Rangers from . . . what system was that? And of course there were the Blue Light monstrosities we all heard about some years back." His expression seemed so thoughtful, so enlightened. "Better for everyone to bring them all to Ajanib and keep them away from the gentle folk of society."

"What philanthropists we have become," Sami said.

Sharif's smile faded down to a thin line. "At times, brother, it seems you are allergic to success." Sharif walked a few slow steps away and turned back, speaking louder as the wail of an engine arose from the track below: "You created something quite special here, I fully admit it. Now, stand back and let Ajanib earn back every guilder you ever invested to get this place where it is. Another scenario or two like yesterday and we will be well on our way to a delightful profit."

Warren limped into Build-Out after the flood of paying clients finally moved on to other pursuits. He had several Buick Gran Sports to re-fabricate after the prior scenario's brutal attrition, but unlike so many of his Build-Out marathon sessions where he labored in utter solitude, Warren noticed one of Benin's stone-faced gladiators observing every vehicle that rolled out of the fabricator. Strayer—that was his name—sat inertly in one of the fabrication kiosks merely watching.

Warren smiled to himself as he keyed his unique selections into the system. Clearly Benin sought to observe any crafty innovations like their own El Camino gun trucks, but all Strayer would see was Gran Sport after Gran Sport rolling off the line along with one new Dodge Daytona.

By the time his building chores neared completion, Gilda and her small group of gladiator volunteers arrived and began shuttling the brand-new vehicles to their assembly area. As Warren finally completed his last task and slowly limped from the darkened Build-Out section, Strayer's quiescent form remained an indistinct silhouette seemingly fixed in place.

Warren took one last look at his shadowy outline and gathered his aching limbs for the painful trudge to the line of new Gran Sports waiting for him. When he reached the assembly area, Gilda and the others had long since retired to their rooms and he walked along the row of gleaming vehicles in near silence and solitude. He stepped to one new Gran Sport and slowly lifted the open trunk, peering within. He sighed in satisfaction. The trunk space lay entirely empty. Cherry had done her part moving their little surprises down to the catacombs.

Now to catch a few hours of sleep before he began the ticklish project of convincing his remaining gladiators to take a last chance on the cunning of one Warren Springer Stowe.

Cathwaite made his way back to the luxury suite, the fumes of too many cocktails blurring his thoughts, though his stride showed only the effects of his slowly healing injuries. His mind, his troubled emotions, had felt unusually in need of anesthesia after watching the blood-soaked spectacle of the prior scenario. The vision of Benin's dour gunners coolly riddling car after car conjoined with the exultant calls and cheers of the gambling clientele in the Members Club.

Benin's own ghastly expression of ecstasy flashed again and again so that Cathwaite rarely reflected on how many guilders he had bet and lost, unable to constrain his mind from the horrific impressions seared within him.

His wavering vision only just noticed the small card that had clearly been slipped beneath his door, and he reached down to grab it while reeling unsteadily about. He steadied himself against one wall and read the scrawl of words, shocked amazement penetrating the chemical haze, line after line.

Stowe asked too much of him this time. After the disaster of the prior scenario, how could he expect Cathwaite to blindly risk almost the entire remaining bankroll in one crazy bet? Had he lost his mind?

⊕ ⊕ ⊕

Fortunately, Cherry was not called upon to aid Warren Springer Stowe until after she had secured a bath and an excellent meal, which was especially important since her late-night tasks required several tedious trips from the gladiator assembly area, through the shadowy corridors of the resort area and into the science quarter. The scramble down through the jagged chute into the catacombs she could have achieved blindfolded with one hand behind her back, but heavily encumbered with Warren's little toys, and forced to make several trips, touched even her reservoir of endurance.

Ascending from the catacombs after depositing the last load of hardware, Cherry began her trek through the somnolent science quarter only to find Peter Maris seemingly lost in thought, staring at the dividing doorway between the resort access and the science area.

Cherry paused some distance away, evidently making some sound that brought Peter around to look at her with startled eyes. "Poppins!" he blurted.

"What's up, Doc?" Cherry said. "Kind of late for you, isn't it? How are you going to defend science from the filly-things if you can't keep your eyes open? Hmm?"

Peter seemed to notice the fresh scuffs on Cherry's garments, his gaze traveling critically over her. "What have you been doing, Poppins?"

Cherry shrugged. "Forgot my good-luck charm down in the catacombs; needed it if I was going to sleep a wink."

Peter barely seemed to hear her, glancing back at the dividing hatch. "I . . . I had trouble sleeping too." He looked back at Cherry, staring fixedly at her face. "Kept wondering if I was a fool to let you through, hoping I wouldn't wake up to hear . . . to hear that . . ."

"That I'd pinched every rich bastard's left shoe?" Cherry supplied helpfully.

Peter swallowed. "Something like that."

Cherry smirked at him. "Told you, Doc. Word of a Poppins. Didn't harm a soul . . . or a *sole*."

Peter didn't smile at her verbal foray, but his expression seemed less troubled. "What are you . . . What are you going to do now?"

"Sleep," Cherry said. "Got a full plate tomorrow and need at least a little rest."

Cherry saw the thoughts sliding through Peter's mind, as he

wondered what hideous items might be on her to-do list, but simultaneously afraid to know the truth, and she perceived the safest way to keep Peter and his conscience contained. With an internal shrug she said, "Say, Doc, you still offering a place to rest my sinful bones?"

"A place?" Peter said uncertainly, understanding seeming to dawn after a moment with a faint blush. "Oh yes, of course ... in my quarters."

Cherry stepped near and patted Peter's shoulder in a companionable way. "I'll take you up on it," she said, pointing a finger at him. "But I warn you, I'm a shameless blanket thief, and ... I mean *sleep only*."

"Well, y-yes, of course," Peter stammered, blushing more until Cherry pushed on.

"Unless I suddenly change my mind. In which case, I'll let you know. But don't get your hopes up!"

CHAPTER 37

Despite Cherry's scathing comments on the topic, Warren felt inclined to agree with Klaus Benin's estimation that tracer rounds had been engineered to hurt more when they hit someone. Though Warren had never been shot with any other antique projectile weapons before, each of the grazing wounds he had received in the prior scenario burned like red-hot irons touched to his flesh.

Now, attempting to get his bruised and punctured body in motion after awakening, it seemed to Warren that every one of his various injuries hurt still more. Even slipping into his racing jumpsuit caused him to catch his breath at each touch of fabric against wounded flesh. Two mere hours of sleep probably hadn't helped, but he could afford no luxury like wasted time now.

When he reached the meeting room, he breathed a sigh of relief: At least the erstwhile gladiators had all arrived, some bearing obvious wounds, most with expressions that did not bode well for his pitch.

Bandar sat glowering, a bandage covering half his forehead. He took in Warren's racing jumpsuit for a moment before speaking. "You can't be serious, Stowe. You're going to go back out there and let those killers finish shooting you to pieces?"

Several gladiators glanced at Gilda as if waiting for her to join Bandar's critique, but she merely leaned over a chairback, her jaws chomping steadily away, her expression neutral.

Warren hadn't explained his full plan to anyone except Cherry, but he had disclosed portions to Gilda to enlist her aid in getting to this moment. Now it all stood upon Warren's weary shoulders alone.

"No, Bandar," Warren said. "I'm not letting these pricks shoot me to pieces. I'm not letting them get away with their dirty tricks. But more than anything, I'm not letting them *win*, especially after they killed our friends that way."

"It's one thing to say all that," Bandar said, "and another thing to somehow become bulletproof in the next few hours."

Others murmured their approval of Bandar's words, and Warren mustered his cockiest smile in response. "Bulletproof, sport? They used the same guns and bullets we've been using the whole time. They just got creative with them, that's all. Our guns have all offered only a fixed aiming point, a fixed elevation, see? And theirs? We all saw what theirs could do, free to elevate and traverse at will."

Gilda stopped chewing and sat up, clearing her throat. "You propose we try to unbolt the guns in our cars and do something fancy with them, hon? 'Cuz I kinda doubt they'll let us, and if they do I don't see me manhandling that big metal cannon and driving along at the same time."

"I agree completely, Gilda," Warren said, then swept his eyes across the puzzled faces of the gladiators. "That's why I plan to feed these wicked sods their own medicine until they bloody choke on it. Allow me to explain..."

As Warren wove the words, he created the vision that comprised more than mere expressions alone, threading strands of revenge with hints of surprising financial windfalls, capping it all with the dark pleasure found only by turning a dirty trick back upon its unprincipled authors.

Long before he finished speaking, Warren knew he had them on board with his plan.

Now he need only deliver the reality of the vision he sold without getting them all killed in the process.

Cathwaite awakened with a splitting headache and a sick feeling in the pit of his stomach far beyond the effects of a night's debauchery. Then he remembered ... millions of hard-earned guilders were about to be pointlessly squandered. Warren wouldn't even know whether Cathwaite had obeyed his absurd commands or not, because Warren would surely be dead, riddled with bullets down in the catacombs, while the smart money bet on Klaus Benin's butchers instead.

It seemed too much—far too much—for Cathwaite to bear, first placing an idiotic bet that would make his wealthy new associates smirk at his foolishness, then seeing that bet squandered even as he would surely watch the sickening butchery unfold. The final shot of poison to Cathwaite's system would be leaving Ajanib in shame, far poorer than when he had arrived.

He wouldn't do it.

He just couldn't . . .

The gladiators around Warren mostly wore concerned expressions on pallid faces as they entered the assembly area, helmets in hand, his visions of a surprise victory competing with vivid memories of slashing machine-gun fire and bullet-perforated friends. Then the complaints from numerous drivers arose as they inspected their respective vehicles.

"Hey, who's been rooting around in my machine?" Muller groused, seeing his usual supply pack opened and disordered.

"Mine too," Gilda said, popping her head up from her Gran Sport.

Warren nodded, glancing back to see the utility lifts opening to permit the Maktoum flunkies and their ammunition carts to enter. "It appears Benin's butchers wanted to be sure we carry no innovations into the fight this time like they did." Warren fell silent as the carts drew near, each gladiator loading the ammunition boxes in and assuring their guns stood ready, ammo belts fed into place, weapons charged.

Engines down the line began to crank into life, one and two at a time until the whole assembly area lay shrouded in swirling smoke. Warren slipped the Daytona into gear and revved his engine as he eased the clutch out, leading the way out of the assembly area a few minutes early, leaving the dormant camera drones behind in their racks.

An unfamiliar voice came over the communicator channel: "*Gladiators, you are ahead of schedule. Wait for your camera drones to activate.*"

Warren keyed his communicator. "We'll wait for them down below."

Warren smiled to himself as he turned from their usual route onto the arterial, instead deviating into a tight roadway to the right, weaving along a short distance before drawing to a halt.

Moving fast, Warren jumped out of his car and led four others to the left, where Cherry had cached the equipment, grabbing items and hustling them into the five chosen vehicles before the camera drones caught up.

In seconds they were back in motion, heading back to the arterial, leaving five Gran Sports idling behind them, each without a driver.

"Alright, Muller," Warren murmured over his shoulder, covering the microphone on his helmet, just in case someone monitored. "Stay low and get ready."

Muller settled low in the back seat of the Daytona and nodded jerkily, his face pale, just as the camera drones swooped into place, circling and weaving around each of the vehicles.

Running up through the gears, Warren accelerated, allowing Gilda to pace him on his left, Bandar on his right, their vehicles roaring to maintain position. They sped together onto the arterial side by side, even as the scenario tone rang out.

The declared scenario didn't matter at all to them. They all knew the true contest had become simply *kill or be killed* and nothing more.

Cherry emerged from the utilitarian shower cubicle provided to the unloved scientists in their cramped little quarters, and stood drying her black hair as Peter Maris sat up on his bed, his own hair askew, blinking at Cherry.

Considering Peter for a moment, Cherry finally said, "You were amazing, Doc."

Peter's eyes opened wider, an expression of confusion chasing an evident bolt of shock.

"Didn't snore, kick, or defend your blankets from theft," Cherry clarified. "Admirable habits in a bunkmate, love."

Peter settled back, his lips shaping a rueful grin. "A bit spiritless of me, I suppose."

Cherry tossed the damp towel aside. "Not at all. Any uninvited border crossings might have painfully tested the tensile strength of your hide, duck. Better all the way around this way." She stepped beside the low bedside and patted Peter's cheek with negligent affection. "Hate to dash away, but the work of a Poppins is never done. Have a few odds and ends to sort out."

Peter's face underwent a change and Cherry wagged a finger.

"None of that now, old fellow. I won't harm a hair on the head of a single soul . . . unless they really ask for it."

Before Peter Maris could think of anything to say, Cherry slipped quietly out the door and made her way to the catacombs, avoiding the scant early risers in the science quarter.

Just as every time she dropped down into the silent labyrinth alone, Cherry wondered if she might meet the body-snatching alien in person and discover if it could successfully digest one of the Blue Light orphans like her. As in every other prior occasion, Cherry found her cached Fireblade untouched, awaiting her, the Thompson submachine gun clipped in its place, and no alien willing to test her mettle. Yet.

Starting the Fireblade's engine, she began to thread her way through the tight, twisting passages, trying to place herself in a key position well before the scenario began. Despite the seemingly shifting geography of Ajanib, Cherry located a choice overwatch position and began her silent vigil, cradling the Thompson as she sat astride her Fireblade.

Over an hour elapsed before she heard the distant, distorted bellow of high-performance combustion engines, their roar growing nearer by the moment.

Peering out, she saw a string of vehicles descending from the circuit track access: Mustangs, including that distinctive green Mustang Catbox favored, Corvettes, and . . . two El Caminos with swivel-mounted machine guns. Cherry continued watching as the El Caminos each went their separate ways, chuckling to herself. "Creatures of habit, clearly," she murmured. "So much the better."

She awaited the scenario start tone before keying the communicator channel in her helmet. "Quack, quack, quack," she clearly enunciated into the mic, keying off and starting the Fireblade.

She needed to carefully reposition and still avoid the static cameras scattered about the catacombs. All she might offer now held value only if she remained unseen.

Cathwaite had spent the earlier part of the day nursing his sore head and sick stomach, finally joining the expanding crowd of gambling clientele in the Members Club, his limping steps more hesitant than ever.

The gleaming wager board already revealed the lines of a dozen early bets, and Cathwaite felt its gloating presence like a baleful gaze, both mocking him and challenging him. He refused to even look at it, instead ordering a cocktail that he didn't even want.

The pressure to act on—or conversely, deliberately disobey—Warren's orders compounded and intensified, and Cathwaite took a sour gulp of his drink as he heard the sudden increase of chatter rising up around him. Against his will, Cathwaite looked up at the holographic scenes filling the periphery of the room. On one side, a line of mixed vehicles trundled along, two El Caminos among them. On the other side four Gran Sports and one Dodge Daytona turned onto the arterial, accelerating hard, a pair of Gran Sports moving up to pace Warren's Daytona on either flank, two Buicks staying close behind.

The pressure in Cathwaite's chest increased as the moment to act or disobey became imminent.

The scenario tone sounded to cheers throughout the Members Club, and still Cathwaite sat frozen, thinking of the millions of guilders that would be his alone once Warren Springer Stowe died in a hail of gunfire... in moments.

The audio channel crackled into life and a woman's voice clearly called out, "Quack, quack, quack," and the odd words ludicrously affected Cathwaite to his core.

As Klaus Benin and Sharif shared a perplexed look, Cathwaite took action as if an animatronic extension of Warren's will, refusing to even think as he placed the absurd, obscene wager.

As expected, a dozen of the more experienced gamblers rounded on Cathwaite, looking at him with a range of expressions from outrage to mockery.

"You are fully realizing the odds are thirty-to-one, dear fellow?" Prabak Bhatt inquired.

"Are they?" Cathwaite said, feeling increasingly idiotic, taking refuge in his drink, draining it in one gulp.

"Do you know something we don't, old boy?" York Rigby asked, looking narrowly at Cathwaite.

"No," Cathwaite said, flagging the server for another strong drink, refusing to look up at the displays, the bravely accelerating gladiators speeding to their doom. "But I wish I did."

CHAPTER 38

Over the roaring engine noise, Warren heard the audio channel come to life, Cherry's voice uttering some flat imitation of a bird call, three distinct quacks. "Alright, do it!" he shouted.

Muller moved, rolling the window halfway down, the wind buffeting him as he fit the freshly fabricated fastener into place and hefted the Lewis machine gun up into position, charging its action and lining up the weapon's sights.

Warren glanced over to see the other Gran Sports following suit, the fat barrels of the Lewis guns elevated and ready. *Any second now* . . .

At the same moment, Warren saw a gleam of light far ahead, a string of incoming tracers arced out, impacting short, and the Lewis guns around him roared back, their odd disclike magazines spinning as they sprayed .30-caliber rounds in three intersecting streams. Only one incoming round struck his car before the opposing machine gun fell silent. As the Lewis gunners reloaded, Warren and his wingmates all fired the fixed Browning machine guns mounted in their vehicles, their six lines of fire sweeping across an El Camino where it sat, thoroughly riddling its body.

It seemed unlikely that either the driver or gunner of the El Camino survived, and Warren looked beyond, seeing a Pontiac GTO and a green Mustang speeding straight toward them. All three Lewis guns began to hammer, the converging streaks of their tracer rounds plunging into Hammerworth's GTO, smoke or steam spewing from the vehicle's hood, the windshield flashing into a spiderweb of cracks. As Hammerworth careened out of control, Catbox jigged his Mustang back and forth, firing bursts from his fixed .30-caliber Brownings as the range closed fast between Warren's crew and Catbox.

Even as all three Lewis guns began to score hits on the green Mustang, Catbox threw it into a hard slide, his guns flashing fire, a sweep of bullets that struck Warren's Daytona and seemed to chase Bandar into a screeching contact with the arterial's wall.

Catbox continued to slide, spinning around broadside, and Warren fired a short burst from his two fixed guns, thoroughly puncturing the Mustang's engine compartment before he juked to the side, slipping past.

A quick glimpse in the mirror confirmed that Bandar still held on back there, struggling to keep up. Warren didn't dare say anything over the communication channel, but Cherry's birdcall indicated that the two El Camino gun-rigs had assumed the same positions as the prior scenario, and he knew they needed to hit the final El Camino all together or risk getting picked apart piecemeal.

Only then did Warren notice the temperature gauge on the Daytona's dashboard beginning to climb into the red, and he cursed quietly. One of the incoming rounds surely scored a hit on a hose or the radiator itself, and the life of his engine was now very short. Warren bit his lip, thinking of the distance, the minutes he needed the Daytona to function or risk losing millions of guilders on Cathwaite's bet—and the lives of his comrades.

Cherry had her own missions to accomplish now and couldn't bail him out. Either he would nurse the Daytona along until they confronted the last El Camino, or his beautiful plan would fail.

Cherry slipped from passage to passage, piloting her Fireblade through torturous paths, bypassing static camera positions and closing as tightly as she dared to the access ramp up to the circuit track.

The Fireblade could take her no farther, and Cherry parked the bike and liberated her Thompson gun along with the small parcel lashed to the minuscule pillion seat. From there, her engineered powers of stealth brought her from shadow to shadow, right to the heart of enemy territory, half expecting that sneaky alien to make its try for her at any moment.

Finally finding a tight alcove in Ajanib's native rock that offered a view of the opposing gladiator assembly area, Cherry opened her parcel, lifting a bottle of adhesive and a salvaged camera free. She had stolen the camera from a drone, smashing it loose, and its outer casing showed signs of its violent liberation; still, it worked for her needs. A thick blob of adhesive applied to the battered casing managed to securely fix it to the aquamarine substrate of Ajanib's rocky skin, and after eyeballing the angle to be sure it covered her target zone, Cherry stealthed back the way she had come. She could not afford to be discovered by any returning foes and their attendant camera drones. Any hint of her presence would eliminate the usefulness of the asset she had just created.

Warren tried to keep the Daytona's RPM gauge under 2,500, hoping he could nurse the car along until they closed with the second El Camino and any other opposing vehicles in its vicinity, but the temperature gauge steadily climbed higher and higher regardless. He was not precisely sure when catastrophic failure was likely to occur, simply because few collectors of Old Earth cars had ever been so foolish as to destroy a priceless treasure with such wanton disregard, but the scent of hot metal increased by the second. His own sweat felt like sulfuric acid oozing into all his many wounds, and the waves of heat beating at him stoked the agony, but he could only lead the attack as quickly as possible and hope the Daytona could survive for . . . maybe two more minutes.

He steered around a sweeping curve, seeing Bandar and Gilda still holding position, their own wingmates trailing behind, ready to branch out at the first available moment.

There . . . ahead the Y-junction approached, and just as Warren spotted the waiting El Camino in its commanding position, its swivel-mounted machine gun spewed fire. Three Lewis guns opened up at almost the same moment, incoming and outgoing tracers flashing, fast hammer blows ringing through the Daytona in quick succession. Warren threw himself painfully to the side below the edge of the dashboard as an arcing line of tracers walked across the Daytona's hood and windshield.

Muller cried out behind Warren at the same moment the Daytona's engine seized up, and Warren blindly threw the transmission out of gear, hearing the continuous firing of machine guns around him, the Daytona rolling on inertia alone.

After a moment, Warren chanced a look through the shattered windshield to see the El Camino dead ahead—literally dead, the gunner visibly slumped across that swivel-mounted gun, the driver not visible anywhere. As he skidded to a halt right beside the bullet-riddled El Camino, Warren looked over his shoulder at a bleeding, white-faced Muller, but a quick assessment showed no imminent sign of flames kindling within the Daytona. "You still hanging in there, Muller?"

"Barely," Muller gritted out. "My elbow got shot. Broken, I think. Hurts like nothing else."

"I'll bet it does, sport," Warren said, painfully freeing himself from the safety harness as he scanned around the Y-junction, seeing Gilda and Bandar speeding off with their two wingmates, hot after a pair of Corvettes, their machine guns chattering, testing the range. The only other motion came from the slow sweep of camera drones around the Daytona and the El Camino.

"Let's see if we can do something with your arm there, chief," Warren murmured as he wrenched himself about in his seat despite the stabs of pain, each wound chafing within the rough fabric of his jumpsuit.

The sudden sound of the Daytona's door being jerked open behind him brought a jolt of surprise, but Muller's terrified grimace, looking over Warren's shoulder, multiplied it by a hundred or so just as a pair of strong hands gripped Warren's collar and leg.

Warren only uttered one startled yelp as he flew backward out through the Daytona's open door, rebounding painfully off the steering wheel on his way to the unyielding road surface. Every wound on his body seemed to detonate with shockwaves of agony, but through the veil of pain Warren looked up into the scowling face of that soldier of fortune, Strayer.

"What the hell, Strayer?" Warren snarled, trying to get up. "We're out of the scenario, with dead cars, don't you—" Strayer interrupted Warren's diatribe with nonverbal communication in the form of a savage kick to Warren's belly.

Warren felt something snap as his body spun to the side, a sharp knifepoint of pain spearing from backbone to sternum through his torso. He clumsily continued the roll, trying for distance from those killing blows, but only managed to curl his knees and elbows across his body when Strayer struck again.

He could not survive much more of this, and Warren knew Cherry could not rescue him this time.

Cathwaite drank steadily, trying to block out the sounds of roaring engines and thundering machine guns, the hoots and cries of the gamblers all around him. He had foolishly, stupidly done the final bidding of Warren Springer Stowe, but he didn't have to imbibe every instant of the slaughter that would bring Warren's demise and his own relative penury at the same moment.

He only looked up from his cocktails when York Rigby clapped him on the shoulder, saying, "Well played indeed, cobber! At thirty-five-to-one!"

A sufficient quantity of intoxicants flowed through Cathwaite's veins to cause some real effort in focusing on the wager board, but he eventually locked onto the key total. He now sported a balance of over 100 million guilders, with more than a billion guilders rolling in total wagers on the board.

As this reality sank in, Cathwaite seemed to isolate Klaus Benin's low, angry voice among the chaos of babble around him, hearing him poisonously cursing. "This is Stowe's doing! He thinks he can cheat me? Thinks he can play me for a damned fool?"

Cathwaite sought Benin's face among the mob, finding Sami staring at Klaus with a critical, measuring gaze that made it clear he also heard Benin's oddly personal grievance. Some nagging recollection dragged Cathwaite's stupefied eyes from Benin back to the wager board. What was it? Oh yes, Warren's ridiculous directive had included a second bet that Cathwaite had barely considered before, since it seemed impossible Warren (or their shared bankroll) could survive long enough to act upon it.

Once again Cathwaite placed the bet, consigning more than fifty million guilders to perdition at merely ten-to-one odds. As he stared into his half-consumed cocktail, Cathwaite tuned out from the ongoing drama of vehicular bellows and thundering weaponry, thinking instead of how many years it would take for him to earn fifty million guilders.

A mixture of startled oaths and a sudden cessation of babble managed to hook Cathwaite's attention yet again, just as York Rigby swore close beside him. "What the hell is he doing?"

Cathwaite scanned blearily through the holographic displays until saw the odd tableau of two bullet-scarred vehicles positioned a short distance apart. One, the El Camino, featured the gory trophy of a slumped body, while the other, Warren's Daytona, bore a pair of wriggling forms that Cathwaite couldn't at first comprehend.

"Is this supposed to be a contest of driving skill?" York called out. "Or is it a pugilism display?"

Klaus Benin's voice interjected, "It is nothing less than that Stowe receiving his just reward." Klaus locked his avid gaze hungrily on the unfolding scene, Savanah Westbrook beside him, her expression revealing a flush of excitement. "How clever will he feel as Strayer stomps the guts out of him? I do wonder this. Teach him to try those fancy, fancy tricks."

Only then did Cathwaite fully understand what unfolded, just as the prone figure of Warren Springer Stowe received a body kick that sent him sprawling across the road surface.

"A million says Stowe survives," York Rigby said, and Cathwaite tore his eyes from the awful display just long enough to see Sami frowning as he looked from Sharif to Klaus, a sick cast coloring Sami's skin.

"Ten million says Strayer kills him," Benin snapped, never looking away from the entrancing violence.

"Fifty million says Stowe survives."

Only a moment after the words were spoken, the immense bet placed, did Cathwaite realize the blurry voice that uttered such a rash pledge was his own.

The kick struck Warren like a sledgehammer and he felt his left shoulder go with an explosive pop as his body rolled, a sound like a cry coming unbidden from his lips.

Strayer hadn't said a word, but now his strangely accented voice spoke out: "Oh? You try this, eh?" Warren looked up, gasping, hoping for a chance to use his most effective tool: his own crafty words. Strayer did not even look at Warren now, smiling faintly, his gaze focused on the Daytona. Warren saw it then, that fat barrel of the Lewis gun edging out through the open window, almost lining up on Strayer.

The blur of movement reminded Warren of Cherry somehow, and in a flash Strayer had the Lewis gun pinned against the doorframe, a twist and a sharp blow bringing Muller's shriek of pain loud to his ears.

Warren seized the brief respite, rolling to his knees, rising up, pawing at his pockets with his right hand, his left arm dangling limp. Fingers clenched tight in a fist, Warren swung with his full strength, that little memento of Torino's jail gripped tight. As soon as his pathetic jail shank bit into Strayer's neck, that super soldier's elbow shot out, connecting with Warren's jaw, sending him flying, his every wound screaming silently, consciousness fading to a pinprick of light. That bead of light lingered, slowly expanding, as sound and pain returned in a crashing wave that had Warren gasping deep in his chest, each breath stabbing him through and through.

Strayer appeared above Warren, staring down, his teeth barred, that ridiculous little weapon protruding from his bull neck. He stomped down hard, his boot crushing Warren's right arm to the unyielding rock as he leaned down closer, his own right hand reaching up to grasp the tape-wrapped shank handle in his neck. "Kill you now . . . with your own tool, eh?" Strayer growled, jerking the shank from his own flesh.

Warren stared right into Strayer's eyes as the shocking spray of blood erupted from the soldier's small, deep wound with the shank pulled free. The eyes widening in surprise dimmed in an instant, the light fading, going blank, and Strayer slumped forward, face-first, his head striking the ground beside Warren's with an audible crack, lifeblood pooling quickly about them both.

CHAPTER 39

"Wake up, Mister Stowe. Wake up now and open your little eyes for me." The annoying feminine voice kept nagging away until Warren finally obeyed.

"There you are," Rose the medico encouraged. "You really must stop fainting this way, Mister Stowe."

Warren tried to correct her misconception but his voice emerged as a gurgling sound. "Probably hard to speak yet," Rose explained. "I shot you full of novafix, and that tends to garble the vocal cords until you get some solid food and drink down your gullet." She poked about Warren's agonized body in her usual fashion as she went on. "I put your shoulder back in its proper place and taped your broken ribs, but the novafix should get it mending quick as can be expec—" Rose broke off, looking over her shoulder.

"Oh? A visitor? A visitor, Mister Stowe." Rose sauntered off and the unexpected figure of Sami appeared above Warren, an expression on Sami's face that Warren had never seen before. It seemed to reveal shame and indignation in equal measures.

"Stowe," Sami greeted, grimacing as he viewed Warren's injuries, "I am very sorry about"—he waved his hand indicating Warren's whole body—"all this. It should not have happened." He hesitated. "And I'm afraid I bring even more bad news."

Sami glanced at Warren's face and then looked away. "While I personally believe it was well within your rights to sneak additional weaponry into the scenario—however you managed that—others have, *ahem*, protested. I hate to say it, but with your bonus from this scenario you could have cashed out of your indenture agreement, but now with this protest and with the, um, approval of my *brother*"—Sami seemed to almost spit the word—"your bonus was suspended. I am truly sorry, truly ashamed."

Warren wanted to tell Sami not to sweat it. If Cathwaite had followed instructions, a rather sizable influx of cash would now be his, reducing his driver bonus to a mere garnish. The state of his vocal cords didn't allow Warren to say anything, so he tried a stiff, pained shrug and a grunt.

Sami shook his head. "It is worse than you think. The whole gladiator scheme will be . . . evolving now, beginning with the next full scenario, and they will not allow you to capitalize upon another such trick, I'm afraid." Sami stared down at Warren. "It will be very, very unhealthy to play the role of gladiator anymore, Stowe . . . on your team at least."

At Warren's inquisitive grunt Sami ran a hand through his dark hair and turned away. "More gladiators arrive today; more of Vogl's sort to oppose you. And for your new recruits? Dozens of unskilled drivers— cannon fodder for the slaughter."

Warren nodded, but his thoughts flew through possibilities, implications, opportunities.

"I will do what I can to moderate the situation for you, Stowe," Sami said, "but my brother holds the reins now. I can only do so much." Sami hesitated, awkwardly reaching out to press Warren's mostly uninjured right shoulder before walking out.

Warren continued to lay thinking for some time before he could only acknowledge that he did not possess enough information to form a new plan . . . yet.

From Sami's perspective, Hammerworth and Catbox should have felt only gratitude for surviving the prior scenario when Stowe's gladiators had clearly held their lives for the taking. The two Bethune-based toughs had accumulated an impressive total in bonus guilders by wrecking and shooting up Stowe's protégés across several prior scenarios, and as deadly as the scenarios had grown, survival had become a prize of its own. But Hammerworth complained now, though not about Stowe or the scenarios.

"Who told these baby-killin' newcomers they get to boss me around, anyway?" he demanded. "That was never part of our contract."

The blackened eye and swollen cheekbone Hammerworth visibly sported made the nature of his complaint quite obvious to Sami, and he shrugged. "I didn't give them any authority over you. I suggest you settle the disputes among your teammates internally, just as you always have before."

Hammerworth scowled. "Being cute, are you?" he growled.

"Not at all," Sami said. "If you dislike the situation, you may take your winnings and go any time you like."

"That's just what I'll do too," Hammerworth said. "And when this bunch of bloody butchers finish with your little game here, you'll wish it was just me and my crew doing what we do."

Sami smiled bitterly, staring at Hammerworth's brutish face. "You know, I don't doubt that you are entirely correct. I already wish it was just you and your, er, crew. Truly."

The transport from Bethune arrived with a far larger company of passengers than ever before. Though only a handful of wealthy new clients lowered themselves to such plebian means of transportation, exiting the dock as quickly as possible and welcomed into Ajanib's luxurious embrace by Belinda Athenos and her team of functionaries, a far greater number of potential new gladiators filed out next.

Sami felt a measure of surprise that these new gladiators looked very little different from many of the construction laborers currently working on Ajanib's numerous improvements. In both groups there were few who stood out as especially attractive representatives of humanity, with far more males than females in evidence. If any characteristic stood out to Sami that differentiated these people from his regular workforce, it was the notable expression most of them wore: a measuring, calculating gleam in their eyes.

The well-dressed, well-manicured man who accompanied this mob looked less like a bureaucrat than Sami had expected, and he strode up to Sharif and Sami with a mixture of confidence and diffidence in his manner that made Sami uneasy.

"You must be Mister Bartson," Sharif said, smiling that warm way that he did so well.

"I am. And you are Sharif Maktoum. Pleasure." Sharif and Bartson shook hands and Sharif nodded toward the line of new cannon fodder being led toward their rough new lodgings.

"All these have spent sufficient hours on the simulator system?" Sharif asked.

Bartson cleared his throat, appraising the alleged gladiators. "*They* certainly seemed to think so. All of them signed the agreement without any hesitation."

Sharif nodded without comment, but Sami listened to Bartson's words with increasing indignation. "Willing cannon fodder is not enough, Mister Bartson. Ajanib features contests of *driving* skill, and if the drivers cannot *drive* it will not be a thrilling sight for anyone."

Bartson flushed, but the glitter in his eye made Sami think it was more driven by anger than embarrassment or shame, accustomed to holding all the power, likely. "Perhaps I should have been more clear," Bartson said. "All of them have spent some hours on the simulator and successfully completed at least one of the simulated racing challenges, so they are *skilled operators*, I would say."

"Very good," Sharif said, seeming to dismiss Sami's concerns without another thought. "Excellent."

Sami felt like protesting more, but knew it wouldn't amount to any real advantage for anyone. The willing bodies had arrived, and very little could now keep them from meeting their grim fate in the catacombs, no matter what Sami said. Prison inmates who raced for a chance at winning freedom might even resent his attempts to aid them.

As the last of these jailbird gladiators filed past, the final contingent of passengers debarked from the transport, and all three men turned their focus on these new figures. Though four of the group appeared to be female, and eight appeared male, they looked more alike than different, not unlike Strayer and Vogl's crew: a group of hard-faced, compactly constructed operatives.

"I saw that bunch keeping to themselves in the transport," Bartson commented, eyeing them curiously. "Who are they?"

Sami didn't look at Bartson as he said, "Those, Bartson? They are the butchers who are going to be slaughtering your *skilled operators* very soon."

"So, tell me, what's your secret?" York Rigby asked as Cathwaite hunched over his late breakfast in the opulent dining parlor, the warm steam from his coffee mug rising to seep into his nostrils, where it slowly melted the block of concrete that seemed to fill his skull.

"Hmph?" Cathwaite snorted in pained confusion. "Secret?"

York plopped down at the table and rested his chin in one palm as he considered Cathwaite. "I hate counting another fellow's guilders, but it is safe to say that you turned a very humble fortune into . . . what? More than five hundred million guilders in an unfashionably brief period of time." York picked up a loose spoon with his free hand and considered its gleaming surface before bringing his gaze back on Cathwaite. "So what's your secret? Does it have something to do with your mysterious injuries that Sami's so eager to avoid discussing?"

Cathwaite felt himself blushing, wishing to discuss anything but how he came to receive his lingering injuries, but his clogged thoughts seemed unable to articulate anything creative under the heat of York's inquiring eyes. "No, not . . . it's—it's nothing like that."

York tilted his head. "No, I suppose it couldn't be. Sami seems as surprised by your success as anyone." His eyes locked onto Cathwaite's. "So, it *is* a secret, then. I can understand that."

Cathwaite thought of that rumor circulating, creating speculations, suspicions . . . trouble. He gulped a little of his coffee, burning his tongue, thinking it through. It dawned upon him: straight truth must be the simplest answer. He matched York's steady gaze. "My secret is— is no secret at all," Cathwaite said. "It is simple, idiotic, blind faith in Warren Springer Stowe . . . and nothing more—God help me!"

With Warren momentarily confined to Medical, Cherry felt the need to keep an eye on his usual bailiwick to the best of her abilities. This required the utmost of her skulking powers, slipping about the shadows of Ajanib's resort areas, avoiding newly installed scanners and cameras as she observed the pieces falling slowly into place.

The drab new recruits from Bethune inhabited a pair of sparse dorm areas, one for the men, the other for women, just like her memories of Torino's delightful jail. They even sported a few Bethune jail guards amongst the standard Maktoum security to contend with any unruly behavior.

At the same moment, Gilda attempted to fill Warren's shoes as well as she could, following his instructions as she labored in Build-Out to create dozens of vehicles, all to Warren's exact specifications, including one distinctive Dodge Daytona. The construction of so many vehicles and the minimum test drives on the oval track meant no full scenario could be considered for at least another day, and the intrusive presence of inspectors looking through every vehicle that rolled out of Build-Out slowed the process even more. Clearly Sharif or Klaus Benin would not allow any unsanctioned weapons to enter the scenario a second time, and the inspectors assured that only two fixed Browning machine guns lay ensconced in each new vehicle.

Unable to invisibly penetrate the medical ward, Cherry could only wonder how long Warren's physical recovery might take and what plan he might hatch to combat Benin's butchers yet again, seeing no ability to fabricate yet another clever work-around with the inspectors nosing about for any hint of a weapon.

At least it appeared that Benin's people only constructed Corvettes and Mustangs for the next scenario rather than something sneaky like their El Camino gun platforms. Perhaps Klaus Benin moderated his violence in the absence of Warren Springer Stowe from this scenario. Certainly no other reason for moderation sprang to Cherry's mind. Neither Klaus nor all the gambling, spectating nobs had drunk their fill of mayhem and bloodshed yet.

When Warren argued so vociferously against Cherry simply eliminating Klaus Benin, he had highlighted her inability to escape Ajanib's confines with billionaire—trillionaire—vigilantes rabidly on her heels. His concern had stoked an unfamiliar warmth in Cherry's innermost workings, and that sensation had done more to curb her plans for Klaus than any dread image of repercussions. She had thought through every permutation of Warren's Big Plan, and, despite what he might think, in none of these eventualities could she perceive an outcome where she left Ajanib alive.

Though Warren clearly could not extrapolate to the inevitable ends, Cherry had accepted her fate.

Here on Ajanib, in this theatre of the macabre, Cherry Aisha would likely face her final day, at last embracing the abyss that had consumed nearly all her Blue Light siblings.

And she was content.

CHAPTER 40

Warren recognized the look-in from Sharif for what it was, assessing Warren's battered appearance where he lay propped up in the hospital bed, his arm bound in a sling. After uttering his sincere-sounding well-wishes, Sharif took his leave, and Warren wasted little time in getting his long legs free from the entangling sheets and making his unsteady way out of Rose's medical torture chamber.

As this odd new scenario drew nearer by the moment, the thoroughfares of Ajanib stood mostly clear of traffic. The few people Warren encountered were all strangers who eyed his bandaged form with curiosity or distaste until he nearly reached his destination. "Well?" The voice speaking practically in his ear made Warren spasm so hard every wound on his body screamed in protest.

"Gah!" Warren yelped eloquently. "Damn it, Cherry! A bell! I'm not kidding! A bell around your neck from now on!"

"Aww, did I give you a fright, Stowe?" Cherry said, looking him over critically. "Oh my goodness, you did get rather socked up, didn't you? It's a skill of yours, I suppose, though *I* rather prefer to give than receive."

Warren glared at Cherry, massaging his throbbing left arm in its sling. "Whatever. We don't have time for all that. Gilda's getting the new drivers assembled, and the new scenario starts in . . . well, very soon." He hesitated before adding, "Did you get the, um, camera in—"

"It's in place," Cherry cut him off. "Looks like they're playing fair so far; all regular cars, fixed guns."

"Hah! Hah!" Warren chortled. "Excellent!" He thought for a moment before asking, "And Cathwaite?"

"Seems I should have negotiated a steeper fee for my abundant services. The old stick is up over a half-billion guilders, I understand."

Warren's humor faded as he stared at Cherry. She stared back, raising an eyebrow. "So? What is it, duck?" she asked after a moment.

The light dawned for him, an unfamiliar sensation rising in his chest. "You've got a secure account somewhere, right? Drop Cathwaite a note with your particulars and direct him to transfer, say, fifty million over to you." Warren nodded half to himself. It was only money, right? "Then you're out, and set for life."

At the pained expression that flitted across Cherry's face, Warren felt a moment of suspicious dread, but she only said, "Very sweet of you, Stowe. Makes me feel all warm inside, but I'll let my chips ride on your little game." Her lips shifted into a cheeky smirk. "Besides, got my romantic sights set on an egghead science bloke, and all that coin is sure to make him pouty, daresay."

Warren continued to fix her with his gaze, trying to understand her true thoughts until she pointed along their route. "Someplace to be, right? Time of the essence and all that?"

Warren gathered himself and dismissed his misgiving for the moment as he began limping along again. "Well, I must congratulate the science fellow someday on his good fortune, but for now, my chariot calls. I shouldn't need you for anything in this scenario unless they add some late arrival to the mix, so just keep a weather eye on that camera, right?"

Cherry rounded on Warren, blocking his path. "You're not thinking of actually driving in this scenario. You're not such an idiot as that . . . are you?"

With his left arm strapped in its sling, Warren shrugged. "Why wouldn't I? Of course I'll drive! But first I've got to get these yokels ready for action."

Cherry shook her head. "Thicker than an elephant omelet!"

Gilda obviously found the process of helping Warren ease into his racing jumpsuit a fertile field for ribald comments, and Warren endured the process with undiminished good humor. Gilda had proven herself both loyal and reliable, qualities Warren rarely found among the teeming hordes of humanity and prized above all. He would happily endure any jokes at his expense in exchange for all that Gilda embodied.

"All our Bethune yobs assembled yet?" Warren asked, drawing a sharp breath as Gilda eased his wounded arm through its corresponding sleeve.

"That smarts, does it?" she innocently inquired. "Seems like it'll feel *way* nicer trying to muscle your steering wheel, hon, right?" Gilda finished the sleeve operation, fitting the arm back into its sling as she answered his actual question, "They should be herded into place about now, but I don't see you teaching them much in the time we got left."

With the agonizing process of dressing complete, Warren wiped a bead of sweat from his brow and nodded. "Lucky I won't have to teach them anything much, then," he said. "Let's go see these paragons, shall we?"

"Your funeral," Gilda groused, starting to lead the way, hesitating a moment. "And theirs," she added, shrugging, "and mine."

Warren laughed, wishing he could roll a cigarette one-handed, but instead he stepped out before the small group of desperate new gladiators, armed with only his smile . . . and of course his incomparable wit.

Guards stood at a few points around the room but Warren knew his audience well, sweeping his gaze across the pale, determined faces, stopping twice at familiar figures among the crowd. What new thoughts sprang up as they saw Warren before them, his face bruised and swollen, arm bound tight in its sling? Did their dreams of driving their way to freedom shrivel upon the vine?

Warren raised his good right arm, and even the buzz of whispered conversation faded. "I'm Warren Springer Stowe, and some of you were actually acquainted with me in the Torino lockup not so long ago." He looked at one particularly unpleasant customer, hailing, "Bailey," and another mound of muscle, "Monk." He smiled. "Since Monk beat me like a dirty rug back in Torino, I've stacked up a fat wad of guilders by driving here and battling whoever they threw at us."

"Looks like you're still getting your ass beat," someone called out from the watchful audience.

"True," Warren said, pointing his index finger toward the speaker. "True, but not for free anymore."

A few laughs broke out from the crowd and Warren kept smiling, feeling the wave of his unstoppable charisma beginning to surge and extend beyond his bruised and injured body, beyond his nagging awareness of unknown variables.

"So, you lot got some time in a simulator and now you think you can drive, right?" Warren said, assessing the sea of skeptical expressions aimed at him. "Hate to bring the bad news, friends, but you really *can't*. Not by Ajanib standards."

The murmur of words were not especially discernible to Warren, but he interpreted the general meaning easily enough, seeing even the guards stirring nervously at the suddenly agitated emotional current.

"But..." Warren said, then raising his voice, "*But!*" The murmurs died down and he scanned the angry eyes aimed at him. "You have a choice today: You can choose to try your amazing driving skills on your own . . . and serve as a really lovely moving target for the bastards out there, or you can do what I tell you and probably survive. It's your choice."

Warren stood there, feeling them all falling into the palm of his hand, waiting for him to lead them.

"You see, the trick to surviving the catacombs today will be less about speed or sheer driving skill, and more about one thing: range!"

The gamblers filtered into the Members Club, eager for this new scenario that promised to be something quite special. Sami retained no heart for it, seeing his beautiful dream seized and distorted by Sharif and Klaus Benin, and he only attended now under relentless pressure from Sharif to play the good host.

Sami sourly eyed the clientele, many of whom were now scarcely known to him, but there among them were almost all of those original clients: Prabak Bhatt, Savanah Westbrook, York Rigby, Klaus Benin, and a number of the others. Even Cathwaite now became something of a notable figure, repeatedly winning against remarkable odds, accruing a sizable fortune and yet seeming to grow increasingly morose even as his wealth multiplied.

The bureaucratic prig from Torino, Bartson, didn't seem to realize how poorly he fit in within this crowd, smiling comfortably as he sipped a cocktail far above his pay grade. He seemed in great spirits as he prepared to watch a slaughter he had helped engineer.

Belinda Athenos materialized at Sami's elbow, leaning close to whisper in his ear. Sami heard her words and nodded in a businesslike manner, dismissing her even as he worked to keep the smile off his face. Belinda surely thought Sami would share her news with Sharif and Benin, and likely even tell Bartson, but Sami saw no reason to enlighten anyone. Stowe's mobility and the plans he had just disclosed to his own pathetic gladiators would remain a secret for at least a little longer, and Sami's own heart felt considerably lighter as he faced the prospect of the fast-approaching scenario.

Cherry waited until Peter Maris yielded to his inevitable work duties before slipping through the bolt-hole down to Ajanib's catacombs, undetected by his overanxious scrutiny. She brought a purloined palm slate with her to monitor her also-borrowed camera where it scanned for any illicit curveballs from Vogl's cutthroats. If they tried any eleventh-hour stunt she would be poised to respond immediately.

As ever before, the Fireblade awaited her in its concealed niche, no alien entity on hand to pounce, the Thompson clipped into place, and Cherry started the 954 engine without a moment's hesitation. She set out to what had become her favored overwatch position, weaving through Ajanib's convoluted and deceptive bowels with easy assurance now. She had become the lone mistress of this domain, with nothing and no one to truly challenge her.

Just after she killed the Fireblade's engine and removed her helmet to begin her surveillance, Cherry discovered *someone* did indeed challenge her lone mastery.

The muted sound of a footfall probably would not have been detectable by any normal human being, but it brought Cherry an instant download of realizations, facts aligning in a flash, so that when she turned to see the figure quietly emerge from a tight alcove nearby she already knew whom she would behold.

"You must be Vogl," Cherry said, eyeing the powerfully built woman without stirring a muscle.

Vogl's cold, emotionless expression did not change. "You are Poppins, and predictable," she said, and drew a large knife silently from its sheath in one slow, smooth motion, her gaze fixed on Cherry. "Very pretty, Poppins."

Cherry thought about snatching up the Thompson from beside her left leg, but the feeling of an uneven contest brought the hideous memory of Panawaat to her mind. "Can't we talk about this?" Cherry asked, leaving the Thompson as she slipped both feet to the ground, her body internally changing in a hundred small ways, responding to a threat.

Vogl did not answer with words, springing forward to attack, the knife held low and close. Cherry leaped to the side, the edge of her hand deflecting the knife a handsbreadth off its thrust, narrowly missing her skin. Like any true pro, Vogl didn't pause or hesitate, the first attack flowing into a second and third, Cherry dodging, slipping back, and deflecting. Only when she knocked Vogl's slashing blade high enough off the centerline did Cherry initiate her own counterattack, her right foot snapping forward with superhuman speed to strike beneath Vogl's left knee. Any normal person struck with such force would have experienced a shattered joint, but Vogl seemed only staggered by the kick, her knee partially buckling.

"Fancy," Cherry said, backing away as Vogl paused, assessing anew. "Reinforced joint. Bone overlays. What? Muscle graft mesh too?" Cherry saw Vogl shift the long knife to her left hand, settling upon a fresh course of attack. "Someone spent a bundle on all your bits, old stick."

Vogl said nothing in response, surging forward again, her left leg visibly wobbling from Cherry's blow... until it wasn't. The feint and the exaggerated injury were perfectly executed, Vogl's razor-edged knife catching Cherry across her forearm, where it cut right through her sleeve and should have flayed her flesh down to white bone. With the symbiote rendering her skin into a sort of flexible armor, Vogl's knife blade barely left a mark.

Only then did Cherry spot any expression on Vogl's face for a frozen instant between them, the sound of an indrawn breath. "You are Blue Light," Vogl stated in a dead tone.

"Right you are, love," Cherry said, turning her entire body into a fulcrum of force, hammering a straight kick into Vogl's sternum that launched the larger woman backward, rolling back into the niche from where she had emerged.

The flash of red illumination and the startled gasp from Vogl caused Cherry to leap recklessly forward. The broad, glittering shape undulating across the stony ground seemed to have consumed Vogl in an instant and Cherry launched her attack, spinning a lightning kick that solidly contacted the dazzling mosaic of glowing rubies. In the next instant, Cherry seemed to be fighting a bewildering battle for her life, her alien opponent absorbing her most powerful strikes, then latching onto a wrist or ankle with iron bands from which she could scarcely break free.

In a moment of dawning desperation, Cherry flipped back and cannoned a powerful kick straight up to a dense cluster of gleaming eyelets even as she flung herself backward. She wrenched free, landing on her feet, and the broad, glowing shape seemed to hesitate for a moment.

Cherry stared, her hands raised to attack or defend, her augmented vision striving to comprehend the creature before her.

"Come on, then," Cherry said, the symbiote stirring through her sinews, tightening her body like a steel trap. "Come have a taste."

The rippling shape pulsed to an invisible current, its form shifting, broadening, the ruby motes moving outward until the creature's center became a dark void, a pool of rippling darkness.

Cherry's brows lowered as she witnessed the slow transformation taking place, her own body easing from its defensive posture, the symbiote reluctantly subsiding within her.

"I see," Cherry whispered to herself, and the glowing entity seemed to fragment into a million glowing flecks, each speck drifting to the floor, walls, ceiling, disappearing back into the aquamarine luminance of Ajanib.

CHAPTER 41

With just a small handful of his original gladiators still riding along, risking their necks, Warren only pulled them up for a moment as the utility lift descended to the catacombs. "Just stick with your assigned group and watch out for Vogl slipping some cars in behind you. If she does, either you'll hold them off or it'll be a slaughter, right?"

They all nodded as the lift doors opened to the crowded assembly area. Warren, battered and bruised, his left arm immobilized in its sling, still smiled at the sight of so many glossy Mustangs and Corvettes assembled in one place, waiting for their painfully inept drivers to take them into battle.

Those novice drivers ambled out to their waiting vehicles in ones and twos, looking about the large chamber uncertainly, helmets clutched in nervous hands as Warren and his core of more experienced drivers strode to their respective vehicles. The cargo carts followed, loading boxes of .30-caliber ammunition into car after car.

Warren leaned painfully down to charge both of his Browning machine guns one-armed, then waited for the new drivers to get themselves ready and strapped in. Unlike every prior scenario, Warren would not lead the gladiators out into the catacombs; instead he was forced to impatiently await the slow, lurching process of drivers experiencing a true mechanical clutch and gears for the first time. Particularly with a dose of nerves in the mix, the process would not feel at all similar to their time on the simulator system, and this was proven as several drivers accidentally stalled out as they attempted to get into motion.

Eventually, Warren's entire element got underway, the camera drones filling the air above them even as that air became hazy from so many engines rumbling, roaring, or spluttering exhaust fumes. Warren drove and shifted one-handed, using his knee to steady the wheel as he downshifted to accommodate one of his new gladiators lurching all over the road.

At least his people all followed his direction—so far at least—keeping their speed low and sticking to the first arterial. Gilda would take her element on the south arterial next, hopefully getting them all assembled before the scenario began.

Thinking through the approaching conflict, Warren calculated their chances of surviving. If Vogl's people hadn't snuck some tricky weaponry down, and if Vogl didn't figure a way to backdoor these poor amateur gladiators, and if these same amateurs managed to keep their vehicles rolling more less straight ahead, Warren thought their odds of winning were substantially better than a coin toss.

With this comforting calculation complete, Warren felt considerably better. Snatching victory from Klaus Benin's pets despite all these obstacles and impediments seemed like a suitable demonstration of Warren's ability to turn any pile of dung into a rose garden. It would be a splendid day... if only a few small details went his way...

The scenario start tone resounded through their shared audio channel, and the moment of truth sped toward them.

Within the Members Club, Cathwaite should have enjoyed the fresh acceptance he received as the most nouveau member of the nouveau riche, now risking fortunes on par with at least the smallest fish in this very exclusive pond, but he now seemed constitutionally unable to truly relax. The odd crosscurrents between Klaus Benin and Sami, Savanah Westbrook's barely veiled hostility toward him, and Sharif's penetrating gaze all served to stoke Cathwaite's unease. Aside from those delightful ingredients, Cathwaite also carried the latest orders from Warren that some unknown hand had slipped under his door, and, as always, Warren's directives provoked no shortage of jitters for Cathwaite.

Adding to the iniquitous sense of risking an immense fortune on a single hazardous bet, Cathwaite also faced an unpleasant degree of skeptical speculation from York Rigby and other gamblers who viewed his near-perfect wager record in an uncomfortable light. Really, who wouldn't?

Never had he possessed a tenth of the fortune that he was about to blindly risk once again.

A murmured conversation and one particular holographic display drew Cathwaite's attention from his grim imaginings. The display flickered into life to feature one lone, stationary Corvette, a camera drone clearly revealing the absence of any driver.

"Isn't that Vogl's Corvette?" Sami inquired. "Where is she?"

Benin's sharklike smile abraded Cathwaite's nerves. "Vogl? She's just handling a little needed cleanup."

Sami frowned. "She wandered away from her vehicle in the catacombs? Does she have an escort drone and—"

"Vogl can take care of herself," Benin said, cutting Sami sharply off.

In just a few weeks, Klaus Benin had lost well more than a billion guilders on wagers, and his very thin cloak of urbanity had all but disappeared with his vanishing bankroll. Even Savanah Westbrook had been the recipient of his biting words, and Cathwaite momentarily pondered the proclivity of beautiful women for tyrannical nutjobs before turning his attention back to the conversation.

"She's going to miss the scenario if she doesn't finish, er, cleaning up soon, Klaus," Sami said, seeming to enjoy baiting Benin more and more as the days passed.

"She'll be there," Klaus said, never taking his eyes off the holographic image of Vogl's waiting Corvette.

Other holographic displays now revealed the host of novice gladiators attempting to inexpertly negotiate their way out into the catacombs.

Savanah Westbrook suddenly pointed at one display. "There's a Daytona; I thought Stowe was in hospital still."

For once Klaus looked away from Vogl's Corvette, grating out, "That's his number." He turned accusingly toward Sami. "What's he doing?"

"Driving one-handed, I presume," Sami said with a shrug, a faint smile hovering about his mouth.

York Rigby spoke up near Cathwaite. "Still risk some coin on Stowe, even if he's driving one-handed?"

"Uh..." Cathwaite said, suddenly on the spot, thinking of the orders resting in his pocket for that very moment. "I don't know. These new drivers with him are terrible."

"But"—York turned to point at Vogl's still-unoccupied Corvette— "Vogl's not even around, looks like. Might have disappeared in the catacombs like the others."

York's comment dragged Klaus back to the display. "Where the hell is she?" Klaus growled through gritted teeth.

At that moment, the scenario start tone rang out and the entire company of the Members Club observed a bizarre sight. Instead of the usual launch of mad acceleration among the gladiator vehicles at the outset of a scenario, or the billiards-like scatter into the maze of side passages, the novice gladiators maintained their low speed, holding to the arterials, stacked three cars abreast.

Cathwaite followed the script, mustering a short laugh. "These people can't even drive. It's going to be a slaughter." He placed his first small wager: fifty thousand on Vogl's cutthroats. In the next few moments the odds against Warren and his band of convict drivers climbed from three-to-one, up and up until it topped ten-to-one.

"You've got to hand it to Stowe," Cathwaite said. "Even driving one-handed, stuck behind all these losers, he's got a certain something." He waited just a moment before adding, "I'll probably hate myself tomorrow, but..." He placed the second-largest wager in his life, as gamblers all around him looked from the holographic displays to Cathwaite, their expressions spanning the range.

Warren saw the big, sweeping curve approaching and silently prayed that the timing would come together... even close to right, though they still advanced at a ridiculously low speed. The first line started through the sweeper, Warren close behind, and as the arterial revealed the long straightaway ahead, he called the first signal through the communication channel: "*Tally whore!*"

If the novice drivers heard him, and if they remembered their instructions, they should reach for that innocent-looking switch each of them carried among the gauges on their respective dashboards...

Warren stared at the three vehicles driving unsteadily abreast just ahead of him, waiting... waiting. First the Corvette on the left revealed a change, then both of the Mustangs, their headlights slowly angling higher and higher as they triggered the air-suspension systems Gilda had secretly fabbed into all the new vehicles at Warren's command.

Warren had only a moment of quiet satisfaction before approaching headlights appeared in the distance before them. As he had directed, the novice drivers of the first line each squeezed their triggers as soon as they spotted the nearing headlights, tracers arcing up high, halfway to the rocky ceiling before raining down in the distance. As the opposing vehicles closed, driving through the hail of long-range fire, Warren's new pupils released their air-suspensions, firing steadily, their twin Browning machine guns sending streams of tracer rounds at lower and lower trajectories.

Before the opposing vehicles ever came within their own firing range, they were riddled with bullets.

Warren grinned. Benin and Sharif thought they could contain his genius through limiting his access to weaponry, but they now received a sharp lesson in just how far beyond them his vision extended.

Now, if only Gilda's group could employ the same technique as flawlessly...

After Warren's inscrutable call of "*Tally whore!*" Klaus Benin stared at the holographic images flooding in, clearly obtaining no joy from the wicked display of all his own antique weaponry in action. Tracers flew at extreme range, pounding Vogl's drivers practically as soon as they spotted distant headlights, rounds slamming through metal and glass, and sometimes through flesh, neutralizing car after car.

Prabak Bhatt seemed immune to the mute rage emanating from Klaus. "It appears your military geniuses could not adapt so well to a tiny innovation from their foes, no?"

Cathwaite saw Klaus Benin's jaw clench, his white-knuckled fists quivering, and wondered how Prabak stood so calmly beside that cold-blooded maniac. Klaus peeled back his lips, speaking slowly, almost mechanically. "Another trick from Stowe—a silly, dirty little gimmick." His head turned. "And he *murdered* my tactical commander before the scenario began."

That bureaucratic stiff, Bartson from Bethune, perked up at the mention of murder and Stowe in the same breath, his mouth half filled with succulent appetizers, but Prabak ignored Bartson, only smiling at Klaus. "Murder, you say? But Stowe went from the hospital straight to the scenario. And how could a half-dead driver like Stowe kill a warrior like Vogl, anyway? Don't you mean the catacombs consumed Vogl, just like the others?"

"No!" Klaus snapped. "Somehow or other that murderous Poppins woman killed Vogl, and she is tied together with Stowe. I'm sure of it!"

Even Sharif began to frown at Benin's angry, unhinged tirade, but Bartson swallowed his appetizers, gracelessly interjecting, "Poppins? Which Poppins woman? What's all this talk of murder?"

Savanah reached out to the tabletop controls, selecting a highlight sequence from earlier scenarios, and flipping through the scenes until she found the camera drone footage displaying that distinctive red-and-black Fireblade motorcycle sweeping up to a halt in the assembly area, the lithe rider tugging her helmet free to reveal a woman of dark tresses and exotic features, freezing the image.

"That's Mary Poppins," Savanah Westbrook declared. "She snuck into Ajanib, tried to kill . . . someone, and escaped into the catacombs."

For once the cocky, self-absorbed expression disappeared from Bartson's face, his jaw visibly dropping as he stared at the frozen image of the dark-haired beauty. "You are wrong," Bartson said after a moment, moistening his mouth, his gaze never leaving the holographic display. "That's not Mary Poppins . . . It's Betty Boop!"

CHAPTER 42

Returning to the assembly area in the company of so many utterly unskilled drivers would normally have taxed Warren's patience to the extreme, maneuvering around lurching, stalling, weaving vehicles, wary of placing himself broadside to any of their gunports. A fumbling, nervous driver might bungle their way into blasting a burst of bullets into the unwary. But despite all that, and the aching, throbbing collection of injuries he endured, Warren felt only satisfaction.

Aside from the future winnings Cathwaite undoubtedly netted, Warren had demonstrated the brilliance of his cunning before the most exclusive, wealthiest audience in the known galaxy, and the sensation felt intoxicating. The waiting wall of Maktoum security formed a lumpy, heavy-handed buzzkill that Warren had not anticipated. The sphere of tenuous respect he had experienced within Ajanib since achieving his accord with Sami had clearly vanished, the uniformed security stiffs illustrating this point by painfully seizing Warren and jerking him from the Daytona without a word of explanation.

"Ow! Easy, Attila!" Warren yelled, his new gladiators looking on, their triumphant smiles fading away in confusion. As they dragged the limping, staggering Warren to the lifts, he caught one glimpse of Gilda staring after him, the ever-present chew-gum a frozen lump in her cheek.

As soon as the lift doors closed upon them, Warren looked to the guard on his right. "Say there, sport, what's this all about, hmm?" he asked as calmly as possible, receiving nothing in response.

They snatched him out of the lift as soon as the doors opened, hustling him in an undignified manner to a portion of Ajanib he had never visited before: the holding cells, where they tossed him like a soiled diaper.

Three hours might generally toll quickly for any middle-aged person with an active mind, but locked within a cell, segregated from all sources of information, and a host of injuries serving as one's only distraction, Warren found time creeping by at a glacial pace. When the sound of approaching footsteps reached his ears he didn't really care who he might face, just as a break from the monotonous silence.

The appearance of the Bethune chief prosecutor, Bartson, beside Sharif Maktoum, certainly provided a moment of surprise for Warren, but his mind quickly chewed through likelihoods even as he measured the censorious expression on Sharif's face. The muscle-bound security shirts completed the ensemble but to Warren they served as mere decoration.

"Ah! Bartson!" Warren greeted with his usual aplomb. "Here on Ajanib? Seems a bit above the touch of a civil servant. What are you doing? Selling these new gladiators to them by the pound?"

Sharif replied for Bartson. "You don't seem to understand the gravity of your situation, Stowe. Mister Bartson here provided useful information regarding your crime partner, Miss Betty Boop, and now we comprehend the depths of your criminal conduct."

"'Crime partner'?" Warren repeated, chuckling. "Wow! Take a pretty girl out for a little unsanctioned test drive and—"

"You can cease all the prevarication," Sharif interrupted. "It might confuse Sami, but it only bores me. And now your fate returns to its natural condition." Sharif only paused a moment before continuing. "Due to your fraudulent actions, your partnership contract with Sami is null and void. You now have only two possible outcomes for the remainder of your life: You will either die laboring as an unremarkable asset of the Maktoum Corporation, or . . . you will die in a Bethune prison while serving a very, very long sentence."

"Huh, seems like a lot of dying planned for me, right?" Warren mused. "Feels a trifle extreme simply because a violent tart trailed me out to Ajanib for some reason and stuck a knife in me. Hardly seems even a Bethune court would sentence me to a *very, very long* sentence for that."

Bartson spoke up now, that self-satisfied grin impossible to conceal. "Courts on Bethune hand out *very, very long sentences* for murder, Stowe."

Warren wondered what game they played at now. "Murder? Is that what this is supposed to be about? For defending myself from Strayer?" He looked between Sharif and Bartson. "Because it obviously can't be from any loss of life during a scenario, or Sharif here would be on the hook for a half dozen contract killings at least."

From the flicker in Sharif's eyes Warren knew his words scored at least a partial hit, but Bartson bulled in. "Don't play ignorant, Stowe—"

"Impossible!" Stowe interrupted. "I could never play ignorant, Bartson. I lack the natural aptitude someone like you comes by from birth."

Bartson flushed angrily. "You are pretending that your crime partner, Betty Boop, has not systematically, violently eliminated your opponents, most recently Karin Vogl."

Lights finally illuminated for Warren, seeing the rough outline that led to this moment, but he needed more information. "Boop? I thought she got body-snatched in the catacombs days ago . . . She show up somewhere?"

Again he saw the telltale flicker in Sharif's eyes, and again Bartson stepped in. "Obviously there's been no time to track Miss Boop down and conduct a full investigation, but you don't know Torino juries like I do, Stowe. After I connect the dots for them, it will be very obvious that Boop has been doing your dirty work behind the scenes. A very nasty duo that will make the average juror's blood run cold."

"I'd like to see that," Warren said. "A trial where I explain exactly how the superrich are exploiting regular folk, killing them off for entertainment . . . That seems like an interesting revelation for these juries that you know so well."

Bartson seemed to almost glance toward Sharif, and Warren pressed his advantage. "But you aren't here threatening me with imaginary murders for nothing . . . Is this all just a game to void my contract with Sami? Or have we got some other grimy hijinks in mind?"

Sharif frowned at Warren. "There's nothing imaginary about the trouble you face, Stowe."

Warren snorted. "Unless you plan to simply murder me yourselves, the trouble *I* can create for *you* is not imaginary, Sharif, so why don't we quit this game of threats and get down to details."

Sharif's expression hardened. "Your confidence is based upon nothing, and there is nothing left to discuss. You are merely another Maktoum indentured asset. You will simply drive in the next scenario like every other gladiator, with no more cheating maneuvers, no more tricks—and no more unsanctioned violence from this Boop woman to stack the odds always in your favor."

Warren smiled. "Is that all? What a lot of chest-beating over nothing. Let's get out of this cell and you fellows can go get to your dinner. It's got to be about that time, right?"

"And as an indentured asset," Sharif continued, ignoring Warren entirely, "you will remain in this cell until you are escorted to the next scenario. If you don't choose to participate you will be delivered to the jail on Bethune and await trial for murder. Those are the only options that remain to you."

Cherry clambered up the rocky chute into the science quarter of Ajanib to find Peter Maris waiting as he had on prior occasions, only now she spotted immediate signs of trouble.

"Doc, you really needn't sit about this drafty cavern like this. Can't be comfortable," she said, measuring the wounded look in his eyes . . . and the communicator clenched in his hands, both with a sense of internal foreboding.

"You lied to me," Peter said in a quiet voice.

Cherry folded her arms and leaned against one craggy wall. "Did I now? I don't recall any lies of significance, so what's got you all in a state, then?"

"Your name's not Poppins at all."

Cherry waited somewhat anxiously for Peter's next words. Which old name had he learned?

"You're—you're Betty Boop. Some old girlfriend of Warren Springer Stowe's."

Everything became crystal clear in an instant for Cherry, including the depths of Peter's wounded expression. "Oh my! Someone's been telling tall tales, I daresay."

Peter stared at her. "Are you claiming you're *not* Betty Boop?"

Cherry shrugged. "I've used the name, but Stowe and I were never an item. How many knives do I have to stick in the man to make that clear?"

Her mind sped quickly through implications beyond Peter's sense of betrayal. If the Boop name had become such an article of interest, then her prior connection to Warren had undoubtedly created real trouble for him too...but at the moment the wounded male ego served as her first hurdle.

Though Cherry's experience in romantic matters mostly dated back to her youth, she could practically see the unhappy imaginings ripple through Peter's mind. He surely visualized Cherry leading him on, laughing behind his back as she snuck off to her *real* lover in Warren Springer Stowe. Then Peter's doubts undoubtedly going on to compare himself unfavorably with the exotic, eccentric Stowe in the most painful ways possible.

She saw the line between Peter's brows as he struggled, wanting to believe what she said, her words colliding with his imagined doubts, his own small zones of inadequacy growing into vast canyons in his tortured estimation.

His gaze bored into her eyes. "I don't think you're telling me everything."

Cherry smiled, tilting her head to one side with a half shrug. "Don't feel bad. I don't tell *anyone* everything."

Peter looked down miserably, various doubts playing across his face. "Tell you what, Doc," she said at last, "what's the most pressing question you've got? If I answer that, can we adjourn to a snack and maybe some access to your little shower?"

Peter looked back up, suddenly intent. "Did you meet Vogl down there?"

Cherry nodded. "We exchanged a couple of words."

Peter's mouth formed a compressed line just before he asked. "And did you...did you kill her?"

Cherry blinked. "While that's *two* questions, Doc, I'll tell you, when Vogl and I parted, she was alive. Word of proud Boop on it!"

When Cathwaite stood from the last fragments of a sumptuous dinner, he found his way suddenly blocked by Klaus Benin, Savanah Westbrook hovering nearby, the triumphant expressions they shared making him immediately uneasy.

Michael Mersault

"Ah, Cathwaite, the luckiest man in the history of Bethune," Klaus proclaimed in place of a greeting. "Turned a few million guilders into, what? More than a billion now?" He shared a smile with Savanah before turning his focus back on Cathwaite, the smile hardening into something far more savage. "But will you still be so lucky now?"

Prabak Bhatt sat nearby, dabbing his lips with a creamy white napkin. "What's this? What are you going on about now, Benin? No one is lucky forever. You should know that better than most, earning such a respectable fortune through one blessing of chance after another in your business, then losing... oh, so many guilders here in Ajanib so quickly."

Klaus shot a poisonous glare at Prabak. "I am speaking of *unreasonable* luck." His eyes returned to Cathwaite. "A luck *created* by, shall we say, *stealthy* methods."

"I—I don't understand what you mean," Cathwaite said, moistening his dry lips, looking uneasily from Klaus to Savanah, then on to Prabak.

Benin's grin expanded. "Don't you? Haven't you heard that Warren Springer Stowe is confined within a holding cell even now?"

"Difficult to bet on a fellow who is barred from competing, isn't it?" Prabak offered.

"Oh, he will compete," Klaus said. "As a Maktoum indenture he will be escorted from his cell to the next scenario, with no more of these shameless cheats and gimmicks." Klaus stared hard at Cathwaite. "And now we will see if the luckiest man of Bethune still bets on Stowe when no cheating is permitted, or if all his great luck was manufactured artificially."

"Hmm," Prabak mused thoughtfully. "Yes, I suppose it will be informative to see—not the extent of dear Cathwaite's luck, which we all know to be so damnably fickle, but the extent of his confidence, which he has displayed over and over, risking great sums. Will the confidence remain?"

Cathwaite looked from Prabak to Klaus, seeing a new, sharklike smile bared. "Yes, Cathwaite, will your confidence remain? Or will it fall, right along with Stowe?" He chuckled, suddenly gleeful. "And you may wish to know, more security and constables are arriving soon. They will comb the catacombs until they find Stowe's murderous partner, that Boop woman."

Cathwaite wasn't sure what Poppins, or Boop, was supposed to mean to him and said as much: "Boop? Good . . . if she's even alive."

Savanah stepped near, wrapping one smooth arm around Benin's waist as she looked between Prabak and Cathwaite. "How about a side bet, lucky man?" Klaus said to Cathwaite. "What would you bet that Boop and Stowe survive to the end of the week?"

Cathwaite wondered if Warren could have imagined he would be confined in a cell when he issued all his prior instructions. Could he have any idea what a position his debacle placed Cathwaite in?

He swallowed doubts and acid.

"What odds are you talking, Klaus?"

CHAPTER 43

Along with even more wealthy clients flooding into Ajanib, Sami witnessed his beautiful creation polluted by dozens of armed constables brought out from Bethune. They went about in clusters, poking and prying through every portion of the worker areas and on down into the catacombs.

Good luck finding anything or anyone in that maze.

Meanwhile Klaus claimed sudden, exclusive reign over Build-Out with Sharif's full permission, working steadily upon what he promised to be the greatest display in Ajanib's brief, spectacular history. Just from his fleeting glimpse of Benin's work, Sami felt not only doubts, but a further sense of eroding vision. The scenarios of Ajanib had originally been a living re-creation of muscular elegance in the form of slick and glossy performance vehicles. What Klaus now created could only be viewed as grim, brutal, or utilitarian—vehicles that communicated a certain blocky militarism.

Rather than voicing utterly useless complaints, Sami left Build-Out and avoided his clientele, going instead to the security cell and Warren Springer Stowe.

"Come to see the condemned, Sami?" Warren greeted, smiling though he sat on his slender bunk with his wounded arm clutched against his chest, his racing jumpsuit peeled down to his waist.

"I came to apologize, Stowe," Sami said, though the security stood nearby, hearing every word and likely making a record to share with Sharif. "Everything is going to hell here, and I've got little say over any of it. Klaus is planning some big splash for this next scenario and he's got Build-Out so stacked that new clients can't get in to create their

277

own cars. Such ugly things he's making too. A Dodge vehicle of sorts, but one that looks like a great, swollen El Camino, kind of."

Warren's eyes narrowed. "Dodge Power Wagons?"

"Yes, er, I believe so."

"Not ugly, then. Not really," Warren said, his expression becoming thoughtful.

Sami shrugged, wondering what Sharif would later say about this conversation. "Well, they're sure as hell not Mustangs or Corvettes or Barracudas," he said. "And Benin is only part of the mess. We've got a small army of Bethune constables searching all over for that Betty Boop, making a damned nuisance of themselves."

Sami couldn't read the expression on Warren's face until a mocking smile appeared. "Wonder how many of them go missing in the catacombs? Will Bartson accuse Boop of murdering every one of them that gets body-snatched?"

"Maybe. Who knows?" Sami said. "I have no idea what to expect anymore."

"Did you expect Sharif to void our contract?" Warren inquired, smiling.

Sami felt the heat on his face. "No. It's—it's that Klaus."

Warren's expression didn't change, staring at Sami.

"Really," Sami said. "Our parents would have disapproved, I know it." The listening security stiffs would really have some juicy stories to tell Sharif.

"Whatever the case, Sami," Warren said, "I'm beginning to take it personally, and as much as I loved the whole idea of Ajanib, I'm thinking of burning the whole thing down."

Though Sami found a dozen questions bubbling up at Warren's haughty threat, already too much had been said before witnesses. Looking at Warren, his skin discolored and bandaged, one-armed, sitting in a sterile cell, it almost seemed the disasters had cracked his intellect. As a helpless indentured asset, locked in a tiny cell, how did he think he could burn anything down?

While Peter Maris still seemed miserably plagued by doubts and uncertainties, Cherry felt a measure of success merely sharing a companionable meal with him, emerging from the shower to find him frowning at a palm slate.

"Do all science blokes invest in strawberry body wash, Doc?" she asked, toweling her dark hair dry. "Or is this your own exclusive genius at work? It's fab."

Peter brought his troubled gaze up, not seeming to hear her. "Warren Springer Stowe has been detained. Locked in a cell."

Cherry settled backward on a chair, leaning her arms across the back as she considered Peter. "Do him good, I'm sure. Could stand to lose some weight in that great swollen head of his."

"Don't you understand?" Peter said in a low voice, his eyes flicking to her and away. "They took him because of you. They—they claim you both conspired to murder Vogl."

"Well, there you are," Cherry replied. "I didn't kill Vogl, so it won't amount to anything."

"That Bartson fellow seems to think otherwise."

Awareness began to dawn. "Bartson," Cherry said with sudden clarity, nodding slowly. "Oh, I see now. That cheeky yob has everyone in a pucker over nothing. Should have guessed it was some such wanker."

"And he's brought a mob of constables," Peter went on. "They're tearing the place apart trying to find you."

Cherry sat up. "A *mob* of coppers? That's not just Bartson, then. Klaus or Sharif Maktoum must be dropping some coin for all that, covering costs."

"Does it matter who's paying the bills?" Peter said, his face lined with growing disquiet. "When the constables start asking questions, they will speak to my colleagues . . . to Doctor Sang. And when she tells them what she knows about . . . our conversation, they'll be looking for answers . . . from me."

Cherry quietly considered Peter Maris until he looked down, avoiding her eyes, revealing everything by this one act. "I see." She stood slowly. "Don't feel too bad, Doc. Chivalry never really died, you know. It just grew very bloody timid." Peter flushed, opening his mouth, but Cherry went on, looking down at the slashed sleeve of her jumpsuit. "You can tell them whatever you wish, old stick, but if you're smart you'll go all stiff-necked and scientific on them; tell them they've got no authority to question you and all that. Answer one question for them and they'll have you confessing your sins back to childhood."

Cherry grabbed up her own purloined palm slate and moved

toward the door. Peter looked up at her one last time, his eyes stricken. "I am sorry."

Cherry paused, flashing him a forced smile as she put her hand to the door. "You won't be, Doc. I've been on good behavior because of your delicate sensibilities. After I'm through with this lot you'll be happy to see the last of me!"

Over the dozen angry wounds throbbing their discontent, Warren tried to concentrate, thinking through Klaus Benin's likely game.

Why Dodge Power Wagons? Surely some variation on the El Camino gun rig was envisioned now, but with such a low-wattage screwball like Klaus it couldn't be anything too imaginative . . .

Outside his plain little cell the sound of confused noises interrupted Warren's musings, an evident argument in progress followed by the scuffle of hurried steps retreating into the distance. A sharp tang of smoke came to his nostrils at that moment. Before anything else occurred, Warren felt a distinct premonition, sitting up on his bunk, his ears straining for any audible clues.

Instead of some distant noise, the cell door suddenly rattled, opening smoothly, a curtain of white smoke billowing in along with the lithe form of Cherry Aisha. She nonchalantly closed the door and sized Warren up before pointing up at the camera in the corner of the cell. "If I take another step they'll see it's me."

"Won't they know it's you anyway?" Warren said, looking her over, seeing an oddly vulnerable expression in her eyes and a notable slice through her sleeve.

"Keep the sods guessing." Cherry winked at Warren, seeming to force a lightness she did not feel. "Only have a few seconds, duck, then I either have to scarper, or permanently shut a load of scream-holes. So here's the program: Nasty old Klaus fabbed up a few of these—"

"I know," Warren interrupted. "Big Dodge Power Wagons. Probably doing gun mounts like he did with those El Camino rigs."

"Not quite," Cherry said. "They've got four fixed thirty-caliber machine guns mounted in the front, and one fifty-caliber in back on a tacky sort of swivel mount."

Warren shrugged, wincing painfully and rubbing his left shoulder. "Like I said, gun mounts."

Cherry frowned. "You don't understand, mate. The Browning fifty-caliber is not just a smidge more powerful than my forty-five Thompson, or the thirty-caliber guns, it is multiple times more destructive."

"How much more destructive are we talking?"

"Like shooting-lengthways-through-a-Grand-Sport more destructive," Cherry said, looking over her shoulder as if listening, then turning back to Warren. "This little setup is certainly intended as a death trap for you and all the poor devils with you, so...do you want me to break you out? Or would you prefer me to finish breaking all the bones in your body so they can't frog-march you into their shooting gallery? Your choice, old fellow, but this rock is crawling with security yobs now, sooo...tricky to stay un-caught once we have you out."

Warren mused for only seconds before saying, "Neither, Cherry, though I thank you for your generous offer. I've got a brilliant plan coming together...but tell me"—he focused on her eyes and that disquieting hint in their depths—"did you, um, permanently shut Vogl's *scream-hole*?"

Cherry stepped back as Warren fumbled out a stub of graphite and scribbled something on a shred of cloth, a fresh cloud of smoke swirling in behind her. "Nope." She shook her head, thinking back. "Alien got her right before my eyes."

Warren froze, looking up. "Interesting. I'll want to know more, when we have a moment to talk." He hesitated but turned back to his scribbling until he completed the small message.

"I saw..." Cherry began, then shook her head. "I think I understand what it's up to, but we'll have to chat later. My time here is spent."

She caught the balled-up note Warren casually flicked her way and held his gaze as she gripped the cell door. "Good luck with your brilliant plan, Stowe. I'll put a nice little arrangement of flowers on your grave...along with Klaus Benin's melon, right?"

Warren smiled as the door quietly closed, the lock snicking into place. Only a minute or so passed before it opened again to admit a suspicious security stiff, measuring Warren for a long moment before retreating.

Alone again, Warren settled back into place, adding Cherry's new information into his calculations. An alien in the flesh? He couldn't figure an angle on the alien yet, but his plan didn't require any aliens.

His plan did require an immense load of luck, though. If Cherry delivered that note to Gilda it might just work, even now. It *had* to work.

News of the disturbance in the security section reached Sami, Klaus, and Sharif all at the same moment, driving Klaus into a strange frenzy. "That Boop woman!" he snarled. "Attempting some kind of escape for Stowe. I'm sure of it."

"Escape to where, Klaus?" Sami asked. "There's nowhere to go."

"Really? Really, Sami? Then where's Boop hiding out then?"

"The same place twenty-odd other missing persons and Vogl all are, probably never to be seen again."

For a moment it almost seemed Klaus would physically attack Sami, but instead he whirled with a mocking laugh. "And this diversionary fire lit itself, I suppose."

Sharif spoke up for the first time. "There are many people who could have kindled that fire; some of them working with Stowe here demonstrated a surprising loyalty."

Klaus swiped his hand, rejecting all that Sharif said. "And one of these loyal underlings evaded or disabled every camera or security device? It can only be Boop! No one else."

Sami felt repulsed by Benin's obsessive energy but Sharif seemed bent on placating him. "Perhaps you are right, Klaus, but if so she will be found out soon enough and her efforts will be finished."

"That Bartson is a fool, and his people are no better," Klaus grumbled, but after a little urging Klaus set out to find the beauraucrat and focus his search in the "correct" direction.

With Klaus dispatched, Sami stared at Sharif, annoyed by Sharif's self-satisfied smile. "*Why*, brother?" he said at last. "Why do you encourage this maniac?"

"Will you never look farther than mere personalities?" Sharif said, smiling. "Benin's obsession has made us a tidy profit here already, and his inattention to business is costing him dearly."

Sami shook his head, uncomprehending, and Sharif leaned close, speaking softly. "I shorted Benin's corporate stock a week or more ago. Let us hope he continues to run it into the ground as he plays his bloodthirsty games with Stowe here—the bloodier the better if that is what keeps his mind fixed on petty vices."

This revelation rocked Sami anew. Not only was this a depth of manipulation that never would have occurred to Sami, it illustrated more clearly than ever Sharif's laser focus on grander things. The beautiful vision of Ajanib never meant anything to Sharif, clearly, forming only a quaint tool that he would employ, casting it off when it suited his own vision, just like Stowe and so many others around him who were about to meet their end.

Sami did not trust himself to reply, and Sharif did not seem to notice, his eyes going distant, obviously lost in the vision of his unfolding plan.

With swarms of Torino constabulary troopers around him, Bartson felt much more in his element, able to command at least hesitant respect from even these rich pricks who had looked down their haughty noses at him for days. Just like back on Bethune, the rich and powerful could all be dislodged from their pedestals using a serious alleged crime for leverage. It was an advantage Bartson would only reluctantly surrender, though he already held grave doubts regarding the supposed murder of this Vogl woman.

The search teams he had dispatched into the catacombs already experienced a few troubling incidents—two constables seemingly lost in inexplicable circumstances—and now the other searchers stuck to only broad thoroughfares, worried about adding to the number of lost souls themselves. But they had located and searched Vogl's abandoned vehicle, leading most to the natural conclusion that she had merely *disappeared* like everyone else.

Still, Bartson flexed his erstwhile power, sifting and questioning everyone that Sharif allowed him to harass, and he finally found a possible nugget of treasure. One of the scientists evidently mentioned that she had actually spoken with Betty Boop *after* Boop had stuck a knife into Warren Springer Stowe. With this hot target in mind, Bartson gathered a pair of his best interrogators, about to go corner this Dr. Sang for the full treatment. At that precise moment, Klaus Benin arrived full of his own fiery zeal.

"I need some of your best people, Bartson," he demanded, immediately setting Bartson's temper alight.

"Ah, Mister Benin, we have a hot lead on someone who interacted with Boop some hours after—"

"You can interview people and scribble your little notes later," Klaus interrupted. "Boop herself can't be far from we're standing at this very moment. You heard about the diversion in the security section just minutes ago?"

Bartson ground his teeth. "Yes, Mister Benin, I heard about the small fire, and Maktoum security has that well in hand now. This scientist, Doctor Sang, may have key informa—"

"Feel free to sort out all her outdated information *after* we seal the area and actually catch Boop, Bartson," Klaus said, talking over him, then turning to one of the investigators. "You there, get some people and seal off every exit on the south side of the security section."

Bartson's blood boiled, but Klaus was footing the bill for this whole hunting expedition so he could only go along. The interview with Dr. Sang could wait a few hours, surely... while he placated the most arrogant member of an insufferable coterie.

CHAPTER 44

Cherry accomplished all the preparation she could, even while slipping and dodging around roving security patrols and wandering constables, counting down the minutes. As Peter Maris had said, when Bartson's people interviewed Dr. Sang they might learn far more than Cherry wanted them to know...like the existence of her private escape hatch from the catacombs. That would spell the end for her ready egress, leaving her stuck down in the catacombs—or worse, stuck above, unable to assist Warren in thwarting Benin's designs in the next scenario. That revelation seemed inevitable and it might arrive any moment.

Though she felt she comprehended the nature of the alien entity now, she didn't fancy trying to contend with it while handling all the responsibilities that already threatened to overwhelm her, but she couldn't afford to be stuck above either.

As soon as she could thread her way through the posh environs of Ajanib's ritzy resort, Cherry made her way to the science quarter, slipping through its mostly barren halls with her senses dialed up to maximum. At the final turn to her bolt-hole, Cherry paused to listen and test the air until she felt sure no human awaited her.

Not even Peter Maris sat poised around the jagged vent, the silent void awaiting her below, and Cherry found herself momentarily gutted by a rare wash of self-pity. Why was she even here? For Stowe? For some sense of recompense for past sins? Or because it had been the only path that held any greater meaning than mere self-destruction? Whatever the reasons, she had not felt as entirely removed from humanity since tumbling into Stowe's schemes, and now the silent exclusion of the catacombs seemed a fitting purgatory for the damned.

As her internal isolation became complete, Cherry clambered down into the waiting embrace of cold solitude.

Eventually, the Build-Out section became available to Ajanib's newest client members, after Klaus Benin's super-secretive fabrication projects had finally completed, and Cathwaite wandered through, both to observe any new cars that caught his fancy and on the off chance Warren had managed to leave new instructions.

A Chevrolet Corvair, a Nova, and a Ford Falcon fulfilled his desires for interesting new builds, but no hint of fresh instructions appeared, and Cathwaite left Build-Out in no better mood than he had entered it.

With more than a billion guilders now in his control, Cathwaite found himself strangely more attached to the idea of immense wealth than he had ever previously felt. While always before in his life the idea of a billion guilders seemed almost a ridiculous surplus of riches, now a billion felt like the *minimum* sum necessary to really capture the life he had begun to not only envision but *embody*. The idea of casually risking much of this new wealth on foolish bets became increasingly nauseating to him. Only one thing kept him from holding back, from ignoring any obligation to Warren Springer Stowe now, and it was not honor or fairness or even his genuine respect for Warren.

The impetus driving Cathwaite to continue this reckless betting streak originated from Klaus Benin's own caustic observation to him. Cathwaite found that he would almost rather die than suffer social disgrace among these new peers who had just begun to accept him. From this almost helpless position, he had retained a slim hope that Warren's comforting insights would somehow still arrive, and for once he would go risk a vast wager with some true certainty of success. This hope remained only a fantasy.

As the minutes ticked down and the time for the scenario drew near, Cathwaite saw no relief, with even less direction or clarity from Warren than he had received on each prior occasion—no mysterious note appeared, no secretive advisor or fresh clue. Cathwaite only knew that when the scenario launched he would place an immense bet, regardless of any risk. He could face the shattering loss of this precious new wealth more readily than the loss of face abstaining would bring him.

One moment, Warren's weary mind was filled with the whirling variables of the approaching scenario; the next moment, the rattling lock on his cell door jarred him from sleep.

The meals provided to Warren all came from Ajanib's workers' kitchen, so remained far more edible than the fare of any real jail where the poor food always served as yet another tool of law enforcement coercion, and breakfast—perhaps his final meal—arrived on the same room service cart as his prior meals. His beverage choice remained limited to juice and water, but both continued to be provided in Ajanib's quaint and expensive custom glass bottles, which remained a delightfully elegant touch. "Don't suppose I could suggest a cup of English breakfast tea? And cream?" Warren inquired of his two dour-faced turnkeys. "The cream is almost essential."

Neither answered, and Warren spread marmalade across toast with a shrug. "Driving without the sustaining powers of tea is very nearly a crime in itself, gents, but . . . you can tell Sharif or whomever you wish, I'm not driving at all without my smoking case, you hear? Pass that along."

They didn't respond to this either, but when they came to escort him to the gladiator assembly area they silently presented him with his battered smoking case, and Warren jammed it one-handed into his pocket. His security escort felt no need to place Warren in restraints, possibly because of his injured arm, or possibly because it would be needless and silly, but they flanked him as they marched straight past the gladiator meeting room to the utility lifts.

Ajanib's old-timey drink bottles had sparked an idea for Warren that he had scribbled down for Cherry to deliver, and he hoped that idea, coupled with his current scheme, might offer some path toward survival through this scenario, but it would require some chance to clue his fellow gladiators in on the plan. Doing this without giving the concepts away to Sharif or Klaus or their lackeys presented a particular challenge.

When the utility lift slid back to reveal the catacomb assembly area, most of the Camaros and Corvettes sat ready to roll, their novice drivers behind their respective wheels, but Warren spotted a few familiar figures still loitering about. Of his original gladiators, only Gilda stood near, but his old jail comrades, Bailey and Monk, both lounged beside their vehicles, observing Warren with pointed curiosity.

"Gilda," Warren greeted as his escorts each placed a strong hand on his upper arm, practically forcing him forward. "Easy, Brutus! That's a wounded wing you're groping!" He looked back over his shoulder at Gilda's troubled face. "Gonna be a long scenario, Gilda. Probably want some extra fuel." Her expression turned thoughtful before Warren was rudely snatched away.

As he stumbled past Bailey and Monk, Warren tried again. "Hey, fellas. Don't mind these authoritarian thugs—*Ouch*! Easy!" Warren turned back after scowling at his escorts. "Reminds me of that day with Dilman and Boxner, remember that? Just like it was then—erk!"

The toughs practically threw Warren into his Daytona before he could finish speaking, but the glimpse he saw of Bailey's and Monk's expressions led him to feel some hope that they did remember that informative day, a particular event during their time dwelling in Torino's jail together.

Within the sordid environment of incarceration, Monk and Bailey had been comfortable operators, knowing the bounds and limitations, able to command a degree of respect from their fellow inmates. Now, in the alien catacombs of Ajanib, Warren saw the signs of their uneasiness, their insecurity. They stood ripe for direction, ready to be led.

As the oh-so-helpful security thugs slammed his door with undue violence, Warren leaned over to arm both of his machine guns, checking to be sure the ammo boxes were in place. He sat up as engines rumbled into life all over the assembly area, drones beginning to lift off from their charging racks and swarm above the gladiator vehicles. Before starting his engine, Warren opened the smoking case and fished into its secret compartment, withdrawing one of his prized data sticks. He linked it to his non-period sound system and cued a tune from that golden era that had defined his entire adult life. Though he scarcely understood the meaning of the song's lyrics, it communicated the feeling of a plunge into deadly uncertainty that matched Warren's feelings exactly. He cranked the volume as that soul-stirring cry rose up, the "Immigrant Song" blaring loud through the car's abundant speakers.

The long-extinct musical act bore the name *Zeppelin*, which seemed appropriate. Those bards and Warren both clearly obsessed over archaic vehicles.

As the music blared out its defiance, Warren cranked up the Daytona's powerful engine, slipped his left arm painfully from its sling, and pressed his helmet on. He hoped the Members Club got an earful of his music through the audio channel, a little of the Old Earth culture Ajanib was always *meant* to supply.

With the Towed Zeppelin—no, *Led* Zeppelin—fellows singing about taking their ships to new lands (zeppelin ships, presumably) and facing the tides of war, Warren chunked the Daytona into gear and throttled his way into the line of cars heading down into the approaching fray.

If Cherry knew her facts—and Warren possessed no doubt on this—many of these gladiators would never return from the scenario. They hurried to their deaths even now, their dreams of freedom nothing but enticement to their doom.

Seated on her Fireblade, the palm slate resting on the smooth fuel tank between her knees, Cherry's augmented senses seemed to detect the alien entity's watchful presence in the aquamarine walls around her. She had no time for its antics now, seeing the feed from her carefully secreted camera where it spied the opposing gladiators. "You'll get your meat soon enough, you ruby sod," Cherry murmured to the alien. "Just give me a few minutes."

Her eyes narrowed as she spied the Power Wagons rolling down from the circuit track, heading into the catacombs, each bearing a huge .50-caliber Browning M2 machine gun on a swivel mount, just as she had expected. But she zoomed in on the swivel mounts, smiling to herself. "Made a novice mistake, Klaus," she said, seeing that the guns could not be depressed below the horizontal plane. This small technical fault in the mount mechanism, however, would not prove too useful for all the poor gladiators.

While she comprehended Warren's plan—such as it was—he could have little concept of the demoralizing power of heavy weapons on the average human psyche. She had witnessed it firsthand more than once among professional soldiers, and Warren's rabble possessed little of the eesprit de corps those soldiers had known. When the first car and driver got rapidly shot into bits, the rest of them would likely sell their souls to get back into a nice, safe prison cell, any thoughts of fighting their way to freedom utterly gone.

Cherry chewed her lip for a moment, then shrugged to herself, reaching down to free the Thompson from its securing clips. Warren didn't want her to intervene and bring the mob of constables hounding after her, but she preferred that challenge to letting that Klaus Benin arsehole slaughter all the gladiators, including Warren. Besides, with the proper urging, Ajanib itself might have the final say in their fate.

She checked the Thompson's magazine and started the Fireblade's engine, smiling at last, remembering that cheerful line from her military days:

While there's lead in the air, there's hope in the heart!

CHAPTER 45

Sami Maktoum should have felt thrilled as the Members Club filled to overflowing with the richest people in the known galaxy, his vision realized, his most risk-filled business choices finally validated. Instead, Sami felt only a sense of foreboding and distaste.

He should also have become comfortable with Klaus Benin's cold creepiness by now, but he hadn't, observing the avaricious gleam in Benin's eyes as these bulky Power Wagon vehicles made their appearance. Sami couldn't help silently noting that Klaus uttered no more grandiose statements about abstaining from the betting, wondering if Klaus felt the financial pinch so keenly that he held his tongue, or if he felt that losing so many guilders in so many consecutive bets absolved him from criticism now.

Above the chatter of excited voices around him, Sami heard the sound of engine noises that the clientele enjoyed so greatly coming over the various audio channels: Warren's jailbird gladiators firing up all those Corvettes and Camaros. In the next moment, a rhythmic sort of song began coming across the line, some fellow singing about a land of ice and snow, and Sharif shared a look with Klaus.

"Let him play his little tunes," Klaus said, smiling savagely as he placed a possessive hand on Savanah Westbrook's waist. "In a few minutes we can play a funeral dirge for him in return."

Sharif shrugged and looked up at the wager board that already filled with dozens of immense bets, mostly on these Power Wagons to win, regardless of the scenario description that would soon be revealed.

"Well, Cathwaite?" York Rigby's voice inquired, and Sami turned farther to see the newly wealthy collector sitting glumly, two empty glasses before him. More than a few gamblers observed Cathwaite with cynical eyes, though Sami felt the rumors of improper behavior from Cathwaite hardly formed the only explanation in continuing his reckless betting trend. Whether someone had previously colluded with Stowe or not, just one glimpse of these Power Wagons with such massive guns would give anyone pause.

As Sami watched, Cathwaite squinted up at the wager board, panned his gaze across the holographic displays, and ended by scowling at York Rigby. "Scen-scenario's not even declared yet," Cathwaite said thickly. "What's the hurry, York, old... old fellow, hmm?" Sami recalled Cathwaite's earlier diffidence and timidity and wondered if it had evaporated under the influence of new wealth, or merely through alcohol-induced courage.

"No hurry, my friend, no hurry," York said, smiling indulgently. "Though by the look of these monstrous vehicles and their weaponry this scenario may be over in seconds, so if you plan to bet, your window of opportunity may be limited."

Cathwaite seemed to barely hear York, calling for another drink, shooting censorious glances at other gamblers until the drink arrived. He took a voluptuous gulp from his glass and stared up at the wager board with a cold, glare, his forehead shiny with sweat. Among the available bets, odds against Stowe surviving the scenario began at two-to-one, and driven by Klaus Benin's heavy bets climbed to four-to-one. "That's it!" Cathwaite declared to no one particular. "That's it. It's all I can do, right? What more... what more could any... anyone expect?"

No one replied, the general chatter of the assembly allowing only the nearest listeners to hear Cathwaite's evidently rhetorical words.

The expression on Cathwaite's face seemed to reveal deep physical pain as he placed a five-hundred-million guilder bet on Stowe's survival. While Cathwaite had passed up higher risk, higher potential reward on Stowe's gladiators to win the entire scenario, Sami thought Cathwaite's massive wager would silence his critics, even if he did utter somewhat suspicious, cryptic statements while in his cups.

It seemed all but certain that Cathwaite would be losing a half-billion guilders *and* some sort of personal idol in a few minutes when Klaus Benin's executioners slaughtered Stowe along with his accompanying horde of jailbird gladiators.

⊕ ⊕ ⊕

Gilda gunned the Gran Sport's engine, racing out of the assembly area into the catacombs well ahead of the other gladiators, prompted by Warren's words to check the fuel depot for "extra fuel" as he suggested. If she read the emphasis of his speech correctly, she might have some important role to serve now, but time would be of the essence. She couldn't be sure what sneaky trick was in store for the rabble of her fellow gladiators, but since the El Camino gambit, she knew it would likely be deadly in the extreme.

She floored it to the fuel depot, sliding in for a screeching stop, and jumped out of the Gran Sport. After only a moment she spotted the small note, palming it as the fuel nozzle unspooled and began to top off her Gran Sport's mostly filled fuel tank. To avoid the prying eyes of her camera drones, Gilda popped the car's bonnet and used the cover to scan through the hastily scribbled message, feeling shock and consternation as she read it a second time.

If she followed his orders they could only rely upon the inattention of any critical observers. There would be no way to hide her actions from the camera drones, but after a moment Gilda realized Stowe's key insight. The fireworks and slaughter were about to explode; with so many targets to select from, surely no one in the Members Club would spare a moment to watch one driver tinkering with her vehicle . . . not unless Sharif or Benin suspected her actions already. It was a chance she must take.

Gilda found the collection of old-timey glass bottles waiting in the waste receptacle just as the note described, snatching them up and hurrying to do as Warren ordered. She needed to be in position fast, and each minute of delay would push any chance of survival further and further from grasp.

Among all the sights and sounds pouring from the displays within the Members Club, the uninteresting actions of one lone Gran Sport should have warranted little attention as it wandered off to a fuel depot, but Sami knew he was not the only one who had learned of Gilda's importance to Warren Springer Stowe. When he spotted the feed from Gilda's camera drones, Sami shot a quick glance at Sharif and Klaus, assuring they remained fixated on the greater conflict, before he casually accessed the broadcast controls.

One moment, the display clearly revealed Gilda filling a number of glass bottles with explosive hydrocarbon fuel, and in the next moment Sami's manipulation switched the display to a static camera feed where fire, death, and mayhem provided a much safer view. Klaus and Sharif glanced over too late to catch a glimpse of Gilda.

Sami could not guess what desperate game Stowe might be attempting in cooperation with Gilda, but it seemed likely that it might only succeed if it remained a secret from Benin's butchers. While he lacked the power—or the courage—to win a direct conflict with Sharif, Sami would do what little he could to give Warren whatever slender chance he might have to survive.

It seemed the very least he could do.

Warren remembered the moment well among the many, many tedious days in Torino's jail. Two of their fellow inmates, Boxner and Dilman, were discovered to be secret informants—spies—for Bartson's screws, and some of the hotheads, like Bailey and Monk, wanted to immediately impress on these two exactly how they felt about this betrayal, mostly using fists and elbows in a rough sort of nonverbal communication. Warren had restrained them, pointing out how miserable they would feel shivering in the punishment cells, offering them a safer path to their goal that didn't involve lumping these two up in the middle of the open dayroom.

Warren had invested a few guilders on a bag full of sugary snacks from the overpriced jail commissary, loudly calling out that he would be freely giving away said snacks, and waited as a crowd of hungry, penniless degenerates gathered before him, with Bailey and Monk waiting on the outer edge of the mob. When Warren upended the bag across his audience, a sudden scramble ensued, Dilman and Boxner right the midst of the struggling knot. It was then simplicity itself for Monk and Bailey to work their way to the two sellouts, and under cover of the surging mob give them the good news—fast, hard, and repeatedly.

Warren bore a strong distaste for disingenuous traitors of any stripe, and possessed a natural instinct for accumulating obligation from the lesser beings in his orbit, so it had seemed a worthwhile investment at the time. Now it served as a perfect example for this pair of potentially useful gladiators.

If Warren left this Bethune rabble to their own devices, they would all pathetically die in the scenario, probably without firing a single shot of their own, and there was simply no way he could save them all, but he might be able to save a few . . . and incidentally beat Klaus Benin at this murderous game.

The scenario start tone rang out, the moment suddenly upon them.

"Gladiators," Warren called over the audio channel, certain that his every word was conveyed to his enemies, "increase speed over one hundred on your gauges. Stay on the main arterial, call out any enemies you see. Speed is your friend now."

Engines increased their individual roars, Corvettes and Camaros around Warren accelerating, pushing forward as they took his words to heart, but as Warren had hoped, Monk and Bailey stayed glued to his flanks rather than rushing forward with the others. They evidently remembered that day with Boxner and Dilman, and its attendant lesson.

Within moments, the mass of gladiator vehicles ran ahead, only glimpses of distant taillights showing on the straightaways. Warren silently hoped that speed alone might give the poor sods a better than even chance of surviving their first contact with the enemy, and buy time for Gilda to get into position. She embodied their only real hope of beating Klaus this time.

For the first time in days, Cherry opted to abandon the tight and twisting side passages, sacrificing stealth for speed. She didn't care if Klaus or Sharif, or Bartson and his constables, got an eyeful of her now. If Klaus was actively cheating, as she fully expected, her appearance might actually draw heat off Warren and his novice gladiators too.

She wheeled out onto a broad roadway and rolled the throttle on, feeling the Fireblade leap forward, the engine's roar bringing that familiar surge of pleasure as she hunkered low over the fuel tank, her speed gauge spooling higher and higher, her left hand and right foot seamlessly clicking up through the gears as the Fireblade's engine rose to a scream, just beginning to redline.

She came to the first sweeper, barely slowing, throwing the motorcycle over, her knee almost scraping the roadway despite drifting up onto the track's banked outer wall. She shot out of the curve at nearly 200 on her gauge, the aquamarine passage flashing past her

Michael Mersault

vision, the symbiote within her increasing her reflexes and perception speed in response, effectively slowing time's passage.

For this moment the horrors of the war, the horrors of Panawaat were forgotten, her bloodlust rising. She smiled within the enclosure of her helmet, hungry for the conflict racing toward her.

Cathwaite blearily glanced at the holographic streams and looked away, groaning, pressing his hands to his face. Those Power Wagon vehicles of Benin's trundled into their disparate positions, their respective gunners pivoting the heavy weapons to cover each approach, while Warren's new rabble of gladiators raced blindly to their doom.

"Appears Mister Stowe may finally have acquired a morsel of judicious caution, no?" Prabak Bhatt said, and Cathwaite looked through his fingers at one particular display featuring that distinctive Dodge Daytona. "He does not so heedlessly race to the attack this time, it seems."

As this sank into Cathwaite's sodden brain he caught the abrupt jerk of movement at a nearby table in the Members Club. Savanah Westbrook had caught sight of something on one display and reached out to grip Klaus Benin's shoulder, pointing. Klaus smiled with wolfish satisfaction. "There she is ... just as I expected."

That officious sod, Bartson, perked up, a half-eaten appetizer in his hand. "There who is?"

Was he always grazing?

"That Betty Boop, of course," Benin said, never taking his eyes off the static camera image as the small figure on the red-and-black motorcycle swept past. "I knew she still lived."

"You're certain it's her?" Bartson said, the serious expression on his face diminished somewhat by a blob of cream cheese gleaming on his lip. "If that truly is Boop, she'll be arrested the moment the scenario ends. I'll have constables waiting."

Klaus turned to Bartson, a mocking twist to his lips. "Have your constables ready, Bartson, but you can be sure they'll only be collecting her in pieces. She has meddled once too often."

Before Bartson could reply, a chorus of shouts erupted and Cathwaite glanced up at the displays despite himself, transfixed by the lurid images unfolding.

One Dodge Power Wagon waited broadside on the wide arterial, the gunner unleashing bursts of fire that rocked the entire vehicle, the fat red tracer rounds streaming out like the powerful pulses of some advanced modern weapon system. A Corvette served as the first target, the first victim, its driver rushing straight toward his doom, both of the Corvette's machine-gun ports streaming fire. Before this novice gladiator ever drew near enough to score effective hits, .50-caliber slugs slammed into the Corvette, exploding its engine compartment, the hood blasting free to slam back over the car's windshield. The Corvette cannoned into a sidewall, rolling over and over as the cars following tried to dodge flaming wreckage, seemingly undeterred by the mayhem.

Cheers erupted in the Members Club as the gunner atop that utilitarian Power Wagon lined up on the next car, a Camaro, shredding it in an instant.

Wagers skyrocketed on the board and Cathwaite sank his face into the crook of his elbow, unwilling to watch either the merciless reaping of lives, or the impending tragic depletion of his vast new fortune.

It was all just so heartbreaking...he could almost cry!

CHAPTER 46

"Monk! Bailey! Stay on me!" Warren yelled as he raced onto the perimeter road, feathering his throttle to allow his wingmates to keep up. They needed all the speed they could manage, but they had to stay together for any chance at survival.

Already over the audio channel they heard the shouts, cries, and thunders of destruction, and Warren knew they had only a tight window to exploit the diversion bought with blood.

"Floor it, damn it!" he called out, lashing them beyond the reach of their untried skills.

They flew down the tight perimeter road, all three vehicles nearly abreast with no room to maneuver, their roaring engines resonating and reverberating from Ajanib's rocky walls.

Warren saw the opening ahead a moment before their three cars swept into the broad cavern. As Warren had expected, one Power Wagon waited here, covering the junction of three roads, and the gunner instantly pivoted to fire, red tracers arcing out. The stream streaked behind them, the gunner misjudging their speed, but before Warren and his wingmates could clear the cavern a fresh burst slashed in from the left.

An explosion of shattered glass and motor oil sprayed Warren's windshield, and Bailey's car jerked to the left. Warren glanced in his mirror to see the shattered hulk of Bailey's Camaro tumbling sideways behind him, sparks and metal chunks shooting up into the air.

In the next instant they flashed out of the cavern, out of sight from that Power Wagon, the main arterial not far ahead.

If Gilda hadn't reached her position, or if Warren's plan failed he would be trapped—a fearsome machine of destruction surely now pursuing him, while its twin awaited him not far ahead.

Gilda killed the engine on her Gran Sport where it sat on the steep ramp, fumbling the collection of fragile glass bottles about for a moment before kicking her door open. The bottles, her car, and her hands all smelled strongly of accelerant, and she feared any spark might turn her into a human torch in the blink of an eye.

In the next moment, she heard the echoing roar of engines drawing nearer and nearer, their direction impossible to determine over the whine of her attendant camera drones, but she took a chance on Ajanib's alien treachery and jumped out of her car, getting into position, lifting one gurgling bottle in her hand. A loud basso hammer of gunfire resounded down the tunnel, the engines roaring louder, closer, and Gilda set the oil rag wick alight, hoping the bottle wouldn't explode in her face as she looked down on the roadway below her.

Another burst of titanic gunfire and the sound of screaming metal preceded two cars whipping by below at top speed, one Warren's Daytona. The cars disappeared to her right in the tunnel opening and the rag wick began to burn out as Gilda stood poised, waiting. She lit a second bottle even as she heard a lower engine sound rumbling nearer.

Gilda bit her lip, ready to lob the bottle filled with gasoline down, knowing she'd have only a split second to react. The engine roared louder, drawing nearer, and Gilda quickly eyed the wick one last time. She looked back barely in time, seeing the Power Wagon rolling along at a good clip, even as she hurled her flaming missile.

The bottle arced down, hitting square on the Power Wagon's roof, splashing back over the gunner crouched in its bed. Gilda saw the gunner jerk his weapon about to bear on her just as the wick ignited the splash of accelerant. There was no explosion, only a strange puff of ghostly fire that engulfed the gunner, setting him writhing in the truck's bed. Gilda stared, shocked, as the Power Wagon roared on, now a flaming comet trailing smoke in its wake as it disappeared into the tunnel mouth.

Gilda hesitated a moment as the glow of fire faded below while a confusing ruby luminance increased, rising up around her in its place. She only had an instant to turn and see the apparition that fell upon her.

"No!" she cried, her voice echoing through the empty ramp overlooking the perimeter road, a few drips of gasoline on the roadway still fitfully burning. Her Gran Sport sat motionless, silent, unattended, only the camera drones stirring in their quiet orbits.

Cherry discovered that her presence had been anticipated by Sharif or Sami or Klaus, when a Corvette shot onto the arterial from a perimeter junction just before her. Cherry narrowly dodged the slow-moving Corvette, whipping past close enough to brush a fender with her elbow, then barely avoided the twin streams of fire from .30-caliber machine guns, tracers whipping around her, shattering her mirror.

She rounded another sweeper at high speed and left the Corvette far behind, but through some trickery, one of the Corvette's camera drones peeled off to stay with her. She saw it there, pacing her, and she tasted Klaus Benin's handiwork as she contemplated trying a shot from her Thompson to bring it down, but the moment of ultimate conflict raced toward her even then with terminal finality.

In a flash she perceived the trap assembled for her alone, waiting ahead. A Corvette sat still in the center of the arterial, its twin weapon ports pointing toward her, while behind the Corvette another Power Wagon squatted, the gunner homed in on Cherry, the .50 caliber Browning machine gun leveled and waiting.

Cherry rolled off the throttle, decelerating as she wondered what they waited for . . . wanting her so close they could not miss? Or to capture vivid, close-up footage of her violent death for the voyeuristic pleasures of the gambling clientele?

Either way, it seemed it would only be seconds until they opened fire on her, and even the most powerful members of Blue Light could not survive a direct hit from those big .50-caliber slugs.

The flaming Power Wagon careened about as ammunition stores in the bed began to cook off, .50-caliber rounds exploding like small grenades in the Dodge's burning bed.

"What lit that vehicle ablaze, I do wonder?" Prabak Bhatt said to the room at large, while most gamblers still watched gladiator after gladiator charging headlong into the fire of the fully intact Power

Wagon on the arterial, most cars getting hammered into flaming wreckage before they could even bring their own guns to bear.

Sami noticed that Klaus Benin paid less attention to the greater drama, instead watching every appearance of that Boop woman on disparate camera feeds. Klaus became rigid with barely suppressed tension as one of his pet cutthroats nearly crashed his Corvette into Boop, muttering to himself as she darted her saucy little motorcycle past the Corvette and seemingly through deadly streams of tracer bullets.

"Good, Boop," Sami heard Klaus murmur, Savanah Westbrook frowning sidelong at him. "Very good, but all for nothing."

Sami gained a dawning awareness as he saw the image unfold on one of the many displays, the roadway blocked, weapons ready and trained on Boop. And it was then Sami noticed a camera drone dedicated to her, circling her motorcycle as it fed the stream back to the Members Club. He frowned, looking to see if Sharif had noticed the extreme liberties Klaus had taken, but Sharif conferred privately with Bartson to one side, seemingly unaware.

Turning back to the displays, Sami saw Betty Boop suddenly slowing, her posture straightening as she looked ahead, and only then did Sami fully comprehend the waiting executioners, weapons poised. Jaw clenched, he was unable to look away from the impending horror.

The lone woman on her motorcycle seemed to coast passively nearer and nearer, evidently resigned to her fate. "Why do they hold off? Why does she not act?" Prabak Bhatt said, transfixed by the unfolding scene as more and more gamblers in the Members Club turned from the large-scale mayhem on other displays to witness this spectacle. "Why do they not shoot?"

Almost as Prabak spoke the words, Boop finally took some evasive action, whipping her cycle to one side, signaling her foes to open fire at almost the same instant. As .50-caliber tracers homed in on her, Boop dumped her Fireblade on the roadway in an explosion of sparks, sliding wheels-first down the roadway, tracers whipping past over her prone, sliding body.

"She's hit!" Savanah Westbrook called out.

"I don't think she is," York Rigby said, squinting at the display, "but after her skin is all peeled off on the road, she might wish she was."

Motorcycle and woman slid together at high speed right up to the stationary Corvette, where her shredded body should have struck with bone-breaking finality. The viewing gamblers around Sami uttered a muted gasp as that road-torn Boop seemed to spring from prone to aggressive attack in a millisecond, flinging her helmet at the .50-caliber's gunner as she continued her forward momentum in a blur, racing up between the Corvette's gunports, her jumpsuit shredded to reveal smooth skin that should have been one massive bleeding wound. Without slowing she leaped from the Corvette, soaring across a gap of nearly twenty paces to land in the Power Wagon's bed.

Sami heard Klaus murmuring something now, over and over, his head shaking, transfixed. "She can't be . . . she can't . . . she can't be . . ."

But Boop did not stop moving, a flurry of blows knocking the gunner into a boneless heap, her hands grasping the .50 caliber's dual grips. The Power Wagon's driver threw himself prone as Cherry pivoted its barrel around, blasting the glass and steel of the truck's cab into a thousand pieces of shrapnel.

She only seemed to pause a moment, her savage smile visible to everyone as the camera drone swept by. Her foot rose and smashed at the gun's swivel mount once, twice, as the accompanying Corvette spun around to bring its guns to bear. The swivel mount broke free, and Boop muscled the huge gun onto the edge of the truck bed, depressing the muzzle down and firing, stitching tracer rounds through the Corvette until it ceased any sign of life, rolling to a halt.

The wild-eyed Boop looked up, straight into the camera drone, straight into their eyes and bared her teeth, laughing.

"What is she?" Prabak Bhatt said, breaking the near silence of the Members Club, his voice filled with awe.

Klaus Benin stared at the holographic feed, frozen in place, his face almost rapturous. "She can be only one thing," he said, his voice uncharacteristically soft. "She is Blue Light . . . and I must have her."

Bartson spoke up, "Whatever she is, she will not escape. I captured her once before, and I will take her into custody again."

Klaus Benin's dry laugh clearly incensed Bartson, but before the Torino prosecutor could say a word, Klaus said, "I wonder why she wanted to be arrested before? I soon hope to ask her that question myself, once she has been safely neutralized."

⊕ ⊕ ⊕

Warren and Monk sped almost side by side down the perimeter road as the sounds of a one-sided slaughter came through their audio feed. Convict gladiators still raced to attack the indomitable Power Wagon on the arterial, some even managing to fire off a burst from their own guns before adding to the growing casualty list. As long as gladiators still kept the gunner busy Warren knew they had a chance, but without other targets, the waiting Power Wagon would pot them with ease ... just like all the other fresh victims.

The last curve greeted them, and as they cleared it, Warren saw the tableau he expected, the waiting Power Wagon stationary on the arterial, right where the perimeter road terminated. The .50-caliber gunner in the truck bed fanned the weapon back and forth, its muzzle pouring out streaks of fire to the right down the arterial, its deafening blast overpowering any engine noise from Monk and Warren ... for the moment at least.

Warren had to time it, measuring the range by eye to fire a burst at the narrow window where his rounds might arc high enough to reach the gunner and driver of the Power Wagon; too far or too near might mean his fire would strike too low to be effective or miss entirely.

They closed the gap, drawing closer and closer, and just as Warren reached for the trigger, the Power Wagon's gunner seemed to catch sight of them, whipping his long weapon around. Warren fired, his tracers arcing in ... too low. In a flash he stomped his brake, then floored the throttle, holding down the trigger, his machine guns hammering tracers that rose up as the nose of his Daytona lifted under hard acceleration.

Even as the Power Wagon's .50-caliber gunner fired, Warren's dual streams of machine-gun fire swept over the gunner, knocking him back while the Power Wagon's windshield flew to pieces.

"Hah-hah!" Warren called out. "Got him, Monk!"

It was only then that Warren saw Monk's Corvette crash behind him, its forward surfaces cratered by fist-sized .50-caliber holes.

He bit his lip as he maneuvered his Daytona onto the arterial, seeing the wreckage of a dozen gladiator vehicles to his right, some of them burning fitfully, others with figures staggering free.

An odd tone came across the audio channel then, followed by an announcement: "Scenario complete. Make your way to your assembly area and cooperate with all constabulary forces who now operate within the catacombs."

Constables in the catacombs? While convicts still roved about in armed vehicles?

If the scenario was deemed complete, that meant someone had accounted for the third Power Wagon: *Cherry.*

Everything became clear. The constables came for Cherry.

Warren turned his Daytona to the left, away from the assembly area, and floored it, trying for all the speed he could squeeze out of the powerful engine even as his camera drones swept along with him.

Now . . . to quickly hatch some brilliant unlikely plan to save them both . . . or die trying.

CHAPTER 47

A firm hand jostled Cathwaite where he slumped on the glistening tabletop. "Hey there, look, old fellow." The voice belonged to York Rigby and the insistent tone brought Cathwaite's head slowly up.

York pointed up at the wager board. "Stowe survived the scenario," he said. "Looks like you'll have to make a good home for a stack of new guilders."

"This scenario was compromised," Sharif interjected in a firm voice, shaking his head. "That wager is compromised right along with it."

Prabak Bhatt turned from the flickering holographic displays. "Oh my, Sharif! Is this not an ill-advised stance?" he said, his expression uncharacteristically severe. "Did this scenario not begin, action—such violent, gruesome action—ensued, many drivers fell? And the scenario ended, the charming announcement stating that it ended. And there"—he pointed his whole hand at the display featuring Warren's Daytona speeding down the arterial—"Stowe still lives." Prabak's hand lowered and he looked solemnly between York and Sharif as various other gamblers watched, Klaus Benin seemingly unaware of the exchange as he stared at just one display. "What element of a proper wager is lacking?"

Sharif's lips compressed into a thin line and he replied in a flat tone, "Perhaps you are correct."

Prabak glanced around the Members Club. "I believe that so many of us will be most interested in your firm conclusion, whether we lost money in this wager or made a great winning," he said, though to Cathwaite's eyes it seemed only a handful of the gamblers paid much heed to the conversation, their attention riveted on the remarkable actions still unfolding in the catacombs.

Cathwaite's bleary vision saw Warren's Daytona on one feed, another revealing that Boop woman in her road-shredded jumpsuit, linking ammunition belts together in the bed of a shattered Power Wagon, while nearly every other holographic image featured the golden illuminators of swarming constables. They motored along in modern utility vehicles or marched in broad skirmish lines, all closing in on one single point of the catacombs.

"We will clear everything up once Bartson has dealt with this... Betty Boop woman," Sharif said, then his lips formed something approximating a smile. "Stowe may have survived the scenario, but it appears he may not actually live much longer." He nodded toward the holographic output. "He is not exiting the scenario as instructed, and those constables will be understandably touchy with so many weapons scattered about down there. The constables are *not* armed with antiques, as you can see."

Even in his inebriated state Cathwaite saw it all coming together, speaking even as the thought formed: "Bartson will kill them both."

Sharif shrugged, jerking his head toward the holographic image. "What choice will he have? Look at her, preparing to fight them all. And if she truly is one of those Blue Light creatures... better for everyone if she is dealt with here and now."

Cathwaite tore his eyes from the rippling holograms, moistening his lips. "Care to place a wager, Sh-Sharif, hmm? Say, a bill-billion guilders? My, uh, my money says... they live!"

With the throttle pegged, the Daytona's engine roaring, Warren raced down the empty arterial. He passed a junction and just glimpsed the golden gleam of constabulary forces closing. The whip-fire bolts from a plasma rifle made it clear they viewed Warren as a target, and a conversation wasn't on the menu, but he flashed out of their sight in an instant before their targeting scopes locked on.

Moments later, Warren saw the last Power Wagon ahead, Cherry manning the .50-caliber machine gun in its bed, her racing jumpsuit clinging to her body in tatters.

Jerking the steering wheel as he stomped the brakes, Warren slid up to the Power Wagon in a cloud of smoke, painfully throwing his door open and staggering out. Before Warren could say a word, Cherry yelled, "What the devil are you doing here, Stowe?"

"Giving you a ride. Come on quick—there're a zillion troopers coming for you."

"I figured that, idiot!" Cherry said, pointing her finger up at the attendant camera drone, her face revealing an unfamiliar feral savagery.

"And I figured you were afoot, Cherry, so come on quick. They're right behind me, and in the Daytona we've got a chance to get clear."

"It's too late for that," Cherry said, looking past Warren down the arterial, suddenly firing a thundering burst from the machine gun, almost driving Warren to his knees from the concussive muzzle-blast.

"God, Cherry! I've gone deaf in my right ear! Are you happy?" Warren shook his head to clear it. "Now come on! Quit arguing and get in the car!"

"There's no way out down this arterial, Stowe. You have to know that—" She broke off to fire another burst with a snarl, this time Warren managing to plug his functioning ear. "But I truly appreciate the gesture." She paused, looking down at him, her expression softening back to the face he had come to know so well. "I guess chivalry isn't as bloody timid as I thought." She looked back up, over the barrel of her weapon. "Now lie down over there and act dead. Chances are these ducky sods will let you live, right?"

Warren shook his head. "Nope. Quit arguing, Cherry."

Cherry sighed. "Idiot. They're on both sides of us by now, and with plasma weapons they will incinerate your car with us inside it if—" She paused, clearly some thought dawning. "Okay, Stowe. I'll come with you . . . but get in and get ready to floor it, right?"

Warren began to speak but Cherry drowned him out, firing a sustained burst down the arterial, keeping the encroaching troopers back, making obedience his only option.

He opened the Daytona's passenger door and leaped stiffly into the driver's seat, slapping the shifter into first gear as he revved the engine, Cherry blasting a final burst down the long arterial. Instead of leaping down to join him, Cherry turned the massive machine gun toward one aquamarine wall, yelling out, "I'm ready! Come and get me!" as she depressed the triggers, raking fire across the native stone of Ajanib, sparking tracer-bullet fragments scattering in every direction even as Warren stared, trying to understand her objective. *There's no time for this!*

At first it seemed the red tracers began to adhere to Ajanib's rock, glowing crimson motes sparkling in a broad ring around Cherry's zone of violent demolition, but a moment later those points of ruby fire flowed out from wall, extruding into a broad, alien shape that swept down on her.

She abandoned the machine gun and dove from the Power Wagon, landing heavily on the Daytona's hood, staring right into Warren's eyes as the amorphous mass of crimson fires came for her. "Floor it! Go! Go!"

Warren dumped the clutch, the throttle stomped to the floorboard, his engine roaring as the Daytona leaped forward, but the alien entity seemed to expand and shift. Before Warren could do more than whip the wheel, it had them. Cherry, Warren, and the entire car fell under its blinding embrace, taken in one flashing instant.

In the Members Club, most of the gamblers had filtered away, only the most bloodthirsty remaining, while Klaus Benin and Bartson argued strategy as Sami and Sharif looked on.

The bickering between Klaus Benin and Bartson seemed to frustrate Bartson's underlings even more than it irritated Klaus himself. "We have them surrounded and pinned in place, *Mister* Benin," Bartson enunciated with barely restrained rage. "But I will not risk my people in some needless ploy. When they have a clear shot, they'll take it and end the threat of Betty Boop for everyone." Bartson's underling looked at Klaus with a haughty expression, waiting on the final word for his troopers.

"Bartson, do you have any idea what a Blue Light survivor would be *worth* to the right people?" Klaus said. "After Panawaat and the war's end, they permanently memory-holed the whole project, and there can't be ten remaining hosts of that remarkable symbiote."

Sami saw Bartson's rage visibly diminish by an order of magnitude. Klaus spoke in terms the prosecutor clearly understood, the language of money, and Bartson's underling frowned, seeing it too. "Well," Bartson hedged, "we can *try* a negotiation in the interest of peace, and see if they will, you know, yield to our superior forces."

Audio output from the holographic displays brought them the sustained roar of a .50-caliber machine gun, and Sami expected to see Cherry and Warren fighting a hopeless battle against superior weapons and numbers.

Instead he saw the impossible suddenly made real.

"Sharif," Sami called out, not taking his eyes from the display. "Sharif! Look at this..." The broad, flat mosaic of eye-searing beads swooped down to envelope Stowe's entire Daytona, and then looped liquidly back against a wall, fading into the aquamarine substrate.

Benin, Sharif, and Bartson turned in time to see only the final moment of the manifestation, but York Rigby, Cathwaite, and a few other members of the gambling clientele witnessed the entire spectacle. "What was that?" Sharif said as Klaus spoke at the same moment:

"What happened?"

Before Sami could formulate any response, York Rigby interjected. "It certainly appeared that Stowe and Boop just got eaten by an alien, along with the car."

The shock of what he had just witnessed immobilized Sami's thoughts for several seconds before rippling ramifications began to sink in, and he desperately wished that York and the other witnesses had not been present to see this glimpse of trouble. One live alien within Ajanib irreversibly changed everything.

"An alien?" Sharif said with a mocking smile. "A man of your parts, Rigby, and you fall for one of Sami's pranks."

York considered Sharif for a long moment, shot a quick glance at Sami, and said, "Not trying to be rude, old fellow, but that story doesn't wash with me. If the holographic feeds are somehow subject to image manipulation, then all our bets, won or lost, were made under false pretenses. Which do you want me to believe? That Sami fabricated an alien abduction? Or that one hundred billion guilders in wagers were cast on the level? You can't get both."

Bartson unexpectedly broke in: "Just as Stowe is about to be captured and punished, he is conveniently grabbed by some kind of alien? This is Stowe's doing; some kind of trick he conjured up, and you can *bet* on that."

"Around here, Bartson," York said in a dry voice, "betting requires deeper pockets than you're likely to be working with."

"None of that matters," Klaus Benin snapped. "If Stowe and his accomplice are on this rock we'll find them. In the meantime, no ship should be allowed to dock until we've got them in custody."

Sami said nothing, waiting for the moment he could sift the camera streams privately. At least three camera drones worked that scene, and perhaps a careful review could provide insights, but he wanted those insights *alone*, without inconvenient witnesses looking over his shoulder. Not that he believed anything except what he saw: an alien being consumed two people and one car, leaving no trace of them behind.

Better for the Maktoum Corporation in general and for Sami in particular if everyone completely believed Klaus Benin's words.

Stowe in the role of consummate escape artist would not get Ajanib shut down or bring the Confederated Worlds down upon them in force, but a live alien most certainly could.

CHAPTER 48

One moment, Warren saw the apparition sweeping over Cherry and the Daytona, Cherry's body jerking back, only her fingers locked in the top edge of the hood keeping her from being sucked away. In the next instant, the whole car jerked, wrenching, the doors flexing inward, the side windows exploding, and Warren looked straight into the wide, ebony pools of Cherry's eyes as darkness swept over them.

Piercing cold leached the heat from Warren's lungs and skin, his gasping breaths and the tortured groan of compressed metal the only audible sound, darkness complete. A glimmer of expanding light revealed Cherry's eyes still there before him, just beyond the Daytona's surviving windshield, growing clearer as the illumination increased.

The entire vehicle bucked sharply, rattling Warren's teeth together as he glimpsed looming shapes around them, a sensation of forward movement, a familiar screeching sound in his ears. He turned the steering wheel and compressed the brake pedal, seeing Cherry jerked to one side as the car slid, some pillar-like objects smashing across the Daytona's bumper, narrowly missing her.

They stopped, and before Warren could budge, Cherry disappeared, snatched upward by something that rattled and hummed. He looked wildly around him, seeing a confusing array of unfamiliar shapes filling some expansive space, then momentarily froze as a neat column of green cylinders resolved themselves, each containing the indistinct shape of a still humanoid form.

"Cherry!" Warren yelled, struggling to free himself from his safety harness, ignoring the jolts of pain from his wounded shoulder. The

313

crumpled door panel forced Warren to worm his way out the shattered window, and as his feet touched the hard ground, Cherry dropped lightly down beside him.

"Cherry! What? Where?" Warren said, gasping.

"Hush now, duck," she said, gripping a manacle-like device seized to her forearm and snapping it free with a twist, tossing it aside.

"What happened to us? What grabbed you?" Warren babbled, getting a grip on himself with difficulty. "I mean . . . where in Ajanib could we be?" he said, looking nervously at the green cylinders in the distance, their human-shaped contents stirring uncomfortable sensations above his mere pain and confusion.

"We're not in Ajanib, I'd say. Gravity feels different. Still have the alien's twiddled geometry, though."

Warren stared uncomprehendingly at her, then turned to give the vast chamber area more searching examination, stopping again on the collection of humanoid forms. "Those look like people . . . like humans."

Cherry nodded. "Looks like it. Body-snatched on Ajanib, most likely, cold-stored here." She jerked her head at the pillar-like structures that surrounded the Daytona. "Tried to cold-store me too, just now. I objected." She rubbed her wrist where the manacle had gripped her.

It began to sink in for Warren. "The alien shoved us into some kind of portal for storage, like a bug collection, right?" He looked at the Daytona's skid marks on the smooth, aquamarine ground, the trail leading back to a pair of sheared stanchions and a slightly elevated dais.

"Not quite, I think," Cherry said. "The alien itself is the portal, I think. Probably some kind of automaton, not working with too much intelligence."

Warren frowned, thinking, his eyes irresistibly drawn back to the tubes and their human contents. "Then are they . . . dead?"

"Doubt it," Cherry said, glancing, "but before we go checking their vitals, let's get your tool kit and do a little necessary tinkering here."

The "tinkering" she had in mind involved liberating one of the Browning 1919 machine guns from the Daytona for her to pack along, a belt of ammunition wrapped around her arm. "In case something nasty objects to us rambling about here, I can forcefully protest."

Easily hefting the weighty machine gun, Cherry glanced about the large space surrounding them before saying, "Can't really see beyond all this clutter, so shall we look to all these human samples before checking in with our hosts?"

Feeling both painfully battered and far outside his element, Warren could only agree. "Kind of surprised our, um, hosts haven't come to complain about our messy entrance. We may wish we were back in the catacombs surrounded by coppers when they do."

Cherry set off toward the glowing emerald cylinders, casting over her shoulder, "Nah, much more interesting here."

Warren could only trail along behind her, walking beneath a complex apparatus that had clearly functioned to grab and package new arrivals . . . until the Daytona's entrance and Cherry's gentle touch wrecked much of it, its shattered members still whining and stirring impotently from time to time above them.

No more than ninety full strides brought them near enough to clearly see the faces through the cloudy enclosures. "Damn! That's *Gilda* . . ." Warren said, recognizing the first face of the gathering, his voice sounding strained to his own ears.

"And there's Vogl and Kira and . ." Cherry broke off, looking through the silent battalion of suspended figures to more distant ranks. "Oh. Huh. New hypothesis: Not cold-storing specimens . . . cold-storing *survivors*."

At first Warren didn't understand what Cherry said, still staring at Gilda's familiar face, her eyes closed, a thick green haze making it difficult to determine if any hint of life still animated her waxen form. Then he looked beyond to where Cherry nodded, seeing ranks of tall, elongated figures, each sequestered in their own identical capsule, each clearly nonhuman.

Cherry walked confidently among the dozens of cylinders, the bulky machine gun nestled in her arms as she examined these alien entities, and Warren followed, his head turning to look at each of the comatose humans they bypassed.

"I can see how it was," Cherry murmured quietly. "Their war goes badly . ." She stopped to examine the first tall alien figure, a bipedal form clad in garments as shredded as Cherry's, one arm missing, the broad, hairless head discolored with what appeared to be wounds. "The survivors scuttle to one of their prearranged escape routes, and no matter how injured or confused they might be, the automated attendant scoops them up and packages them here for safekeeping until reinforcements arrived."

"Only reinforcements never arrived," Warren said, wondering how many millennia these beings had rested here . . . wherever *here* even was.

Cherry turned to look at Warren, her brows lowered. "Oh? I'm thinking reinforcements did arrive, all eager to snatch up their survivors . . . and fell into a trap. Had their landing gear shot off before they could get clear, even."

Warren drew in a breath, staring at her. "Are you saying we're on Bethune . . . now?"

Cherry shrugged, the machine gun in her arms flopping. "Adds up that way."

Warren shook his head. "But people have been searching Bethune, sifting it for alien hardware for more than a century. How could they miss this place?"

"Bigger on the inside than it is on the outside, remember," Cherry said. "Just like Ajanib. And it's a sneaky hidey-hole, right? Probably shielded every which way. Hard to find . . . even if you have the juice to shoot the landing gear off a huge alien battlewagon."

Warren looked around this alien safe house, his mind leaping through one possibility after another, implications spreading like chain lightning. "If you're right, Cherry, then we've got to find the way out of here, unless our exit is buried under fifty thousand years of Bethune sediment. And then . . . we've got to see if we can revive the poor blighters snatched out of Ajanib. Or even better, get them out of here, and *then* revive them." Warren smiled suddenly. "If we can accomplish these two miracles I think we can put this whole experience to, um, excellent use."

Cherry eyed Warren, rolling her eyes. "You mean *profitable* use, don't you, Stowe?"

Warren shrugged, his gaze already distant, imagining new altitudes of greatness. "Same thing."

Although Warren had used the word *we* when enumerating the tasks set before them, almost all the superhuman efforts they would employ surely fell upon Cherry's shoulders alone. As she carefully searched the ancient subterranean outpost, seeking some exit that might bring them up to Bethune's surface, Cherry found herself strangely lighthearted despite it all. Not many hours earlier she had resigned herself to a pointless, violent death within the catacombs of Ajanib, and now new challenges, new possibilities seemed to draw her further from self-destruction every moment. Now, if only she could locate some exit out of this place—preferably one not situated at the bottom of an ocean . . .

Warren called out, his voice echoing across the dimly glowing expanse, "Look! See this thing?" He held up an odd device that might be a tool or weapon, scaled for hands much larger than standard human issue.

"What is it, then?" Cherry yelled back, turning to continue her search, running her fingers over a rectangular impression on the curving outer wall.

"I don't know!" Warren shouted. "Isn't it amazing?"

The tall rectangular section clicked at Cherry's insistent pressure, pivoting open to reveal a broad passage angled upward, the walls glowing green just like Ajanib. "Amazing indeed," Cherry murmured to herself, reaching down to grasp the Browning machine gun at her feet before moving up the incline.

Only a hundred paces brought her to the end of the passage and a massive hatch sealing the exit. Fortunately, the hatch opened inward, releasing a small flood of soil and rocks, but above the minor avalanche Cherry saw the mouth of a natural cave, thick foliage allowing only a trickle of green-tinted sunlight, but it was enough.

"Better and better," Cherry softly declared, permitting the machine gun in her arms to sink to the floor with a solid clank.

A few moments later, Cherry rejoined Warren, finding him still collecting an assortment of smallish alien knickknacks as he poked about every nook and cranny he could find, the rows of bottled humanoids ranked like a silent audience around him as he hunched over his careful looting.

Cherry cleared her throat, provoking a startled yelp and spasm from Warren.

"Found our way out," she announced before Warren could utter the remonstration regarding her habitual stealth that clearly lay on the tip of his tongue.

Warren's face cleared into a broad smile. "Hah! I knew you could do it! Now ... everything else is pure simplicity!" He paused, wrinkling his brow. "Any idea where it comes out? Hopefully not a half continent away from any decent restaurants ..."

Cherry shook her head. "Nope. Looks like we're not that far from Torino at all, just a bit of a stroll from the eastern Gear."

"The eastern Gear?" Warren repeated, chuckling. "This treasure trove under their noses the whole time!" He spun slowly around, surveying the alien chamber with obvious satisfaction. "Like I said, pure simplicity."

Cherry snorted, crossing her arms. "Simplicity. Right. We've got to get Gilda and the others out of their odd little coffins here without awakening them in the middle of your filthy loot, *somehow* transport them someplace where we *may* still revive them, we've got to pack your"—she waved a hand at his growing collection—"gewgaws out of here, and we've got to keep any Torino cop from getting a glimpse of you while we're doing it."

Warren nodded enthusiastically. "Yes. You describe it perfectly. So simple."

Cherry sighed. "Okay, Stowe, why don't you explain how this becomes so simple for me."

"First," Warren declared, holding up one finger, "one of us legs it out there and rousts up some suitable transportation." A second finger jutted up. "Then we pull Gilda and ... whoever else we feel like out of their little test tubes and bring them someplace, er, cozy before we revive them."

"Because you don't want anyone to see your little prize here, right?" Cherry dryly clarified.

Warren drew himself up. "For their own protection, Cherry ... and because I'm not a fool, yes. Can you imagine the pressure that would be brought to bear on them to reveal what they know?"

"You are nothing if not a humanitarian, Stowe."

"True, Cherry. Very true. But"—Warren held up a third finger—"lastly we have got to find some clever place I can squirrel away some of this amazing loot!"

"Oh we do, do we?" Cherry said, thinking of far more that she would need to accomplish than Warren even imagined.

⊕ ⊕ ⊕

Gilda awakened, her eyes opening to an unfamiliar room, her mouth feeling like each of her teeth wore tiny, filthy sweaters. As consciousness sank in, she remembered lobbing a firebomb at the gunned-up Power Wagon, turning to confront an alien creature...and then nothing more.

She rolled stiffly from what seemed to be a hotel bed and staggered unsteadily to a brightly lighted window, blinking down at the familiar sight of a Torino city street. She stared at the people and vehicles milling about below for what seemed an hour, her mind trying to reconnect to some kind of reality. Had she ever really been racing cars in Ajanib? Or had that been some sort of fever dream?

The thoughts flashed and rolled, her recollections of countless details flooding back in, and Gilda slowly turned to survey the hotel room, her eyes fastening upon the provided hotel slate. She stumbled to the slate and numbly entered her personal account identifier.

She held her breath, hoping the dream of Ajanib had been real, that she was not still a manual laborer with nothing to show for a lifetime of work... Her banking totals appeared and Gilda let out her breath in a single gust. She chuckled quietly, shrugging off the mystery of how she came to be in Torino.

She was here, alive and a woman of substantial financial means, her Ajanib winnings filling the bank with delightful zeroes. For once in her life she would be living in style...as soon as she found a toothbrush and brushed her teeth about ten times in succession.

Cathwaite puttered around his converted warehouse, lovingly polishing the first of his new collection—a blue 1960 Ford Thunderbird. He had only been back on Bethune for a week, but with the kind of wealth he now commanded he could afford fast results, no longer teased by classic vehicles that he could never afford to own himself.

The sound of a step close behind Cathwaite brought his head around, his satisfied smile freezing. "It's *you*!" he said in a choked voice, staring.

"It's me," Warren Springer Stowe agreed, "come to collect my half of *our* winnings, sport. By my estimation it should be one-point-five billion guilders."

"But...but, Warren, how?" Cathwaite stammered. "It looked like an alien gobbled you up and—and no one could get a straight answer out of the Maktoums—" He broke off, swallowing. "And—and Bartson wants you to rot in prison for a million years. How are you just walking around Torino like this?"

Warren smiled, shrugging, his eyes piercing Cathwaite with a hard glint. "It would be such a shame—for you—if Bartson grabbed me and discovered our little business relationship. I'm sure the Maktoums would assume the worst and set their lawyers to repossessing all your Ajanib winnings without delay. Such a delicate situation, when you think about it."

Cathwaite swallowed, his mouth suddenly dry. "Yes. Delicate. I can see that."

Warren produced a slate and stepped forward, offering it to Cathwaite. "Here you are. You can make the transfer to my secure account. One-point-five billion even is sufficient. I won't sweat you for any extra millions of spare pocket change you accrued."

Cathwaite hesitated, contemplating telling Warren that he had done a fair bit better than Warren seemed to think, then internally shrugged, taking the proffered slate and entering the necessary information, validating with a thumbprint and retinal scan. Thinking quickly, he decided to take one small extra step and a chance. Cathwaite activated the image capture setting on his account and casually tilted the slate toward Warren. If Warren wanted one-point-five, Cathwaite certainly would not argue, but he wouldn't allow Warren to disappear without a trace either.

As he handed the slate back to Warren, Warren's eyes probed narrowly. "I'm sure you got all accustomed to that stack of guilders in your name, tiger, but do be philosophical about it, if you can. You can only admit that I made you filthy rich, even if you're half as rich now as you thought you were a few minutes ago."

Cathwaite shrugged, struggling to maintain a neutral expression. "I'll get used to it, I guess."

Warren chuckled as he took out his battered smoking case and rolled a cigarette. "That's a boy. Look at the bright side, right?" He puffed the cigarette into life and blew a cloud of noxious haze around Cathwaite as he gestured to the gleaming blue car. "That's a damned fine Thunderbird, by the way, old boy. See you around some day."

Warren strolled out of the warehouse, smoke wafting in his wake as he laughed, and Cathwaite stared after him for a moment, frowning until he was certain Warren Springer Stowe had cleared the vicinity, undoubtedly scurrying out from Torino before Bartson got his claws on him.

Cathwaite reached into a pocket and produced his own slate, making a quick call. "It's Cathwaite, put me through to him." He waited a moment until the voice rang out across the line into his ear. "Just wanted you to know... Warren Springer Stowe is alive and I got the proof on my secure account. Time to pay up, Sharif. The figure is two billion as I recall... What? No, I have no idea how he got out of Ajanib. He didn't say a word about it as he left the Bethune system, but his ship has got to be long gone by now. What do I care? I just want to get the money that's coming to me." Lying to Sharif did not bother Cathwaite one bit.

As Sharif's voice murmured calmly about the details, Cathwaite shook his head. "Whatever, Sharif. Just have it in my account by tonight. And one more thing: How can I get ahold of Klaus Benin today? He owes me money too!"

Sharif said a few words and Cathwaite jerked the slate back, staring at it. "What? *What do you mean Klaus is broke?* He owes me a billion guilders!"

CHAPTER 49

Sami Maktoum stood before the vast window of his office overlooking Torino, seeing the Gear jutting up out of sight above his view, one hand in his pocket, the other lightly drumming fingers on the crystalline pane as Sharif droned on behind him, going on and on about this new political landscape.

"... And this broad alliance of interests was wholly unexpected, even by our best predictive models," Sharif said. "It provides an opportunity that we must capitalize upon immediately."

Sami turned with a sigh. "So you're trying to say ... what? You want to be some kind of politician now?"

Sharif smiled. "I ask you, Sami, is a king just a politician? An emperor?"

Sami held his brother's gaze for a moment. "You're serious, aren't you?" The silence stretched a few seconds and Sami laughed. "So you *encourage* Bethune to declare their independence and create some kind of capitalist free-for-all, and now you and your coterie of friends think to duplicate the model and just set up your own competition for the Confederated Worlds?"

Sharif shrugged tolerantly. "For generations our family has thrived by identifying and meeting human needs of one kind or another, and now the galaxy calls for an alternative to the Confederated Worlds. This is merely a ... *product* we can provide."

"Unless the Confederated Worlds feels its existence is threatened somehow," Sami said. "Then you will experience a whole different sort of *hostile takeover* from the corporate games you enjoy."

"Certain subtlety is required," Sharif said placidly, looking off to some imagined glory.

Sami stepped nearer. "And if the Confederated Worlds gets wind of the alien on Ajanib? If they somehow connect the dots from a mysterious alien discovery to your sudden new interest in hegemony?"

Sharif turned his focus on Sami again. "What alien discovery? Stowe popping up all alive and well has become a valuable boon to us, well worth the billion guilders he cost me." Sharif examined the sleeve of his tailored jacket. "Clearly Stowe engineered some trick to escape Ajanib, and that will be evident to anyone who looks closely at the situation."

Sami digested this a moment, rubbing his chin. "And this means you won't be hounding after him, trying to throw him in a dungeon?"

Sharif stood and began to collect his few personal items from the desk. "Warren Springer Stowe alive and free remains a self-aggrandizing display that can only allay any rumors of an alien abduction in his disappearing act."

Sami mused over Sharif's words for a moment before strolling back to the window, looking out at the massive piece of alien technology lording over the skyline. "I see ... And what do you want from me, then?"

The sounds of Sharif's soft steps preceded the touch on Sami's shoulder. "Is it not obvious?" They stood side by side, their hazy reflections conjoined upon the clear pane. "Despite the various critiques I leveled against you, Sami, you demonstrated true initiative with Ajanib, real command."

Sami turned to search Sharif's profile. "Oh?"

Sharif smiled broadly and clapped Sami on the back before heading toward the door. "Absolutely. You will head Maktoum Corporation now, Sami. And I will take the family name to its next logical point of growth."

The sensation in Sami's chest was not entirely pride, nor even entirely pleasure—an oddly mixed feeling for the culmination of a lifetime's effort and frustration. "The *next logical point*, Sharif? Emperor Maktoum?"

As the thick office door sighed open, Sharif merely glanced back at Sami, a thin smile on his lips. "Something like that, dear brother."

⊕ ⊕ ⊕

Warren paced around the waiting smuggler ship, alternately checking the advancing time or looking about the periphery of the rugged launch apron out in the countryside.

"Hey, friend," a surly voice called from the ship's open outer hatch. "We're getting past optimal here . . . Needing to launch if we don't want a damned interceptor on us before we clear orbit."

Warren scowled, scanning the short breadth of horizon available to his vision. "Five minutes more, *friend*," he said without looking back.

"Now, guvnor," the voice reproved in a coaxing tone, "you know how hot the provincials are to lay hands on you, so can't we—"

"Yes," Warren snapped, "in five minutes."

The unseen speaker retreated, muttering under-voiced curses, and Warren returned to pacing. *Where is she?*

Cherry knew the tight launch window they faced, and Warren had felt sure she had intended to accompany him off Bethune, though her responses remained as elusive as ever. So where could she be?

The list of potential disasters began to march through his head. Had she decided that Bartson's smugness needed a sharp, pointed, painful lesson? Or worse, had she visited the Maktoums and tangled with something beyond her own lethal abilities?

His thoughts turned to an entirely different track . . . could she have succumbed to the symbiote psychosis that had destroyed so many of her Blue Light comrades since the war? Had she made Bethune her final, *permanent* resting place after all?

"Who are we looking for, then, duck?" Cherry's voice inquired from directly beside Warren, causing his entire body to spasm in a most undignified manner.

"Gah! Cherry! I—I!" Warren fumed, waving his hand about. "It's about time, damn it!" He stared down at her smiling, placid expression, feeling a surprising warmth in his chest. "Well, you're here, so come on before these rascally smugglers leave us behind."

Cherry looked at him, still smiling faintly, her dark eyes reflecting more peace than he remembered seeing before. As they walked up into the small, fast vessel, Warren glanced back at her several times, trying to read her expression.

"You look rather pleased with yourself, Cherry. You didn't do anything . . . unkind, permanent, or fatal to anyone I know, did you?"

The hatch sealed behind them, the smugglers hustling to launch, clattering from place to place in a sudden zeal to get away from nagging authorities.

Cherry shrugged, acting far too casual for Warren's comfort. "Nothing fatal. But unkind? Permanent? Hmm. Depends on your perspective, love, doesn't it?" The ship began to lift clear and they staggered into their seats, but Warren never took his gaze off her.

"Cherry?" he said, suspicious.

She smirked. "You looted enough of your little odds and ends from the alien hidey-hole to keep you happy for a while, didn't you, old fellow?"

Warren slumped back, putting a hand to his forehead. "Cherry, my alien treasure trove? What did you . . . ? You *didn't*!"

The ship kicked into full acceleration then, and Warren could only be content that they were clear of Bethune, on their way back to the Confederated Worlds, and he held a fat bankroll ready to execute his biggest plan ever. It was almost frightening how brilliant it all was.

But strangely, as he looked at Cherry there beside him, smiling in her mysterious way, he found more joy in the smile at that moment than in all the guilders he had just acquired. So what if she had frittered away the most valuable repository of alien technology ever known to humanity, right?

Pure bloody insanity!

Dr. Peter Maris had not really enjoyed a single day since that fateful morning on Ajanib when he had allowed his fears to override his . . . what? Heart? His code of chivalry, such as it was? Love? Something.

For the first time in his life he lived with a regret that seemed to undermine his own validity as a human being, and this combined with a very unsatisfactory professional result on Ajanib to crush Peter's view of any future path. All the scientists, including Peter, had been hustled off the Maktoums' asteroid base shortly after some dramatic happenings in the catacombs. He had heard rumors that Stowe and Boop had been gunned down, their bodies ejected into space, then other rumors that they had somehow escaped . . . and even a few whispered rumors that they had been body-snatched by an alien.

The truth of that now only mattered to Peter in that it seemed to set an exclamation point on his failure that day—his obeisance to fear.

The scientific failure on Ajanib also rankled and added to the overall sense of futility with which Peter now viewed his entire life, so he idled on Bethune, wrapping up the uninspiring academic papers that he and Dr. Sang authored together. They did not anticipate the acclaim—or really even the notice—of their peers for the Ajanib project, but they still went through the tiresome professional motions.

Like so many other moments in the previous weeks, Peter found himself lost, thinking about dark, intelligent eyes, the quirky humor and remarkable courage of a woman who had somehow seemed to genuinely like him, finding it almost impossible that she had actually curled beside him, sleeping, her dark hair fanned across his pillow. It all seemed a brief, remarkable dream that he had scuttled himself through pathetic fear.

This bolt of self-revulsion drove him to his feet, mindlessly moving to the drab door of his humble Torino apartment with no particular destination in mind. He froze, looking down. The strange packet lay jammed under the door's edge, and Peter almost stepped over it before he paused, catching a glimpse of one scrawled word adorning its outer face: *Doc*.

A moment later, he clutched the crumpled sheets, his eyes racing through the incomprehensible message down to the one-word signature at its base: *Boop*. Only then did he draw a deep breath and work his way through the obscure wording, her description of an "egghead's rare treat," and his lifelong mission to "defy all desecration from the filly-things" finally beginning to sink in. The crude map's coordinates at the bottom set the final hook.

Despite the late hour, without a word to anyone, Peter set off to the destination Boop had marked, hoping more to see her there than any real expectation of a great scientific discovery. The thought that she might turn her renowned violence upon him touched him only for a moment before he shook it off. Fear would not own him again.

Only a fifteen-minute shot in his cheap, rented scuttle brought him to the spot on the opposite side of the unexcavated pyramid from Torino's glowing lights. Though it lay in a rough, undeveloped area abutting a low plateau, Peter spotted an odd pile of fresh wreckage to one side, as if someone had chopped a sizable vehicle into manageable portions and stacked the rough chunks in an untidy heap.

Standing beside the wreckage, Peter scanned in a slow circle with a bright hand light, the beam sweeping along an unremarkable stretch of the plateau's near edge, a glimpse of a tattered garment catching his breath. "Boop!" he called out before realizing that the jumpsuit he had last seen her wearing was not only badly shredded but absent its owner.

Of course he could not stop himself from walking to this last token of her, and as he reached out to touch the fabric, he saw the clear marks, the open hollow yawning beneath trailing vegetation. He leaned down, playing his light, seeing the rocky channel leading downward, his breath catching in his throat.

An hour later, back in the scuttle, his hands shaking, Peter knew his life had just been transformed with the scientific discovery of the century—of the millennium—gift-wrapped for him alone. But as he looked at the memento laid across the seat beside him, remembering... remembering... he knew his sense of fulfillment would forever remain some measure short of complete.

He laid the shredded jumpsuit aside, trying to focus upon the monumental opportunity before him, trying to release the fruitless questions... Where could she be now?

Her farewell gift was certainly more than he deserved, and wherever she might be, Dr. Peter Maris very unscientifically spoke a blessing on the soul of a proud, proud Boop.

Acknowledgments:

The Redline Heist came to life through the input and assistance of several people, most notably among them: Aubry William and Rebekah Joanna, my agent Kimberley Cameron of Kimberley Cameron and Associates, Gray Rinehart of Baen, and Steven Roman.